COUNTDOWN TO THE PERFECT WEDDING

BY

TERESA HILL

First published in Great Britain 2013
by Mills & Boon, an imprint of Harlequin (UK) Limited,
Eton House, 18-24 Paradise Road, Richmond, Surrey TW9 1SR

ISBN: 978 0 263 90638 7
ebook ISBN: 978 1 472 01206 7

23-0613

Harlequin (UK) policy is to use papers that are natural, renewable and recyclable products and made from wood grown in sustainable forests. The logging and manufacturing processes conform to the legal environmental regulations of the country of origin.

Printed and bound in Spain
by Blackprint CPI, Barcelona

Teresa Hill tells people if they want to be writers, to find a spouse who's patient, understanding and interested in being a patron of the arts. Lucky for her, she found a man just like that, who's been with her through all the ups and downs of being a writer. They live in Travelers Rest, South Carolina, in the foothills of the beautiful Blue Ridge Mountains, with two beautiful, spoiled dogs and two gigantic, lazy cats.

To my niece, Rachel, who has welcomed her first child, Ashley Nicole, into the world and brought incredible joy to my parents, now the happiest great-grandparents ever.

Prologue

Eleanor Barrington Morgan smiled and nodded, she hoped with nothing but a mixture of happiness and acceptance showing in her face, as her most favorite person in the whole world, her godson, Tate Darnley, told her he'd met yet another woman.

This one was an investment banker.

"Mmm." She nodded, having to grit her teeth beneath her smile. "Someone from your office?"

"Yes," Tate said.

Eleanor could just picture her, disciplined as could be; fastidious in her dress, diet and exercise plan; highly intelligent when it came to numbers and strategy; working her little fanny off to get ahead.

She probably came to bed clutching a spreadsheet, not quite able to let it go completely.

Eleanor's husband used to be that way. He was an investment banker, cool, calculating, highly intelligent and with the warmth and interpersonal skills of a deep freeze. She'd endured thirty years of trying like a fool to change him, to figure out what was wrong with her that she couldn't make him love her or want her the way she wanted to be loved, and she wanted so much more for Tate.

Instead, he'd been raised by a stockbroker, become a venture capitalist himself, and showed all the signs of following in all of their footsteps.

Especially in his choice of women.

She wanted to weep, to scream at him, to try to knock some sense into him, to tell him there was so much more to this world and to life other than money, the latest business deal and numbers. But of course, a Barrington-Holmes woman simply did not do those kinds of things. She'd been raised to be too dignified for that.

So she sat there and smiled and nodded, until he kissed her on her cheek and left. Her best friends at Remington Park Retirement Village, Kathleen and Gladdy, saw him go and came to hear the news right away.

"He found another one," Eleanor told them. "Just like the last one and the one before that, it sounds like. How can men be so stupid?"

Kathleen and Gladdy shook their heads and sighed, having heard it all before.

"That first woman like that? Did she make him happy? No," Eleanor said, answering her own question. "The second one? Was he happy with her? No. The third one? Not even close, and now, here we are. Number four, who sounds like a clone of the first three. I could tell by the way he talks about her. No real emotion there at all, no excitement, no warmth. Just all this bunk about compatibility and shared goals. Please! It sounds like they're going into business together."

Kathleen frowned. "What exactly is your objection to…

trying to gently nudge him toward someone else? Someone you think would make him happy?"

"Well, Mother always said we shouldn't meddle," Eleanor said.

"Oh, please." Gladdy dismissed that with a huff and a smile. "What kind of mother is that? And besides, you told me your mother died twenty years ago. It's not like she's going to come scold you for anything now."

"I know, but…well, the honest truth is I've tried before to steer Tate in a different direction, and…I'm afraid I'm just no good at it," Eleanor admitted, much as it cost her to say so. She was raised to never admit any kind of inadequacy she might have.

"Oh, honey." Kathleen laughed. "We can fix that. Gladdy and I are terribly good at meddling. Just ask anyone. What we pulled off with my darling granddaughter Jane…"

"It was a thing of beauty. A master feat," Gladdy bragged. "And now, Jane's happy as can be, and believe me, we despaired of Jane ever truly being happy. In truth, sometimes we despaired of her ever so much as going on a date."

Kathleen nodded. "It was bad. Very bad. I don't think anyone but Gladdy and I ever thought we could save Jane, but we did. We can save your godson, too. Just say the word, and we'll go to work."

Eleanor sighed. She'd heard this story. Practically the whole of Remington Park had been involved in the matchmaking scheme and had a blast doing it, she'd been told.

Her people, the Barringtons, and her husband's, the Holmes, were just repressed, stuffy, private people, crippled emotionally and quite possibly beyond all help, Eleanor sometimes thought, and it was hard, breaking the patterns of decades, the ones imprinted on the very DNA in every single cell in one's body.

"I wouldn't even know where to start," she said.

"Don't worry." Gladdy patted her hand reassuringly. "We do."

Eleanor tried to be good. Truly, she did. She stayed out of Tate's supposed love life, although honestly, she doubted there was any kind of love involved, emotional or physical. Poor thing.

And what did her noninterference get her?

Six months after first mentioning her, Tate announced he was engaged and finally admitted the woman he'd been seeing all that time was none other than Victoria Ryan! A girl he'd known for years. They'd practically grown up together, acting more like brother and sister than anything else. And Victoria, unfortunately, had the most disagreeable mother. Eleanor shuddered at the thought of ever having to face that woman over a holiday dinner table or, even worse, at a wedding.

Still, Eleanor thought it wouldn't last. No woman ever really had with Tate. She wasn't worried, wasn't sorry she'd stuck with her plan of not butting in.

Six months after that, the wedding—a huge extravaganza in that mausoleum of a place Eleanor once called home—a mere two weeks away, she was hungrily searching for any signs that the nuptials would somehow fail to take place.

Two days before the first of the family guests were scheduled to arrive for the five-day event, she was desperate and went to Kathleen and Gladdy.

"Well, the simplest thing, of course, is another woman," Kathleen said quite calmly in the face of Eleanor's outright panic.

"But, he's not seeing anyone else," she explained. "Not that I know of."

"No, I mean, we have to find him another woman—a real one, not an ice sculpture," Gladdy told her.

"Where are we going to find him a real woman in two days? He's been dating for fifteen years and hasn't found one yet," Eleanor said. "And even if we did find one, what then? It's not like we can guarantee he's going to fall for her. I mean, he's a man, and we all know what most of them are like. But he's not a rat. I just don't think he's going to be looking for another woman on the weekend of his wedding."

"We put them together and see what happens. That's all it should take," Kathleen said, sounding remarkably confident.

"Yes, and we all know just the woman!" Gladdy announced, glancing into the kitchen, where Amy, their sweet, most favorite former employee, newly graduated from cooking school, had arrived with a special birthday cake for one of the ladies in their cottage who'd always been a favorite of hers. "Eleanor, didn't you say you were going to hire a chef for the weekend? To feed all those guests staying at your house?"

"Yes, I did. A lovely man named Adolfo."

"He's going to come down with something at the last minute," Gladdy said, pointing to the woman in the kitchen. "And you're going to replace him with her."

Chapter One

Tate Darnley was later than he'd planned getting to the house Wednesday night and a little bit tipsy. Victoria's father and some of Tate's colleagues had thrown a little cocktail party in honor of their upcoming wedding, and the champagne had flowed freely.

He came in through the side door leading past the servants' quarters and the kitchen, as he always did, hoping to avoid any friends and family members who might have already arrived for the long weekend, looking forward to a bit of peace and quiet before things got too crazy for the wedding.

What he'd hoped would be a small, family-only affair had turned into an extravaganza, and Victoria, normally the epitome of calm and grace under pressure, now seemed like a woman trying to steer the Titanic through a vast, bottomless ocean, fraught with all sorts of confusion and peril.

It was a little disconcerting, but not overly so. Tate had always heard weddings made just about everyone crazy. It would all be over soon, and he and Victoria could get on with having a life together, which he expected to be nothing but smooth sailing—two intelligent, hardworking people with the same goals, same values, who'd known and respected each other for years. How could they go wrong?

Tate checked himself for any twinge of impending nerves, happy to find none. He was even whistling a bit, striding down the back hall when the most amazing smell hit him.

Tangy, citrusy…lemons, he decided.

Something sweet, too.

Lemons, sugar no doubt and…some kind of berries?

He groaned, it smelled so good.

Someone preparing food for the wedding, he supposed, and yet, he didn't remember anything that smelled that good at the various tasting menus they'd sampled, at Victoria's insistence.

He lingered in the hallway, thinking if he couldn't get a bit of that sweet lemony thing right now, who could? After all, he was the groom. So he turned around and headed into the big, open gourmet kitchen, finding a slender young woman clad in a starched white apron, her copper-colored hair tied back in a braid, testing the firmness of a plate of lemon bars she'd just pulled from the oven. That luscious smell was even more irresistible here in the kitchen.

A boy of maybe seven sat on a high stool beside her, pouting for all he was worth. "One?" he asked. "Come on, Mom. Just one?"

"Max, you already had two from the earlier batch. Any more and you'll be sick, and I can't have you sick this weekend, because I can't take care of you and cook for all these people."

"But—"

"No." She didn't let him get out another word, as she slid her lemon bars one by one onto a waiting cooling rack. "Now stay here, and guard these for me. I just used the last of the powdered sugar, and I have to search the pantry for more."

The boy pouted mightily but held his tongue.

Tate waited until the cook disappeared into the butler's pantry and the even bigger pantry closet in back of that and then strolled into the kitchen, saying, "Wow, that smells amazing."

The kid looked up and frowned. "Yeah."

Just then, from deep inside the pantry, Tate heard a woman's voice call out, "Tell me you're not eating those, Max? Because I counted them already. I'll know if you do."

The boy sighed and looked resigned to following that order. "I'm not."

"Just not fair, is it?" Tate said quietly to the boy.

The kid shook his head. Judging by his expression, he was trying to convince Tate he was a poor, abused child, left to starve among all this bounty.

Tate finally got a good look at the things. Lemon, indeed, and something pinkish mixed in. "Lemon and strawberry?" he guessed.

"I dunno. They just taste really good."

"I'm sure," Tate agreed, sniffing again. "Raspberry. That's what it is, isn't it? Do you remember?"

"I think so," Max said, looking none too sure of himself. "Mom calls 'em sugar daddies."

"Oh." Tate nodded. Interesting name. "Because she's going to sprinkle powdered sugar on top of them?"

"'Cause of Leo," Max said.

Leo?

Sugar daddies?

Surely the kid didn't mean what Tate was thinking? "So, Leo is…your dad?"

"No." Max shook his head. "A friend of mine and my mom's. She cooked for him and stuff, and he liked her a lot."

"Oh." Tate didn't dare ask another thing.

"She got to go to cooking school 'cause of it," Max said, obviously a talker. "She always wanted to go to cooking school. And I get to go to school, too, someday. I mean, I didn't really want to, but Leo left me some money for that, too. Not cooking school, but…the big place? You know?"

"College?" Tate tried.

Max nodded. "I guess I have to go."

"So…Leo was a good guy, I guess," Tate said, at a complete loss as to what else to say to the kid about that particular arrangement.

"You ever have a sugar daddy?" Max asked.

Tate grinned, couldn't help it. It was like trying to have two completely different conversations at once. The kid was talking about his mom's dessert, wasn't he?

"No," Tate said. "I haven't had the pleasure."

"They're the best thing my mom cooks," Max confided. "And she didn't even have to go to cooking school to learn to make them. She already knew."

"Wow," Tate said.

Max leaned in close and whispered, "She won't give me another one, 'cause she thinks I'll get sick if I have one more. But I won't, really. Maybe she'll give you one, and you can…you know…share with me?"

Tate loved it. What a little schemer. Life would never be dull with this one around. He reached out and ruffled the kid's hair, thick and dark reddish brown and just getting to the unruly stage where it really needed to be trimmed.

"I'll do my best," Tate promised.

"So, did you ever have the other kind of sugar daddy?" Max continued.

"Other kind?"

Max nodded. "Like Leo?"

Tate cleared his throat to stall for time. "I...I don't think so."

"Know why mom called him that?"

"No, Max, I don't," he said carefully.

"'Cause he was so sweet, and he was like a dad. He took care of us."

"Oh." Tate nodded, thinking that was about as good of a G-rated explanation as he could think of. "Well, I'm glad for you. And your mom."

From their hiding place in the dining room, ears pressed to the wall shared with the kitchen, Eleanor groaned softly, throwing a horrified look to her friends and companions in meddling, Kathleen and Gladdy.

"Sugar daddy? Tate's going to think Amy's just awful!"

Kathleen, Leo's loving widow, sighed and admitted, "Okay, so it's not going particularly well at the moment."

"Well? It's a disaster!" Eleanor exclaimed.

"Not completely," Gladdy pointed out. "I mean, your godson is surely not going to think we brought Amy here to fix her up with him. Not from what he just heard from our dear Max."

"No, he'll think she's a gold digger! A kept woman, looking for her next sugar daddy to take over where Leo left off!" Eleanor could have cried right then and there.

The wedding was less than ninety-six hours away.

"Just give it a moment," Kathleen said, calm as could be. "See what happens. Your godson barely knows Amy, but he's clearly interested in her cooking and quite taken with Max."

"Why would he even want to know her now?"

"For the lemon bars, if nothing else," Gladdy said, sounding absolutely sure of herself.

Eleanor sighed, feeling doubtful about the whole mess, but stayed where she was, her ear pressed once again against the wall.

Amy found the powdered sugar, finally, but only after climbing on a rolling ladder that slid from one end of the tall pantry wall to the other and nearly climbing onto the top shelf to reach into the back and get it.

This was the most amazing pantry she'd ever seen. And the kitchen was a chef's dream.

She climbed back down the ladder, powdered sugar in hand, her nerves still zinging from the first moment she'd seen the house—mansion was a better word, castle not far from her thoughts when she'd first seen the giant, weathered stone building—and realized what she'd gotten herself into.

She didn't have the experience for this, having literally just graduated from her single year of cooking school last week. She'd gotten hardly any prep time at all, because she'd come in at the last minute, filling in for the unfortunate Adolfo. And just for fun, she hadn't been able to find a sitter with so little notice, so she'd had to bring Max. Eleanor swore that one of the three nannies expected to accompany various invited relatives would be happy to watch over Max, and that there was another seven-year-old boy coming for the long weekend wedding, so he'd have a built-in playmate, too.

At least Amy had gotten a good bit of the baking done tonight. Making the lemon bars—her favorites, her specialty—had helped calm her down.

She was opening the bag of powdered sugar as she walked back into the kitchen, hoping Max had actually listened to her and hadn't scarfed down another one, and there he was, sitting on his stool, guarding her desserts, with an absolutely beautiful man, dressed in what she was sure was a very expensive suit, talking earnestly with her son.

Amy paused there for a moment, unable to help herself. The man was standing in profile, dark blond hair, cut short and neatly, a bit of a tan on his pretty face, contrasting nicely with the stark white shirt and deep blue tie and suit. His whole image positively screamed of both money and privilege, and he looked like he'd been born to live in a place like this.

Completely out of her league, Amy knew in an instant.

Still, a woman could look every now and then, couldn't she?

The last man in her life had been Max's father, and look how badly that had turned out. She'd been understandably cautious since then.

Max spotted her and called out, "Hey, Mom! Guess what? This is my new friend Tate, and he's never had a sugar daddy before!"

Amy stopped short, thinking she'd really done it with that name. At least the beautiful man in the hideously expensive suit didn't know the whole story behind it.

And then, Max, who just didn't know when to close his mouth, piped up and added, "Not one of your lemon bars or one like Leo."

Amy winced, closed her eyes tightly for a moment and

cursed inside. She must have blushed at the same time, and then she started trying to explain, talking with her hands, as she often did, forgetting all about the powdered sugar.

It slipped from her hands.

She grabbed for it and so did the man, but they both missed.

The package hit the hard tile floor with a big thump, and the next thing she knew, an explosion of finely powdered sugar rose up into the air, in her and the man's faces.

Amy and the gorgeous man both froze, leaning over what was left of the bag, the cloud having enveloped them, sprinkled over their faces, their hair, getting in their mouths, even up their noses.

She blinked. Yes, there was a bit on her eyelashes, too.

The man coughed. Amy did, too, sending tiny puffs of white powder into the air.

Max laughed so hard he nearly fell off his stool.

It was like something out of a cartoon he would watch, this puffy cloud of sugar rising up and enveloping them like a sweet fog, coating everything in a fine sheen of white.

Max started to get down off the stool, but Amy stopped him. "No. Stay right where you are!"

"Mom—"

"I've already made a huge mess. The last thing we need is you over here making the mess even bigger," she said, then turned to the man. "I am so sorry. I don't know what happened."

Okay, she did, but no way she was admitting it.

He didn't look mad. He looked ridiculous with sugar all over him, and no doubt, she did, too.

"Oh, my God, I've probably ruined your suit," she

said, afraid it cost more than several months' rent on her apartment.

"Don't worry about it," he said.

Sugar drifted off him as he smiled and shook his head. Even his eyebrows were coated in white.

She couldn't help it. She reached for him, trying to brush some of the sugar off his suit. Not that it was really working. Powdered sugar was indeed the texture of powder, too fine to brush off, mostly just sinking into the grain of the fabric and leaving a faint imprint of white.

"I'm afraid I'm making it worse," she said, still trying anyway to get the stuff off him.

He held up his hands to get her to stop, which she did, feeling even worse about how she'd had her hands all over the man. Just trying to help, truly. She honestly feared the cost of the ruined suit.

"Sorry," she said again.

"I'll just take this off right here," he said, shrugging out of it, more powder flying as he did it.

"Wait, let me get you something to put that in, or you'll have powdered sugar all over the house." She pulled out a fresh kitchen garbage bag and held it out to him as he put the folded suit jacket into it.

He peeled off his tie next, depositing that in the bag, too.

Looking down at his shirt and pants, he brushed himself off as best he could, started to unbutton the shirt, but then quit when he had it half off. "Is this…do you mind?"

Amy shook her head.

Mind was not the word.

A more accurate one would be…

Appreciate the sight before her?

Oh, my.

He had no way of knowing what she'd promised herself

long ago, when Max was born. That one day, she'd have a man in her life again. First, it had all been about Max, overwhelmingly Max, and the work she needed to do to support them both. Then she'd gone to cooking school and had no time for anything but that and Max. But she'd promised herself that once she graduated, had a good job and things calmed down, got a little easier, she'd let herself… at least think about a man again.

She hadn't thought that would be any kind of problem. Her first and only real experience with men had been such a downer. But seven years had gone by. More than seven, since she really had a man in her life, and here she was, newly graduated, working her first real, if short-term, job and…

Maybe she was more ready than she knew, because he…

He just looked so good.

She groaned just a bit at the sight of him, lean as could be, and yet… Well, she hadn't seen such a perfect specimen of man outside of an advertisement for cologne or men's jeans in ages—maybe even her whole life.

He wadded up the shirt and put it in his bag of clothing, looked down at his pants and then smiled back at her. "I think I'll stop there."

Max laughed from his perch on the stool. "You have eyebrows like Santa."

The man looked from Max to Amy, puzzled.

"They're white, too," she told him.

He brushed at them, not really getting the job done, then looked to her questioningly.

"No. Not quite, I'm afraid," she said. "Plus, it's in your hair."

He dipped his head toward her, standing perfectly still then, waiting. She had made the mess. She supposed she was responsible for cleaning it up, even the part that was on him.

Cautiously, she moved close enough to brush the sugar off him, catching a whiff of aftershave, something minty and yummy smelling, somehow coming through the overwhelming aroma of sugar and lemon that permeated the room. With the side of her thumb, she reached up and stroked her thumb across his eyebrows. Nothing too scary there. But then she had her hands in his hair, his truly gorgeous hair.

Lord, it had been a long, long time since she'd touched a man—an attractive man anywhere near her age—in any way at all.

Never thought it would happen in a borrowed kitchen with her son looking on and one of the biggest messes she'd ever made in her life all around them.

She finished with his hair, trying to ignore the softness of it, the thickness, the luxurious feeling of touching him.

Darn.

She dropped her gaze, clearly a mistake as her breath stirred some of the powder that now clung to the little springy curls of hair on his chest. Not gonna go anywhere near that, she promised herself, gazing at the pretty swell of tanned skin and taut muscles that made up Mr. Perfect's absolutely perfect-looking chest.

Max laughed again. The man, who'd looked completely at ease only moments ago, looked a little taken aback now, a little surprised, a little uneasy.

She caught a whiff of champagne on his breath. She was that close.

So, he'd been drinking. The whole long weekend was a giant party, after all.

"I think I just made it worse," she confessed.

"I'll live. Promise. I've made messes of all kinds in this kitchen and survived them all."

"Oh, no," she groaned. "I just remembered the housekeeper, Mrs. Brown. She told me not to dare make a mess of any kind, that she'd spent weeks getting the house ready for this, and…well…she scares me."

"Me, too," Max piped up.

"Me, too," the man said. "She scares everybody. Always has."

"You better clean up your mess, Mom," Max said.

"Yes, I'd better," she said, looking around once more to assess the situation and figure out where to start.

That's when she realized how far and wide a cloud of powdered sugar could travel. It had even gotten Max, his clothes, his hair, his adorable, grinning face.

"I've never made a mess this big," he claimed, making it sound like he should be rewarded for that.

"Good for you, Max," the man said. "But your mother's right about Mrs. Brown. We don't want to make her mad, especially on a weekend like this. So you and I need to help your mother clean this up."

Max frowned. "I'm not good at cleaning up messes. Mom says I usually just make a bigger one while I'm trying to fix the first one."

"He does," Amy agreed.

"Well, then let's think about how to do this." The man looked around the room, then back to Max. "Are you and your mom staying back there in the bedroom off the pantry?"

Max nodded.

"How about I carry Mad Max to the bathroom, trying not to get powdered sugar on anything between here and there, and then Max gets in the shower."

"I already got clean once today!" Max protested.

"We know, Max," Amy said, "but the only way all that sugar is going to come off you is if you do it all again. So, let Mr…?"

"Tate, please," he said. "Tate Darnley."

"Hi. I'm Amy. I'm filling in at the last minute for the personal chef who was supposed to be here for the long weekend, to keep everyone staying in the house fed, and Max…."

"I just came to play," Max said. "There's gonna be another boy here, and we're going to play."

"It would be great if you'd haul him into the bathroom for me. Max, be still, and let's try not to make a mess along the way, okay?"

Tate Darnley carried her son as if he weighed nothing at all, through the bedroom she and Max were sharing and into the attached bathroom, then stepped back out of the way for Amy to take over.

Max grumbled, but a few moments later, he was in the shower. Then there Amy was, standing in a tiny bathroom, still coated with sugar, Max on the other side of the shower curtain and Tate relaxing as he leaned against the doorway, grinning back at her.

"You have powdered sugar all over you, too. Worse than Max did. Maybe even worse than I did," he told her.

She turned and looked in the bathroom mirror, wincing at the image reflected back at her. She was covered in powdered sugar, too.

"Are those suitcases on the bed yours and Max's?" Mr. Perfect asked.

She nodded, and he grabbed them both, setting them just inside the bathroom door.

"Thank you." Amy pulled out Max's pajamas, ready to tuck him into bed. "Max, remember soap and shampoo. It doesn't count if you don't use those."

"Awe, Mom!"

"I mean it, Max," she said, raising her voice to talk over the sound of the shower, trying to put fantasyland firmly behind her.

"Great kid," Tate said softly.

"Thank you."

"I bet there's never a dull moment with him around."

"Never."

"What is he? Five? Six?"

"Seven," Amy told him, then could read exactly what he was thinking.

She'd started young with Max.

"I was sixteen when he was born, living on my own with him by the time I was seventeen."

Tate nodded. "That must not have been easy."

"No, but Max was worth every bit of it."

"Then I'd say Max is a lucky boy," the man said.

Chapter Two

Okay, that *was* a comment right out of fantasyland.

Maybe she was dreaming after all.

Because most men were freaked out by the idea that she had a son she was raising on her own, and none of them seemed too concerned about whether she was a good mother to Max—one reason she'd stayed far away from men for the past seven years.

"Thank you," she said, as she looked up at this man, Tate Darnley.

Where did you come from? she wanted to ask him. How could you be so perfect? Or at least, seem so perfect?

There had to be a major flaw in him somewhere, something she just hadn't seen yet but would no doubt discover at any moment. Some crushing flaw. She told herself to focus, that there was work to do, a giant mess to clean up, and yes, she really had been a little afraid of Mrs. Brown and her spotlessly clean house, her admonishment to Amy not to dare mess up anything.

Amy started unbuttoning her white chef's coat, wanting to leave it in the bathroom, because it really was coated with sugar and wearing it while trying to clean up the mess in the kitchen would only make more of a mess. Glancing up, she saw that Tate was still there, backing out of the doorway to the bathroom now, a little flare of something in his eyes, as she watched him watch her.

"Don't worry," she said, laughing a bit. "I'm not… I have something on under this."

"Of course." He nodded, still watching, still looking a bit puzzled and confused.

What she had on was a plain black tank top with spaghetti straps and a built-in bra—nothing fancy, nothing too revealing and exceedingly comfortable. It got hot in a kitchen in a chef's coat.

So why did she feel as self-conscious as if she'd just peeled off her clothes down to the skin? What a weird night.

"So," she said, looking up at him and trying to pretend a nonchalance she certainly didn't feel. "I should get back to the kitchen."

He nodded, still standing in the doorway, took a tentative step forward, watching her as he did, like she might want to run away and wanting to give her a chance. "You've still got powdered sugar in your hair."

"Oh. Forgot." She started swiping at it, sugar going this way and that as she brushed her hands through her hair and along the braid. It just wasn't working, and she finally took her hair out of the braid.

"Bend forward," he said. "I'll get it."

And then he had his hands in her hair.

Nothing overtly sexy about it, just that she loved it when

anyone fooled with her hair. Even the hairdresser. It was one sad but true little secret thrill she'd allowed herself over the years. Letting a really cute guy cut her hair. And now, Mr. Perfect had his hands in it, brushing out a cloud of powdered sugar onto the floor.

She whimpered a bit, hopefully nothing that could be heard. And yet, she couldn't help herself. Mr. Perfect had his hands in those little curls of hair at the nape of her neck, then brushing along her shoulders, her collarbone and then her chin.

He backed up suddenly, like a man who'd been burned, then said, "Looks like some of it got down the collar of your chef's coat."

Okay, that was it. She had to get out a little bit more. Obviously it was time, when she started to melt from a guy brushing sugar out of her hair.

He finally stopped, stepping away from her. "I did what I could, but…"

He certainly had. More than enough. And the way he was looking at her…she moved quickly, ruthlessly, to tug her hair back into place in the braid.

"I have to get back to the kitchen," she said firmly. "I don't want anyone else to see the mess I made. Max?" she raised her voice to make sure he heard. "I'm going to leave the bathroom door open just a crack, and I'll be right next door in the kitchen, okay? Your pajamas are right outside the shower. Come find me when you're dressed?"

"Mom, I'm not a baby!" Max protested.

Mr. Perfect laughed and said, "Come on. I'll help you clean up."

Don't, she thought. *Just…don't.*

But he followed her back into the kitchen. Powdered sugar was on the countertops, the sink, the floor and, in what seemed like some cosmic joke, coating the top of the lemon bars.

"Look at that," she said, pointing to them. "That's why I went and got the extra bag of powdered sugar. To coat the top of the lemon bars, and somehow, by dropping it, I managed to do just that. Do you ever feel like the world is just sitting back and laughing at you?"

"Not very often. Although," he said, staring at the lemon bars, "I will cop to coming in here planning to beg, borrow or steal one of those."

She grabbed a dessert plate from the cabinet, a fork and served one to him at the breakfast bar that was part of the big island in the middle of the kitchen. "I think you've earned it."

He held up a hand to refuse. "I promised to help you clean up."

"I know, and I appreciate it, but right now, the lemon bars are still warm. They're even better when they're still warm from the oven."

He hesitated, sat on one of the high stools, picked up the fork but didn't use it. "The other thing is, I kind of promised Max I'd help him get another one, too. Or maybe…just a bite of mine."

She shook her head. "The kid never quits. Never. Not with anything."

Tate Darnley shrugged. "I had to ask. We bonded over our desperate desire for dessert."

"I'll save him some crumbs," she said. "Unless you want to share yours with him."

"I don't think I like the kid that much," he said, holding a forkful to his mouth and sniffing it like it was some kind of fine wine and he was drunk on it already.

Amy had grabbed a hand towel, planning to start cleaning but couldn't help herself. She had to watch him take that first bite. She loved watching people who really loved her food, and she wanted very badly for him to absolutely adore hers.

He put the forkful in his mouth, his lips closing around it, eyes drifting shut and groaning in an exaggerated but highly flattering way, savoring every bit.

"Oh, my God. That's amazing!" he proclaimed.

Amy laughed like she hadn't in years, feeling silly and free and just plain happy.

"Thank you, but I know it's not that good," she insisted, leaning against the other side of the kitchen island from him, purposely keeping a good foot and a half of counter space between them.

"No. I mean it." He groaned again, the sound to her lonely ears seeming decidedly sexual in nature. "I could die happy right now. It's that good."

"Then you'd never get to finish eating it," she told him, gazing up into the most gorgeous pair of chocolate-brown eyes with lashes a woman would kill for, thick and full and dark.

"You're right. I can't die yet. I'll eat the whole thing, and then…" He took another bite.

Amy laughed again, thinking it was an absolute joy to feed some people, to feed this man, especially.

He licked his lips, groaned again and now he smelled like lemon bars.

He'd taste that way, too.

She couldn't help the thought. It was just there. She loved those lemon bars, and it occurred to her that she'd never tasted one on a man's lips. And she wasn't going to let herself start now.

She wasn't even sure if he was just happy and having a good time, enjoying something sweet, or if he was flirting with her. Honestly, it had been that long since she'd been out in the man-woman world that she wasn't sure.

This could all be wishful thinking on her part, nothing but a little bit of champagne and a great dessert to him. Although he did have a look that said perhaps he shouldn't be sitting here laughing and having such a good time while eating her food.

She glanced down at his hand, looking for a wedding ring and finding none. Okay, he wasn't wearing a ring. So what? Some men didn't. And even if he was free as a bird, it didn't mean anything.

He took another bite of his lemon bar, still appreciating every bit, still being very vocal in that appreciation, then adding, "I mean it. Never in my life have I—"

All of a sudden, Amy heard a hard tap-tap-tap of high heels across the hard tile floor of the kitchen. Tate obviously did, too, because they both turned toward the sound. She hadn't heard anyone come in, had been sure they were alone.

Now, standing just inside the kitchen door was one of the most polished, perfectly put-together women she'd ever seen—a tall, regimentally thin blonde, wearing what Amy suspected was a very expensive designer suit, a cool, assessing look on her face and a hint of fire—possibly outrage—in her eyes.

"Never in your life have you…what, darling?" she asked.

Amy gulped, thinking this woman might be even more frightening than the housekeeper, Mrs. Brown, and feeling as if she'd been caught red-handed and not with a mess that had anything to do with sugar.

"Victoria?" Tate said, getting to his feet and going to her side, giving her a little peck of a kiss on her perfectly made-up cheek. "I didn't know you were here."

She laughed, clearly not amused. "Obviously."

"I was going to say," Tate told her, "that I've never tasted anything as delicious in my life as these lemon bars Amy made."

A beautifully arched eyebrow arched even higher at that, Victoria's look saying she didn't believe a word of his explanation, although her gaze had to take in the fact that he had indeed been sitting here eating a lemon bar, Amy firmly on the other side of the kitchen island, not doing anything but…

Well, admiring the sights and sounds of him eating that lemon bar. But that was it. Everything else had been pure fantasy. Amy stepped back, clutching her dishcloth and wishing she could disappear behind it.

Victoria turned to Tate and asked, "Where are your clothes?"

Okay, that didn't look so good—the fact that he was standing there in nothing but his pants.

"They're right here," Amy said, grabbing the white garbage bag that contained his things. "I had a little accident with some powdered sugar, and it got all over his shirt and…the rest of his things. Sorry."

He walked over to her and took the clothes, mouthing "sorry" and looking like he meant it. Then he said out loud, "Thank you, Amy. I didn't introduce the two of you. Victoria, this is Amy… I'm sorry, I don't think I got your last name?"

"Carson," Amy told them both, trying to look like someone who didn't matter at all, someone here just to cook and stay out of the way and certainly not cause trouble.

"Victoria, this is Amy Carson," Tate said. "Amy, this is Victoria Ryan, my fiancée."

Fiancée?

"You two are the ones getting married?" she asked, smiling desperately.

"Yes. In four days," Victoria said coolly, nodding barely in Amy's direction. "And you are…?"

"House chef for the weekend. Something came up at the last minute with the man Eleanor hired, and she asked me to fill in," Amy said, still clinging to that smile.

Victoria gave her the once-over, much as she'd done her shirtless fiancé, a most thorough assessment, then said, "You certainly don't look like a chef."

Amy felt her cheeks burn and felt decidedly bare everywhere else. "I made a mess of my chef's coat, too."

And then realized it sounded like they'd had some kind of crazy food fight, which she supposed was better than what it might have sounded like, with all that moaning and groaning Tate had been doing when his fiancée walked into the kitchen.

This was bad on so many levels.

She looked down at the floor, at the mess she was standing in, up to the ceiling, to the wide swath of countertop between her and Ms. Perfect, the perfect companion for Mr. Perfect. And then Amy's gaze landed on the lemon bars. Thinking she had nothing to lose, and that the silly things did tend to put most anyone in a good mood, she picked up the platter they were on and held them out to Victoria.

"Lemon bar?" she asked.

"No, thank you," the woman said.

"Well, we should let Amy get back to her work," Tate said, then looked down at what was left of the lemon bar on his plate. Looked longingly, Amy thought, despite what had just happened.

His fiancée saw him, too, and shot him a look that said, "You're kidding, right?"

He just smiled, grabbed the thing and practically shoved

the rest of it in his mouth, and then led his fiancée out of the kitchen.

Amy stood there, watching them go, not listening in but not really able to keep from hearing as they walked away, either.

"What was that?" Victoria asked.

"Nothing. She told you that she spilled some powdered sugar. It was like a mushroom cloud, rising up and enveloping everything in its path—"

"Sugar? That's what you have to say? Sugar? Tate, we're getting married in four days—"

Tate tried to respond. "My clothes are right here in the bag. You can see for yourself—"

"You can't do this now. Not now."

"I didn't do anything. Nothing happened. I stopped to talk to her little boy—"

"I didn't see any little boy—"

"He was a mess, too. We put him in the shower—"

"We?" Victoria asked.

"Yes… I mean… Victoria, I am not this guy. You know that. I am not this guy—"

"I thought I knew that—"

"You know it. I'm not."

And then Amy couldn't hear any more.

They were gone.

Whew.

The weekend—and especially the job—had to get better from here, she told herself.

Eleanor felt a tad guilty when she saw how upset Victoria was, although it was reassuring that Victoria was at least capable of showing enough emotion to be upset. Maybe she wasn't entirely as unfeeling as Eleanor feared.

"See, we told you to just let it be and see what happened,"

Gladdy told her, having stood there beside Eleanor the whole time and listening to the whole encounter.

"It's a start, I suppose," Eleanor admitted. Still, time was so short, and she just wasn't sure if anything could truly change the planned wedding at this late date. Tate loved plans, loved making them and then meticulously carrying them out, and the plan was to marry Victoria on Saturday.

"Suppose?" Kathleen gave a dismissive huff. "Look at Amy's face right now, now that your godson's gone, and tell me you can't see exactly what she's thinking."

Eleanor peered around the corner once again and into the kitchen. Amy stood leaning back against the cabinets, eyes half shut, head tilted up toward the ceiling, a dreamy look on her pretty, young face.

"She's thinking…it's been a long time since she's been anywhere near a man—any man—let alone one so gorgeous."

"You got all that from one look?" Eleanor asked.

"No," Gladdy admitted. "I know that from talking to her. Believe me, it's been a ridiculously long time, but she's had Max to take care of all on her own and work that barely pays their bills, and there just hasn't been time for herself or anyone else. I doubt she's had so much as a date in the last year."

"Gladdy and I used to beg to be able to babysit for her while she went out," Kathleen explained. "And the poor thing just wouldn't do it. Said she's sworn off men or some ridiculous thing like that."

"Sworn off men? You brought someone here to lure my godson away from his fiancée within four days' time, and she's sworn off men? You didn't tell me that," Eleanor complained.

"Well, Amy obviously knows that was a mistake right

now. Remember the way she looked when Tate took off his shirt? Or when she brushed sugar from his hair?"

"Yes." Kathleen sighed, looking wistful. "Nothing like the sight of a beautiful man or the feel of running your fingers through his hair, that delicious feeling of anticipation of so much more."

"It's a beautiful thing," Gladdy said.

Eleanor had to admit, "I don't think Tate's ever looked at Victoria like that."

"Like he wants to drag her off into some dark corner and have his way with her?" Gladdy offered.

"Yes. Although, I'm sure he's not a drag-her-off-into-a-dark-corner-and-have-his-way-with-her kind of man," Eleanor admitted.

"What a pity."

"Maybe we can change his mind," Gladdy said. "Or maybe Amy can."

Later that night, Tate sat outside on the patio, talking to one of his oldest and best friends. He still felt befuddled and was determined to lay out his supposed crimes in the most straightforward way possible in order to evaluate the seriousness of his offenses.

"So," he concluded his scary tale of sugar-filled bliss in the kitchen that had turned to near-disaster in the blink of an eye, "let me have it. How bad do you think it was?"

"You got sugar all over you, took off a lot of your clothes, helped her get her kid in the shower and moaned and groaned while eating her lemon bars as Victoria walked in?" Rick asked, leaning back in the wicker patio chair.

Tate nodded. "That was it."

"This other woman…she didn't touch you?"

He frowned. "She brushed some sugar off me. Off my hair and my clothes."

"And you didn't touch her?"

"No," Tate said quickly, then had to backtrack. "Wait. I did. I helped brush powdered sugar out of her hair. And off her neck. Maybe…yeah, her collarbone, I'm afraid."

Rick frowned. "And you liked it, right?"

"I did." Tate shook his head, the point where he crossed the line, right there. The neck. The collarbone. "That's when I knew I was in trouble, when I knew I was doing something I probably shouldn't have, as a man who's engaged and getting married in four days."

"Yeah, I'd say that's where you messed up," said Rick, who'd been married all of a year. "Tate, it's not like you suddenly don't notice other women or like you're just… dead inside. It's just that, you don't get yourself into that kind of situation with another woman—"

"I didn't think I was. I mean, those things she baked just smelled so good. That's all it was. I swear. I couldn't ignore that smell, and when I went into the kitchen, it was just the kid there, and I talked to the kid. Funny little kid—"

"Who told you about the whole sugar daddy thing?"

"Yeah." Tate shook his head. Weird. Very weird. "And then, she came walking into the kitchen and poof! Before I even said anything to her or sensed any kind of impropriety in the situation, we're enveloped in this cloud of powdered sugar."

Rick shook his head. "That's a story I haven't ever heard before. Attacked by sugar. I had to take my clothes off, honest—"

"It's not a story. It's what happened. I swear," Tate claimed, still feeling confused and fuzzy-headed from all the champagne. How had this happened to him?

"Were you drunk?" Rick tried. "Because, hey, it happens. We get drunk, we do things we wouldn't normally do…."

"No, I wasn't drunk. I was…just a little loose and happy. You know. Everything was good. I'm just going along living my life. Victoria's father and all those guys from work keep making toasts to me and Victoria, and when your future father-in-law is making the toasts, you drink. You know?"

Rick nodded.

"And then…it's like… I don't know. It just happened."

Rick leaned closer, whispering in case anyone else might be listening, because a dozen people had descended on the house. "You didn't kiss her?"

"No! Nothing like that—"

"But you wanted to."

Tate winced, not wanting to even think about that. "I… like—"

"Yeah, you wanted to," Rick concluded, shaking his head like it wasn't even a question.

"She had really nice hair," Tate said. "It was reddish, and she had it in this braid. The sugar got in it, and I liked… trying to brush the sugar out of it. And then, her neck was right there. These little tiny curls that had escaped from her braid, right there against her neck, and she smelled so good. Like sugar and those damned lemon bars, and it's been a long time since I kissed another woman. A long time. And all of a sudden, I'm thinking…I won't ever kiss another woman again. I mean, not really kiss one. I mean, I shouldn't. I don't intend to…."

"But you wanted to," Rick said again.

"Yeah, okay. For a second, I did. And then I thought…" *Wait a minute. Stop. Back up. Trouble here. Get out. Get out right now. You are not this guy. You are not going to be this guy.*

"So, you're thinking…for old times' sake? Last chance as a single man and all that?" Rick said.

"No. Really, no. It just kind of freaked me out that I wanted to. That I was curious about…what it would be like, and that…you know? I'm going along living my life, about to get married, and poof! Cloud of sugar, and I've got my hands in this woman's hair, wanting to kiss her neck, even if it was just for a second or two. So, come on, tell me. How big of a jerk am I?"

"I don't know. You're in a gray area here," Rick concluded. "It sounds like you really didn't do anything awful—"

"I didn't. I swear."

"And we're all human. From time to time…you know. You're going to want to do things like that, but the key is that you don't actually do it, and the way to do that is not to put yourself in the position to want to do it. So you don't turn into that guy."

"Right," Tate said, taking some comfort in that. "Don't get in that spot. Don't be that guy. I should have just walked away."

"Yes, you should have."

"It was those damned lemon bars," Tate said.

"Oh, please," Rick scoffed. "They couldn't have been that good."

"You didn't taste them. You didn't smell them. I mean… they have to be in there, in the kitchen, right now."

"And you are going nowhere near the kitchen, my friend. The kitchen is definitely off-limits to you."

"Yeah, you're right. I just have to stay out of the kitchen. That's all. But you could go down there and get some for both of us. You just don't know how good they were."

Chapter Three

Amy did not sleep well.

She kept having nightmares in which she was being chased by a really scary bride wielding a giant hand mixer as a weapon. Really powerful mixers had always freaked her out a bit. And then the scene shifted, and she was some sort of human baked good, naked, rolled in powdered sugar and then put on display at the reception for the whole wedding party to see. She would swear she still had sugar all over her, despite having scrubbed herself completely in the shower last night. She thought she could still smell it on herself, too.

There might have been another dream where someone had been licking sugar off her body, but she refused to even think of that one, grimly forcing all such thoughts from her head.

She hadn't allowed herself any thoughts remotely like that since Max was born, and that had worked just fine for her for so long. In fact, it had worked perfectly until a few hours ago. Right then, it was suddenly not okay that she hadn't had a man's hands on her in years, hadn't sighed over the sight of one's body or felt that little kick of anticipation that said something was going to happen.

Delicious, magical things.

It couldn't have waited another three days? Tate would be safely married; Amy would be safely done with this first professional chef's job. That was all she was asking for. Just a few days!

She'd imagined it all quite logically. She'd get a good job, the first one she'd ever really had, a little money in the bank, a safety net against hard times and unexpected expenses. Life would be good, settled, safe for the first time in years. And then, she'd see someone, a man, mildly interesting and attractive and she'd think… Okay, it's time. She'd imagined herself tiptoeing, quite cautiously and sanely, back into the dating scene.

Not diving in, headfirst and naked, into a bowl of powdered sugar for someone to lick off her!

Amy willed herself to go back to sleep. She had to be up in a few hours to face Tate, Victoria and all their relatives; feed them; and hopefully become all but invisible to the entire wedding party for the duration.

She'd almost gotten back to sleep when she thought she heard someone fumbling around in the kitchen.

Amy sighed and looked at the clock.

Four o'clock in the morning?

She'd planned on getting up at 6:00 a.m. to feed any early risers who might show up in the kitchen soon after that, but 4:00 a.m. was ridiculous.

Still, someone was in there, banging the cupboards shut, fumbling with utensils. She feared if she didn't get up and see what was going on that she might wake up to an even bigger mess than the one she'd made with the sugar.

She left Max sleeping soundly beside her, grabbed a fresh chef's coat off a hanger in the closet and put it over her plain, cotton pajamas. She padded into the kitchen and found…

Oh, no!

Victoria!

Amy would have turned and run as fast as she could, but the woman spotted her first, looking like she might throw up at the sight of Amy.

She was still wearing that ultraperfect suit, except it wasn't so perfect anymore. It was rumpled and wrinkled, the blouse unbuttoned by one too many buttons and coming untucked from her skirt, her hair falling out of that perfect knot it had been in earlier.

Amy decided right then that taking this job was a big, big mistake—a colossal, ultrahideous mistake. She had to find a way out of here right now. She and Max could go running off into the night, never to have to worry about Tate Darnley licking sugar off her again. But then Victoria, looking grayish in the face and clutching her stomach, spotted Amy and looked as miserable to see Amy as Amy was to see her—maybe even worse.

"Are you okay?" Amy asked finally.

"I'm afraid I don't feel well," Victoria whispered back. "I was looking for something to settle my stomach, and I couldn't find anything in the guesthouse where I'm staying. Do you—"

"Let's try some soda crackers to start with," Amy suggested, because she knew where those were already. She took the box from the cabinet and handed them to Victoria. "Just nibble, very slowly. And I'll look for some tea. Ginger is good for settling your stomach. Or mint."

Amy found chamomile tea. That would do. She quickly grated a bit of fresh ginger to blend with it. There was a tap that dispensed hot water at the touch of a handle, and she soon had medicinal tea brewing in a small pot for poor Victoria.

Had she really made the woman sick? Just from the stress of Victoria finding Amy with Tate?

Then Amy had an even worse thought. Victoria hadn't eaten anything Amy had cooked, had she? Because already, there were a number of freshly prepared pasta and vegetable salads in the refrigerator, each clearly labeled for the guests to help themselves. Being suspected—or responsible—for giving the bride food poisoning at her first real catering job would be a genuine nightmare.

Victoria nibbled her cracker, looking like she was afraid of every bite she took, like it might come back to haunt her. Amy stared at the tea, steeping it again and resigning herself to waiting a bit longer. With the fresh ginger, it needed a few minutes to brew, and minutes now felt like hours.

"I am so sorry about earlier," Amy finally said. "I swear, my son was with your fiancé and me most all the time. Even when it didn't look like he was, he was right back there in the bathroom, taking a shower. He's only seven, and I left the door open so I could hear him in case he needed anything. He walked back in right after you left."

Surely Victoria would get the fact that Amy wasn't going to do anything inappropriate with a man with her son right there. Of course, her son had told Tate that Amy had a sugar daddy who took care of them both, so, if Victoria had heard about that, she might well think Amy would do just about anything.

"Your fiancé was a perfect gentleman," Amy said.

Victoria made a face, closed her eyes and pressed a hand

to her stomach again. Was she that insecure? That worried? That jealous? Was her fiancé that much of a jerk?

Amy steeped the tea bags again, thinking that surely in the entire course of human history time had never dragged by so slowly during the brewing of a single cup of tea. Finally, she thought it was ready. She'd have added sugar but was afraid to even touch the stuff in front of Victoria, so she just got out a mug and poured.

The woman picked up the mug, looked at it like it might contain some deadly poison. Honestly, did Amy look like some kind of food-poisoning home wrecker?

Victoria finally overcame her fears and took a sip of her tea.

Amy waited, Victoria waited, both holding their breath.

"Oh, no!" Victoria groaned as she turned around and threw up in the sink.

Amy fussed over her, brought her a warm, wet hand towel to wipe off with, brought her plain water to drink, got rid of all the crackers and tea in the vicinity, thoroughly flushed the mess in the sink and found some air freshener to try to kill the smell lingering in the kitchen.

Finally, she leaned back against the counter and waited, asking, "What else can I do?"

Victoria sniffled, wiped away a stray tear, looked as if she was trying to think of anything she might say and then just blurted out, "Do you know if, maybe, there's one of those drugstores that stays open all night anywhere around here?"

Amy nodded. That wasn't hard. "I passed a drugstore on my way here, but I didn't notice if it stayed open all night or not. I could search the house for some medicine, if you'd like. There are ten bathrooms, at least. Surely I could find something to settle your stomach."

Victoria shook her head, more tears falling. "I wish there was something that would settle my stomach."

"What?" Amy didn't get it.

"I didn't think anything about it in the last few weeks, with all the stress of the wedding and everything, but tonight, I checked over my to-do list? It was not my daily to-do list but my master to-do list for the wedding."

Amy nodded, as if it was perfectly normal to have daily to-do lists, master to-do lists and probably to-do lists in between.

"That's when I realized," poor Victoria said. "That… well…I think what I really need is…a pregnancy test."

Amy waited, letting that fully sink in, managing to say nothing but a noncommittal "Oh."

Perfect.

She was going to help Mr. Perfect's fiancée find a pregnancy test? After fearing she might have broken up the wedding with the little sugar incident?

"And I know this isn't fair at all," Victoria said, sounding quite human now. "And I don't really know you, and I wasn't that nice to you before, and I'm sorry. Honestly, I am. This wedding…this wedding is about to make me crazy."

"I hear they do that," Amy said, trying to provide some comfort, wondering how Mr. Perfect felt about kids, hoping for Victoria's sake and the kid's sake that he liked them.

"Yeah, well, the thing is…could you possibly not tell anyone anything about this? I know it's a lot to ask, and I'm sorry, but…could I trust you not to do that?"

"Of course." Amy nodded. "You'll want to tell people when the time is right, and I absolutely understand that it's something you'll want to tell your fiancé yourself, that it should be something private between the two of you. A beautiful moment for you."

But Victoria didn't look like she was expecting a beautiful moment. She looked like she was going to throw up again.

"Does he not want children? Because he seemed great with Max. Really comfortable and sweet with him."

Victoria shook her head. "No, it's not that."

"Well, I know the timing might not be what you expected or planned, but still… You're in love, and you're going to have a baby." Victoria looked even more grim. "Do you…not want children?"

"Of course," Victoria confided, then backtracked a bit. "I think so. Someday. I just… I never thought that day would be now—or a few months from now. I just… I really don't know what I want right now."

"Well, okay. You need time." Amy remembered well how that felt, from when she found out she was pregnant with Max. Adorable as he was, and as much as she loved him, he was the last thing she'd expected at that point in her life, and she had likely felt even less prepared than Victoria did now.

Amy took Victoria by the arm, guided her over to one of the high stools at the breakfast bar and urged her to sit, which Victoria did. Nothing else to eat or drink, not with her stomach as touch and go as it was at the moment, but she could at least sit. The woman looked like she was about to fall down.

"I don't know what I'm going to do," Victoria cried.

"Well, first you have to find out for sure if you are pregnant," Amy said.

That made sense. Amy doubted it would help, because she'd found that most women who were sobbing and saying they were afraid they were pregnant were well and truly pregnant. And they knew it. They'd just been too scared to have it confirmed. She knew that feeling well, from having tried to avoid for three solid months the knowledge that she was pregnant with Max.

"You know, I'm sure I'll have to go out anyway in the morning," Amy offered. "One of the guests will get up and ask for something I don't have in the kitchen, and I'll end up going to the grocery store. And when I do, I'll get you a pregnancy test, okay?"

Victoria sniffled and stopped crying for a moment. "You'd do that for me?"

"Sure," Amy said.

"Thank you. Thank you so much. I couldn't stand to tell anybody I knew really well. I mean—"

"I understand perfectly."

"They all think Tate's perfect and that I'm perfect and that we're perfect together. Which we are, actually. We're just…perfect. We make perfect sense. We want the same things, have the same goals, have the same life plan and we even work in the same industry, so we understand all the pressures that go along with it and the sacrifices people make, and…it should be perfect. You know?"

Amy nodded, although honestly, she'd never been close to perfect in any aspect of her life. But she could see that Victoria obviously felt like that was the standard she needed to meet. Victoria certainly gave the initial impression of a woman capable of being perfect. And now, she was faced with failing in the perfection department, which seemed to be every woman's lot in life, as far as Amy had seen, but she wasn't going to explain that one to Victoria right now.

"One step at a time, okay?" Amy advised, because that did make sense. No sense looking two or three steps ahead. "I'll get you the test in the morning, and I'll bring it to you. Where did you say you're staying?"

"The guesthouse, just down the driveway, past the pool

and the tennis courts. Me and my parents. Eleanor, Tate's godmother, thought we'd like the privacy of not being in the main house. Although, honestly, she and my mother have never gotten along. Something about a man, ages ago. I've always been too scared to ask. But Eleanor put us in the guesthouse. Which is fine, except… I'm scared my mother's going to hear me throwing up. Oh, God, if my mother hears that… You don't know what my mother's like."

"Perfect?" Amy guessed.

"She thinks she is," Victoria said wearily.

And now, Amy really didn't want to know Victoria's mother.

"Okay," she said, trying to keep Victoria focused on what was at hand, on the plan. "I'll look for you in the guesthouse and try to avoid your mother at all costs. I just have to make sure everyone gets a good breakfast first, and then I'll go to the store and I'll bring the test back to you."

Victoria nodded pitifully. "Thank you. Thank you so much."

Tate woke up to a house that smelled even better than it had the night before, when the lemon bars were still warm and gooey and absolutely perfect.

How could that be? How could the woman, Amy, make something even better than those perfect lemon bars?

And he remembered the room he'd always occupied in his godmother's house was almost directly above the kitchen. So whatever luscious things that happened to be cooking there he'd be smelling all weekend long.

He considered bashing his head against the big wooden headboard of the bed, hoping if not to drive the smell out of his brain, to perhaps knock himself unconscious, so as not to be tempted by whatever was going on in the kitchen.

Tempted by the smell, not tempted…the other way. The bad way. He was just hungry, he told himself. Hungry the regular way.

What was he supposed to do? Tate reasoned. Starve all weekend? Staying out of the kitchen was one thing but actually staying completely out of the kitchen for three more days was not going to work.

He'd just make Rick go into the kitchen and get Tate whatever he wanted. That was all. It made perfect sense. He could eat a woman's food without wanting anything else from her, without getting into trouble or doing something stupid or making Victoria suspicious. Sure he could.

It was just food.

He got up and put on his sweats, because the grounds of Eleanor's house were gorgeous, especially in the spring, and he loved to run here. He'd run far away from the kitchen, all the guests, Victoria and everything else. And then he'd have a perfectly reasonable breakfast without ever setting foot inside the kitchen.

It was a good plan, Tate decided. He ran until he was about to fall down, he was so tired, and without even thinking, he headed for the back door to the house to go inside and get cleaned up.

That's when he saw Amy leaning over the trunk of a car, unloading groceries to carry inside.

Tate had already slowed to a walk, and now he slowed even more, to a pace more akin to a crawl. A gentleman would certainly help her carry in those bags, but a gentleman would also not have upset his fiancée mere days before their wedding and would certainly not break the promise he'd made to himself just last night by heading into the forbidden kitchen again.

He hesitated there, trying to decide what to do, and that's when she looked up and saw him, looking not just uneasy at seeing him but downright guilty, he feared.

Ah, hell, he owed her an apology, too. Surely a gentleman would do that, at least. Apologize and then stay away. Maybe after getting a huge plateful of whatever she'd been serving for breakfast as he woke up, some luscious bacon thing. There was nothing like the smell of bacon to make a man ravenous in the morning.

Tate gave her a wary smile, a not-too-interested-but-not-too-guilty one, he hoped, then walked over to the open trunk of the car and said, "Let me help you with these."

"No, it's fine. I didn't get much. Just a few special requests for some of the guests." She hung on stubbornly to the bag he'd planned to take from her.

"Really, I insist. Eleanor would scold me if I let a lady haul these things in when I was right here to do it for her."

She now had the one bag clutched to her chest like she'd fight him to the death for it, if it came down to that. "Okay," she said. "But I've got this one. You can get the rest, if you really want to."

Tate gave her a smile that he hoped didn't look completely forced, took the rest of the bags from her trunk and followed her inside to the scene of his downfall the night before.

It was spotlessly clean, he noted, no traces of powdered sugar anywhere, and yet it smelled divine. Fresh bread, most certainly. A hint of bacon remaining. Eggs, he thought.

His stomach rumbled as he set the bags down on the countertop by the huge refrigerator. Amy shot him a look that said he had to be kidding to be back here, right now, at the scene of the almost-crime, just the two of them alone, and him wanting breakfast.

"Sorry," he said, thinking if she offered him anything he'd just take it and run. No time for temptation of any kind. No guilt necessary. No upsetting Victoria or anyone else.

She sighed, put the small bag she'd been carrying down in the farthest corner of the kitchen and said, "You missed breakfast."

"Yes, I did," he said, staying carefully in his spot, far away from her.

"And I'm here to feed the guests, so I suppose I'll have to feed you."

He swallowed hard, his stomach thrilled at the offer, his taste buds, too, his head telling him to be smart, to get out. But it was three days until the wedding. He'd have to eat sometime, wouldn't he?

It wasn't like the woman held some kind of special powers over him. She was just a woman who'd been momentarily covered in powdered sugar while he'd been tipsy, rethinking his soon-to-be lost bachelorhood and had a momentary lapse, nothing more. Surely he could eat her food and not want to do anything else to her. It was a new day, after all. He was himself again, a good guy, a logical, reasonable guy, getting ready to marry a wonderful woman, perfect for him in every way.

So it wasn't some crazy, intense, hormone-fueled kind of passion between them. It was something infinitely more substantial than that. An honest respect and affection that had grown slowly over time into what he believed would be a dynamic, powerful, long-standing partnership, something that had a shot of withstanding the test of time far greater than any silly infatuation.

What could possibly go wrong with that?

"Thank you," he said, smiling with nothing but politeness, he hoped. "I'd love some breakfast."

"Sit," she said, pointing to a high stool at the breakfast bar on the far side of the kitchen, putting cabinets and a couple of feet of highly polished black granite between them.

Perfect.

He'd stay on his side, and she'd stay on hers.

And he'd get fed and leave.

No harm done.

He went obediently to his side of the kitchen and sat, hoping no one walked by and saw him there, just… because.

Because he didn't want to look guilty. Didn't want to feel guilty. Didn't want to do anything that required him to feel guilty. Because he was a good guy.

This could be like a little test he gave himself, he decided. He was a man getting married to a wonderful woman, and he could sit in this kitchen with an attractive redhead who cooked like a dream and not do anything but appreciate her…food. Yeah, this was all about the food.

He'd been bewitched by her food.

She had a nice smile, he admitted to himself, because he always tried to be honest with himself. And she smelled good, but that was mostly about the food, too, because she always smelled good enough to eat.

Oops.

No, he was okay. He was going to get it back, that Zen-like calm of a man certain of his decision to be married in three days, certain he'd done the right thing.

"Just give me a minute to put these things away, and I'll find you something to eat," Amy said, making quick work of that chore and then facing him from the side of the big stainless-steel refrigerator.

"Fine. Great. Thank you."

Yeah, he was okay.

She hummed while she worked, he realized while staying far, far away from her, as far as he could get and still be in the kitchen. Her hair was back in the braid, but obviously didn't want to stay there. It looked as if it was constantly fighting to get out, little red tendrils of curls going this way and that.

Delicate, fiery-red circles on the pale skin of her neck.

He closed his eyes, trying to block out the thought, but it was a mistake, because it made him remember being up close and personal with that neck the night before. Remembering a fine coating of powdered sugar on that neck and the urge he'd had to lick it off.

Tate winced, groaned, shook his head to block out that image, and then found Amy had turned to stare at him.

"Are you okay?"

No, he was crazy, he decided. Wedding-derangement syndrome. Surely such a thing existed. Other perfectly sane, reasonable people just went nuts. Look at Victoria, after all, and how wacky and uptight she'd been the past few weeks.

"I'm fine," he insisted to Amy, telling himself to get out, now, while he still could.

But then Amy said, "I made bacon and spinach quiche, fresh croissants, fried potatoes and fresh-cut fruit this morning. I could warm up something for you."

He felt every bit of his resolve to save himself slipping away, as he once again lied to himself, pledging that he was strong enough and smart enough to simply eat this woman's wonderful food and not get into any other sort of trouble with her.

"Okay," he agreed.

"So what would you like?"

"All of it," he said.

She looked back at him questioningly.

"I'll just..." Was that bad? It all sounded so good. It had all smelled so good. He wanted it all. He shrugged, as if he could still pretend he didn't want her food so much that he was risking his entire future by being here in the kitchen with her to get it. "My run this morning... You know? I'm always famished after a run. Anything you have is fine. Anything quick and not too much trouble."

Was that agreeable enough? He hoped so. He certainly didn't want to cause any more trouble. Please, let him not cause any more trouble for anyone, especially himself.

"Okay." She nodded, pulling a big bowl out of the refrigerator and scooping out a serving of mixed fruit. "You can start with this while I warm up a plate of quiche and potatoes for you."

She put the bowl down in front of him, along with a pretty cloth napkin and polished silver utensils, then she promptly turned her back on him to go to work on the rest.

Tate dug in to the fruit like a man half starved to death. Just plain cut-up fresh fruit. Nothing special about it, he told himself. She hadn't done anything to it, so it had to be his imagination that it was really, really good. Or maybe the sheer anticipation of what was to come, what he'd smelled this morning—bacon, eggs in the quiche, fried potatoes, freshly baked croissants. He soon smelled it all again as she warmed things in the microwave.

He sat obediently on his stool, still having gone undetected in the kitchen with her, not doing anything untoward at all, feeling quite proud of himself. He was back, Tate the good guy, soon-to-be married, and all was right with the world. She put a plate of luscious-smelling, beautiful food down in front of him. He could smell the bacon, the golden crust of the quiche, the onions and spices mixed in with the potatoes, the warm croissant.

"Anything else I can get you?" she asked politely.

He smiled, again not too friendly, and said, "No, thank you. This is perfect. Just perfect."

She put a small dish of butter in front of him, a salt shaker, then frowned at the pepper shaker in her hand. "Just a second. I bought fresh peppercorns for the grinder. I just think fresh pepper tastes better."

She turned to find the little plastic grocery bag she'd stashed in the far corner of the kitchen, picked it up and pulled out a little jar, but when she went to put the bag back down on the counter, she didn't quite make it. The bag caught half on the edge, half off, and then slid to the floor. A little spice bottle rolled toward him, and Tate bent to pick it up.

"Oh, it's okay. I'll get it. Really," she said.

"No, I've got it. Pumpkin spice," he said, thinking it would probably smell great, too, in anything she made. And he didn't even like pumpkin. Not really.

He saw one more thing on the floor, reached for it just as she did, but he got there first, and then saw…

Yeah, it really was.

One of those home pregnancy tests.

Chapter Four

Amy froze.

Victoria—who'd stopped short in the doorway to the kitchen when she'd seen Tate—had caught Amy's attention at just the wrong moment, when Amy should have been making sure the stupid grocery bag ended up on the stupid counter. She'd missed it.

Victoria froze, too.

Tate gingerly picked up the little pink box with the pregnancy test in it, as if it might contaminate him or something, his attention firmly on that and then Amy. Amy gave the slightest little nod off to the left to Victoria, telling her to get out of there. If Tate saw her now, he'd know everything in an instant, just from the look on her face. Victoria mouthed a "thank you," then tiptoed back out of the room.

"Sorry," Tate said, getting up from the counter and walking over to Amy with the box, then holding it out to her.

She took it, forcing a smile. "No problem."

"Are you okay?"

She nodded, putting the little box behind her, firmly on the counter this time, and turning back to face him, ready to try to brazen this out, as if there was nothing unusual at all about her buying or needing a home pregnancy test.

He looked as if he didn't believe her one bit. "Well, I guess… Max will be happy. I mean, when I was his age, I always wanted a little brother or a little sister."

"Max?" Oh, no! One little favor for his bride-to-be, in trying to atone for the sugar fiasco, and look where it had gotten Amy. "You can't tell Max. Max doesn't know anything about this. I don't know anything, really, about this. No one knows anything for certain."

"Okay. Of course," Tate said. "I would never… I mean, you can tell Max whatever you want, whenever you want—"

"If there's even anything to tell," she reminded him. "I mean, I'm really not…it's just…it's not even mine, okay?"

He frowned. "Not your baby? How could it not be your baby? You're having a baby for someone else?"

"No, the test. It's not my test. I—" What else could she say, after that brilliant *It's not even mine?* Her brain had just fumbled this completely. "It's just… I bought it for a friend. Really."

"Okay," Tate said, not buying a word of it, she was sure.

Amy shook her head. "Look, just forget about this, okay?"

"Of course. I didn't see anything. I won't say anything. Promise."

"Good. Especially not to Max!"

"Wouldn't dream of it," he said. "I'll just take my breakfast and go."

"Good," Amy said.

He picked up his plate, his utensils, his napkin, then looked even more troubled than before when he turned to her and whispered, "It's not… I mean, Max said Leo was… it's not Leo's, is it?"

"No!" she said, almost yelling.

He still looked confused but gave up, took his breakfast and fled.

Amy groaned and buried her head in her hands.

Victoria peeked around the doorway to the kitchen ten minutes later, looking scared and maybe still queasy.

"It's okay. He's gone," Amy said, motioning for Victoria to come on in.

"I'm sorry," she said. "I'm sorry. I just…couldn't wait any longer, and I thought I'd just come over here and see if you were back from the store yet, and if you got it, and then…I'm sorry."

"He thinks I'm pregnant. Maybe with someone else's baby. As in another woman's baby, I guess, which has him really puzzled," Amy said. "But I had to say something, because I was afraid he'd say something to Max or maybe just hint at something with Max. And then he wanted to know if it's Leo's baby, which is truly hilarious, considering Leo is dead now and was eighty-six years old."

"Wait, you had a fling with an eighty-six-year-old man?"

"No! But even if I had, he died a year ago. So to be having Leo's baby…well, that would be a really neat trick."

"I heard. I hid in the dining room, listening. I feel just terrible. Not sick-terrible, although…well, yeah, that, too.

But what I meant was, I feel terrible about dragging you into this, when you were just trying to help."

"As long as he doesn't say anything to Max, I'm fine," Amy reassured her. "Or Kathleen or Gladdy or Eleanor, now that I think about it. Not that they'd believe anything about me having Leo's baby. It's just…well, Kathleen was Leo's wife, and she'd know there was no way it could be Leo's. But then she and Gladdy and Eleanor would all be interested in exactly whose baby I was supposedly having. They wouldn't stop asking until they got answers."

"Oh, God!" Victoria said, looking all done-in.

"But don't worry. Tate promised not to tell, and hopefully, he's a man of his word."

"He is," Victoria reassured her. "Always. He's just—"

"What?" What did he do? There had to be something wrong with him. He was a man, after all.

"He tends to try to…take care of people. To want to fix things for them, and if he thinks you're in trouble, he might…well, he'd want to help."

"Oh, great." Amy groaned.

"I'm sorry. I'm really sorry. I am. I should never have dragged you into this in the first place. I'll take care of it. I swear, I will. I just…"

She broke off as Amy opened one of the kitchen drawers and pulled out the pregnancy test, stealthily wrapped up in a plastic grocery bag.

"Have to take this," Amy said slowly, hopefully kindly, but handing it over all the same. "Really, it's the only way."

Victoria got that I-might-throw-up-at-any-second look again and couldn't seem to even take the test from Amy.

"I'm afraid it's not going to get any easier," Amy said, remembering the test she'd taken that had told her she was pregnant with Max. Four tests, actually. It had taken that many to convince her she was truly pregnant, even though every single test she'd taken had come back positive.

Victoria nodded, whimpered just a bit and even then, Amy had to push the test toward her midsection and wait for Victoria to take hold of it.

"Just do it. Right now."

"Okay. I'll try," she said.

"You can use my bathroom. No one goes in that bedroom or bathroom but me and Max, and Max is off playing with one of your cousin's little boys. So if you do this now, you don't have to worry about anyone seeing you or ever knowing what you're doing."

Victoria looked ready to beg for more time.

"Go on." Amy forced herself to go on, to be a part of this little prewedding adventure. Victoria obviously needed a friend, and it looked as if Amy was it. "I'll be here after you're done, in case you need someone to talk to."

Tate was devouring his breakfast on the back terrace when his godmother and two of her friends she'd invited to the wedding came outside.

"Good morning, my dear," Eleanor said. "How was your run?"

"Perfect, as always. You know how much I've always loved this house." He stood up and kissed Eleanor on her cheek, then looked to her friends. "Ladies, I'm so glad you could join us for the weekend. I hope you're enjoying it here."

"Oh, it's beautiful," the one named Kathleen, a pretty white-haired woman, said. "It's a shame Eleanor will be giving up the estate after this weekend."

"Please, it's much too much for one person and a handful of servants. Feels like a museum. I should have done this years ago," Eleanor insisted.

"Still, it has to be hard to let it go completely. All the good memories?" Gladdy, also pretty and white-haired, asked.

"But I'll still have all the memories," Eleanor said. "And we have wonderful ones, don't we, my dear?"

"Yes, we do," Tate agreed, explaining to her friends, as he held out seats for them all at the table on the patio. "My mother died when I was ten, and my father traveled a lot for his work. Eleanor was my mother's best friend and stepped in and made sure I always had a place to stay when my father was away. This was like a second home to me, and when it came time to pick a spot for the wedding…well, this place is so beautiful, and Eleanor has always thrown the best parties."

"I have to agree. It's been nothing but lovely, so far," Kathleen said, sitting back and sighing with contentment as she looked over the grounds. "I just wish my dear Leo was here to enjoy it."

Tate frowned. "Leo?"

"Her husband," Eleanor explained.

"We lost him not long ago," Kathleen said with a sad smile. "No one loved a party like Leo."

"Your…husband?" Tate couldn't help it. He had to be wrong about this. Kathleen had to be at least sixty-something, maybe even older. She was a pretty woman in great shape, so it was hard to tell. Surely they were talking about different men named Leo.

"Yes. He was a dear," she said. "I treasure every moment we had together."

"They met at Remington Park Retirement Village, where I went to recuperate after my knee surgery. I told you it's a lovely place," Eleanor claimed. "With any number of eligible, older men, although from what I've heard, I doubt any of them can claim to be as full of life as Leo."

Tate just blinked, feeling like he'd walked into some kind of carnival maze of conversation, too bizarre to be believed. Surely the lovely young woman who'd made his breakfast wasn't carrying his godmother's friend's late husband's child! And surely the two women—the bereaved widow and the possibly pregnant woman having the widow's husband's baby—weren't both here for the long weekend together!

Still, hadn't Eleanor said she knew the chef she'd hired to fill in at the last minute because Amy used to work at Remington Park? Tate thought he remembered something about a connection to that place. But just because the two women were involved with a man with the same name didn't mean a thing. It couldn't.

"I hope the wedding doesn't bring up sad memories for you," Eleanor said to Kathleen.

"Oh, dear, I was doing just fine until sweet little Amy made those lemon bars. The minute I smelled them yesterday I thought of Leo. They were his favorite. Leo just adored her and Max, and Amy made lemon bars for Leo all the time."

Tate made a choking sound, the ladies clustering around him, patting him on the back and fussing over him. He tried to claim he'd swallowed something the wrong way, although he hadn't taken a bite since before the ladies showed up. So it was an exceedingly poor lie but was all he could come up with at the moment.

How many Leos could there be who loved lemon bars?

And did they know about each other? Did Amy know that Kathleen was here, and did Kathleen know that Amy had been involved with her late husband and, even worse, that she was carrying Kathleen's late husband's baby?

Surely not.

Come to think of it, Eleanor's two friends had been late additions to the invitation list. Eleanor said she'd like for her new friends to have a chance to see her soon-to-be former home and for her to have their company over the long weekend. And she'd hired Amy at the last minute, so maybe Amy didn't know they were here yet, and maybe Eleanor didn't know that Amy had been involved with Leo at all.

How utterly bizarre.

"You know, Eleanor, we could work on finding someone for you," Gladdy said, looking excited by the prospect. "Kathleen and I need a new project to keep us busy. Assuming you'd like to have a man in your life?"

"Well, if he wasn't too much trouble," Eleanor said. "Let's face it. Men our age tend to be a needy lot."

"Yes, they do. But we could try," Gladdy said. "It might be fun."

Tate felt like choking again.

They were going to find Eleanor a man now? Hopefully one much different from that scoundrel Leo, messing around with a woman half… no, surely a third of his age? Leaving her pregnant and alone to raise their child, when she already had another child of her own. Was that what the money Max said he left them had been about? The baby on the way? Max said it was for school, but Max was seven. What did he know?

What did any of them know about each other?

Tate saw the possibility of some very bad things happening over the weekend if certain secrets came out. Looking at Kathleen, he thought about how awful that would be for her. The poor woman had lost her husband and was now about to find out he not only cheated on her with someone much younger than she was but left that younger woman pregnant!

* * *

Eleanor was getting ready to leave with her friends when Tate put his hand on her arm and said, "Would you mind staying a bit? I need to talk to you about something."

"Of course, dear." She bid her friends goodbye, promising to catch up with them in the study to give them a tour of the house and grounds.

"Okay, no," Tate whispered urgently as the two women walked away. "No tour. You can't do that."

Amused, Eleanor whispered back, like they were involved in some sort of mock conspiracy. "Why not?"

"Because they can't go into the kitchen," Tate said, not looking at all like a boy playing a silly game.

Eleanor repeated. "Why not?"

"Because that woman is there. The cook you hired. Amy."

"Of course Amy's there. Where else would she be? She's cooking. Isn't she wonderful. That breakfast this morning? Wasn't it divine?"

"No," he stammered, very unlike himself. He was always so poised, so polished, even as a teenager.

"Tate, what's wrong?"

"I just think it would be better if your friend Kathleen and Amy didn't see each other. Especially not now."

Eleanor was lost at first but then thought back to the day before, eavesdropping in the kitchen listening to Max and his tales of the sugar daddy, Leo. Now that she thought about it, Eleanor didn't remember Amy ever denying the part about Leo being her sugar daddy.

"Oh, dear," Eleanor said.

"So you do know?" Tate whispered urgently. "About Amy and Leo? It's the same Leo, isn't it? She was involved with your friend's husband? A man in his… what? Sixties? Seventies? That Leo?"

"Tate, darling, I don't know what you heard, but—"

"I heard everything," he claimed. "From her and her little boy, Max. Max likes to talk, and he loved Leo, told me all about him. And I know Amy's your friend, but you should know, she heard Max telling me about Leo, and she didn't deny anything."

Eleanor sighed, thinking she was really bad at meddling. She'd known it all along, and now, here she was, her meddling gone bad and Kathleen and Gladdy nowhere near to help her.

What could she do? What could she say?

"Truly, it's not what you think, dear," she began.

"It's exactly what I think. I got it straight from her kid, Eleanor. Does your friend Kathleen know? Because if she doesn't, I'm afraid this might be the weekend she finds out, and if she does know…things could get really ugly here."

"I can assure you that Kathleen and Amy are not going to come to blows with each other over Kathleen's dead husband in my house this weekend. Tate, really—"

"Well, I don't understand how you can be sure of that—"

"I can. I've known them both for the past few months. They get along perfectly well."

He looked completely baffled by that, stating emphatically, "No way."

Given what he thought of the situation, two women sharing the affections of one man—one married to him, one his sweet young thing—and them both getting along perfect? Of course, it sounded ridiculous like that.

Eleanor sighed, looking toward the house where Kathleen and Gladdy had disappeared only moments ago, thinking they'd probably stopped just inside the door and were peeking out, wondering what Tate was saying. They should have all worked out some kind of signal, if one of them needed help. But they hadn't thought that far ahead, and now, here Eleanor was, baffled as to what to do and seeing no possible explanation that might make sense.

"You'll have to just trust me on this," she finally said, a lame try but all she could come up with. "They like each other very much."

"And yet, they were both involved with the same man? At the same time?"

"No," Eleanor began, then caught herself. Amy hadn't denied it. Not at all. So what could Eleanor say? "Yes, I guess. What I mean is this is really none of our business. I'm surprised at you, dear. It's not like you to gossip."

"I'm not gossiping. I'm trying to keep what seems like a nice widow lady and a little boy from facing what might be a very uncomfortable situation for them both," he insisted.

"Of course, you are," Eleanor agreed. "I don't know what I was thinking. Of course, you're only trying to help. Just don't worry. I'll take care of it."

Tate hesitated, still looking troubled.

What in the world?

"Dear, is there something else? Something you're not telling me?"

Something about Amy, Eleanor thought. Tell me about you and Amy, that spilled sugar and those long, longing looks? Eleanor got excited just thinking about it. Maybe she wasn't that bad at meddling.

"I promised her I wouldn't tell anyone," Tate said.

Eleanor smiled, waited, not saying anything.

Tate made a face, one that spoke of pain and honor and true indecision. Then he said, "There might be… things going on that no one knows about yet. Things that would…complicate…things. Between Amy and your friend Kathleen."

"Darling, the man is dead and buried. I don't see how he could possibly cause trouble between the two of them now."

"There might be…things…he left behind."

"You mean, the money? For Max and Amy? Kathleen knows all about that."

He frowned. "She does? And yet…she's fine with that?"

Eleanor had gone and done it again, gotten herself into trouble, fumbling with her words while trying to keep straight the truth and the fiction she and her friends had created to try and get Tate together with Amy. And the fiction Amy and Max had interjected about Amy's relationship with Leo certainly wasn't helping.

"I don't think I could truly explain women and the things that upset them and don't upset them or how they manage to get along, even when…things with men threaten to intercede," Eleanor said, not even sure what she was trying to say herself. "I don't think I'll be alive long enough to explain that one to you, Tate. So you'll just have to trust me on this one, too. The money is not a problem."

Poor dear boy looked even more confused then—and no wonder, given the mishmash of facts parading along here.

"What if there was…something else?" he asked. "Something else he…left behind. Something…of himself…with Amy?"

Eleanor looked again toward the house, helpless and wishing someone would come along and save her or that the skies would open up and a convenient downpour would come along at this very moment, so she'd have an excuse to run away, run for help from her friends.

"Darling, there's really nothing I can imagine that Leo

might have left behind that would upset either Amy or Kathleen."

"Not even…a baby."

"Baby?" What in the world? "You mean, Max? Max is not a baby. Max is seven—"

"No, a real baby. I mean, maybe a baby. One day soon… or not so soon, but one day. Leo's baby."

She laughed, couldn't help it. "You think Leo Gray—eighty-six-year-old Leo Gray—left someone carrying his baby?"

"Eighty-six?" Tate looked like it hurt him just to think it.

"I mean, I heard he was an incredible man, but I doubt even the infamous Leo Gray, at eighty-six, could…"

And then she realized the other part that was so startling. The first, that Leo at his age might ever have left anyone pregnant, had so surprised and amused Eleanor that she forgot for a moment about the second part that was equally startling.

"Amy? You think our dear Amy's pregnant?"

Tate looked ashamed of himself but concerned, too, like he was truly worried about the situation. He nodded this way and that and then threw up his hands in surrender and said, "I don't know. Maybe. I just thought, if she is and it's Leo's…he was really eighty-six?"

Eleanor nodded.

"Ooh." Tate winced.

"I really have to go," Eleanor said. "I'll talk to you later, dear."

"But… I promised Amy I wouldn't tell. I wasn't going to, really, but then I heard that Kathleen's husband's name was Leo and that Leo loved lemon bars, and I thought… this could be bad, you know? Really bad."

"I'll take care of it," Eleanor promised, hurrying off

toward the house and hopefully her friends, who'd talked her into starting this whole mess in the first place.

Victoria was alone in Amy's bedroom, the dreaded pregnancy test still in its little box in her hand, as she paced back and forth in front of the door that led to the bathroom.

She honestly wasn't sure she could go in there.

Her, one of the most sensible, confident women in the world, as she liked to tell herself in her little private pep talks. Everyone needed a pep talk every now and then. Victoria made sure she got her share. So what if they came from herself? A pep talk was a pep talk. She tried one now.

You can do this.

You can do anything.

You are Victoria Elizabeth Ryan, after all.

She looked toward the bathroom door, feeling sick just gazing at it, and whimpered like the frightened little girl she felt like at the moment.

Forcing several deep, deliberately slow breaths, she tried once again, one foot forward, just one step toward that room, to answers.

Amy was right. This was the first step to any sort of decision she had to make, unquestionably the first item on any to-do list from now until she had the answer to this one question.

She took another breath, walked shakily into the bathroom, closed and then locked the door.

Chapter Five

After talking to Eleanor, Tate was even more perplexed than he had been before. No problem? Two women sharing the same man, one maybe carrying his child and one in mourning for him, was no problem?

How could that possibly be?

Women did not share happily, he'd observed.

He didn't tangle with more than one woman at a time, but he'd had friends who'd tried it. They'd always gotten caught eventually, and the situations had never ended with the women happily becoming friends and hanging out for long weekends together for a wedding.

There was something very strange about this.

And he felt really bad about blurting out Amy's secret—or potential secret—like that. He could normally be trusted with all sorts of confidences. It was just that his godmother didn't seem to realize how potentially dangerous and hurtful the situation was—having both Amy and Kathleen here. And he thought someone who knew and cared about both of them should be warned about what might happen should the two run into each other and then certain information come out. Which seemed a likely possibility over the course of a number of days with both women in close contact with one another.

He stood up from the patio table, feeling guilty and very, very confused.

He should at least own up to what he'd done with Amy. Even if it did mean risking a trip back into the kitchen. Plus, he had his empty breakfast plate and utensils sitting on the table in front of him. It would be impolite to just leave them there, and Tate was nothing if not polite.

Picking up his breakfast dishes, he headed for the kitchen to confess to what he'd done.

Eleanor indeed found her friends just inside the house, having surely been peeking through the lace curtains of the back windows, trying to figure out what was going on with her and Tate.

They both looked at her excitedly and expectantly as she walked in, and she touched her index finger to her lips to silence any questions they might have right here, fearing Tate would soon be following her inside. Instead, she gestured for them to follow her through the next room and then into her late husband's study. No one used that room anymore. She got them inside and closed the door behind her, staying right there with her back against the door for good measure, not wanting anyone to interrupt them, either.

"This is a disaster!" she whispered urgently.

"Oh, it can't be that bad. Practically the first thing the boy did this morning was head to the kitchen for one of

Amy's delicious breakfasts, after all," Gladdy reminded her.

"No, it is. It's worse! He thinks Amy really had a sugar daddy! He believes that about her, poor sweet girl. And…" Good Lord! Eleanor realized she'd assumed that if anything like that had happened, Kathleen would have known. And she'd never suspected anything like that of Amy, but still one never knew. "I…I'm sorry. Truly sorry, but…I have to ask. Leo wasn't really her sugar daddy, was he?"

Kathleen and Gladdy both laughed. "Of course not," Kathleen said.

"Well, I didn't think so, but Tate does, and when he said that, I realized she never denied it, not while we were eavesdropping on them in the kitchen last night. Why would she let Tate think something like that about her?"

"She's an attractive young woman who had an older man's money to help her get through school. Rumors have a way of getting started. At first Amy was so mad and hurt by it, but then I guess she figured if she couldn't stop the rumors that she might as well take advantage of them. People assumed certain things about her…like that she was involved in a relationship with an older man—"

"That she was taken," Gladdy jumped in.

"So the men her age left her alone, which, sadly, is what she wanted when she was in school," Kathleen continued.

"Apparently, there are a lot of good-looking men who want to learn to cook. Lots of testosterone floating around in those kitchens. We should have gone to visit her there," Gladdy said.

Whew! That was a relief. "So, Leo was nothing but a convenient little white lie?"

"Of course." Kathleen seemed perfectly confident that he was nothing more to Amy.

"But she's over that now? Right? Pushing men away? Because what we need is a woman who at least wants a man, if she's going to try to take Tate away from his fiancée this weekend!"

"Well—"

"And yet, she just used the Leo-the-sugar-daddy excuse with Tate." Eleanor sighed. It was all so complicated, so difficult.

"She didn't bring up the whole sugar daddy thing," Kathleen reminded them. "Max did."

"But she didn't deny it, either," Eleanor pointed out. "She let Tate think she was for sale to the highest bidder, even if he was an eighty-something-year-old man."

"Okay, so it's not the most perfect start to a relationship," Gladdy said.

"Perfect start? It's the furthest thing from a perfect start." Eleanor stopped, remembering the part she hadn't brought up. "I haven't even told you the worst of it yet."

"There's more? Oh, dear," Kathleen said. "What else?"

"Tate seems to have gotten the idea…and I really don't know how or why, because I was so flustered about the whole thing that I never got around to asking. But he thinks…do you think it might even be remotely possible that…that Amy might be pregnant?"

Gladdy and Kathleen gasped, threw puzzled looks at each other, then took a moment. Eleanor could see them trying to make sense of that piece of information.

"I haven't seen her with anyone," Eleanor began. "Or heard her talk about anyone, and—"

"Surely if she was seeing someone, she'd tell us. I mean, who else would she tell? She hasn't been doing anything but working, going to school and taking care of Max. I think we're her best friends," Gladdy said.

"Her family was just awful to her once she got pregnant

with Max, so she wouldn't tell them. Yes, I think Gladdy's right. I'm sure we'd be the ones she'd tell. You said he thinks she might be pregnant?"

Eleanor nodded.

"I just can't believe that could be, without us knowing," Kathleen said.

"Although, the idea of having a new baby to fuss over and spoil..." Gladdy got a dreamy look on her face. "We could have so much fun, helping to spoil a new baby—"

"Gladdy, please," Eleanor said. "We brought her here to keep Tate from getting married this weekend!"

"Well, how does he feel about children? I mean, maybe the baby's father, whoever he is, is long gone, and you said Tate likes to rescue people. Amy will certainly need help, if there is a new baby, and Tate seemed awfully taken with Max last night in the kitchen."

Eleanor groaned and covered her face with her hand. "I told you, I've never been any good at meddling. Never. And I forgot to tell you, the worst thing of all, the reason my dear godson is distressed enough to blab about Amy's business is that he fears Amy may be having Leo's baby!"

Amy was in the kitchen, staring at the closed door that led to her room. Barley soup was simmering in a big pot on the stove, fresh bread baking in the oven.

Had Victoria fallen in or something? It wasn't a complicated test, done in minutes. No way it would take this long.

She must have chickened out, Amy decided.

Or maybe she took the test and the results had her hysterical or weeping, maybe even passed out on Amy's bathroom floor.

She supposed she'd have to go in there and check on poor Victoria. There wasn't anyone else around to do it, might not even be anyone else who knew about the possibility of Victoria being pregnant. Still, how Amy had gotten herself drawn into wedding drama like this was…

She heard footsteps behind her, strong, confident, decidedly masculine footsteps. Ridiculously, she felt like she already knew just by the sound who it was. Or maybe by the way some internal radar system of hers kicked up a notch.

Not him, she wanted to tell her radar. He's getting married this weekend. He may well have a baby on the way, too. Anybody but him!

Amy turned around.

Of course, it was him.

He was carrying his breakfast dishes and trailing along beside him was Max, dirt rubbed into the knees of his jeans, on his shirt, even on his face, which was beaming with happiness.

"Max!" Amy began.

"I didn't mean to," Max claimed. To hear him tell it, he never meant to do anything like this. Things just magically happened to Max, usually in the worst possible places and at the worst possible times.

"If it helps, his companion in cave exploring looks just as bad," Tate offered, putting a hand of support on Max's shoulder, like they were two guys in this together, understanding things like the necessity to get filthy every now and then.

"Cave exploring? You were in a cave?"

"Not really," Tate whispered.

"Just pretend," Max said. "In a buncha leaves, in this spot where there's lots of bushes and tree branches down low, and it's all dark and… You know, like a cave."

"I could never resist cavelike enclosures when I was a boy," Tate said, again jumping in to defend Max.

"Were you a part of this?" Amy asked.

"Oh, no. Not this mess. This was all Max and his new friend Drew, Victoria's cousin. They had a delightful morning, the nanny said. Messy, but delightful. She's trying to sneak Drew into the house and into his room without Mrs. Brown spotting them, and I was headed this way anyway and said I'd try to get Max past the Drag—"

"Shh," Amy cut him off, then mouthed to him, "If you call her names, Max will, too, except he'll forget and do it to her face."

"Sorry," he mouthed back.

"Do I hafta take another shower!" Max asked, groaning.

"You look like you need one."

"Mooooom! I'll just get dirty all over again!"

Amy sighed. "Yes, you probably will."

"This place is way cool," he said. "Like a big park. We're going to explore some more after lunch."

"Lovely," Amy said.

This was going to call for serious bribes to the nanny, for taking care of two boys instead of one.

"Do I hafta put clean clothes on?" Max said, sounding as if it was a ridiculous thing for a mother to expect.

"Tell you what, we'll skip the shower. But the hands and the face have to be washed and as for the clothes…take those off, put on something else just while you're in the house. You can't drag that kind of mess inside this house, Max! Not this weekend. And then when it's time to go back outside, you can put your dirty clothes on again, and we'll take you out the back way."

He sighed heavily. "Okaaaaayyy."

As they headed for the door to their room, Amy remembered… Victoria.

"Oh, wait!" She ran and got between Max and the door. "You can't go in there."

Max looked puzzled.

Tate looked way too interested in this new twist. He cocked his head to the right and just stared at her, like he might be able to see through both her and the door.

"My clothes are in there, Mom."

"I know. I'll get them, okay?" she offered, rushing and trying to think as she spoke. "How about this. Tate can help you wash up right here in the kitchen sink...."

Amy couldn't help but wince at that as it came out. Not that sinks didn't get dirty or that she wouldn't clean it. Just that in this house, as fancy as it was, right now with all the wedding guests coming and going, her dirty son washing up in the kitchen sink was not something she wanted to ever happen or for anyone to ever see. But she couldn't send him in there with Victoria and her pregnancy test, either, not with Tate right here.

"Yes, if Tate will help you with that, I'll go get you some clothes, and I'll be right back."

Max was puzzled. "But you don't like for me to clean up in the kitchen sink—"

"I know, but just this one time, it's okay," Amy said.

Max still looked unconvinced.

Tate, she could just imagine, was thinking of all sorts of things that might be going on behind that closed door that she didn't want Max to see.

If you only knew, Amy thought.

But Tate didn't say anything. He just found a footstool for Max to stand on and grabbed the clean kitchen towel hanging on the handle of the stove, telling Max, "Come on. This will be completely painless and over in seconds. I promise."

Behind Max's back, Amy mouthed "thank you" to him.

Tate just shrugged.

He was angry, she thought, that she might be pregnant with some old man's baby or that she might have a new man and have brought him here, with her son here, too, and while she was working! He probably had thought of any number of possibilities about her, all of them bad.

Oh, well. She couldn't tell him anything different—not now. Not that it mattered what he thought of her. He was getting married, after all!

Amy disappeared into her room and quietly locked the door behind her. He'd surely find that little tidbit interesting—her locking that door to keep him and Max out.

And then she found herself feeling ridiculously like crying and maybe as if she couldn't even breathe.

It was infuriating!

He was just a man. A good-looking, seemingly kind-hearted man who happened to think her son was adorable and Amy was a…a promiscuous girl and maybe still a promiscuous woman who'd entertain a man in her bedroom, while on a job where her young son was present.

That she'd flirt with Tate one night, while he was engaged, while having another man come to visit her the next day, a man who might have recently gotten her pregnant for the second time in her life without her being married!

How could she be attracted to a man like that? And how could he possibly be attracted to her?

God, she'd been out of this whole man-woman thing for so long that all her man-woman vibes had short-circuited. Nothing she was thinking was making the least bit of sense.

He was good-looking. So what? And charming and nice to her kid. Again, so what? He was also rich and engaged. Nothing else really mattered, did it?

* * *

Tate shook his head, completely perplexed, watching Amy disappear behind the closed, then locked door.

So it wasn't the old man's baby? Because the old man was dead and buried, so it wasn't him in that room with her right now. But whose baby was it? And did the guy know about the baby? Think it was his? And he just couldn't stay away from her? Not even for a few days while she worked this wedding?

Honestly…women? Tate really didn't understand them and was feeling uncharacteristically mad about the whole thing, when it was obviously none of his business.

Why would he even care? He was getting married on Saturday, after all.

He'd made a decision, a very carefully thought out, logical decision, at a time when he'd actually been capable of thinking logically and carefully, when his brain had been functioning in a perfectly fine manner.

Not like now, when he felt as if he was trying to think through a haze of powdered sugar and a kind of hunger that had nothing to do with sugar at all.

"Moms are really weird sometimes," Max said, standing on the stool and leaning over the sink, washing his hands while Tate stood by.

"Yeah, they are," Tate agreed, considering giving the boy a lecture about the importance of not losing his head around women when he grew up.

Someone had to do it, after all. Max didn't have a father to explain things like women to him. And Tate wanted that for Max. He wanted Max to have everything a boy needed or wanted.

"You want to go exploring with us after lunch?" Max invited.

Tate laughed, thinking hiding out in a cave sounded

good to him right now. He could probably stay out of trouble hiding in a cave with Max.

Amy heard a tiny shriek from inside the bathroom before she could even get to the door and knock on it. Now she approached it even more cautiously, waiting on the other side of the door and whispering, "Victoria?"

The door was flung open, a pale, weepy, crazed-looking Victoria standing there, appearing like a woman who had no hope at all in the world, as she whispered, "It's just you? I thought I heard Tate! I was sure I heard him!"

"You did. He's out there—"

She whimpered, bottom lip trembling, tears glistening in her pretty blue eyes.

"But don't worry. He doesn't know you're in here, and I'm not going to tell him. And he can't get in. I locked the door behind me."

"Okay. Good. Thank you."

"Just breathe, Victoria. Don't stop breathing, because you look like you're about to pass out, and if I couldn't catch you, you'd hit the floor, and he'd hear and come charging in here, locked door or no locked door."

"Okay, I'll breathe. I promise."

"So," Amy said, getting to the really hard stuff, "did you take the test?"

Victoria nodded, looking so sad. "Finally. I did it. I took it!"

"And?"

"And time was up, and I was getting ready to read the results when I thought I heard Tate's voice, and I got so startled that I dropped it." She started to cry softly.

"So…you are?" Judging by Victoria's reaction, probably.

"I don't know!" Victoria wailed.

"What do you mean you don't know? Pick it up and see," Amy said. It wasn't that hard to figure out. The woman was pregnant or she wasn't, and that wasn't changing, no matter how hard she tried to keep from knowing.

"I can't. I mean, I guess I could, but…I don't think it would do any good. The little stick hit the countertop and skidded across it and then plopped into the toilet!"

"Oh." Amy frowned.

"I probably couldn't trust what the results said now, right?"

"Probably not," Amy agreed, shaking her head. "I should have got the little box with two tests in it. Every woman needs a second one, anyway, to make herself believe the first one's not a fluke. Don't worry. One of the guests just asked for artichoke hearts for his salad, so I have to go back to the grocery store anyway. I'll get the box with two tests in it, and then…we'll know."

"Thank you," Victoria said, taking a deep, shaky breath and then trying to hold back more tears.

Amy left Victoria hidden in the bathroom, red-eyed and solemn-looking, grabbed some clean clothes for Max and then went back to the kitchen, finding Max a bit wet, but mostly clean, getting what appeared to be cave-exploring tips from Tate.

"Here you go," Amy told Max, handing him the clothes, then had to steer him down the hallway to the laundry room to change.

"But, Mom," he protested. "Our room is right there."

"I know," she told him.

"Why can't I just change in our room?"

"Because you'll make a mess," she claimed.

"But won't I make a mess in the other room, too?"

"No. I won't let you. And…I saw it earlier. It's already

kind of messy, so you won't make as much of a mess in there."

When they got to the laundry room door, she held open the door for him and promised to wait on the other side, to make sure no one came in. Max took his clothes and went, giving her an odd look but not protesting further, probably in fear that he still might end up being ordered into the shower. But Tate…Tate followed them, waiting in the hallway with Amy and giving her a firmly disappointed stare.

Frustrated, irritated and wanting nothing more than to tell him this was his mess, not hers, but simply unable to betray poor, weeping Victoria that way, Amy did the only thing she could think of.

She crossed her arms in front of her and stared right back at him, daring him to say a word.

He shook his head and swore under his breath. "I know it's none of my business—"

"No, it's not," she said, knowing that wasn't going to stop him, either.

"It's just that…your kid is right in there."

"I'm aware of that."

"He could have walked in, any minute, and you've got… you've got. Who have you got in that room?"

"Not who you think," she told him. "I can guarantee that."

He huffed and looked indignant and a little self-righteous and maddening. "Really?"

"Yes, really."

"Then why can't your own son go in there?"

"Because it's private. It's a private situation. Not mine. Someone else's—"

"Oh, right," he said.

"Yes, that's right. I'm protecting someone else's privacy. I'm trying to be someone's friend, and help—"

"Right. How did your test come out?"

"I didn't take it. I told you. It's not mine—"

"Sure, it's not."

"No, it's not." She glared at him. "And just who are you, anyway? The morality police?"

"I just…I like your kid, okay? He seems like a really good kid, and you're…you're—"

"Please, tell me. What am I?"

"Really young to already have one child, on your own, it seems."

"Yes, I am." She was furious now—not that she hadn't heard any of this before, but not from him. Not from a man she actually found attractive before he'd opened his mouth just now. Not one she'd daydreamed about.

Served her right, looking at a man like him and thinking the things she'd thought. About how perfect he was, and how he looked carrying Max. No man had ever scooped Max up and hauled him into the bathroom to get cleaned up after Max had made one of his messes. There was no man who teased him, who shared treats with him and tried to talk Amy out of even more sugary treats for Max. No one ruffled his hair or spoke to him in a big, deep, kind, manly voice.

Amy didn't have a man to groan with sheer pleasure as he bit into the food she cooked, to lavish praise on her for the meals she put on the table. No one flirted with her, grinned at her, gave her those looks that said he not only liked the way she cooked, he liked the way she looked, too.

In short, there was no man in their lives. She hadn't let any in during the past hard, lonely years of raising Max. It had all been about surviving and doing the right thing and dreaming of a day, a far-off wonderful day when she might feel like a woman again and not be scared of that. When she might feel as if it was okay to have a man in her life again, and maybe she could enjoy that man, that relationship. That maybe she could do it right this time, and when it ended, not be left with a million regrets about the relationship gone wrong and one small, adorable boy to raise on her own.

One day.

She'd had this silly idea that the day she saw Tate was that long-awaited day.

And now he'd shown her exactly what he thought of her.

"You have no right—" she began, voice trembling.

"I'm sorry, okay?" he said. "You're right. None of my business. And I don't want to be anybody's morality police. It's just…raising a kid… It's really hard, isn't it?"

"Yes, it is."

"Even harder on your own, especially when you're so young."

"Yes. I know that firsthand."

"And it just seems like…you wouldn't want to make that any harder for yourself or Max."

"No, I don't. So I really shouldn't blow this job by yelling at the groom in the first wedding I've ever worked—"

"You're not blowing the job. I don't…I'm not talking about that. I just…" He sighed heavily, then shook his head. "Just forget it, okay? I shouldn't have said anything. I…I didn't come here to give you a hard time. I came because I have to tell you something—"

"You really don't. You've said quite enough already."

"No, I… Oh, hell. I'm sorry. Really. But, the thing is, when I thought you might be pregnant and that it might be Leo's baby—"

"I told you it's not Leo's baby! It couldn't be—"

"It's just that his widow is here. Did you know his widow is here?"

"Of course I did. I fed her breakfast this morning."

Tate nodded. "Okay. Well, I didn't know if you knew she was here or if she knew you were here."

"There's nothing to know!" Amy yelled at him.

"Well, I didn't know that, and I was worried that you and Kathleen might…not be on good terms, and that if it came out that you might be pregnant with Leo's baby… She's a sweet old lady, and I didn't want her to get her feelings hurt if she heard the news."

Amy just gaped at him, furious at him for jumping to conclusions and refusing to believe anything she said and at the same time, finding the whole situation so ridiculous that it was all she could do not to start laughing and never stop.

She chuckled once, then clamped a hand over her mouth to stop it.

He glared at her, incredulous. "You think this is funny?"

"It's beyond funny. Way beyond—"

"How can you think that? You pregnant, and Leo's widow in the other room—"

"Well, for one thing, Leo Gray was eighty-six years old. He really got around well for a man his age, but I don't know if he was up to impregnating anyone. And for another, I couldn't possibly be carrying his baby. Not only did we never sleep together but the man's been dead for over a year—"

"A year?"

"Yes, and if you know how long it takes to have a baby, you know it's impossible for me to now be pregnant with his child."

Tate looked taken aback. "Kathleen said she'd lost him recently. I thought…a few months, maybe?"

"It may still seem recent to her, but believe me or don't believe me. Ask someone else, if you need to. It's been more than a year. I am not having his baby. I'm not having anyone's baby. And Kathleen isn't going to swoon or anything like that at the sight of me. She knows me. We're friends—good friends. She and Gladdy babysat for Max sometimes. They adore him. They even adore me, hard as that might be for you to believe."

Tate just stared at her. Obviously it was hard for him to believe.

"You know what, you can ask Max if you want to. Max knows and adores them, too. He'll tell you," Amy said. "Although if you mention one thing about this ridiculous idea of me having Leo's baby to Max, I swear, I don't care if this is my first real cooking job and you are the groom, you will live to regret it. It would be easy as could be for me to slip something into a lemon bar and leave you hurling in the bathroom for hours. And don't you think I won't."

Chapter Six

He just stared at her, thinking nobody had ever messed with her kid, not ever, and liking her for that, in spite of the threat she'd just made of revenge by lemon bars.

She had to be the most confusing woman he'd ever met, making him like her or at least admire her, for the fiercely protective way she stood between her son and the rest of the world. A man who grew up without a mother for most of his life couldn't help but admire that. He was happy Max had a mom like that. Every kid should.

She was like some exotic puzzle he desperately wanted to solve, one he thought would be very interesting to decipher. He could spend a whole lot of time figuring her out and be really happy doing it.

She'd be fiery at times and fiercely protective at others, and he'd have to be on his toes around her, and he'd like it. Really like it. She'd challenge him and sometimes argue with him and make him crazy, but that would be okay, too.

More than okay.

It would be really good.

If this had happened at any other time in his life, and he wasn't the reasonable, careful man that he was… If he could somehow wave a magic wand and make time stop for everyone but them, he'd do it. He'd take some time to get to know her, away from all this, especially his impending wedding and the very real fact that he was engaged to another woman.

He'd take the time, and who knew what would happen?

Maybe he'd see that this was some trick of smoke and mirrors and clouds of sugar. That she was just some other woman with a cute kid and amazing skill in the kitchen. Nothing else.

But a man couldn't stop time. He couldn't go to Victoria and say, *Sorry, I just need a few days, maybe a few weeks,* and then expect everything to go back to normal when he was finished with this little adventure known as Amy.

He'd made a promise to Victoria. He knew Victoria. He understood her. He appreciated all the good qualities she had. He knew exactly what he was getting into with Victoria, and it would be good. It would be perfectly fine.

It just wouldn't be…this.

This little zing of wildness and yearning.

Surely he wasn't going to wreck his life over something as insubstantial as that—an awareness, a curiosity, a sexually charged zing.

So he had to back off.

Back off now.

Let this whole mess be.

"Okay, you're right," he began. "I'm completely out of

line, and I would never, ever do anything to hurt Max. I was just worried about a sweet old lady getting her feelings hurt. That's all. I swear."

She relented the slightest bit, not looking at him like she completely loathed him at least. "Well, I do adore Kathleen, and I have to admit I'd want to protect her, too, if I ever thought she'd get hurt."

He nodded. "Thank you for that."

"And I suppose I have to take some responsibility here, too. Max told you about Leo and the whole ridiculous sugar daddy thing, and I just let it stand, rather than go into the whole story. I tend to do that, because…well, it's really not anyone else's business and because it makes me mad how people assume the worst and then don't want to believe the truth when you tell it to them—"

"Like me?" he admitted.

"No, not you, exactly. People who are a lot meaner than you." She almost smiled then.

He was getting somewhere with his apology. "So, you could tell me the whole story, if you wanted to."

She sighed, still looking a little annoyed, but definitely not as if she loathed him, at least.

"Leo lived at Remington Park, too, where Kathleen and Gladdy lived and I worked. He was outrageous, flirted with anything that moved, including me, I have to admit. But it was just the way he was. He saw a woman, he flirted. It might have been really annoying in a younger man, but at eighty-six, he was adorable and so much fun to have around. And he adored Max and my lemon bars."

"I certainly understand that," Tate told her. "Both adoring Max and the lemon bars."

"Yeah, we all still miss Leo. And when he died, he left a little money in his will for Max for college and some more money in a fund to help single mothers who are going back to school. He specified that I be the first recipient."

"Wow," Tate said. "Nice guy."

"Yes, a wonderful man. I was shocked. No one's ever helped me like that. It's just been me and Max since I got pregnant and my family kicked me out. So I went to cooking school, and with Leo's money I didn't have to work while I was in school, which would have been nearly impossible. Max would have been in day care around the clock, and I would have never seen him between working and going to school. I'd have hated that, and I don't really know if I could have done it—school—that way. But Leo fixed it so I could. It's an incredible gift that he gave me and Max."

"So that's why people thought you had a sugar daddy? Because Leo left you money to help you go back to school?"

Amy nodded. "Word gets around, you know? People heard someone else—an older man—was paying my bills, and no matter how I explained it, no one believed the truth. Someone said something in front of Max one day, about us having a sugar daddy, and I wasn't about to tell him what it really meant. I told him it was something good, like Leo being our friend and helping us both get through school. Of course, now he thinks it's a good thing, and he tells people all the time about Leo, our sugar daddy!"

Tate burst out laughing.

"I know." Amy actually laughed, too. "My own fault, right? And then I saw that it kept men from hitting on me, which is a good thing, because I really don't have time for that between school and Max. I saw that the whole gossip thing could work for me, and after a while, I stopped fighting it and let people believe it."

"Well, that I can understand. Not fighting the rumors. I'm sorry I made things harder for you."

She shook her head. "Forget it. It's nothing, really. Besides, I told you I adore Kathleen. Anyone trying to protect her is fine with me."

Tate nodded, feeling better for a moment, and then not feeling better at all.

"So you haven't given up on men completely, right? Because we're not all worthless." Said the man who was supposed to be getting married this weekend, the one who hated the idea of her just giving up, a woman as young and beautiful and good at cooking as she was. He tried desperately to save himself, to sound casual and friendlike. "I mean…nobody really wants to be alone forever."

"No, but…things are a lot less complicated that way."

"Granted," he said.

"And I have Max to think of. A lot of men don't really want to take on a woman and a child."

"Some of them don't," Tate admitted.

"And I'd hate for Max to get attached to someone I was dating and then have us break up and Max get hurt," she reasoned.

"No. Max is a gem. Can't have Max getting hurt," he agreed. "But you get to have a life, too, don't you?"

"I have a life. I have Max and my work and good friends."

Tate nodded. "And that's really enough?"

"It's… I'm fine," she insisted.

"Maybe." But Tate really didn't think it was. Didn't everyone want more than that in life? And then he thought he'd figured it out. "Or maybe you're just scared—"

"I am not scared of men. That is one of the most ridiculous things I've ever heard in my life. Men are nothing to be scared of. They're—"

"Not of men. Of yourself. Of making another mistake with a man…"

She looked as if she could happily bash him in the head with a frying pan. "Max is not a mistake!"

"No, not Max. Max could never be a mistake. I wasn't talking about Max. I was talking about Max's father. About you being scared of making another mistake in a man you chose to…love. Did you love him? Max's father?"

"I was young. I was stupid. I believed everything he said to me, and yes, I thought I loved him."

"Well, you're not young and stupid anymore," he reminded her.

"One would hope not, although I'm starting to wonder."

About him, Tate knew.

She was worried about making a stupid decision about him, just as much as he worried about being really stupid and reckless with her. Him, a man who didn't think he'd ever been reckless or stupid in his life.

If anything, he'd hardly ever taken a risk at all.

No time to start now, he told himself.

Not now.

"Maybe it's time you stopped punishing yourself," he said anyway. For her, he told himself. Not for him or for the nonexistent her and him. "Because it looks like you made one mistake and have spent the last six years trying to make up for it."

"I haven't been punishing myself. I've been making a life for myself and my son, and that hasn't been easy."

"No, I know. I'm sure it hasn't. Especially doing that alone."

"It's taken everything I've had in me to take care of myself and Max," she said, tears glistening in those pretty eyes of hers.

"And now maybe it won't," he said. "And you'll have some time and energy for yourself and maybe...someone to share it all with."

But not with him.

Definitely not with him.

Tate shook his head and swore softly under his breath. "I'm sorry. This is none of my business."

"No, it's not," she said, looking as surprised as he felt about where this whole conversation had gone.

He forgot himself with her, just lost himself and who he was and what he was supposed to be doing, and the next thing he knew he was treating her like a woman he wanted to get to know, acting as if he was a man with every right to get to know a pretty woman.

Which was just ridiculous.

He was a man getting married.

Here.

This weekend.

How did Amy do that to him? Get him all turned around and mixed up and lost?

He felt dazed and confused and, yes, stupid. Hungry, too. What was that smell? What had she been cooking today? Could he get some of it, after insulting her and then butting into her life this way?

Probably not.

He felt hungry around her, too. Always.

A bad thing to think about.

"I should go," he said, finally trying to save himself.

"You should," she agreed.

"I... Oh, hell, I forgot." He groaned to himself, remembering the whole pregnancy-test thing and what he feared and what he'd done about it.

"What did you do now?" she whispered furiously at him.

"I…I'm really, really sorry about this next part. Really," he said again. "But when I was worried about Kathleen finding out you might be pregnant with Leo's baby, I'm afraid—"

"You didn't!" Amy said. "You told?"

He nodded.

"Kathleen? Because—"

"No, not her."

"Whew!" Amy said. "Because Kathleen wouldn't leave me alone until she knew exactly what was going on."

"No, I didn't tell her. I'm afraid I told my godmother, who will probably tell Kathleen."

Amy groaned, frustrated, angry—he couldn't exactly tell what.

"I'm sorry. I'll tell her I got it completely wrong. I'll tell her anything you want me to tell her, I swear. Just tell me what I can say."

"Nothing," she said. "Don't say another word to anyone about anything."

"Okay," he promised. He'd been doing so well there for a moment, had almost made up for every bad thing he'd said and done.

Now she just looked annoyed with him again.

"Don't you have a bachelor party or something to get ready for?"

"Yes," he remembered. He did. Tonight.

Because he was getting married on Saturday.

To another woman.

And yet here he was, in the kitchen again, trying to figure out Amy and to make things better of the mess he'd made for Amy.

He didn't even know where Victoria was today—hadn't seen her at all, hadn't thought about her.

It was puzzling, surprising, troubling all at the same time.

He so seldom took a wrong turn in his life. At least, so far. He'd never thought agreeing to marry Victoria could be one of those wrong turns. In fact, he'd thought it was one of the safest, most reasonable decisions he could have made. He understood Victoria, could swear he'd know exactly what she'd do in any given situation, that he knew her that well, took comfort in knowing her that well. Most of life's surprises, after all, did not turn out to be good things, he'd found. Knowing, understanding, trusting, predicting the road ahead…that had always seemed like a good thing to him. A very good thing.

Until right this minute, Amy standing in front of him looking annoyed at him one minute, threatening to give him food poisoning, in fact, and looking…interesting, really interesting and surprising the next.

Victoria didn't surprise him in the least, except in the way she was stressing out about the wedding of late. He'd always thought that was a good thing, that he was a man who really didn't need surprises in a relationship, in a marriage. It had all made so much sense at one time.

Of course, he would marry Victoria. Of course, they would be happy together, the perfect partners for each other, so much understanding, so much respect, all the years of friendship they shared. And she was an attractive woman, an appealing one. Of course she was.

Granted, it wasn't a relationship that set his blood on fire. He was honest enough to admit that, but it worked for both of them, he thought. It was something that would last long after any crazy passion would burn itself out, and he wanted something that would last.

Why was that thought so unsettling now?

That she didn't absolutely set his blood on fire?

And that…that he feared the woman standing in front of him could?

Amy looked up at him, a little frustrated, a little amused.

"What?" he said.

"Bachelor party," she said again. "Remember? Your bachelor party. Tonight?"

"Yes," he said. He remembered.

"Then go. I'll take care of everything with Eleanor and Kathleen and this silly pregnancy rumor somehow." She sighed heavily, shaking her head, definitely annoyed at him again.

"Okay. I'm going. Right now." Then he remembered his fiancée. "Hey, have you seen Victoria this morning? No one seems to know where she is?"

"I really don't know where she is," Amy claimed.

And he would have sworn she was lying.

Which was even odder.

But no way he was going to take that up with her.

"Okay. I'm gone. Right now. Sorry."

And then he turned around and fled.

Amy made a quick picnic lunch for Max, his new friend Drew and the nanny, throwing in all sorts of sweet treats in a separate package just for the nanny as a thank-you for taking Max off her hands.

It was almost eleven o'clock by the time she was done with that. If she hurried, she could go to the grocery store and be back by eleven-thirty to put out the lunch buffet. It was lasagna, which was already in the oven, and a salad she'd made this morning, so not much prep work was left to do except bake more fresh bread. It was already in the pan and rising.

She ran back to the grocery store for artichokes and a two-pack of pregnancy tests, got the same clerk as before, who gave her a knowing smile that said, *Didn't believe the first one, right?*

Of course not.

Back at the house, Amy crept in the back door, trying not to get cornered by anyone regarding her mistakenly possibly pregnant state. She made it, too, until she walked into the kitchen, and there Kathleen and Gladdy stood, looking as excited as little girls who'd just found out the circus was coming to town.

Amy would have turned around on the spot and left, except they were in the kitchen, and if she knew them, they wouldn't leave until they found out exactly what was going on, and avoiding the kitchen long-term was simply not an option for her. So she wrapped her plastic grocery bag more securely around her artichoke and the pregnancy tests—they'd have to wrestle her to get the bag away from her and see what was inside. She quickly composed herself, then walked into the kitchen.

The two older women positively glowed as their gaze went pointedly from her face to her midsection and back to her face again.

"Darling," Gladdy said, "do you have something to tell us?"

"No," Amy said, stashing the grocery bag in the far corner of the kitchen and then walking over to them. "Nothing. I swear!"

They still glowed.

"It's all a big misunderstanding," she tried. "I mean... you know me. You know my love life is nonexistent."

"Well, we thought so, but then we thought maybe we were wrong. You're much too young to give up on men, my dear," Kathleen told her.

"I haven't given up. I'm just on hiatus from dating. That's all. Now that I'm out of school—"

"Yes," they said hopefully.

"Once I get settled into a job and put a little money away, you know, just in case, then I'll think about dating. But for now, there's no man, and there's definitely no baby. I promise."

The two women looked at each other, confused, unhappy, still doubtful, Amy feared.

"There was a pregnancy test. We know that," Gladdy tried, shooting a stubbornly satisfied look toward Amy. "And if there's a pregnancy test, there's a woman who thinks she might be pregnant."

Amy sighed. "Okay. Yes, there was a test. But it wasn't mine. I swear! I had to go to the store anyway, and…someone needed one, and I offered to get it. That's all. Really. The sum total of my involvement with any possible pregnancy and pregnancy test."

Gladdy looked disappointed. Kathleen looked as if she still knew she wasn't getting the whole story.

"Tate was obviously worried about you," Kathleen tried.

"Such a nice boy," Gladdy added.

"Nice boy?" Amy couldn't believe this. "He's getting married on Saturday. We're all at his wedding celebration weekend."

"Uh-huh," Kathleen said, still wearing a huge grin on her face.

Wait a minute. What were they doing? Amy gaped at them. "Surely you're not trying to fix me up with a man who's getting married in two days?"

Gladdy shrugged, smiled. "You never know, my dear. He's not married yet."

"Never know?" This was beyond ridiculous. Amy reminded them, "Two days from now, he's getting married, and you're both friends with his godmother. What are you two trying to do?"

"Nothing," Gladdy said.

"No, nothing."

Those odd smiles stayed right there on their faces, along with the guilty looks.

Amy remembered then just how the two ladies had worked to get Kathleen's granddaughter together with Leo's nephew last year. Amy had even helped with their efforts. And it had worked, despite Amy being sure that meddling in such ways never worked out well. But the granddaughter and the nephew were married now and, from all Amy had heard from Gladdy and Kathleen, perfectly happy.

Still, people didn't try to fix up anyone with the groom of a wedding to take place in two days, did they? Because that was just nuts. The man was engaged. His fiancée was right here, maybe even still in Amy's bathroom, waiting for the next two pregnancy tests Amy was bringing her.

Of course, Kathleen and Gladdy didn't know that.

"You two look like you're up to something," she said.

"So do you, dear," Kathleen said. "So do you."

"Well, I'm not. I'm not up to anything. And the two of you, don't you do anything. Promise me, right now, that you won't do anything."

"We're not. We're just here as Eleanor's guests, to enjoy ourselves and keep her company, to help out with anything that she might need help with. And to enjoy this beautiful home of hers before she sells it. That's all."

Amy frowned as she thought of something, another possibility that might make this whole thing make sense. "Eleanor doesn't want Tate to marry Victoria?"

Gladdy sighed. "She's turned her home over to them for the wedding. That's not what one does when one disapproves of the marriage, dear."

Maybe not, but still something was going on.

"Does she like Victoria?" Amy asked.

"Well, she's not the one marrying her. Tate is. So the question is, does Tate like Victoria? Does he love her?" Gladdy shrugged, looking to Kathleen, who shrugged, as well. "I suppose he does. I really haven't asked him. I mean, that would be terribly rude, my dear. Asking the groom-to-be if he's in love with his bride-to-be. That would definitely cross the line, don't you think?"

"Yes," Amy agreed. "That would cross the line between good and bad behavior at a wedding celebration."

"Have you actually asked him, dear? If he loves Victoria?"

"No, I haven't asked him."

"Do you think we should?" Kathleen asked, looking concerned now, like a woman who truly wanted to do the right thing.

"No. I didn't say that. I didn't say anything like that. I don't even know how we got to this point in the conversation."

"Although, I have to say that Victoria does seem rather… cool to me," Kathleen began.

"Reserved," Gladdy added.

"Distant."

"Serious."

"Stop it!" Amy insisted, praying now that Victoria wasn't still hiding in her room and hearing this whole conversation.

"I'm sorry. You're right. We shouldn't be talking about the poor thing this way. She just…doesn't seem to be a very happy bride," Kathleen claimed.

Of course not. She'd been throwing up all night and feared she was pregnant, and the groom didn't know anything about it yet and might not want children or might not want them now! No bride would look happy under those circumstances.

Not that Amy could tell them any of that.

"I'm sorry. I'd love to gossip some more about the bride and groom and exactly how they feel about each other, but people will be showing up for lunch any minute, and I have so much to do," she said.

"Oh, we'd be happy to help," Gladdy said, looking around the kitchen to see what might need to be done.

"You made lasagna, did you? It smells so good. I adore your lasagna. So did my dear Leo," Kathleen said.

"You just tell us what we can do to help, dear. You know, we're always happy to help you and that dear, sweet boy of yours."

Amy bit back a groan of resignation and told them she just needed a moment in her room, and she'd be right back to get things started. Much as she tried, she couldn't get them to go away. They were pulling out plates and silverware for lunch as she grabbed the grocery bag and headed for her room.

But the door wouldn't open when she tried the handle.

It was locked.

She could feel Kathleen and Gladdy staring at her back, would swear they picked up on the sound of her trying to open her own locked bedroom door. No way was she explaining that to them.

Whispering into the crack between the door and the door frame, she said, "Victoria? It's Amy. Let me in."

The door opened in front of her, and Amy walked through, only to have Victoria quickly reach over and lock the door behind her once again.

She was still dreadfully pale and crying once again. "They're right. Eleanor doesn't like me."

"No, no, no," Amy tried to soothe her.

"It's true. She's never liked me. Most women don't like me. I don't know why. I mean, I am too serious. I don't think I'm cold, I just don't really get the whole warmth thing. I mean, I try, it just… I don't think I know how to do it, which means I have no business being a mother. I'll probably be lousy at it, and my kid will end up in therapy telling his shrink his mother is cold and distant and way too serious—that no one likes her. He'll never have any fun and grow up to be a serial killer or something, and it'll all be my fault—"

Amy threw the bag with the pregnancy tests on the bed, then took Victoria by both arms to steady her and to get her attention. Looking her in the eye, Amy said, "Victoria, breathe, okay? Just breathe and stop talking—"

"But it's true. I know it. Tate adores Eleanor, and she most definitely does not adore me. I don't know what kind of woman she wanted for him, but I am not it!"

"Maybe she does feel that way. Maybe she doesn't. We don't know that. And it really doesn't matter. All that does matter is how Tate feels about you, and he loves you. I mean, he asked you to marry him, didn't he?"

"Kind of," Victoria said.

Kind of?

"What does that mean?"

"It means, we'd been dating for a while, and we'd worked together for three years, and we're always so busy. He said I'm the first woman he's been involved with who understood the pressures and the time involved with the job. That we want the same things and are just so like each other. I mean, it just made sense, you know? That we'd end up married. I don't even remember him asking exactly. It was more like we agreed this is what we'd do, that we did make sense together, and then we went shopping for a ring."

"Oh." What else could Amy say to that kind of a

nonproposal proposal? Surely there'd been more to it than that.

Victoria froze, looking as if she was going through things in her head, and then her bottom lip started trembling. "That's how it happened. Exactly like that. I don't think he even said he loved me. I don't remember if I said I loved him, either. I mean, I think I do."

"Okay," Amy said as calmly as possible.

"I mean, I absolutely adore Tate, and I trust him completely. I know he's a man I can depend on, a reasonable, kind, hardworking man. A wonderful man who understands me and really cares about me, and…and… I mean, of course we have strong feelings for each other. We'd never get married without feeling…strongly about each other. Right?"

Amy was thinking that through the whole rambling explanation Victoria had never actually said she loved Tate.

Amy would never get married if this was what it did to people. Victoria didn't seem ditzy at all. Amy would never say it to anyone, but had to admit to herself that Victoria did seem a little serious, a little reserved but still very, very smart. If Victoria could find herself getting engaged and married in such an illogical way, what kind of chance did that give people who weren't as smart as she was?

Did love just make people stupid? Amy thought maybe it did.

She took a breath, tried to focus on what needed to be done, right here and now, to start figuring out this mess, and when she did that, the answer seemed obvious. She let Victoria go, picked up the grocery bag, pulled out the pregnancy tests and handed them to Victoria.

"I don't believe you're thinking all that clearly right now, Victoria."

"No, neither do I," she admitted.

"Which is understandable, because you're under a great deal of stress, much of which I'm sure started when you began to suspect you might be pregnant. So I think the first thing you need to know, before you figure out how you really feel about Tate and how he feels about you, is whether you are really pregnant. Because you never want to try to make big decisions without having all the facts, right? I mean, I'm sure that's how you always make important decisions. By gathering all the facts?"

Victoria nodded, seeming to be able to grasp the logic in that, her normal approach to decision making.

"Okay. Good."

Amy proceeded as if they were in perfect agreement. She took Victoria's hand and wrapped it around the box with the pregnancy tests. Then she turned Victoria around and gave her a little nudge toward the bathroom.

"I'll lock the door behind me, and I'll be right outside in the kitchen if you need me."

Amy made good her escape before Victoria could cry more or protest or tell Amy more about her life and upcoming marriage than Amy wanted to know. Kathleen and Gladdy, as promised, were helping, having set out the plates, utensils and napkins for lunch, which would again be served buffet style, so the guests could come and go as they pleased. They gave her an expectant look as she came back into the kitchen. Amy just stared back, not saying anything.

Kathleen finally broke down and asked, "Everything turn out okay?"

Amy frowned. "You mean—"

"Yes, dear. The test. Did it come out the way you wanted?"

"I told you. It's not mine! I'm not pregnant! I have no

reason to think I might be pregnant! In fact, it's impossible. It would be on the order of the eighth wonder of the world, because I haven't been anywhere near a man in I don't even remember how long. Men are just trouble! All of them are so much trouble…."

She trailed off as they looked frantically over her shoulder and started motioning for her to stop. With a sinking feeling, she turned around, and there was Tate, standing in the doorway. He looked guilty about what he'd overheard and surely about the secrets he'd told that weren't his to tell. And maybe—just maybe—he was finally starting to believe Amy when she said she was most definitely not pregnant.

But he smiled in the end, forced as it was, and greeted them all. "Ladies, something smells wonderful, doesn't it?"

"Lasagna," Amy said, ready to rescue him this once.

"Great. I'm starving."

Kathleen gave him a look of complete approval. "You know, dear, most women don't have any idea how to satisfy a man in the kitchen these days, but our Amy certainly does."

Amy hung her head and swore silently. Surely she hadn't just heard what she thought she heard.

Shameless. They were completely shameless!

"So true," Gladdy agreed. "And so nice to see a young man with such a healthy appetite. Let me get you a plate, dear. You'll just love Amy's lasagna. It's one of her best dishes."

Tate smiled and held his tongue until he paused for just a moment at Amy's side and whispered into her ear. "Don't hurt them. They're old and very sweet. You told me so."

"This is all your fault," she whispered back.

He just kept smiling. "Ladies, I hope you'll join me for lunch. I hate to eat alone."

And then he deftly made sure they got plates of their own, filled them with salad, lasagna and fresh bread and followed him out of the kitchen and into the dining room.

He turned back to look at Amy as they left, and mouthed, "Sorry. Best I could do."

She waved him out of there with an impatient gesture and then turned back to look at the door of her bedroom, no doubt still locked, Victoria likely inside and weeping.

How she'd gotten caught up in the middle of this, she'd never understand. She'd been told people got crazy the closer the actual wedding date got. She'd had no idea just how true that was.

I am never doing another wedding, she promised herself. Never!

Chapter Seven

Guests trickled in, off and on, for the next hour and a half, leaving poor Victoria trapped in the bedroom and Amy unable to get away to check on her.

Truth be told, Amy dreaded what she would find when she went in there. But the woman couldn't stay locked in Amy's bedroom forever. She had to come out and face her fate eventually. Amy decided it was time, mostly because she was exhausted from staying up so late prepping food for today, getting up in the middle of the night with Victoria and starting her day so early today.

She went back to the door, tapped softly on it and went inside when Victoria opened up for her. One look at Victoria's face told Amy what she suspected was true.

Victoria nodded, not even able to say the word *pregnant*.

"What am I going to do?" she wailed instead.

"Tell him. Tell him the truth right now. This is something

you decide together. If he's going to freak out at the idea of being a father, you need to know now. If he's going to walk away—although, honestly, Victoria, he really doesn't seem like the kind of guy to freak out and walk away—you need to know that, too. Or is it that you just really don't think you're ready? That you can be a good mother to this baby?"

Victoria looked aghast. "You don't understand. This is not part of my plan. I always have a plan! I make plans every day. I make lists of things I plan to do, and I just go down my list, checking things off. But this…this was not on any list of mine!"

"Okay." Amy took a breath, picturing a freaky little kid with tons of lists of his own, day after day, crossing things off with a crayon before he could even read, trying to make his list-making mother happy.

And how had this become Amy's problem? Did Victoria have no friends? She had bridesmaids, Amy knew. Where were the damned bridesmaids when the bride needed them?

"You know, this is probably something you'd be more comfortable talking about with…a good friend," Amy tried. "One of your bridesmaids, maybe?"

Victoria shook her head, looking horrified. "I can't tell them. I can't tell anyone I know."

Great, Amy thought.

"You don't understand!" Victoria cried.

"Understand what?"

"Tate went to Tokyo last month!"

"So? What's Tokyo have to do with anything?"

"He was gone for three weeks, closing a deal, and I was…working. I work so hard. We both do. It's been a month at least, maybe longer, since we were…together. I was planning this wedding. My mother was making me crazy. All these stupid details. Everything had to be just right, and I had it all under control. I had my lists, and everything was fine. Then he had to go to Tokyo unexpectedly, and I wasn't supposed to take care of the band for the reception. He was. He did. But the band he booked broke up while Tate was in Tokyo, and I had to find a new one. Why did I have to find a new one? Why did I have to do everything? I should have been the one to go to Tokyo and left him here with my mother and the wedding and all my stupid lists!"

Okay, the band was bad. The band had canceled. Tate had left, and Victoria's mother was scary, really scary. This Amy knew from encountering the woman in the kitchen this morning.

"So you had to find a new band for the reception?" Amy asked.

Victoria nodded.

"And that's bad…why?"

"I've always been a good girl. A very good girl."

"Yes, I'm sure," Amy agreed. She'd been a good girl, too.

But good girls ended up pregnant, too. They fell in love, took silly risks, didn't think bad things could happen to them. Amy knew this story well.

"I'm just really not this woman, okay? Tate said that to me last night, when I thought the two of you were…you know. He said, 'I'm not that guy. You know that Victoria.' And I thought, yes, I do know that. He's a great guy. But the thing is, I would have always said I wasn't that kind of woman, either. Except… I can't say that anymore, because I am. I've turned into that kind of woman, the kind who'd… who'd…"

And she started absolutely bawling.

Okay, this sounded bad. "You mean—"

"The band I called…there weren't that many I could get at the last minute, and I didn't even know it was his band until he showed up."

"You already knew one of the guys in the band?" Amy guessed.

Victoria nodded. "From high school. My little walk on the wild side. My only walk on the wild side, ever! And my mother was horrified. She hated him."

"Okay. I believe you," Amy reassured her.

"He is so cute, so sexy and a little bit dangerous, and I just…you know the type."

"Yes, I do." Amy knew. What was it about the dangerous ones? Although Amy would have said Tate was definitely one of the nice guys, and yet he still made her feel that way, like there was a hint of danger inside of him that could prove very dangerous to her.

Oh, God, Amy realized. She was thinking like *that.* About Tate! While standing here with Tate's fiancée, who was in the middle of confessing all her sins to Amy of all people!

This was all so very bad.

"But it didn't mean anything," Victoria said.

"Right." Neither had wanting Tate to lick powdered sugar off her body, Amy had tried to tell herself. Why couldn't she just forget about the sugar? And the licking?

It was all just so bad.

"So, I just tried to hire a band," Victoria continued, "and it turned out to be his band, and I hadn't seen him in years, and…he still looked so good!"

"Oh, I know. Believe me, I know," Amy agreed, sadly not thinking at all about Victoria's dangerous band man.

"And he still had that whole little dangerous edge, and he acted like he really regretted that we never…you know? In high school?"

"I know," Amy said.

"The bad guy who wants every woman he sees. That it was just a game to him. I thought I was so much smarter than that," Victoria said, in her own little world, telling her own sad story, fortunately oblivious to the fact that Amy was thinking her own sad, guilty thoughts about Victoria's fiancé.

"We all think we're so smart when it comes to men, and so few of us are," Amy said.

Victoria nodded, then sniffled, looking as sad as could be.

"The thing was that all those old feelings I had for him? They were still there, and I've never felt like that, and I was about to get married. I was supposed to be in love and stay married forever. I didn't see how I could feel that way with him when I'm supposed to be in love with Tate and marrying him."

"Right. Of course," Amy said, then thought she should just stuff a dish towel in her mouth to keep quiet. She was not going to give Victoria advice on dangerous men or dangerous thoughts. She was in no position to do that, given the things she kept thinking about Victoria's fiancé.

"Not that that's any excuse, really. I know that."

No, no excuse for either of them, Amy agreed.

"So Tate was off in Tokyo, and James was there, and all those bad, dangerous feelings were still there, and… I slept with him. I slept with James. The guy from high school, from the band. God, I said it! I slept with James."

"Okay, well, if it was just that one time," Amy began.

Victoria wailed again. "But it wasn't! It wasn't just that one time."

"Okay." She just patted Victoria on the shoulder, thinking that was the safest and kindest thing she could do at the moment.

"So, what do you think I should do?" Victoria asked Amy, finally, after her sobs subsided.

"Oh, Victoria. I am really not the person to ask about that. I mean…that's a question only you can answer. I mean, could you forgive yourself? Could you forget about it? Could you just go on with your life, like nothing happened?"

"You mean, marry Tate and not tell him the baby isn't his?"

Amy was sure she hadn't heard correctly.

Baby isn't his?

"Wait… What did you say? The baby isn't his? Isn't Tate's?"

"Yes. I told you he was in Tokyo. For three weeks. The important three weeks. The time when… I don't see any way this could be Tate's baby."

"Oh," Amy said.

She'd been so caught up with her own traitorous thoughts, her own guilt, that she'd missed the whole point of Victoria's confession. Not that she'd merely slept with the guy in the band but that she was likely carrying that guy's baby.

Okay.

"So, what do you think?" Victoria asked. "What do I do?"

"I…you…I can't tell you what to do," Amy said. "I'm not the person. I'm sorry. I just can't."

And then Victoria started to cry again.

Tate hadn't wanted to have a bachelor party.

At least, not one of *those* bachelor parties.

Half-naked women he didn't know crawling all over him, while a bunch of other drunken guys watched and shouted encouragement, just didn't do anything for him.

So he'd tried, really tried, to negotiate for something much more low-key, maybe courtside seats for a basketball game, some good scotch and reminiscing about old times with a few buddies. That's what he'd wanted.

But no one had listened to him.

Plus, he hadn't been able to find Victoria all day. It was as if she was hiding out somewhere. He didn't understand what was going on. Was she still mad about finding him with Amy in the kitchen the night before? Or were the wedding and her mother just making her crazy? Hopefully, just her mother, he thought. It was normal for her mother to make her crazy.

So when he got back to the house late that night, with a faint hum of alcohol in his body, despite his best efforts to only look like he was drinking and having a good time, all he'd planned to do was find Victoria. He had the limousine driver they'd hired for the night let him out at the guesthouse and ended up tiptoeing around the place, trying to figure out which room she was using. The guys with him, from the party, gave him hell about it, but he brushed all that off, too. He just needed to talk to her, to make sure everything was okay. Because it just didn't seem like everything was okay.

Like some Peeping Tom he peered into windows all the way around the little guesthouse, but if Victoria was in there, she had to be asleep. No way he was going to risk knocking on the door and waking her mother at this hour. She hadn't been answering her phone all night, either, so he supposed whatever was going on would have to wait until the next morning.

He ended up walking back to the main house, creeping in through the back entrance by the kitchen, as he always did, out of mere habit alone. He didn't even think of how that might not be smart of him until he was already there, walking past the kitchen.

Tate wondered briefly how Max was, if he'd gotten to do more of his pretend cave exploring. He wondered if Amy was still furious with him, if she'd managed to convince Kathleen and Gladdy she wasn't pregnant after all, and if—

Whoof.

He'd walked right into someone coming out of the kitchen.

"What the hell?" a deep, masculine voice asked.

"Hey, sorry," Tate said.

Who was that? He didn't know that voice, and he thought he knew everyone who would be staying on the property this weekend. Tate flicked on the overhead light in the hall, winced as the light hit his eyes. So did the other guy—tall, lanky, a little rough looking.

"Sorry, man," the guy said, looking oddly familiar. "Didn't know anyone else was here."

"It's okay. I didn't either." Tate frowned. "Do I know you?"

"I have no idea," the guy said. "James Fallon. My band's playing for the reception."

"James Fallon?" Why did that name sound familiar? Why did the face look familiar? Wait a minute. "Trinity Prep? You were a year or two ahead of me and Victoria, right?"

And how the guy had ever gotten in or stayed in, Tate would never understand. Not that he wasn't smart. It was just that all the guy ever wanted to do was play his guitar, and everything else got in the way. Girls had gone nuts for him, Tate remembered. That whole dangerous-artist-musician thing made women crazy.

"Yeah, I went to Trinity," James said. "Although nobody

ever believes me when I tell them that now. It was the only way my old man would pay for my music lessons. If I stayed in that stuffy prep school he went to when he was a kid."

"Yeah, my dad went there, too. So did Victoria's."

"Small world, huh?"

Tate nodded. "I remember now that Victoria told me she'd found a new band to play the reception. Glad we could get you on short notice—"

"Yeah. Something fell through for the band at the last minute, too. So I guess this was meant to be."

"Yeah, guess so," Tate said, then realized it was almost two in the morning. What the hell? "So what are you doing here so late?"

"Uh…just finished up a gig somewhere else, and…it was the only time I had to…check the place where we'll be playing. Make sure we have enough room, enough electrical outlets for the amps, the lights, the instruments, you know?"

"Oh. Okay." Sounded a little odd, but Tate supposed musicians lived on different schedules than most people in the working world.

"So…you and Victoria, huh?" James asked.

"Yeah, me and Victoria."

James nodded, waited as if he might have something else to say, then shook it off and just said, "Guess I'll see you on the big day, huh?"

"Guess so," Tate said, standing there and watching as the guy crept down the hallway and out the back door.

Amy could have sworn she heard people in the kitchen again. She'd already found Victoria's musician, James, wandering around, supposedly looking for Victoria to discuss the playlist for the wedding reception. Amy didn't know if Victoria was ready to see him or not, so she didn't tell James anything.

At—she squinted bleary-eyed at the letters on the bedside clock—sometime after two in the morning?

What was wrong with the people at this wedding? Did they never sleep? And if it was Victoria out there throwing up again…? Then what? Amy groaned, stared at the ceiling, could still hear low voices in what sounded like the kitchen. Beside her in the bed, Max slept on, happy but exhausted by cave exploring and other messy, little-boy pursuits.

Tonight was bachelor and bachelorette party night, Amy remembered. Did she have a bunch of tipsy revelers in the kitchen with the late-night munchies? And was she supposed to feed them? Or just let them forage for themselves? If it was Victoria instead, would she ever go away? Or just stay there until Amy came out?

Growling softly in frustration, Amy got out of bed, smoothed down her hair as best she could and grabbed a chef's coat—big enough and long enough to cover what absolutely had to be covered—to put over her pajamas. Buttoning it up, she braced herself for whatever she might find and went out into the kitchen.

Tate, she saw first.

Great.

She really needed a late-night encounter with the groom, who might not turn out to be a groom since he wasn't the father of the bride's baby. And someone was with him, a guy out in the hallway whom she couldn't quite see at first. She took another step into the kitchen. Okay, she had seen him before. The guitarist, she remembered. Victoria's guitarist, the baby daddy. He'd been through the kitchen twice today looking for Victoria.

Everyone had been in the kitchen looking for Victoria today.

Had Tate caught them together?

Uh-oh.

Not in the kitchen, Amy thought. Please, just not in the kitchen, so she didn't have to have any part in it.

She eased back into the doorway, where unless they turned around, they wouldn't see her, thinking she'd just go back to her room and put a pillow over her head, ignoring this whole thing. But before she could do that, the guitarist left, and Tate came into the kitchen and saw her. He gave her one of those odd little grins of his, curious, surprised, happy but not happy, and she thought he was a little bit tipsy once again.

"Sorry if we woke you. Didn't mean to." He fell silent for a moment, his look getting odder, more curious, more confused, maybe. "If we did wake you."

"What?"

He glanced off to the right, to the doorway through which the guitarist had just disappeared.

Amy gaped at him. Were we back to this again? He thought the guitarist was here to see her? At two-thirty in the morning?

She took a breath, ready to just explode with fury and frustration at him and this whole stupid, mixed-up wedding. But he must have seen what was coming and backed off instantly.

"No, no," he said. "Forget that. We've done this. None of my business, I know. I just…ran into that guy, and believe it or not, I went to high school with him. Victoria and I both did."

"She mentioned that," Amy said, then realized that might make Tate think she was interested in the guitarist. And she didn't want Tate to think that, ridiculous as that was. "Victoria said that someone from the band should be coming by today to check out the place where they'll be playing and that you both went to high school with one of the band members."

"Yeah." Tate nodded. "So…he's an…interesting guy. At least, he was back then."

Amy frowned at him. "Are you going to tell me he'd be a bad boyfriend? Or a bad father?"

"Nope. Not going there. No way," he said, although he wasn't leaving, either.

She waited, wanting to defend herself, maybe to warn him about what was coming or to at least tell him to find Victoria and talk to her. Surely Amy could tell him that with a clear conscience.

Tate lingered, just standing there and looking at her, a million questions in his eyes.

I like him, Amy thought. *He seems like a nice guy, one who has no idea what kind of mess is about to drop down out of the sky on top of him.*

"Have you seen Victoria?" he asked. "Because I've been looking for her all day, and I can't seem to find her."

"She's been in and out of the kitchen a couple of times today," Amy said, which was true.

"Hmm. Busy, I guess. All this wedding stuff. Seems like an awful lot of fuss."

Amy agreed, nodding her head. "Is there anything you need?"

He shrugged, considered it, then sniffed. "You baked something tonight, didn't you?"

"Yes.

"Not those lemon things. What was it?"

"Strawberry pillow cookies," she said. "Fresh strawberry glaze on a little bed of puffy cookie dough. You're hungry? Now?"

He shrugged. "I could eat."

She pulled a plastic container out of the refrigerator, put three cookies on a dessert plate and put them in the microwave for the least bit of time, just enough to warm them, and then set them before him with a napkin and a glass of water. He eased onto a high stool at the breakfast bar and slowly tore one of her cookies apart, watching the strawberry goo swell up and run over the sides of the cookie. Then he tried a bite, his eyes closing in sheer pleasure, groaning a bit, taking his time, like he didn't want to let the taste of that one bite leave his mouth.

"You know," he said finally, "how you think you know what something is going to be like, and you're ready for that? You think you're right about it? And then, it turns out just not to be at all what you thought it would?"

Amy frowned. "You don't like the cookies?"

"God, no. I love the cookies." He took another bite, as if to show her how much. "I was talking about…you know… everything. This."

"Getting married?" she guessed.

"Well, getting ready to get married, I guess. Because we haven't gotten married yet. We're just in that…getting ready to get married stage. It just…doesn't feel the way I thought it would."

He said it like he was testing the words. How bad did it sound? How much had he said without really saying it? And how did it feel to almost say these things out loud?

"You should talk to Victoria," Amy said firmly. Something she'd been saying to Victoria all along. Talk to Tate. Until Amy found out Tate wasn't the baby's father. But the advice still applied. Especially now.

Did these two ever talk?

"I'm trying to talk to her. I just can't find her," he said. "It just feels…wrong, you know? Something feels…wrong, and I don't know what. I don't know if this is just how people feel, the closer the wedding gets. If it's just normal jitters or…something else. Does it feel wrong to you?"

Very, Amy thought.

"You should talk to Victoria," she said, trying to sound even more firm about that than before.

"I will," he said, "as soon as I can find her. I was considering sneaking into the guesthouse, but her parents are sleeping there, too, and if her mother caught me, she'd have a fit. And the last thing anyone wants this weekend is for Victoria's mother to have a fit. Appearances and all, you know? The woman cares a great deal about appearances."

"Mmm." Amy could just imagine how she'd feel about Victoria having the guitarist's baby.

"I'm really sorry about earlier, about what I did, telling my godmother that you might be pregnant with Kathleen's late husband's baby. Really sorry for that."

Amy just nodded and smiled. "It's okay."

Then she had the most horrible thought.

Did anyone else know Victoria was pregnant? And that the baby wasn't Tate's? Was that why they were trying to fix her up with the groom at his own wedding? Was she like some consolation prize for him? Some distraction from losing his bride in such a bad way on the weekend of their wedding? Because, honestly, it was crazy to try fixing her and Tate up otherwise.

Maybe they did know.

Of course, if they knew and wanted to keep Tate from marrying Victoria, all they'd have to do was tell him the baby wasn't his, right? That much made sense, Amy was sure.

No, they couldn't know.

Maybe they just didn't like poor Victoria. Or maybe

they knew she was fooling around with the guitar player behind Tate's back. But then, all they'd have to do was tell Tate that, and they hadn't. So they probably didn't know about Victoria and James at all.

So what in the world were they up to?

It just didn't make sense.

Nothing about this wedding or these people made sense.

And here she was, in the kitchen with the groom at two in the morning, feeding him sweets and watching him eat them, listening to the little sounds of satisfaction he made while he ate.

She just wanted to keep feeding him and watching him eat. That would be enough, she thought, just feeding him and watching him take bite after bite. She could do that and not cross any of those tricky little lines between good and bad behavior.

Because she hadn't really been bad.

Not yet.

Not with him.

She hadn't been bad with anyone in so long. *Victoria had felt like this until the guitarist came along,* Amy thought. *Where had it gotten her?* In a much bigger mess than Amy was in so far.

She might find herself telling her story one day, hers and Tate's, and she'd start out by saying, "I just wanted to keep feeding him and watching him eat my cooking." It might well all start as innocently as that.

"You need to finish your cookies and go," she said finally, finding the strength to say it now before she really got in trouble.

He looked surprised. "You're kicking me out? Of my own godmother's kitchen?"

"Yes. Eat. And then go," she said. "You know you need to."

"Yes, I know I do."

But still, he didn't go.

He ate, very slowly, watching her as she watched him. It was crazy. Absolutely crazy.

"Get up," she told him. "Go."

She thought he was actually going to do it, just go, and then she thought she heard something else.

Voices, deep voices and soft laughter, fumbling steps, a door opening and closing.

Damn.

Guests from the bachelor party? If she was lucky. If she wasn't, the bachelorette party? Maybe the bride herself?

Great. Just great.

In a split-second decision, Tate slid off the stool, took Amy by the arm and pulled her into the pantry with him.

"Wait a minute. What are you—"

"Just until they're gone!" he begged softly. "I just don't want to see anybody or have to talk to anyone right now, and I don't need to get caught with you again in this kitchen late at night."

Well, that was certainly true.

"Okay," Amy said, giving in. "But just until they're gone."

Chapter Eight

It was pitch-black in the pantry with the door closed, and this was probably a really bad idea, Tate conceded. Maybe even a worse idea than staying in the kitchen and getting caught alone with Amy there.

He'd brought her in here on sheer impulse alone. He'd been thinking about doing things with her, things he definitely had no business doing, when he'd heard someone coming and panicked out of nothing but guilt over what he'd been thinking. As luck would have it, now he was probably in more danger of doing something with her, rather than merely thinking about it.

He should have eaten those cookies and left. Or never eaten them at all, never come in here at all. He should be with Victoria right now, confessing all and trying to figure out what to do.

Instead, he was alone in the dark behind a closed door with Amy.

He groaned softly. He still had her by the arms, so he knew where she was, that she was right in front of him and a little bit too close.

This was bad, he told himself. So bad.

"I'm sorry," he whispered, staying right where he was, a good six inches between him and Amy, but keeping a hand on her arm so he knew where she was in the dark.

Didn't need to go bumping into her in here, after all.

Not that the distance was enough to keep him from thinking about bumping into her.

His friends made it into the kitchen. He could hear them. They found the cookies in the container on the countertop and foraged through that for a few minutes and then talked about looking for something else to eat.

"Oh, great," Amy whispered. "They're going to stay a while. Do people in this house never sleep? Do you never get tired? Never have things to do the next morning?"

"I'm sorry. I'll just…if they're not gone soon, I'll just… go out there."

"And tell them you were hiding in the pantry for reasons you can't explain?"

"Okay, you're right. I'll… I don't know, I'll—"

"Oh, just be quiet," she told him.

He hung his head down low and ended up with his forehead against hers. Not at all what he'd intended. And she was nice and toasty and warm, just up from her bed, no doubt, and she smelled so good.

Who was he kidding?

She smelled great. Like sugar and spices and strawberry jam right now.

He groaned.

"Don't," she said. "Don't you dare—"

"The thing is," he whispered, just blurting it out before

he could stop himself, "I am not this guy. I swear to you, I'm not."

"So I've been told, and yet here you are, hiding in the dark in the pantry with me, and I know what you're thinking. I do. I know! And I'm telling you right now, don't you dare do it!"

"Yeah, okay. Sue me, I'm thinking about it. I'm sorry. But the thing is, I'm supposed to be getting married in two days—"

"One and a half now," she reminded him.

"Okay, one and a half, and I don't know how I can do that when…when I—"

"Don't say it," she warned.

"When I keep thinking about kissing you."

She growled at him and went to pull away, but he didn't let her. They were still nearly forehead to forehead, and he took the opportunity to run the tip of his nose along the side of her face, right up against her hair. Even her hair smelled sweet.

"I know. I'm a bad man. So bad. I just… I don't know. Is it just some crazy last-minute wedding panic thing? Or something else?"

"I have no idea. I am never doing another wedding in my life. I swear. No weddings. Not ever. People get crazy at weddings."

"Exactly. I know that. I've seen it before. I just didn't expect it to happen to me. Things like this do not happen to me. But now that it has… I don't know what to do."

"Talk to Victoria," she said again.

"I don't want to talk to Victoria about it. I want to kiss you. Just once, okay?" He was practically begging, but he didn't care.

"No, it's not okay. I am not here for you to experiment with."

"I know. I'm sorry. But..." Damn, he wanted to have it out, and here was his chance, even if he was with the wrong woman. It was still a chance to have it out. "The thing is, I don't know if I can go through with this wedding feeling like this. I mean, maybe it's all just crazy last-minute jitters, and maybe it's something else. But it's better to know now, right?"

"Which I'm guessing is a line that grooms-to-be have been using since the beginning of time on women who just happen to be handy when the time came for them to get married."

"No! It's not that, I swear. If it was that, I would have done it already. I mean, okay, this sounds bad," he admitted. So bad. "But I just came from my bachelor party. Believe me, if any woman would do... Because there was a woman, a stripper, and she was more than willing. I wasn't."

"Oh, well," Amy said. "That does it. What a great guy you are? You didn't kiss the stripper. Let's give you a medal for that one. A good-guy medal."

"I don't want a medal. I just want you. I didn't kiss her because I just kept thinking about you. About your lemon bars and how they tasted and you all covered with powdered sugar and how you'd taste, and—"

"Don't," Amy told him. "Don't do it. We'll both regret it if you do."

"I'm afraid I'll regret it more if I don't," he said.

And with that, he leaned down and kissed her.

She wedged her arms in between them, so he couldn't hold her too close, but her back was against the pantry shelves, and she couldn't get away completely, either. So it was just her mouth opening beneath his, despite any protests she'd made before that moment. She was cautious, tentative, but she let him kiss her. And she did indeed taste like those cookies she'd given him moments ago. She must have been eating them, too. Or maybe licking the batter as she cooked them.

He could see her, in his mind, dragging a finger through cookie batter and then slowly bringing it to her lips and sucking the batter off. Or maybe him sucking cookie batter off her finger.

She just made him so hungry, all the time. Tate felt ravenous, like a man who hadn't fed his senses in ages. It felt wrong and very right, bad and very good, dangerous and yet exactly where he wanted to be.

He eased his body closer to hers, and the hands in between them turned from trying to push him away to palms pressed flat and hot against his chest, clutching his shoulders, one sliding into his hair to hold his head down to hers.

He felt heat zinging through him, pooling low in his belly, and he groaned, thinking it was like an oven in here, with her. Every place she touched him, he was hot, so hot it felt like he might start melting, melting into her, at any moment.

Stop, he told himself. *Just stop. Now.*

But he didn't. He kissed her again and again, trying to get every inch of his body pressed tightly against hers, feeling her soft and yielding against him, swearing at him even as she kissed him back.

And then he laughed.

He forgot everything else and just laughed for the sheer joy of it.

She might have told him to get away. She could swear at him if she wanted, but she was hanging on to him for all she was worth, and she was kissing him like crazy now.

He laughed again, thinking this was a mess, but now he

knew, and he'd really needed to know, before he'd made a terrible mistake he'd surely have come to regret.

Things were bad right now and would get worse before they got better, but in the long run, it was all good.

All very good.

So good.

He had his arms wrapped around her, his whole body plastered against hers, and he was happier than he'd been in ages. Ecstatically happy, joyously bad and relieved and—

He froze, hearing the slight creak of the pantry door. He opened his eyes to bright light where before there had been none, lifted his face from hers, his mouth from her soft, sweet lips, and there, standing in the doorway to the kitchen, stood his best man and two of his groomsmen.

They had the stupidest grins on their faces, or maybe that was shock, surprise and confusion.

"Sorry," his best man, Rick, said. "We thought we heard…something in the pantry. Interesting choice of venues, you two. Looks a bit uncomfortable, but…hey, whatever works for you and gets you away from Victoria's mother."

Tate had moved instinctively to shield Amy from view, but he could tell the minute Rick realized it wasn't Victoria hiding in the pantry with Tate.

"Oh," Rick said, nodding and backing away. "Sorry. We'll just…we'll all go now."

"Do that, please," Tate said.

"Right now," Rick said.

"Hey, before we do that, are there any more of those cookies with the jam in them?" Todd, one of the groomsmen, asked.

But Rick shoved him back into the kitchen and closed the door, plunging the pantry back into darkness.

Tate stood there, hearing Amy breathing, feeling the tension build, knowing this was his to fix.

"Okay, I'm really sorry about that last part," Tate began.

"The last part? That's what you're sorry about? The fact that you got caught?"

"Yeah. I am."

"But not anything else?"

"Not that I kissed you. No, I'm not. And you weren't all that upset about it, either, while it was happening. Don't even try to tell me you were."

"Get out of my kitchen," she said. "Get out now."

"Fine, I'll go. I'll stay away, until I've talked to Victoria."

"Yes, please, talk to Victoria."

"And then, I'll be back," he said. "And I'll have a lot more to say then."

Amy hardly slept a wink the rest of the night—her thoughts, her body in complete turmoil.

She couldn't believe he'd kissed her like that, Mr. I-am-not-this-guy! Or that it had felt so good, that she'd made it through everything she had in this world and never been kissed like that in her life.

It was completely unsettling and just…wrong.

Nothing should feel that good, that right, that essential.

He was a man engaged to another woman who happened to be having another man's baby, and he and Amy had been caught wrapped around each other in the pantry at two in the morning. So all kinds of hell was about to break loose in this house in the morning, she was sure, and she just wanted to grab Max, take him to the car and disappear as fast as she could.

Leave Tate Darnley, the good guy, to explain and do whatever he wanted to do with Victoria and her baby and the wedding. Amy was just the woman who caught his eye at exactly the right moment, nothing more. The woman who'd let him kiss her in the pantry and then, unable to help herself, in her surprise, her shock, her sheer pleasure, kissed him back.

But it wasn't any more than that, she knew. She was through making stupid mistakes with men. She was certain she'd been through with that years ago, with Max's father. So how she'd ended up in the pantry kissing Tate, she did not understand.

Amy was either dreaming or Eleanor was in her bedroom, leaning over her, looking concerned and whispering, "Dear, are you all right?"

"Hmm?" Amy sat up, momentarily confused about everything.

Where was she? What was Eleanor doing here? Where was Max? She turned and looked. Okay, Max was right beside her, sleeping soundly, in the big bed in the cook's quarters at Eleanor's house. For Eleanor's godson's wedding, which was likely off now, considering all the things standing in the way of that cursed wedding.

Was that why Eleanor was in her room?

"Oh, my God!" Amy said, wanting nothing more than to pull the covers over her head and hide in here all day.

"Are you not feeling well?" Eleanor asked. "Because if that's the case, don't worry. We'll manage just fine, dear."

"What?" Amy looked from Eleanor to the bedside clock. It was almost 8:00 a.m. "Ohh. I'm so sorry. I guess…I overslept."

Could it be nothing but that? That look of concern

on Eleanor's face? The fact that Amy was still in bed at eight?

"Well, if you're sure you're okay," Eleanor said, then waited, like she thought there might be something more.

Amy glanced at the clock again, her sluggish, sleepy brain starting to function. No way the bachelor party boys were up yet, she thought. It had been so late when they came in, which meant surely there was no way Eleanor could know anything about what happened in the pantry last night.

Could she?

And yet, when Amy turned back to Eleanor, Eleanor was still waiting, looking on expectantly, maybe even hopefully.

This was all so weird.

"I'm fine," Amy told her. "Just give me fifteen minutes, and I'll be in the kitchen making breakfast. I'm sorry."

"Dear, it's fine, truly. Kathleen and Gladdy and I are the only ones up right now, and we're quite self-sufficient, I assure you. Not as gifted as you in the kitchen, but not in any danger of starving. So you take your time."

"Okay," Amy said, now that she was more awake, thinking perhaps she could just pack her things and Max's and they could still disappear out the back door without having to face anyone else this morning. Even if it did mean walking out on her first real job.

Eleanor left, and Amy dragged herself into the shower and got dressed. She made it to the kitchen in eighteen minutes flat. Not bad, she decided, considering the night she'd had.

It was indeed just Eleanor, Kathleen and Gladdy at first, all giving her odd looks this morning. Either that or Amy was paranoid. Which, granted, she might be. All three of them were clearly fishing for information, and Amy refused to give up any. She felt pretty good about that.

And then Victoria's mother walked into the kitchen.

Amy winced. So did Eleanor, who Amy had already figured out did not care for Susan Whitman Ryan, and Mrs. Ryan obviously didn't care for Eleanor. They'd been icily polite to one another, Mrs. Ryan acting like this was a movie set and she was the director, producer and studio head who'd bankrolled the whole thing, despite the fact that the festivities were taking place in Eleanor's house. The gossip floating through the kitchen this week involved something about a former husband of one supposedly having a fling with the other decades ago, and Mrs. Ryan desperately coveting Eleanor's house, which likely had come with the man. Maybe that Eleanor had ended up with the house, Mrs. Ryan the man, at least for a while. Amy hadn't asked, didn't want to pry or gossip, but people had been all over her kitchen all week long, and she hadn't been able to help but hear.

Mrs. Ryan swept into the room like visiting royalty, waiting for them all to drop into a curtsy at the sight of her, and announced, "Good morning, all."

"Morning," the four of them muttered.

Then she addressed Amy alone, "I'd like some coffee, please, cream, no sugar."

"Yes, ma'am," Amy said, turning and hurrying to do the woman's bidding.

"And I'll just have some mixed fruit this morning. Nothing too heavy for the mother of the bride this close to the wedding," she said, once Amy had served her coffee.

"Yes, ma'am," Amy said again, willing to do anything as quickly as possible to get the woman out of the kitchen.

"In the dining room, please," she ordered.

"Of course. I'll bring it right in."

She could hear the low whispers of Eleanor, Kathleen and Gladdy behind her. They didn't care for the imperial attitude, especially directed toward Amy and in Eleanor's own house, but Amy didn't care—especially not this morning. She was just terrified Susan Whitman Ryan would hear about Amy and the groom in the pantry last night. If Amy could just get through this fiasco of a weekend without that happening, she'd consider herself lucky.

She served Mrs. Ryan her bowl of fruit in the dining room, where she could eat in solemn splendor, and then she went back to the kitchen, where the three ladies were whispering away.

"I feel sorry for poor Victoria," Gladdy said. "How could anyone grow up happy and warm and loving with that for a mother."

"I feel sorry for Tate," Kathleen said, "to have that for a mother-in-law."

"Well, I feel sorry for both of them and for me, having to put up with her, here, acting like she owns my house. What's worse, as things stand, I'm facing years to come of family celebrations with her."

They fell silent then, all of them staring at Amy.

"I don't like her, either," Amy said finally.

Still, they stared and waited.

Finally, Kathleen asked, "Amy, darling, is there anything you'd like to tell us?"

"No," Amy said.

"You look like you hardly slept a wink last night, dear," Gladdy jumped in. "Not that you don't look lovely this morning. You always do. Still, it seems like something must be bothering you, to keep you up all night. Why don't you tell us all about it. Maybe we can help."

"I doubt it," Amy said.

They all started talking, insisting that they were capable

of helping with all sorts of problems thanks to the wisdom they'd gained over the years in all sorts of situations.

"Not this one," Amy insisted.

That really got their attention. They were practically salivating, waiting for what she might say.

"Anyway, it's not my problem," Amy insisted. Not really. Not the biggest part of it. "It's someone else's. Really."

They nodded, waited.

"You know, we adore you, dear, don't you?" Eleanor tried. "You can tell us anything. Honestly."

"No, I can't. It's not my secret to tell."

"Secrets?" Gladdy looked very pleased. "I just love secrets."

"Me, too," Kathleen said. "Tell us everything."

"No, really. Can't do it."

"Amy, whatever it is, we'll understand. I promise. There's nothing you could say that would shock us or—"

Someone gave a little shriek.

Amy looked up and there was Victoria, looking dreadfully pale and frightened, just frozen into her place in the doorway. Eleanor, Kathleen and Gladdy turned to stare at her, too, giving her some of those same odd looks they'd just been giving Amy.

"Good morning," Amy said, smiling brightly at Victoria, trying to convince Victoria with nothing but the look on her face that everything was fine, all secrets still intact, no need to panic. "How's the bride this morning?"

Okay, probably not the thing to say, but Amy wasn't at her best, either, and that was just what had popped out of her mouth.

"Fine," Victoria murmured, and, if Amy wasn't mistaken, swayed a bit on her feet.

"Victoria, you're awfully pale," Eleanor observed. "Up late for the bachelorette party?"

Victoria nodded.

"Have a bit too much champagne, dear?" Eleanor went on.

Again, Victoria nodded, although Amy was sure she was lying about the champagne.

"Why don't you sit down," Eleanor began. "Your color is—"

But it was too late.

Victoria slid into a dead faint.

Amy grabbed for her.

So did Eleanor.

And the guitarist. *James.*

Where had he come from? He must have been listening outside the doorway to have gotten there that quickly. Or been with Victoria before she'd rushed into the kitchen, no doubt intent on making sure Amy didn't spill any of her secrets to Tate's godmother.

James got to Victoria first, managing to keep her from cracking her head on the floor, at least. Victoria's mother came running, fighting her way through the crowd to get to her daughter, only to find her lying on the floor with James bending over her.

"What happened?" Mrs. Ryan yelled. "Is she all right? What did you do to her?"

"We didn't do anything," Eleanor said. "She fainted."

"My daughter has never fainted in her life!" Mrs. Ryan exclaimed. "And who is that man? Are you a doctor? What are you doing to her?"

"I'm trying to figure out what happened," James said, feeling for a pulse, checking her forehead for a fever, leaning down and whispering softly to Victoria.

He didn't look up. All his attention was focused on Victoria. But Mrs. Ryan either recognized him or maybe his voice, because she looked, at first, curious, and then, horrified.

"You!" she cried. "You're that…boy! That awful boy!"

He looked at her then, looked her right in the eye and said, "I'm thirty-two years old, Mrs. Ryan. I'm not a boy anymore."

Okay, Victoria had said her mother had been outraged by Victoria's involvement with James years ago. Apparently, Mrs. Ryan hadn't forgotten. A terrible argument might have ensued, if not for Victoria starting to stir.

"There we go," Eleanor said. "She's coming back around."

James, kneeling on the floor over Victoria, took her hand and held it, whispering something to her again. Victoria moaned softly and turned her head toward James, blinked up at him in disbelief and maybe horror, and then promptly burst into tears.

Okay, that was bad.

Mrs. Ryan looked horrified, like James had tried to behead Victoria or something equally hideous. James looked equal parts baffled and concerned.

Amy thought things couldn't possibly get any worse, but then Tate walked in.

Chapter Nine

Tate heard the commotion and hurried to the kitchen, thinking some really scary thoughts about someone from the bachelor party maybe getting up this early to mix a hangover remedy and instead blabbing to Victoria about Tate and Amy in the pantry before Tate could get Victoria aside and confess everything.

But what he found when he got to the kitchen was half a dozen people encircling Victoria, who was on the floor sobbing with her mother standing over her looking thunderous and… Was that James? On the floor half holding Victoria up.

"What the hell is going on here?" Tate asked, aiming most of his ire at Victoria's mother, because, honestly, if anyone in the world could possibly drive Victoria to tears, it would be her mother. Tate didn't think anyone else had that ability.

"That man, he did it!" Mrs. Ryan said, pointing at James.

"Did what?" Tate asked.

"Oh, hush," Eleanor told Mrs. Ryan. "That man didn't do anything. Victoria fainted, and he got here in time to catch her before she hit the floor."

"I told you, my daughter has never fainted in her life!" Mrs. Ryan insisted. "We're made of much sterner stuff than that. So I repeat, what did he do to her, and what is he doing here in the first place?"

"His band is playing for the reception," Tate said, as he, too, knelt at Victoria's side.

"Why ever would she hire his band for the reception? We had a perfectly wonderful band lined up—"

"They canceled more than a month ago," Tate told her. "And Victoria hired James's band to fill in. Not that any of that matters right now. Couldn't we table this discussion until we know Victoria's okay?"

"Yes, please," James said, still holding Victoria's head in his lap, as he said softly to Tate, "I'll give you a hundred bucks if you can get that woman out of here right now."

Tate rolled his eyes, whispering back, "I'll give you anything you want if you can get her away from here for the next twenty-four hours."

Telling Victoria's mother about last night was going to be worse than telling Victoria herself, Tate feared. He could just imagine Victoria demanding that if he wanted to call off the wedding, he had to be the one to explain it to her mother. It would only be fair, he feared, and despite his actions of late, Tate tried to always be fair.

Victoria whimpered and touched her hand to her head.

"We should get her up off the floor," Tate said. "Could we have a little room, please?"

"You can put her in my bed," Amy offered. "It's the closest."

James finally stood up, and after consulting with Amy on the direction of her room, he cleared a path. Tate lifted Victoria into his arms and carried her to Amy's room, where Max was still sleeping. Amy lifted him up and took him into the kitchen.

Tate sat down by Victoria's side on the bed, holding her hand and smiling down at her. "There you go. Is that better?"

She nodded, barely, then looked up and over his shoulder and winced.

"Your mother?" Tate mouthed to her.

"Yes," she whispered weakly.

"Could we have a moment alone, please?" Tate said, turning around to stare at Victoria's mother who was giving them both a look of frosty disapproval.

Mrs. Ryan didn't budge, looking even more stubborn than usual.

"Mother, get out!" Victoria said, in a tone Tate had never heard her use with her mother before.

Go, Victoria, he thought.

Mrs. Ryan looked aghast and like she was winding herself up for a doozie of a lecture about children showing the proper manners and respect toward their parents.

Tate didn't let her even get started, jumping in and saying, "Victoria and I need to talk. Privately."

James, who was still standing in the doorway, came in, turned Mrs. Ryan around and steered her out the door, saying, "This way. You can tell me how horrible I am and what a terrible influence I was on Victoria back in high school. I know you'd enjoy that."

Tate frowned as they left, then turned to Victoria. "You

knew him well enough for him to be a bad influence on you in high school?"

Victoria looked pale and weak again. "Apparently. According to my mother."

"Of course, according to her, most everyone on the planet is a bad influence," Tate said.

"I know. I'm sorry. She really is awful."

Tate squeezed Victoria's hand. "Not your fault, really."

"Still, it's a wonder you were willing to take her on along with me, knowing we've always been a package deal, and she's probably never going to change."

Tate gave Victoria a sad smile. He really did hate hurting her this way. She deserved better than this. Still, he had to hope that he was saving them both from more pain in the future. Short-term though, it would not be pleasant. Even worse if she was ill right now. But he really had to tell her, before someone else did. He owed her that much, at least.

"Victoria, we need to talk about some things—"

"I know," she said. "Just…not now, okay? I just can't do it right now."

Tate hesitated. He'd love to take the out and delay this a while longer, but the wedding was also less than forty-eight hours away. It couldn't wait.

"Just until this afternoon, I promise," Victoria said. "And then, no matter how I feel, we'll talk. We'll get…everything out."

Okay, that didn't sound good.

Had she already heard somehow about him and Amy in the kitchen? "Uh…okay."

She did look awfully pale and somehow…fragile, he would have said, if it was anyone but Victoria. She was the antithesis of fragile.

"What happened in the kitchen?" he asked, "They said you fainted?"

"I guess. I just got dizzy, and then I couldn't stand up anymore."

It still didn't sound like the Victoria he knew. "Is it the wedding? The stress?"

"I'm not sure," she said. "I wasn't feeling well yesterday, either."

"Well, stay here for a while and rest. Amy won't mind. Can I get you anything? Something to eat? Something to drink? What can I do?"

"I…I hate to ask, but if you could keep my mother away from me? Please?"

Tate made a face of mock horror, which won a little smile from Victoria.

"I just can't face her right now," Victoria said. "I'm going to try to slip out the back way and to my car before she sees me and can come chasing after me—"

"You sure you're all right to drive?"

"I think so. I have to get out of here, just for a little while." She went to sit up and then looked like she might faint again.

"Okay, that's not going to work," Tate told her, easing her back down. "Victoria, what's wrong?"

"This afternoon, okay? I promise. I'm not even sure myself yet, but… Look, I'm going to the doctor. Just a quick checkup, to make sure…that everything's okay, before the wedding and before we take off for Greece for the honeymoon. I mean, I wouldn't want to be sick in a foreign country."

"Doctor?" he repeated, feeling as if he might be getting ready to take a blow, might be getting light-headed himself.

Victoria was never sick.

Of course, she hadn't said she was actually…sick.

And she'd fainted.

Which meant…

"No, no, no! Don't look like that," she begged. "I'm just… I'll explain everything this afternoon. Just get my mother out of the way, please. And maybe someone could give me a ride? Maybe…Amy?"

"Amy?" He gulped. Of all the people in this house, Amy was the one she wanted? His voice was tight and high as he asked, "Why?"

"She's so nice," Victoria said, looking completely sincere.

Tate definitely felt queasy now. Victoria didn't look mad, didn't look like an outraged fiancée at all, and yet why Amy, of all people?

And then he started to put it together again, unable to help himself.

She was dizzy, fainting, looking weak and maybe queasy.

Nervous and uncharacteristically unsure of herself.

And he'd caught Amy with a pregnancy test that she claimed was not for her, could not possibly be for her and he hadn't believed her. And now Victoria wanted Amy with her, Amy who'd already been pregnant and been through the experience of having a child.

"Oh, my God!" Tate said.

"No, really! Don't do that!" Victoria said. "I know what you're thinking, and it's not that! I mean, I'm pretty sure, it's not. Honestly. So just wait. I'm going to the doctor. I'm going to make sure, and I'll know really soon. So…just don't freak out. Okay?"

Tate wished he could faint dead away and not be thinking about what he was thinking. If Victoria was pregnant, and he'd just been in the pantry kissing Amy last night and about to call off their wedding…

He gasped, finding it hard to breathe all of a sudden.

"We were careful," he insisted. "We've always been careful. About everything. Our whole lives we have been careful!"

"I know, which is why I really believe…it's not what you're thinking. I promise. But we don't have to wonder, because all I have to do is get out of here and get to the doctor, and we'll know. So there's no reason to do or say anything, except for me to go right now and find out for sure."

"Okay," Tate said, feeling as if it really wasn't okay. Not at all.

Not that he didn't like kids. He did.

But right now? With Victoria?

"Oh, God!" he said again.

"Okay, right now you are not helping, Tate. And I need you to help me. Now. Go get Amy and send her in here, and then go find my mother and lock her in a closet or something until I'm gone."

He closed his eyes and winced.

Amy.

The kiss.

The guys from the bachelor party who'd caught them in the pantry last night.

"This is ridiculous," he said finally. "I'll drive you to the doctor."

"No," Victoria insisted, quickly and with some heat he didn't understand. "I mean, sorry. I'd…I'd like a woman to go with me. You know…it's a woman's thing."

It was a couple's thing, Tate thought, but took the cowardly way out she'd offered and promised to do as she'd asked. The time until she got back was going to seem like an eternity, one of pretending to be the happy bridegroom and maybe physically restraining his mother-in-law-to-be, who he really, really disliked, and she certainly disliked him right back.

Oh, God!

Maybe this was his punishment for his sins of late. Having to keep Victoria's mother out of the way for a while. Oooh. The wages of sin and all had nothing on this.

"All right. I'll do it," he said. "I'll get Amy and send her in, but…Victoria…about Amy?"

"Yes?"

Just then, he remembered Amy telling him again and again to talk to Victoria, practically begging him to talk to Victoria.

That all made sense now.

Because she knew.

Amy must have known.

He hung his head in shame and felt a queasy mix of nerves and guilt.

"Never mind," he said. "We'll talk when you get back."

People lingered conspicuously in the kitchen, getting coffee and more coffee, nibbling on the food Amy put out for breakfast, talking, waiting, most certainly hoping they might overhear the conversation in Amy's bedroom between the bride and groom, if they just stayed there long enough.

Amy wanted to shoo them all away, but as nothing but the woman hired to cook for them didn't think she had the authority. Plus, three of the main eavesdroppers were Eleanor, Kathleen and Gladdy. They'd been trying to corner her ever since Tate and Victoria disappeared into Amy's room, no doubt wanting to know what Amy knew about what was going on. But so far, Amy had managed to evade being cornered by them.

Victoria's mother had stationed herself in the hallway that led to Amy's room, as close as she could get without actually pressing her ear to the door, which Amy was sure Mrs. Ryan wanted to do. James wasn't far from Mrs. Ryan, although Mrs. Ryan had repeatedly told him there was no need for him to stay, that he had no business here.

"I want to make sure Victoria's okay," he said stubbornly, more than once.

Mrs. Ryan did everything but order him out. Amy suspected the only thing that kept her from actually doing that was having Eleanor, who did own the house after all, in the same room and voicing no objections to James being there.

It was the most hideous breakfast Amy had ever endured. All it needed was for Tate's buddies from the bachelor party to show up and think everyone was so tense because they knew about Amy and Tate in the pantry last night and to start blabbing about that.

"Never another wedding," Amy promised herself, while she got out more fresh fruit to slice for the guests. *Never, never, never.*

"What's that, dear?" Eleanor asked, smiling that tell-me-everything-you-know smile.

"Nothing," Amy said.

"I was sure you said something."

"Uh, I think I need to go back to the grocery store. Everyone's eating more than I thought they would this morning. We won't have anything left for breakfast tomorrow."

That was it! She'd escape. Whatever happened in the kitchen when Tate and Victoria came out that door could happen without her, coward that she was.

"Surely you're as curious as the rest of us," Eleanor said softly.

"No," Amy said. "Not at all."

"Which can only mean that you already know what's going on," Eleanor concluded.

"No." It was an outright lie but justified, Amy thought. Victoria's secret to tell, not Amy's. At least, the biggest one was Victoria's.

Mrs. Ryan must have had bionic hearing, because she managed to pick up enough to come rushing over and demanding, "You know what this is about? Tell me this instant."

Amy shrank back against Eleanor, who put her arm around Amy and answered for her.

"Good grief, Susan, you're not going to interrogate the poor girl. I won't stand for it. Just try to be patient for once in your life and wait until your daughter's finished talking to her fiancé."

Mrs. Ryan gave a scary-sounding huff, her whole body going stiff, shot Amy a look that had her wanting to hide somewhere and not come out for hours. Then Mrs. Ryan retreated back to her position in the doorway, where she went back to glaring at James once again.

"Thank you," Amy whispered to Eleanor.

"Of course, dear. And now, I think you should tell me everything you know about this, as payment for fighting off that vile woman for you."

Before Amy could answer, she heard the sound of a door opening. Everyone in the kitchen fell quiet and turned toward the sound. Tate appeared, looking pale, maybe queasy himself, much as Victoria had only moments before. Seeing the crowd gathered, awaiting him, he muttered something under his breath, then took a breath and faced them all.

"Well? What is it? What's going on? Tell me this instant," Mrs. Ryan demanded.

"You and I need to talk," Tate said to her, looking as if he'd rather jump off a cliff, if he had a choice. "But first I need Amy for a moment, please?"

It was Amy's turn to feel sick now. Everyone turned to look at her, their curiosity even higher now.

"Amy?" Mrs. Ryan practically roared. "What does Amy have to do with anything?"

"Victoria would like to see you," Tate said, ignoring Victoria's mother and looking pleadingly at Amy.

Amy gulped.

What did that mean exactly? *See her?*

"Oh, dear," Eleanor said, sounding both surprised and dismayed.

Mrs. Ryan glared at her now. James looked completely baffled by Victoria's request, and Eleanor and Gladdy looked a bit guilty, Amy thought.

"I really don't see—" Victoria's mother began.

"Not now!" Tate said, as sharply as Amy had ever heard him.

Mrs. Ryan seemed to grow three inches taller before their eyes, puffing herself up full of her own importance and most likely getting ready to blast Tate and anyone else who dared interrupt her or interfere.

"You will not speak to me that way—" she began again.

But Eleanor, the only person here who wasn't afraid of Mrs. Ryan, took the woman by the arm and practically dragged her into the dining room. "We'll be waiting, as soon as you're ready to talk, Tate darling," she said.

Amy, seeing no choice in the matter, walked over to Tate and followed him down the hall, feeling the eyes of everyone in the kitchen following them every step of the way.

"Does she know?" Amy whispered.

"No," he claimed.

"Then what does she want with me?"

"A ride to the doctor's office."

"Oh," Amy said, stopping when she reached the closed bedroom door.

"It was her test, wasn't it? You got it for her?"

"Yes, but it's not..." *Oh, hell. Not her secret to tell.*

"Not what I think?" He laughed bitterly. "You mean, I wasn't here kissing you last night, while my fiancée was off somewhere sweating the results of the home pregnancy test you bought for her?"

"Shh," Amy said. "Just...just wait, okay? And don't say anything to Victoria's mother. Not yet."

"That's what Victoria said." He didn't look so much freaked out as completely baffled then. "How could you know so much more about this than I do?"

"I couldn't begin to explain that to you right now."

"Wait," he said. "Even more than that, how could you let me kiss you, knowing my fiancée is pregnant?"

"You did that. I didn't," she reminded him, whispering furiously.

"Maybe, but you kissed me back. You know you did!"

"Okay, yes, I did. But I didn't make this mess. You and Victoria did, and you both somehow dragged me into it all. And you don't even know what's really going on yet—"

"The hell I don't!" he roared back.

"No, you don't," she whispered.

He fell silent then, looked as if he found that impossible to believe, although he'd really like for it to be anything but what he thought he knew.

"Look, I'm going to take Victoria to the doctor, because that's what she needs to do, and you need to just let us go do it. Try not to freak out. I know that seems impossible right now, but try. And whatever you do, don't say anything to anybody until we get back, okay?"

He gaped at her and shook his head. "But—"

"I know, it doesn't make any sense, and I'm sorry, but just do it, okay?" Amy insisted. "And in a couple of hours, you'll have all the answers you need."

Amy opened the door and went into the bedroom before he could ask her anything else, deciding that at the moment it was easier to face Victoria than her poor fiancé.

Chapter Ten

It was the longest two hours of Tate's life.

He walked back down that hall, feeling like a man going to his own execution, walked toward the crowd gathered in the kitchen who'd obviously found his argument with Amy very, very interesting. How much had he given away with that little encounter?

Tate pointedly ignored everyone else except Victoria's mother, who'd gotten away from Eleanor and made her way to the front of the eavesdroppers gathered there. If looks could kill, Tate would be in the morgue in minutes. Sadly, his heart kept right on beating and he'd have to deal with this woman.

"You know," she began. "I never liked you."

"What a surprise," Tate said, taking her firmly by the arm and steering her toward the opposite end of the house, where she hopefully wouldn't see a car leaving the estate with Victoria in it.

"I told Victoria you weren't right for her, right from the start. I told her you'd embarrass her and disappoint her, and look what's happened now. I was right, wasn't I?"

"That remains to be seen," he said, determined to do this penance, endure this woman's presence for poor Victoria's sake. He suspected the only thing that could make her visit to the doctor more stressful was having her mother along.

"I insist that you tell me what's going on this instant," she demanded.

Tate stopped where he was, deep in the east wing of the house, where there were no windows looking out on the drive in front. He took his time, leaning back against a big marble-top buffet, trying for the life of him to look relaxed and surely failing miserably. And then he waited some more, stalling for time.

All they had to do was get to the car and out onto the street, and they were clear, as long as Mrs. Ryan couldn't torture him into giving out their destination. She'd try, he knew, but surely he could take it and not spill their secret.

"Well?" Mrs. Ryan bellowed.

"Well, what?"

"What is it that we need to talk about?"

Tate shrugged. "Nothing, actually."

"Nothing? You just said back there that we needed to talk. You practically dragged me here, away from all those busybodies, so we could have some privacy—"

"No, I didn't," he said.

She huffed, she puffed, she nearly blew her stack. "Don't toy with me. Not now! Something is going on between you and my daughter and that woman, the cook! I know it. And I demand to know what it is this instant!"

"I'm afraid you're just going to have to wait like the rest

of us," he said, realizing he didn't have the strength to lie to Mrs. Ryan about this for as long as it would take Victoria to get back, and once he thought about it, why should he?

All he'd had to do was give Victoria a chance to get away, and he hoped he had.

"Wait? I'm not going to wait. I'm her mother—"

"Yes, you will wait," Tate insisted. "Victoria had some things to take care of."

"What do you mean 'some things to take care of'?"

"I mean some things. And when she gets back—"

"Gets back? What do you mean 'gets back'?"

"I mean she's gone. She left the minute I got you out of the way. And don't ask me where she's going. I don't know." It wasn't exactly a lie. He didn't know her doctor's name or where the office was.

Mrs. Ryan looked too outraged to even speak, then turned around and looked at where they were, where he'd led her. Tate feared she was about to make a break for the other side of the house, to try to stop Victoria, and wondered if he had the nerve to hold her here by physical force, if necessary, to ensure Victoria's getaway.

He'd probably get slapped if he tried it. He might have to get married with a handprint on his face or maybe a black eye, if there was still a wedding on Saturday. Mrs. Ryan would just love that.

But Victoria's mother didn't run. She fumed, shot daggers with her eyes. For a moment he thought she was going to smack him, even though he hadn't tried to restrain her.

Then she drew herself up, as big and important as could be, and said frostily, "We'll just see about this."

We certainly will, Tate thought.

Amy got Victoria into the car, and at Victoria's insistence, she floored it down the driveway, careened out of the gate and onto the lightly traveled road. Only then, when she was sure they were not being pursued, did Victoria finally relax.

She leaned sideways against the door, laid her head against the back of her seat, facing Amy, and said, "This has got to be the worst day of my life. And I haven't even told my mother yet."

"So you told Tate?" Amy asked.

"Not really. He guessed. Just that I was pregnant. Not that it's not his."

"Oh."

"Poor thing was freaked out enough just thinking I might be pregnant that I ended up telling him I was sure it wasn't what he was thinking. Which was obviously that I was pregnant and that it was his baby. So I didn't really lie to him." Victoria sighed, hiding her head against the passenger window. "I mean, okay, I didn't tell him the truth, but all I was trying to do was keep him from worrying too much until I know for sure. Just another hour or so, and I can tell him I am pregnant but that it's not his baby. And I'll tell him, as soon as I know."

"Well, that's a start," Amy said.

"Yeah." She laughed pitifully. "And after that, I can either tell James or my mother. James first, I think, so he can have a chance to get away and think and figure out what he's going to do. So my mother doesn't get hold of him, once she knows. He shouldn't have to deal with her on top of everything else today. Maybe we could call him on the way back to the house and have him meet us somewhere, so I can tell him and then he can get away. I think I owe him that."

"A chance to get away?" Did she think so little of James? That he'd immediately run away?

"No, just a chance to hear the news and then have some

peace and quiet to figure out how he feels about it on his own, without being attacked by my mother."

"That's kind of you," Amy said, touching her hand to Victoria's, wanting to comfort her.

Victoria sighed. "I'm glad you're here. You've been so nice to me. I don't know how I can ever thank you."

Amy felt awful, then. As crazy as the whole mess had been, she did like Victoria. Underneath all that polish and starch was a real human being, and Amy felt for anyone about to become a mother when she least expected it. Which made it even worse that she'd been in the pantry kissing Victoria's fiancé last night.

"Victoria, I have to tell you something," Amy said. "I'm really sorry. I don't know how this happened, and… I know exactly what you meant when you told me that you are so completely not this woman, because neither am I. And yet—"

"Tate does like you!" she said, sitting up in her seat and showing some signs of life for the first time since she got into the car.

"I don't know about that, but—"

"He's interested in you," she said. "I could tell. He's really not a flirt. He's just a really nice guy and not one of those guys who's constantly staring at every woman who walks by or saying things or coming on to women. Just a nice guy. I always felt like I'd be so safe with him, like I'd always be able to trust him."

"God." Amy winced. That just made it even worse. "Well, then I really hate telling you this, but he was in the kitchen really late last night and…he kissed me."

"Oh," Victoria said, looking surprised and as if she wasn't quite sure what else she might feel.

"He said it was one of those experimental kisses. You know? The I-can't-marry-someone-else-unless-I-know-just-once-what-it-feels-like-to-kiss-you? And I'm sure some guys would make the most of that line, but with him… Maybe I'm crazy, too, but it didn't feel like a line."

"Well, that's a surprise," she said, looking a bit stunned at first, then just sad. "I guess I was thinking of Tate as my insurance policy in all this. That if James freaked out and left me, Tate probably wouldn't, even once he knows the truth. That he'd feel sorry for me and not abandon me to face my mother and this baby and everything else alone. Which really isn't fair, I know. It's just… He's a good guy, and we've been friends for ages."

It was Amy's turn to feel queasy then.

Tate, the insurance policy?

He deserved a lot more than that, Amy thought. A whole lot more.

Inside her, it was as if something was rising up and wanting to demand a whole lot more for him than to be Victoria's backup plan, demand it for Tate's sake and maybe even for her own.

"I'm not going to lie to you," Amy said. "I kissed him back. I mean, I really kissed him. I didn't mean to, I just… I don't know what happened. One minute I was backing away from him, and the next, I was all over him like shrink-wrap. And that's not the worst part."

Victoria took a breath. "It gets worse?"

"I'm afraid some of the groomsmen coming in from the bachelor party saw us together."

"Oh, no!" Victoria shook her head, then hid her face in her hands and finally laughed a bit, sounding overwhelmed and edging toward hysteria. "Well, that does it. If there are any weapons on the estate, they should be confiscated, because if my mother hears about that, there's no telling what she might do."

"I'm really sorry," Amy said. "I hate to think I made things even worse."

"No, don't. The real damage was done weeks ago, when I saw James again. I felt the same way about him as it sounds like Tate feels about you. I couldn't stand to get married and not know what it was like to kiss James at least one time, and when I did, I ended up doing a lot more than just kiss him."

"Do you regret it?" Amy asked.

Victoria shook her head, tears shimmering in her eyes. "Crazy as that sounds, no. I mean I regret the mess, that I was engaged to Tate when I did it and that I let weeks go by, feeling guilty, not knowing what to do, not confessing everything to Tate and letting the wedding get closer and closer. I just kept thinking life would get back to normal. That it had to, and the thing with James was just a crazy fling I'd get over. And now here I am, supposed to be at my wedding rehearsal and rehearsal dinner in a few hours, and instead, I'm on my way to the doctor's, pregnant with another man's baby. That's…crazy. Absolutely crazy."

"And the woman taking you to the doctor was kissing your fiancé in the pantry last night," Amy added.

"Yes! My life is like a bad circus right now!" She sighed, groaned, then leaned her head back against the headrest as if it was too much for her to even hold her own head upright at the moment.

"Well, I hate to tell you this, but…I think we've arrived," Amy said, pulling into the parking lot at the address Victoria had given her.

"Oh, God!" Victoria looked as if she might bolt from the car, from the parking lot, from the planet, if only she could.

Amy took her hand and held on to it, well remembering this feeling of being pregnant and terrified.

Victoria looked down at their clasped hands and said, "You have been so nice to me this whole time, and I'm grateful. I'm even a little bit happy for Tate that maybe he's found someone. I've felt awful about cheating on him and not loving him the way I should. He deserves to be crazy in love, too. To feel as crazy about someone else as I feel about James, and Tate doesn't feel that way about me. I know it."

Amy didn't know what to say about that, except, "I don't want him to be crazy in love with me. I don't want to be crazy or in love, and I wouldn't wish those feelings onto anyone."

"Neither did I, but I didn't have a choice. Not about my feelings. I know I had a choice about my actions, that we all do, but not about the way I felt. Give Tate a chance. And don't worry about me and the baby getting in the way of anything. I meant what I said a moment ago—Tate may well offer to marry me anyway, and I might be scared enough to want to take him up on that offer. But I won't. I won't let him marry me just because he cares about me and he feels obligated to try to help, when things are so crazy."

"You know, I'm just going to stay out of this until the two of you both decide what you want," Amy said.

That was sensible. That was the right thing to do.

"Okay," Victoria said. "I just want you to know, too, that I love Tate in a way that means I want him to be as happy as he can possibly be. And I know now that doesn't mean him being with me."

"I'm still staying out of it from here," Amy insisted.

"Okay." Victoria sighed, then stared at the sign on the building with the doctor's name on it. "I guess I really have to go inside now, and I'm really scared. I probably don't deserve this, but if you'd come inside with me and maybe hold my hand while they do this test, I'll consider us completely even on the you-kissing-my-fiancé-right-before-my-wedding thing."

Amy laughed. "Deal."

Victoria's mother nearly called the police, looking for her daughter, until someone showed her that Victoria's car was in the driveway. They'd taken Amy's car, and no one knew what Amy drove. Although Mrs. Ryan said she had the connections to find out.

Eleanor talked Mrs. Ryan down, telling her that her ranting was drawing attention from the other guests, who were up and mingling around the estate. And at this point, no one really knew anything except that Victoria had left on a short errand. But if Mrs. Ryan kept acting like a crazy woman, all the wedding guests would know something was up.

So Mrs. Ryan shut up, for the moment, and busied herself by pacing the driveway by the side entrance to the house. Eleanor told everyone she was nervous about the caterers being late, and most people, smartly, kept their distance from the visibly upset Mrs. Ryan.

Tate chose his spot on one of the second-floor balconies with a view of the driveway. He was pacing as well, although trying to be discreet about it and trying not to hyperventilate.

Rick, his best man, found him after nearly an hour had gone by, took one look at Tate and said, "Oh, my God. Victoria knows?"

"Huh?" Tate said.

"About last night. You and Amy. She knows?"

"No. I don't think so."

Rick frowned. "Then what's wrong? Her mother looks

like she's ready to set someone on fire. I was afraid it was going to be you."

Tate shook his head. "Oh, she hates me, but she's not sure if I'm to blame for this or not."

"Blame for what?"

Tate felt sick once again at the predicament in which he found himself. "I think Victoria's pregnant."

"Oh," his friend said, then thought about it some more. "Oh! You mean, Victoria may be pregnant and doesn't know yet that you were in the pantry with another woman, kissing, last night?"

Tate frowned, shrugged. "Yeah. That, too."

"That, too? What do you mean, that, too? What's going on here?"

"I really liked kissing Amy in the pantry last night," Tate confessed. "I really didn't want to stop. Don't get me wrong, I like kissing Victoria. I've always liked Victoria. But not like that. Not like I'd rather have someone cut off my right arm rather than stop. And I can't really marry Victoria, feeling that way about Amy. That's what I was going to tell Victoria this morning. Except I didn't get a chance. She told me or, she didn't tell me, but let's just say, I'm pretty sure Victoria's pregnant, and that came up before I had the chance to tell her I can't marry her tomorrow."

"Oh, sh—"

"Yeah," Tate said, then turned and glared at his best friend. "And if you ever tell a soul I said that, I'll run you over with a bus. Got it?"

"Got it." Rick looked properly serious and saddened. "So what are you going to do?"

"I have no idea," Tate said. First time in his life, he had no plan, no idea what to do, what was right. "Wait for Victoria to get back and see what she has to say, I guess. Take it from there."

"Anything I can do?" Rick offered.

"Get her mother out of the way somehow, so that Victoria and I get a chance to talk alone when she gets back."

"Sure, I'll just…tell her we're under a nuclear attack or something. She might move for that."

"Tell her something's wrong with the wedding plans," Tate said. "That's the only thing she might listen to right now. And that there's someone, say the florist—she hates the florist—threatening to cancel or something."

"Consider it done," Rick promised.

His friend disappeared, and Tate started pacing again.

It was twenty minutes more before Tate's cell phone rang. He didn't recognize the number but picked it up anyway, surprised to hear Amy's voice.

"We're heading back to the house now. Victoria wants to know if you can get her mother out of the way again, so the two of you can talk," Amy said.

"Already planned for that. What kind of car do you drive, and when will you be here?"

"An old faded blue Honda sedan. We're at the light on Wilmont Road right now, so…"

"Got it." Then he thought of one more thing. "Can we meet in your room? I don't think Victoria's mother would think to look for us there, at least not for a while? Plus, it's close to the side entrance to the house?"

"Sure," Amy said. "Good luck."

Tate laughed. "I'm going to need it, aren't I? Amy, I'm so sorry. I swear, I had no idea any of this was going on."

"I know. Just…talk to Victoria. Don't worry about the rest of it right now."

He got off the phone, then called Rick to tell him to put the distract-the-mother-in-law-from-hell plan into action, watching from the front of the house until Rick convinced Victoria's mother to follow him somewhere. Then Tate rushed down the stairs, out the front door and to the side of the house to meet Victoria and Amy as they arrived.

Victoria looked pale, but calm, thanked Amy for going with her and then headed with Tate toward the house, only to be waved off frantically by Eleanor, who stood at the back door gesturing furiously for them to head to the guesthouse.

"Go, hurry, right now," Eleanor said. "Victoria's mother's right behind me. Rick can't hold her back forever. And Amy, you don't want her to find you, either. Get back in your car and go somewhere else. I'll call you when it's safe to come back. Don't worry about Max. He's fine."

Amy turned around and took off just as Tate held the door open to the guesthouse, which was thankfully empty.

"This is good," Tate reasoned. "Your mother won't think to look for us here, because she knows we're desperately trying to avoid her."

Victoria nodded, looking sad and serious.

"It's ridiculous for two successful, intelligent, well-educated adults to be so afraid of one woman," Tate said, trying for levity or maybe just to avoid what had to be said for another moment.

"I know," she said. "I'm going to do something about that. It's on my list. But the first thing on the list is you and me. I need to sit down. You should, too."

"Victoria, it'll be okay," he said. He had to. "You and I, we can make this work somehow—"

"I knew you'd say that." She smiled at him, despite everything else. "I even told Amy you would."

"Well, I mean it. I have to tell you something first, but I want you to know that you and I will take care of this baby together. Nothing will get in the way of that—"

"I know about you and Amy in the pantry last night."

She jumped in, really surprising him. "She told me on the way to the doctor's office."

Tate closed his eyes for a moment, feeling like an absolute cad. "I'm sorry about that. I have no excuse—"

"Neither do I, and I've done a lot more than you have," she said.

Tate sat down in a chair opposite the one she'd chosen, seeing how uncomfortable she was, even after he'd promised he'd be there for her and the baby, realizing only then that something else was going on here.

"What do you mean?" he asked finally. "What have you done?"

"I never meant for this to happen. I hope you believe me when I say that. It's like he just dropped out of the sky and landed in front of me, a complete surprise. The band we'd hired canceled, and I had to hire another one. You were traveling, and I had a million other wedding details to take care of. I didn't even know it was his band when I called to book them—"

"James?" he asked, incredulous.

Victoria nodded, looking so sad, so afraid.

Tate could hardly believe it. How in the world had he missed this? True, he'd been in Japan for three weeks, and they had been more than a little crazy with wedding plans, and they did both tend to work insane hours. It had been at least a month, maybe even six weeks, since they'd spent a night together. It was hard to believe Victoria had fallen into bed with someone else.

Still…

"You and James Fallon? Really?"

She nodded, blinked back tears and then went on with her confession.

"We had a little…thing in high school."

"That is so hard to believe," he said. "You and James?"

"I feel the same way. I just couldn't quite resist him. Even though I was about to marry a guy I just adore, one I trust with my life, one who makes me feel so safe."

"Too safe, maybe?" Tate guessed.

"Maybe. I just went a little crazy."

Tate knew that feeling. Knew it exactly. *Damn*. Life was so strange sometimes. And they weren't done sorting this out yet. "So you are pregnant?"

She nodded.

"And the baby is…?"

"His."

"You're sure? Absolutely sure?"

She nodded. "I know exactly when you and I were together last. It was before you left for Japan, and I'm not that pregnant. That's why I had to see the doctor today, so I'd know. She said the ultrasound shows the baby was conceived right in the middle of your trip."

"Okay," he said, feeling the most incredible sense of relief of his entire life. What a mess that would have been, if it had been his baby, but it was James that Victoria wanted to be with.

And then he felt guilty about how damned relieved and happy he felt, when Victoria was obviously so miserable. He took her hand, held it in his. They had been good friends forever, after all.

"What are you going to do now?"

"I don't know. Tell everyone the wedding's off and then…" She started to laugh. "Maybe run? Hide? Anything I can do to avoid having to deal with my mother."

"Yeah. That's not going to be pretty," Tate agreed. "But I meant what about James? Does he know?"

"I think he might suspect, after I fainted in the kitchen this morning, but there's no way he could know anything for sure."

"But you're going to tell him, right?"

She nodded. "I was going to tell him first, but then I chickened out and told you instead. Thank you for being so understanding. For just…being you."

Tate came to sit beside her, put his arm around her and held her for a long moment. She was trembling, just all torn up inside, and there was still so much hard stuff that had to be done.

Poor Victoria.

She'd never met a problem she couldn't handle with grace and confidence. Except her mother. That one always got the better of her. Her mother would not take this well, but Tate knew the real worry for Victoria now was how James would react to the news.

"Okay," he said, while she still had her head buried against him. "No time like the present to get this done. Do you know where James is right now?"

"No," she whispered, not even raising her head from Tate's chest. "But he's been calling me nonstop ever since I left the house this morning."

"All right. Give me your phone," Tate insisted.

"No, you don't have to do this. You don't have to be nice to me right now. You don't have to help."

"Of course I do." He leaned down and kissed her forehead. "I think we just avoided making a big mistake. We should both be grateful, and we'll always be friends. Give me the phone."

"You're the best," she whispered.

"Hey, I could be the godfather."

"Not five minutes ago you were terrified of the idea of being a father," she reminded him.

"Yeah, but the godfather gets all the fun stuff. I can do that."

She finally pulled away from him, dug into her purse,

found the phone and handed it to him. He flipped through her missed calls, found one from James and returned it, saying only that Victoria was fine but needed to talk to him somewhere quiet and nowhere near her mother.

James agreed immediately.

"Okay," Tate said, disconnecting the call. "All set. The coffee shop is two blocks from here. Come on. I'll drive you to meet him."

Victoria got to her feet, picked up her purse and then stopped in her tracks. "Wait, what about my mother? I can't leave you to face her all on your own. What in the world are you going to tell her?"

"I don't know. I'll stall. I've held out this long against her. I can make it another hour or so."

Amy stayed away for thirty minutes until Eleanor called and told her it was okay to come back.

"What happened?" she asked the minute she walked into the kitchen and found Eleanor.

"I'm not sure," Eleanor whispered. "Tate's here, but Victoria's not, and he won't say where she is."

"But they talked? Victoria and Tate?"

"I have no idea," Eleanor said. "I would have tortured him until he talked, but Victoria's mother showed up, even more furious than before about not knowing what's going on or where Victoria is. Tate took her away somewhere—Victoria's mother, I mean. I haven't looked for her. I don't want to be anywhere near her right now, not even if it meant finding out what's going on."

Well, Amy could understand that.

She didn't think she'd brave the wrath of Victoria's mother to find out exactly what was going on with the bride and groom.

Eleanor was getting ready to grill Amy some more—Amy

could tell by the look in her eyes—when a man walked down the hall carrying a huge bouquet of flowers.

Wedding flowers, obviously.

Amy looked to Eleanor.

"Tate told the florists to go ahead and put the flowers in place, as planned," Eleanor said. "The minister's due in a few hours for the rehearsal, the caterers even sooner, to get everything ready for the rehearsal dinner. It's all very strange."

Yes, it was.

Amy wondered for a moment if Victoria had told Tate the whole truth, and he'd still offered to marry her, just as Victoria predicted he would. And if maybe Victoria had panicked and agreed. Which felt just terrible, when Amy stood there and thought about it. Tate marrying Victoria anyway, for the baby's sake.

She felt funny, as if she was choking or something, her throat tight, as though she couldn't breathe. It was the worst feeling. Her heart started racing. She felt unsteady on her feet, as if her whole body was turning to mush.

"I need…I'll be right back, Eleanor. I need some air," she said, walking as fast as she could down the hallway and back outside, where she sucked in a big breath, then another and leaned weakly against the side of the house.

What in the world?

"Amy?"

She turned around, thinking it had to be Eleanor, but it was Victoria's mother instead.

Uh-oh.

"You!" Mrs. Ryan said, rushing outside and over to Amy, stopping about an inch from Amy's nose. "What have you done with my daughter?"

"Nothing," Amy said.

"Where is she?"

"I don't know. I brought her back here thirty minutes ago."

Mrs. Ryan's mouth dropped open at that. For a moment Amy thought the woman was about to call her a liar, but instead, she turned beet-red, as if she was about to blow her top, and demanded, "Where did you take her earlier?"

"You'll have to ask her that, Mrs. Ryan."

Amy was relieved to see Tate come rushing from the house to intervene, afraid she was about to be pinned against the house by Mrs. Ryan until she spilled all Victoria's secrets.

"Amy," Tate said, sounding firm and determined, "my godmother needs you in the kitchen. Something about a problem with dinner."

"She's not even cooking dinner," Mrs. Ryan snapped at him. "The caterers are preparing the rehearsal dinner."

"Well, maybe it was something about lunch," Tate said.

"Lunch is over. Hardly anyone ate it. No one cares about lunch anymore. Where is Victoria, and what is going on here?"

"I really wouldn't know," Tate claimed, taking Amy by the hand and pulling her to his side, as if he would protect her if need be.

"You two," Mrs. Ryan said, following them. "I've seen the way you look at each other. Did you know each other? Before this weekend?"

"Nope. Never saw her before," Tate said.

"Well, I don't believe that. Nothing you could say would make me believe that. There's something going on with the two of you. That's what it is. There's something going on, and Victoria's found out about it. I told her you would never be the man for her."

Tate turned around at that but kept his hold on Amy's hand.

"And your daughter," Tate told the woman, "when she has a problem, goes to someone else. She doesn't come to you. In fact, she's spent the day deliberately hiding from you. Think about that. Think about why and what kind of mother you want to be."

With that, he turned back around and led Amy to the house.

"Well said," she whispered to him, squeezing his hand.

"I've been dying to tell that woman off for a decade," he said. "Victoria's a few blocks away. She'll be back soon, so all we have to do is stall her mother a little longer. I promised I'd give it my best shot. She just…has some things to figure out."

"Okay."

"Amy, I don't know what's going to happen here today. There are just…a lot of things up in the air right now, but… we should talk later, okay? Promise me we'll at least get to talk at some point tonight."

Amy felt like crying again, as if she'd been kicked in the stomach.

Talk?

That kind of *talk* was never a good thing, in her meager experience with men.

"Wait," she said, as they stood in the hallway, alone for the moment. "Tate? Did she tell you—"

"She told me everything. She's with James right now, telling him, and after that…I don't know what's going to happen."

"You offered to marry her anyway, didn't you?" Amy asked him.

She could tell by the look on his face that he had, just

as Victoria had said he would. He'd come to Amy's rescue just a moment ago, standing firmly by her side and defending her to Victoria's mother, and it had felt so good. It had felt amazing to have someone stand beside her that way, looking out for her. To have a man treating her that way.

In her limited experience, men did not do that.

Men got scared or bored and walked away.

Now he was going to stand by Victoria through this whole mess, too? Just as he'd done a moment ago for Amy? And Amy couldn't find the words to tell him that was wrong, couldn't even help but admire him in some ways for it.

This was what a woman needed a man to do. She needed him to stand beside her, take her hand, tell her everything was going to be okay and do whatever it took to make that happen.

What woman didn't want a man exactly like that?

What woman ever found one like that?

Not Amy. She'd never expected to.

And she couldn't even tell Tate no, that he could not marry Victoria, because nothing had really happened between Amy and Tate. It had been one kiss. That was it. One crazy kiss that had practically left her melting into a puddle on the floor; it had been so hot, so sexy, so necessary to her entire being.

But it wasn't anything but a kiss and some crazy, fast, hot attraction. That was it.

Victoria was in trouble, and she needed him. Victoria, whom he'd known forever, cared about forever, even thought he'd loved.

What was one crazy kiss and some unexplained attraction when compared to that and a baby on the way?

"I just don't know what's going to happen now," he said again.

Looking like a man full of regrets, he squeezed her hand, then led her down the hall and into the kitchen, turning her over to Eleanor and saying, "Victoria's mother's after her."

"I'll protect her from that old witch," Eleanor promised, putting a kind, supportive arm around Amy.

"Good. Thank you." He leaned over and kissed Eleanor on the cheek.

"Tate, darling? What in the world is going on?"

"I don't know yet," he said sadly, looking from her to Amy, opening his mouth to say something else and then changing his mind once more. "I really just don't know."

He walked down the hallway, then stopped, turned and came back to Amy. When he reached her side, he took her by the arms and gave her a quick, soft kiss, full of restraint and regrets and longings. It was the saddest kiss she'd ever received. It felt as if he'd torn her heart in two, with nothing but the softest brush of his lips against hers.

"Don't give up on me yet," he whispered.

That time he walked away and kept going.

"Amy?" Eleanor said, looking concerned. Amy burst into tears and fell into that sweet older woman's arms.

Chapter Eleven

An army of wedding workers descended upon the house, as Eleanor watched, surprised, puzzled and with a million questions. There were tons of florists, caterers, servers, bartenders, the photographers, the videographer, the wedding planner, the pianist and the soloist.

Finally the minister arrived, entertained in the music room by a very nervous Mrs. Ryan, who was determined that everyone act as if nothing was wrong, like the wedding would go on as planned. Eleanor didn't have the nerve to argue with her. Not at the moment, when it seemed no one really knew what was about to happen anyway.

Eleanor had heard that much from Tate himself, before Amy had burst into tears and then refused to explain anything more. And if Tate didn't even know what was going to happen, who possibly could? It was all very confusing.

Finally Eleanor left Amy alone in the kitchen, confident that she was at least safe from attack from Victoria's mother, who was petrified most of all that the minister might figure out what was really going on, whatever that was. So Victoria's mother wasn't leaving the minister's side, which meant Amy was definitely safe from her at least.

Eleanor walked into the dining room, where Kathleen and Gladdy were waiting to find out what she knew, which was mostly nothing. She was hoping they knew more than she did.

"I'm at a complete loss," Eleanor said.

Once again she'd failed miserably at meddling. Although she thought she'd done a good job of comforting Amy, even if she hadn't been able to get the poor girl to talk about what was going on.

"What's going to happen…with Amy and Victoria's mother?" Gladdy asked. "Or with the wedding? Or the wedding rehearsal?"

"I don't know!" Eleanor said, frustrated beyond belief as she watched this disaster of a wedding come closer and closer every minute. "What do you two think happened?"

"I don't know, but something obviously did," Kathleen said. "Something big. Something very strange."

"And our Amy most definitely had something to do with it," Gladdy concluded. "Although honestly, Victoria's mother doesn't like anyone, so it's not like her being mean to Amy has something to do with Amy and Tate."

"You're right, of course," Eleanor had to concede. "We have to discount the entire bit about Victoria's mother being mad. She's always mad. But the way Amy was crying…that was definitely something. What do you think that was?"

"I don't know, but I keep coming back to Victoria and her grand swoon in the kitchen. I'll never believe that a bride-to-be would fake a faint as a ploy to get herself alone with the woman she thinks is trying to steal her fiancé,"

Kathleen said, looking completely lost. "At least, I've never done that, and why would she? There are much easier ways to get Amy alone. All Victoria had to do was wait until the kitchen was empty of everyone but Amy and then walk in and talk to her. So I don't think the faint was a ploy."

"And I don't think anyone can fake being that pale," Gladdy added. "You were something of the actress in your day, Kathleen, but I don't think even you could have pulled that off."

"So, nerves, lack of sleep, lack of food?" Eleanor considered all those possibilities. But the real disaster was the final one. "Or it could be that pregnancy test Tate said he saw. The one he was so worried was Amy's, that she swore wasn't hers."

"Oh, dear," Gladdy said. "I thought you said Tate and Victoria weren't particularly…attracted to each other? That she probably came to bed clutching her spreadsheets every night?"

"She probably does, but I guess she put them down at some point. I mean, everyone, no matter how enamored of his or her work, would have to put down the spreadsheets every once in a while." Eleanor sighed. "This is terrible. If this is true, and now Tate does want Amy, but Victoria's having his baby… This is awful! I told you both I was bad at this meddling stuff. Very bad! And now look where we are. We've created a disaster!"

"Now, now, we don't know what's happened yet." Gladdy tried to comfort her.

"But we know it's bad! Poor Tate looks so worried, so stressed, and then there's Amy. She was weeping in my arms! I'll never forgive myself if we ruined everything for all of them!"

"Nothing is ruined yet. We just have to stay calm," Kathleen said. "Things are happening right now. We just don't know what."

"So what do we do?" Eleanor cried.

"Wait."

"I'm not good at waiting!"

"Neither am I," Gladdy said.

"Wait. Someone's coming. I think… Oh, dear. I think those are the bridesmaids! Is it time for them to be here, already?" Eleanor asked, looking at her watch.

"They're coming early to get ready with Victoria at the guesthouse," Gladdy said. "I heard Mrs. Ryan yelling at someone about it."

"So no one's called this wedding off yet, I suppose."

"Not yet," Kathleen said.

Eleanor sighed. "Tell me the truth. Best guess. Will we have a wedding tomorrow or not?"

"I'd say the odds are fifty-fifty at best," Kathleen said.

And the three of them kept watch, as member after member of the wedding party and guests at the rehearsal dinner continued to arrive.

Tate eventually had to go upstairs and get dressed for the rehearsal dinner. There was still no Victoria, and in her absence, her mother had decreed that everything would go on as planned.

No way Tate was going to stand in the way of an angry, suspicious, determined Mrs. Ryan and single-handedly tell her what was going on. She was Victoria's mother. It was up to Victoria to tell her what Victoria decided she wanted her mother to know, when Victoria wanted her to know it.

So Tate went to his room alone to get dressed, telling

his groomsmen that he needed the quiet and the privacy to clear his head.

All they wanted to talk about was him and Amy, anyway. Did Victoria know? And had Victoria actually fainted she was so mad? And why was Mrs. Ryan wound up so tight that she was about to explode?

In the end, he never saw Victoria return, although he'd been told she was there, getting dressed, and that it was time to take his place downstairs in the grand foyer, where the rehearsal, and tomorrow perhaps the ceremony, would take place.

So he took his place, finding about thirty people on hand to watch and to stay for the rehearsal dinner. The atmosphere was tense, everyone staring and whispering, waiting.

Tate shook hands with the minister, who took him aside and asked, "What in the world is going on here, son?"

"I have no idea, Reverend."

The reverend looked skeptical at that response but didn't come right out and call Tate a liar.

Eleanor looked frightened, as she sat in the front row with her two friends, waiting. He gave her what he hoped was a reassuring smile, which seemed to leave her puzzled all the more.

He'd hoped there would be time for him and Victoria to talk before this, but apparently he was out of luck there. All he knew to do was play along until he knew what Victoria wanted to do. What did it really matter if they had the rehearsal or not? So he stood there with the minister, trying to smile and play the part of the happy groom, waiting for his bride.

Victoria arrived in a rush, practically running on her high heels, her mother clutching her arm like she was afraid if she let go, Victoria would bolt. Poor Victoria was dressed in a pale yellow dress that made her look even paler than she had in the kitchen. Her bridesmaids clustered around her like they were trying to protect her as best they could from her own mother.

Good luck with that, Tate thought.

Reverend Walker took over from there, noting they were running late and that he could already smell the lovely dinner that had been prepared for them. They should move this along quickly and get to dinner, he said, calling for everyone in the bridal party to take their places.

Victoria, from the back of the room, gave Tate a pleading look and—not knowing what that look meant—he took his place in front of the minister.

Tate let a bunch of talk about music and pacing and how to walk—as if people needed instructions in how to walk—go right over his head, and finally, Victoria made her way down the aisle and to his side.

He took her trembling hand in his, and she whispered, "I am so sorry. I got back here and everyone was here, and I couldn't get a moment alone with you. The only way I could get near you was by walking down the aisle."

"I know. It's okay. Really."

"I don't know what to do," she whispered back, looking more vulnerable than he'd ever seen her.

The reverend cleared his throat, looking down at them to shush them without actually shushing them.

"Sorry. Please go on," Tate said, squeezing Victoria's hand, and after paying attention to another few lines of instruction from the reverend, he whispered back to Victoria. "We don't have to do anything right now, do we? I mean, it's just a rehearsal. And it's not like we want to tell your mother anything with this audience watching and listening in—"

"Ahem," the Reverend said, much louder than before.

"May I remind you that the two of you have the rest of your lives to talk. But for now, we're going to rehearse. All right?"

"Yes, sir," Victoria said obediently. "Reverend, I mean. Yes, Reverend."

"My dear, you are awfully pale. Do you need to sit down?"

She shook her head no, then ruined it by swaying a bit on her feet.

"Oh, dear," the Reverend said. "I didn't realize you were ill. Let's get the bride a chair, someone, please?"

"She doesn't need a chair," Mrs. Ryan said through clenched teeth, as one of the groomsmen went to take one from the row Mrs. Ryan was sitting in and put it into place where Victoria was standing. "She's fine. Just get on with it."

The reverend, obviously not used to being spoken to in that way, gave Mrs. Ryan a hard look that actually quieted her down, a feat Tate had never seen anyone accomplish, not in all the years he'd known Victoria and her family. Maybe the reverend could stay and help them explain things to Mrs. Ryan. Or at least shoot her that look when things got ugly and she got loud.

Victoria got her chair, which was placed beside her. She declined to use it at the moment, but thanked the reverend anyway, saying she would sit if she truly needed to.

They got to the vows. Tate stumbled through his, earning a frightful glare from Mrs. Ryan and a puzzled look from Eleanor.

Victoria whispered, "Thank you."

Reverend Walker turned to Victoria and asked, "Do you, Victoria Elizabeth Ryan, take this man—"

"No, she doesn't!" a man yelled from the back of the room.

Victoria sank down into the chair beside her, squeezed her eyes shut and couldn't even bring herself to look.

Meanwhile, everyone else in the room did, turning around almost as one giant wave. Mrs. Ryan, especially, put a particularly frightening look on her face as she whirled around.

If looks could kill, Tate thought.

And in the back of the room stood James Fallon, the bad boy rock-and-roller, in the flesh, looking half-crazed but determined to have his say.

It was sheer pandemonium for a few moments, and it looked as if Mrs. Ryan might climb over rows and rows of chairs to get to James and shut him up, if need be.

But then he started calling Victoria's name, as if he couldn't survive another moment without her, and it was like the parting of the Red Sea in that room. The crowd moved to open up a path between him and Victoria, who couldn't seem to manage to even stand up.

And then he was at her side, down on one knee.

The crowd gasped as one, then fell silent.

All except Victoria's mother.

"What is he doing?" she yelled, from the other side of the room, where she'd been blocked in by Tate and his best man, who weren't letting her get any closer. "We're having a wedding rehearsal here! She's marrying him—" she poked Tate in the shoulder "—tomorrow!"

"Shh," Tate told her.

"Don't you shush me! Do something! That's your fiancée he's trying to…trying to… What is he doing?"

"Let's give him a chance to do it, and then we'll know," Tate reasoned.

Victoria had tears streaming down her cheeks. James had her hand in his and seemed to have eyes only for her.

"I know this is a little bit crazy," he told her. "And I know it's not what any of us planned, but you can't marry him tomorrow, Victoria."

"She most certainly can!" Mrs. Ryan yelled, and then Tate asked two of the groomsmen to get her out of the room. Former football players, both of them, they lifted her up and carried her, shrieking all the way.

"I am so sorry," Victoria told James.

He shook his head. "It's okay. Everything's going to be fine, Victoria. I know this is sudden, but…I think you should marry me instead."

Victoria smiled weakly through her tears, looking very fragile and sweet.

"I'll be a good husband, I promise, and a good father," James said. "I know what you're thinking. That I'm just some crazy musician, and that you don't think I can take care of you and a kid."

Gasps rose from the crowd at the word *kid*, but James kept right on talking.

"I'll admit that the whole baby thing does freak me out. But I've thought about it, and as long as the kid can have a guitar, I can do it. I'll have him playing by the time he's three. We'll bond over our music. We'll understand each other perfectly and have all kinds of fun together. What do you say?"

Victoria turned to look at Tate, as if she needed his permission or maybe just that she wanted it. He smiled, nodded his head toward James, who looked petrified and a little crazy, but sincere.

Then Victoria looked back at her bad-boy musician and slowly began to nod—yes, she would marry him—as she smiled tentatively through her tears.

Then it seemed as if no one in the room knew whether to break out into applause for the happy couple or wait for a fight to break out between James and Tate. Tate went to Victoria's side, gave her a kiss on the cheek and then shook James's hand, telling James in a loud voice that he was very happy for the couple.

Then he whispered to just the two of them, "How about I get everybody out of here and into dinner, and the two of you can have some privacy. And just so you know, we do have a wedding planned for tomorrow. I have no problem with the two of you going ahead with the ceremony here."

Victoria thanked him profusely. James thanked him, too.

Tate felt for a moment as if his entire life flashed before his eyes—the careful, predictable one he'd believed he'd have with Victoria gone in the blink of an eye. Before him, a vast, unknown array of possibilities with Amy and Max. It was as though he'd stepped off the edge of a cliff to find nothing but air beneath his feet—him, a man who loved nothing more than a well-thought-out plan. But he couldn't say he was sorry either.

He was a completely free man, free for the first time in a long time, a sense of wonder and awe and sheer joy rushing through him.

He'd get rid of the people here, herd them out of the hallway and into the room where the caterers should be set up to serve the rehearsal dinner.

Then he was going to find Amy.

Tate started steering everyone out of the entryway and into dinner, leaving Victoria and James to figure out what they intended to do.

He could see Mrs. Ryan through one of the windows, giving the groomsmen holy hell and trying to break free so she could get inside and find out what was going on, but the groomsmen held on tight.

Poor James, he thought.

Mrs. Ryan would get free eventually, and then he was going to have quite some official introduction to his mother-in-law-to-be.

Amy thought her heart was going to thump right through the wall of her chest as she stood in the back of the room, half hiding behind a big palm plant, watching and waiting to see what happened.

She cried softly as she saw Tate appear at the minister's side to start the rehearsal. Was he really going to go through with this?

Stop, she wanted to yell. *I object! He doesn't really love her. I don't think he does, at least. And she doesn't love him, and the baby she's carrying isn't even his!*

It was as if her body had a mind of its own, her feet inching her forward from her hiding spot, to get out in the open, from which she could voice her objection. Her throat tightened. She wasn't sure if she could even speak.

Victoria made it down the aisle, looking as though she might pass out again at any moment. Amy thought for a while that would solve the whole problem. They couldn't do this if the bride couldn't stay conscious and on her feet.

But then it seemed Victoria was indeed determined to go through with this, and that Tate wasn't going to stop her. Although they were talking about something.

Amy inched forward again, opening her mouth, trying to get some sound out. It was the worst feeling in the world, wanting to say something and not being able to make so much as a squeak of sound. She had nightmares like this, where she had to save herself, save her life sometimes it seemed, and still, she couldn't make a sound.

This was like a nightmare!

If she couldn't stand up and say something today, at

the rehearsal, she'd never manage to do it tomorrow, at the actual ceremony, if things ever went that far. And just when she'd given up, just when she'd decided she was about to lose something very important, something precious and real, something she'd probably likely spend the rest of her life regretting, the guitarist showed up!

Hallelujah!

What joy! What relief! She sagged back against the wall behind the big fake plant, cheering James on as he made his touching, very public declaration.

Victoria cried. Tate looked relieved, Amy thought, her heart starting to pound like mad again. He was relieved, wasn't he? Victoria's mother was hauled out of the room kicking and screaming, and then… Yes! Victoria said yes! She was going to marry James instead tomorrow!

Amy cried, too, happy tears. Joyous tears. Wonderfully relieved tears.

And then Tate started herding the whole crowd out of the foyer and into the solarium, where the rehearsal dinner was being served.

Amy suddenly got scared, slipping out one of the side doors to hide in the kitchen, with no idea of what to do next.

It wasn't as if anything had really happened between her and Tate, she told herself as she waited, trying to be reasonable and smart and not get her hopes up.

They'd had a few conversations, most of them about mistaken beliefs he had about her, and then with her trying to help him buy a clue about what was really going on with his fiancée. They'd laughed a bit. He'd been kind to Max, and they'd shared one blazingly sexy kiss.

That was it.

These things did not a relationship make, Amy told herself very firmly.

Heightened emotions or not, all impending-wedding-craziness aside, nothing had really happened.

She was still telling herself that forty minutes later when the house had quieted down, the guests safely seated at the rehearsal dinner, and Tate zoomed into the kitchen, looking frantically for her and calling her name.

She'd been contemplating hiding in the pantry, to think, to be alone and quiet, to get hold of herself and her silly emotions, when he got there, his eyes searching the darkened room, until they finally landed on the shadows in the far corner by the pantry door, where she was. He skidded to a stop, relief and then what certainly looked like complete, absolute, overwhelming joy spreading across his handsome face.

"I was afraid you might have disappeared before I could get out of that dinner," he said quietly, staring at her the entire time, grinning like crazy.

Amy shook her head. It was still hard to talk. "I wouldn't leave. Not without talking to you."

He nodded, looking very pleased with himself.

She couldn't breathe again, a riot of emotions flooding her body, all these crazy thoughts. He took a step toward her, and she put up a hand to hold him off.

"The thing is," she began, "we don't really know each other."

He nodded, accepting, then said, "We haven't known each other for long. I'll give you that."

"And we don't really know each other," she said again, because that seemed like an important point to make, a crucial one, for any careful, cautious woman who'd been burned before in love and had come out of it with a son to raise on her own because of it.

"But we could take some time to get to know each

other," Tate said, still just standing there grinning hugely at her.

"We could," she admitted, her hand still up, as if that could have stopped him if he'd wanted to rush to her and grab her and kiss her silly. "But I just want to be clear that nothing's really happened here. Between us, I mean. And I can't just rush into anything. I don't do that. Not with Max. I have to think about him, to protect him."

"Of course," Tate agreed. "We have to think about Max."

"Because he gets really lonely sometimes, and he needs a father, and that's a commitment that's absolutely huge and not to be taken lightly. And I won't have him getting his hopes up, getting attached to every man who shows up wanting to…wanting to… I don't even know what you want from me, and I doubt you do, either, because we don't really know each other."

"Well, right now I want to tell you something, and then I want to kiss you," Tate said, looking absolutely sure about that.

Amy pressed her back against the wall, part of her wishing she had hidden in the pantry, so she could have thought this through in private and maybe come into this conversation, which was likely a very important one, with at least a few clear thoughts in her head. But she hadn't hidden in time, and now Tate was here, and he wanted to kiss her.

Well, it wasn't as if a woman would consider herself to be crazy or anything over one kiss. Not in this day and age.

She took a breath, bracing herself, as if she could defend herself properly against how it felt to kiss him. But she tried, because she was careful, and she did have to think about Max, and…well…nothing had really happened.

Tate took a step closer, then another, and then he was

right there, his body pressed up against hers, her back to the wall. She raised her arms to hold him off but ended up clutching at his shoulders instead. He smelled so good that she wanted to eat him up, and he laid the side of his face against hers, his mouth brushing softly against her ear.

"The thing I wanted to tell you," he whispered, his warm breath skimming over her ear, down the side of her neck, sending shivers through her whole body, "is that I'm not getting married tomorrow."

"Oh," she said, because that was all the sound she could get out.

"And that I'm not engaged anymore. I am now, officially, a completely free man."

Amy nodded ever so slightly, his face still right there against hers. "Well…that's good."

"It's very good. It would have been a huge mistake to get married to someone else, feeling the way I do about you."

He rubbed his jaw against her cheek as he said it, his mouth skimming along her neck, there but not quite there. She felt weak in the knees, felt blood rushing from her head and pooling in her body. Her breasts got heavy and achy, pressing against his chest, and then it was like her whole body throbbed in time with his.

"That's what I wanted to tell you," he whispered, then bit gently into the lobe of her ear.

She gasped, the weight of her body sagging against his, him holding her up easily with his body and his arms. What did a woman say to something like that?

But she didn't have to say a thing.

Because then he kissed her.

Chapter Twelve

Tate kept thinking of sugar.

That she tasted sweet, like sugar, and he wanted to know if that was his imagination working overtime right now or if that was just the way she tasted and how she smelled. If it was just her. *Sweet.* Unless he was mentally unbalanced from all the crazy wedding wackiness, she tasted sweet, too.

He pressed her up against the kitchen wall, wanting to devour her right then and there, feeling amazingly free, giddy with happiness and believing that in this moment absolutely anything was possible.

"I just didn't know," he said, between kisses all over her face and her delicious neck. "I didn't know I could feel this good. I kept waiting for it to happen over the years, and it just never did, and then I thought maybe for some people, it never does. That maybe there was something wrong with me."

He lifted his head, gazed down at her for a long moment, just to make sure this was real, at last.

"What?" she asked, smiling and breathless.

"I told myself maybe I just wanted too much or expected too much or that smart people eventually stopped looking for something like this and grew up and settled for something safe and sensible."

"So you're saying you've lost all your normal, sensible thought processes, and you want me?"

He laughed, because he was still kissing her, and he still had her in his arms, and he didn't have to feel guilty about that in the least. "I'm saying you make me crazy, in a very good way, and I like it. I like it a lot."

"Okay," she said, breathing in little gasps, still kissing him, despite her protests. "For now, you like it. But that doesn't mean—"

"Yeah, I know. Could we possibly talk about this later?" he asked, his hands sliding down her back to take her hips in the palms of his hands and pull her up against him.

She gasped but didn't pull away.

"Not a lot later," he promised. "Just a little later."

She frowned, hesitated. "I…I just have to make it clear that…I am not going to have sex with you in this kitchen. Or the pantry. Or in the cook's quarters."

"Okay. Deal."

"Or anywhere else right now."

"I understand," he said, disappointed for sure but not really surprised. As she'd pointed out, she had a kid. She had to be careful. And they really didn't know each other. "I was just hoping we could get to know each other a little better. Right now."

He sank his teeth into her neck, taking a little, bitty bite of her that had her gasping. In a good way. She sighed, in what sounded like surrender, and clutched at his shoulders with her hands, kissing him back in a way that had his body feeling like molten lava.

"It's just that…this is the thing that doesn't last. You know? This crazy feeling?"

"Maybe," he agreed. "But maybe not. I mean, we could get really lucky. It might not fade at all. There are people in this world who are happy together, you know?"

"No, I don't. I don't know anybody who's really happy together. Not in the long run."

"Amy, honestly, right now I'd settle for five good minutes. Five good getting-to-know-you-but-no-I-will-not-have-sex-with-you minutes. What do you say?"

And then she laughed, nuzzled her nose against his chest, pressed her whole body up against his and then tilted her face up to his. Things were definitely heating up in the kitchen.

A minute later she pulled him into the pantry and shut the door.

Feverish kisses followed. Struggles to breathe. Hearts racing. He lifted her off her feet and pressed her up against the closed door. She wrapped her legs around his waist and her arms around his shoulders.

He was thinking he might get much more than five good minutes when he heard someone in the kitchen. Swearing softly, he lifted his head and tried to concentrate on something other than what was going on in the pantry.

"What?" she asked softly, sexily.

"Someone's out there."

She groaned.

"Shh," he said, kissing her once more to keep her quiet. "We've already been caught in here once. It would be unchivalrous of me to get us caught in here again."

"As long as it's not Victoria's mother."

Tate laughed softly. "Come to think of it, I've escaped

from Victoria's mother for the rest of my life. Or at least, for the next few hours. Life is so good right now that I can hardly stand it. That's reason to celebrate, don't you think? And I want to celebrate with you."

She laughed, too.

He kissed her once more.

And then the pantry door opened.

"That's odd," Eleanor said, looking at the empty kitchen. "I know I saw Tate go in here, and I know Amy was in here at the time."

"Well, there are other ways out of this room," Kathleen said.

"And other places to go. Amy's staying in a room right down the hall, right?" Gladdy offered.

"Well, yes," Eleanor said. "Do you really think…?"

Kathleen smiled. "She likes him. He likes her, and now he's free to do as he wishes."

"Could it really be that easy?" Eleanor certainly hoped so.

"Of course," Gladdy said. "The wedding's off, after all. That was your main concern. And Victoria's completely out of the picture, now that she's marrying that young man who plays the guitar and is having his baby. I'd say the weekend has been a complete success."

"I told you we could do this," Kathleen added.

"Well, I will be forever grateful to you both. But I think Victoria sleeping with the guitarist and ending up pregnant was the turning point."

"I still think we had a hand in it, and I think Tate is with our sweet Amy right now. In fact, I thought I just heard something. Someone laughing. Maybe more than one person."

They looked all around the room. The cook's quarters

were right down the hall—not far at all—but didn't seem close enough for them to have heard what might be going on in there. Eleanor was about to give up on hearing anything, thought Kathleen had to be dreaming, when one of the caterers came into the kitchen, saying they'd had a guest ask for balsamic vinegar as a dressing for her salad, something the caterers hadn't brought with them.

"Feel free to look in the pantry. It's right through there," Eleanor offered, pointing out the door.

They heard an odd thump as the door opened.

Tate came falling out, Amy on top of him. They landed together in a heap on the floor, clothed for the most part, a few buttons unbuttoned, a sweet, embarrassed glow to Amy's face, Tate looking happier than Eleanor had seen him in years.

"Uh, I am so sorry," the poor caterer said, then stared at Tate, whispering urgently, "Aren't you the groom?"

"Not anymore," Gladdy said, answering for him.

"Told you so," Kathleen said. "Things worked out just fine."

It was hours later before the puzzled rehearsal dinner guests departed and the house quieted for the night.

Amy had been the recipient of all sorts of curious looks, more than one rudely intrusive question, a warm, genuine thank-you from James Fallon for helping Victoria get through the weekend, a big hug from Victoria and one really scary glare from Victoria's mother. She'd apparently decided the only way to handle this was to brazen it out and try to save face, as if this was a glorious, impulsive match of love that would not be denied. Nothing else to do when the pregnant bride had been the recipient of a proposal from another man in front of her intended groom at their wedding rehearsal.

Eleanor, Kathleen and Gladdy looked like the happiest women on earth, Max was bunking with his new friend Drew in a fort they'd made of blankets in Drew's room upstairs and Amy was thinking she'd lost her mind, all in the space of the past four days. Years of careful, responsible living and trying to be a good mother to Max had all exploded in a cloud of powdered sugar.

Her life hadn't been the same since then.

Tate, standing by her side in the kitchen, said, "You're worrying again. I can tell."

"Tate, this is crazy," she said.

"I know. You've said that. I agree. I just don't care," he said, coming to stand in front of her and wrap his arms loosely around her waist. "Sometimes things just happen, you know? Sometimes crazy things just happen."

Amy was finding it was hard to have a rational conversation with him. He kept distracting her, touching her, kissing her, making her want him, right then, in a way that no careful, cautious woman would after an acquaintance of only four days.

She let him stay there. She was wrapped loosely in his arms but put her own in between them to keep him from getting too close while she explained.

"See, that's the thing, I don't think it just happened. I think people may have been plotting against you and Victoria," Amy admitted. "You know Kathleen and Gladdy think they're matchmakers, ever since they got Kathleen's granddaughter together with Leo's nephew last year. I… well, I even helped them a little."

"You helped?" Tate laughed, seeming not the least bit upset about it.

"Yes. A little." Never thinking one day she'd be on the other end—the recipient of all that plotting.

"You're telling me you think Eleanor called those sweet

little old ladies in to break up my wedding to Victoria? In a single long weekend?"

"Maybe. They've been hovering around me the whole time and acting a little funny. Don't you think?"

"I don't know. I guess…maybe. I don't really care," he said, leaning down to take a little nibble on her ear and send shivers down her spine. "I'm just glad things worked out the way they did. I could have made a very big mistake, and so could Victoria. I'm very glad we didn't. I'm very glad to be exactly where I am right now with you. And I think you should be my date to the wedding tomorrow."

"James and Victoria are really going through with it? Getting married tomorrow? Just like that?"

Tate nodded, then nuzzled the tip of his nose to the side of her face, his breath warm against her ear. "And you thought you and I were moving too fast?"

"We are. I mean, I'm afraid we will."

"We still could," he said, like a promise, as his head dipped to that space where her neck melded into her shoulder.

He wasn't even kissing her, wasn't doing anything except breathing on her, and it was as if the surface of her skin, everywhere he touched, perked up and took notice, as if her whole body was begging for his touch.

"But we don't have to move too fast," he said, still doing that nuzzling thing to her and knowing exactly what it was doing to her, wicked man. "I think you'll find I'm a very reasonable man—"

"Once I get to know you?"

"Yes." He lifted his head, flashed her a beautiful grin. "So let's get started with this careful, cautious courtship. Amy, would you care to be my date to a wedding here tomorrow?"

"That's just crazy," Amy said. "Until a few hours ago, Victoria was supposed to be marrying you."

"She's having a baby, Amy, and she doesn't want to do that alone. James doesn't want her to do that alone. Maybe it is a little crazy, but maybe it's just the two of them taking a leap of faith. Seeing a life they want, a chance, and grabbing it. I think she's always had a thing for him, from the time they dated in high school. So it's not like they just met a couple of days ago."

"Like us."

"Yes, like us."

"Well, that's generous of you, to tell them they were welcome to go ahead with what was supposed to be your wedding."

"I'm a really nice guy," he said, starting to slowly unbutton her chef's coat, one button at a time. "Are you wearing one of those little tops on under this, like you had on that first night? Because I liked that. I liked it a lot. I liked you in it."

"Yes, I am."

He gave her a wicked grin.

"Tate, we're in the kitchen," she protested. "And every time we do anything in this kitchen, we get caught. Have you noticed that?"

He got the coat unbuttoned, pulled the ends open wide and just stared down at her and the clingy, white spaghetti-strap top she wore, watching every breath she took as if he was absolutely fascinated by every inch of skin he'd uncovered.

"We could go somewhere besides the kitchen," he suggested.

"Oh, sure. The pantry, maybe?"

"I don't think the pantry has a lock on the door. I mean, who locks up a pantry? Although, I think when we have our own house and our own pantry, we should definitely put a lock on the pantry door. You know, just in case. You never know what we might want to do in the pantry."

She would have laughed, but he was skimming a fingertip along her collarbone. Her breath was shaky, breasts feeling so full and aching to be touched.

This man made her crazy.

And it had been so long....

"You know," he said, "now that I think about it, I offered James and Victoria the wedding tomorrow, but I never said anything about the honeymoon."

He was tracing the neckline of her top then, just following it with two fingers, nothing more, skimming along the surface of her skin, up and down over the curves of her breasts, rising and falling with each agitated breath she took. She couldn't even complain. He was moving very, very slowly after all.

"I don't suppose you'd like to fly off to Greece with me tomorrow for two weeks?"

Amy laughed, but the sound was more like a choke. "Right. Because, I could just take off for a couple of weeks at a time at the drop of a hat, with a man I just met, taking what was supposed to be his honeymoon trip to Greece with him."

"I know," he said as his hand skimmed up and down one of her arms and then the other, still going so slowly. "But it's Greece. Have you ever been to Greece?"

"No," she admitted, thinking if he didn't kiss her soon, she'd just die from wanting it, from wanting him.

"It's beautiful." He tugged up on the bottom of her top, exposing the soft skin of her belly, drawing little circles on it with his fingertips. "Great old buildings, great food, great beaches."

"Tate, I have a child, remember?" She had to remember that, to be smart about this.

"Want to take him?"

Amy blinked up at him. He didn't seem to be kidding, and he was still skimming his hands along the skin of her belly, his touch setting off a path of heat and awareness everywhere he touched.

"I bet Max would love it," he said.

She went weak in the knees. His thumb was dipping into her belly button, making little circles there. "I…I… but—"

"Yes, Amy?" he asked, sounding infinitely patient with the fact that he'd rendered her incoherent and unable to speak.

"I…I'm afraid Max doesn't have a passport," she said, as if that was the real problem here.

"Darn, I guess Max can't go."

"No." She shook her head, managed just barely not to whimper as his hands settled on the side of her hips. "Max can't go."

"What about you?"

"I don't have a passport, either."

"Well, that does it. We can't go to Greece," he said, not looking that upset about it as he rubbed his palms against the side of her hips, making more little circles there.

He'd barely touched her. Barely. And she felt as if her whole body was on fire. It was all she could do not to beg him to just get on with it, to take her, right here and right now, to not care anymore what she did or did not know about him or how long she'd known him or that until a few hours ago, he'd been ready to marry someone else.

She simply did not care.

"Tate," she whispered raggedly.

"Hmm? I'm not going too fast for you, am I? I'm trying really hard to do what you asked, to take this slow."

"Oh, yes, you are. I can tell. You're trying to make me beg. That's what you're trying to do."

A huge grin flashed across his face. He really was the most adorable man. "Does that mean too fast? Or not fast enough? Just tell me. I'm a man who aims to please."

With that, his hands slid around to cup her bottom and ease her against him. He was every bit as aroused as she was. Pressed up against him this way, there was no mistaking that. And that damned sense of calm, the excruciating slowness with which he'd been moving this whole time, was all a facade.

"Whatever you want, Amy," he said. "I mean that. It's your call. Just don't cook anything sweet and don't feed me anything sweet, and I think I'll be okay."

She laughed. "I'm not supposed to feed you? I like feeding you."

"Yes, but I've gotten to the point where I absolutely crave sugar all the time, and you are the sweetest-tasting thing in this whole kitchen. Anything else that tastes sweet just makes me want you, and you can't make me want you any more than I already do. That would just be cruel."

Amy stood there, pressed up against him, savoring the feel of a man's big, hard body against hers for the first time in what felt like ages. She didn't want to want him this way, and she certainly didn't want to need him, was terrified of starting to count on him, to trust him.

But she was a woman, and a woman got lonely at times. She'd fought off that feeling for so long, denied it, hidden it away and sometimes just been tormented by it.

He stood there, waiting patiently and yet showing her how much he wanted her, how much he needed. She wasn't used to such patience from a man, such understanding, such kindness. She'd never had a really good man, had even doubted sometimes if such a thing existed.

If he kissed her—really kissed her—just one more time now, she'd be lost, and he had to know that, too. And yet, he didn't do it. Which made her want him even more.

"I'm scared," she told him finally.

"Oh, honey, I know." He pulled away, just enough to be able to see her face, and smiled understandingly. "I know. Really, I do. I'm sorry. I'll go now, but…come to the wedding with me tomorrow, okay? I think I need to be there, to show everyone I'm fine with it, and I'd like for you to be beside me. We can consider it our first date."

"To what was supposed to be your own wedding to Victoria?"

"Hey, never doubt that I know how to show a woman a good time," he boasted.

"Oh, yes. You do."

"You'll come with me? I know Victoria would love to have you there. She's going to need all the friendly faces she can get."

"Okay, I'll come with you. Now go on. Get out of here."

He kissed her once, quickly, deeply, then said, "Dream of me. I'll be dreaming of you."

Chapter Thirteen

Eleanor, Kathleen and Gladdy might have been bugging the kitchen, Amy suspected, when they showed up the next morning like fairy godmothers to kidnap her to help her get ready for the wedding. Otherwise, how could they have known she was going as Tate's date?

They took her to the fanciest salon she'd ever been in, had her hair snipped a bit and shaped and given some sort of shine treatment, her makeup professionally done. Then they headed for a department store, where she was given no choice but to model a full half-dozen dresses for the three of them, with all of them discussing and debating the merits of each one before settling on one that felt like a puddle of silk on her body.

She'd never looked anything like this. The dress was the palest of peach colors, not too revealing, but faithfully hugging every curve on her body, curves she was definitely not used to showing off. It had a wide scoop neckline, a belted waist, and when she walked, a slit on the side showed off more of her thighs than she was truly comfortable with. She was given strappy sandals to wear and the promise of a necklace of Eleanor's that would look perfect with the dress.

Her fairy godmothers beamed at her, looking very satisfied with themselves and the outcome of the wild wedding weekend.

"Told you we could do it," Kathleen said finally, once they were all happy with Amy's wedding look.

"We are so good. We could rent out our services, don't you think? It could be a whole new career for us. Matchmakers Incorporated. What do you think?" Gladdy asked.

"That's perfect!" Kathleen exclaimed. "I bet there are tons of people at the retirement village who are unhappy with their children's and grandchildren's choices of partners. We'd have a built-in base of clients. And this has been so much fun. Don't you think, Eleanor?"

"Oh, yes. Love with the right person is a wonderful thing."

"Ladies, I am not in love with Tate!" Amy insisted. "And he is not in love with me! We just met four days ago!"

"We know," Eleanor said.

"Of course, we do," Kathleen said. "We're just…hopeful. Eternally hopeful. My Leo would be so happy for you today, dear. And so proud!"

She teared up and then so did Gladdy and Eleanor. Amy might have, too, but they all threatened her if she shed so much as one tear and ruined her makeup. So they settled for a group hug instead.

The afternoon of Victoria's wedding turned out to be warm, sunny and perfect for the indoor ceremony and the reception on the expansive patio in back of the house.

Amy stuck close by Tate's side, smiling the whole time, despite how ridiculous the circumstances were. So what if it was supposed to have been his wedding to Victoria and Victoria was marrying James? The guests were all comically confused, suspicious and infinitely curious about exactly what had happened and how it had all come to be.

Victoria looked radiant; James looked nervous but happy. Mrs. Ryan might have been on tranquilizers, Amy suspected, because there were no outbursts from her all day. Once everyone got over the shock of the change in grooms, the day went surprisingly well. There were tons of good food and an abundance of drinks. James's band played both with him and without him and sounded great.

And Amy danced slowly, happily in Tate's arms, content as could be. It was like being in their own little world. All she had to do was close her eyes and snuggle up against him. She drank a little too much, let Tate lick cake frosting off her finger and caught the bouquet, which Victoria hurled straight at her.

Tate walked her back to her room, gave her a positively steamy kiss good-night, then pushed her inside the door and told her to lock it, so he couldn't get in, even if he wanted to.

She did as she was told, lying in her bed, her whole body buzzing with desire, finally drifting off to sleep and dreaming of sweet days to come with him.

Amy made a light breakfast for the departing guests Sunday morning, then found herself alone in the kitchen at midmorning with Eleanor, who'd just come from the guesthouse, very pleased to report that Victoria's mother was indeed gone. The only other people left in the house were Kathleen, Gladdy, Max and Tate.

"Well, I should finish cleaning the kitchen and then pack up my things and Max's and get us ready to go home."

"Oh, dear, I wish you wouldn't."

Amy grinned, thinking more matchmaking was coming her way. "Max and I can't just move in here, Eleanor."

"No, of course not. I know that. It's just that I've been talking to Kathleen and Gladdy, and I've missed my house. It's been so nice to be back here this weekend and have it filled with people. This is the way the house should be."

Amy gave her a little hug and said, "It is a beautiful house, but you said you'd been terribly lonely here the last few years—"

"Because it was empty. I wouldn't be lonely if it wasn't empty. Kathleen and Gladdy had such a good time, too. I've asked them to stay on for a while, to keep me company while I think about what to do with it. And we were thinking you and Max could stay, too. Just for a few weeks, maybe? Max adores it here. And we'll all need looking after, someone to cook for us. What do you think?"

Amy saw right through that. "I think there's more to this than you're saying right now and that you're still matchmaking."

Eleanor pretended to take offense, and Amy laughed at her.

"All right. But we're not matchmaking. We've made our match."

"So Tate has nothing to do with this?" Amy asked.

"Well, he does have to move out of his apartment. He'd given it up already, planning to move in with Victoria after the wedding. But of course, he can't move in with her now."

"No, not now," Amy agreed.

"And we have all this space here. I told him he could stay in the house. He didn't feel comfortable doing that, but he did agree to take the guesthouse—"

"Ahh, there we go. Now I see what you're up to."

"Nonsense," Eleanor insisted. "I am not up to anything. I'm just…confused about whether I can truly sell my house, and while I think things through, my dear friends are going to stay here with me. Tate is going to be in the guesthouse, just until he finds a new apartment, and I thought, why not have you and Max here, too?"

"I don't need anyone else pushing me toward Tate. I'm sold on him. I think he's fabulous, and we're going to…date," she said. "And take things slow and see what happens."

Eleanor frowned, as if that just wasn't enough. "But if you were here, I could watch Max for you, and you could help Tate move his things into the guesthouse and go on dates, if that's what you really want. We all have so many things to figure out. You, too, of course, now that you're out of school. We could all figure out things together."

Amy was surprised to actually find herself reluctant to leave here. It had been crazy and stressful, but wonderful, too, and Tate was going to be just down the driveway in the guesthouse.

"You want to stay!" Eleanor exclaimed. "I knew it!"

"Maybe just for a few days. I'd be happy to help Tate move and get settled in, and I suppose Max could use a few more days of exploring. He's been telling me all about the different play places he's found on the estate."

"Oh, I'm so happy!" Eleanor said, beaming at her.

"Just for a few days," Amy insisted.

"Of course, dear. Whatever you say."

* * *

"They're incredibly manipulative," Amy told Tate later that night as they were unpacking boxes of his things in the guesthouse.

"But sweet and well-meaning," he reminded her.

"Well, yes. I suppose," she said, handing him clothes to hang in the closet of his temporary lodgings.

"And it's not the worst thing in the world, to be living in the same place, without living together, which I know would be a no-no on your list—"

"Well, yes," Amy said.

"So this is the next best thing. And you only agreed to a few days. It's not like you've made a life-changing decision or anything."

Something about the way he said it made her suspicious of him, too.

"You're in on this with them!" she said.

He denied it vehemently, but his grin told her all she needed to know.

"You are. You're plotting with the three of them to keep me here, with you!"

He laughed. "I don't need to plot with three little old ladies. You already like me. You like me a lot. And I know it. I just happen to think we all have to be somewhere, right? And there's plenty of room, so why not here?"

"Tate—"

"Amy." He kissed her quickly then backed away. "Eleanor's spent most of her life in this house, and she loves it. She's trying to figure out if she can stand to let it go or if there's something she can do to keep it without living here all by herself and being lonely. It's a big decision for her, and she would like for us all to be here with her while she makes her decision. You're not going to deny her that chance, are you?"

"Oh, you are so working with the three of them. I know it!"

"I had to have a place to stay. This place was empty, that's all. I am completely innocent in all this."

"I don't believe that for a second."

Then he kissed her and didn't stop for a long, long time.

She held him off for two more weeks, and how she did it, Amy really didn't know. It would have been so easy to fall into bed with him at any point along the way. She'd been, quite simply, at war with herself.

Be careful.

Give in.

Be careful.

Give in.

But two weeks was all she could stand. He was kind, funny, sexy, great with Max and their three fairy godmothers and delighted with every new day that came along.

Eleanor had the house filled with architects, hotel people, wedding planners, people who planned and hosted corporate retreats, a few restaurant people, even a couple of matchmaking services, trying to figure out what she wanted to do with the property. Kathleen and Gladdy were still in residence. Max never wanted to leave. Tate hadn't done anything that she'd seen about finding a new apartment. He'd mostly been sitting in on the meetings Eleanor was having, because she wanted his help with her project, whatever it turned out to be.

And Amy was… She truly feared it was too late for her already, that she was in love with him, and both terrified and thrilled about it. About giving in and giving herself to him, too. She didn't think there'd be any holding back for her emotionally once she did, but it seemed there was no holding back now, either.

He'd planned to take her to dinner that night, but when he showed up, he had a picnic basket and a blanket with him.

Oh, I am in trouble, Amy thought.

But maybe, too, she was just where she wanted to be.

He took her to a secluded spot on the back of the estate, a garden where the various trees and hedges kept her from seeing the house at all. Which meant, no one in the house could see them. It was nothing but green grass, green trees and bushes, and a breathtaking, clear, starry sky above them.

He spread the big blanket on the grass, put the picnic basket on top of it. He waited for her to sit down, then seated himself beside her.

"Tate Darnley, I think you have done this before," she said.

He arched a brow. "I haven't brought you here before or taken you on a picnic."

"I meant with some other woman," she explained.

"No," he insisted.

"The spot's too perfect, too beautiful and secluded."

"I have never brought another woman here, I swear."

She gave him a look that told him to come clean.

"I dreamed about bringing women here. No, girls. I dreamed about bringing teenage girls here, when I was a teenager myself."

"Okay, that I believe."

"But I never managed to make it happen," he said, as if she should feel sorry for him or something. "Which makes this a dreams-come-true moment for me. I got the girl. I got her here, all alone. It's a beautiful night. We've got the stars. It's not too cold. We have great food. I have everything I need."

"Everything?"

"Well," he said, considering, "I guess you could feed me."

"Feed you?"

He nodded.

She thought about him licking wedding cake frosting off her finger. If there hadn't been dozens of people around at the time, she might have dragged him down to the ground right then and there, no resistance left at all.

It made her think of sugar, of the first time she'd seen him, them both covered in sugar. Made her think of her and him together, once he knew he wasn't going to marry Victoria, him nibbling on the lobe of her ear, stroking the tip of his tongue along the sensitive skin of her neck. She took a breath, took another one and was still trembling and weak with need.

He opened the picnic basket, pulling out a small container of something she didn't understand at first. Then he pulled off the top, and she could see it, smell it.

Powdered sugar.

She laughed joyously. He grinned wickedly.

Then he held one of his fingers to her lips and she licked it, to wet it. He dipped it in the powdered sugar and then stroked it ever so slowly across her lips, and then his mouth was on hers, hot, needy, insistent, impatient, even.

She loved kissing him. It was like plugging into their very own source of energy, of heat, of desire. Together they generated all of that.

Amy eased onto her back on the blanket, and he stretched out beside her, leaning over her, still kissing her.

He put sugar in her mouth and then devoured her, stroked it along her neck, his mouth following his finger and the little white, powdery-sweet path. He held a pinch of sugar between two fingertips and then rubbed his fingertips together, sending little sprinkles of sugar all over her throat, chest, and then his tongue. His mouth was everywhere.

The night was a tiny bit chilly, but his body was hot, his mouth spreading a sizzling trail of sensation across her skin.

She unbuttoned her dress. He unsnapped the front closure of her bra. She felt cool air on her breasts, watched as he sprinkled a bit more powdered sugar on her, as she blushed like crazy, then reached for him to pull him back to her.

He teased and teased and teased, trailing the tip of his nose along skin that was begging for his touch, nuzzling the underside of her breasts, the outside edges, the valley between them, before he finally took one nipple and then the other into his mouth, toying with them with his tongue. It was a touch that zinged in a line straight down her body to the spot between her legs, which was throbbing in an instant, her body wanting him inside of her.

She clutched at his hair, his shoulders, his hips, wriggling and squirming beneath him, trying to get him to give himself to her completely right that instant. She tore at the buttons on his shirt and pulled it off of him, undid the buckle of his jeans and then he rolled off her and got rid of everything else they had on.

Then he eased himself on top of her, eased that warm, wonderful weight of his body down to hers, nestling his chest against hers. That first touch of skin-to-skin contact all over was almost more than she could bear. And then he started kissing her again until she absolutely begged him to take her.

He paused, looking down into her eyes, his body poised,

and whispered, “Amy, I will never hurt you, and I will never leave you, I swear.”

It was the last thing she expected. Her eyes pooled with tears that seeped out of the corners of her eyes and down her cheeks.

“Hey, no, no, no, not that. Don’t do that,” he said urgently, going to pull away from her.

She shook her head, holding him where he was, moving and shifting beneath him and then finding that spot where she wanted him, needed him, and then she raised her body up to meet his. He swore softly, groaned and then slid home.

And it felt perfect, absolutely perfect finally having him there.

It felt like heaven, like something she’d have dreamed that couldn’t possibly come true.

He kissed the tears from the side of her face, kissed her mouth, and she tasted her own tears and the sweetness on his lips now. She was still crying, and she couldn’t begin to explain that to him, even though she could tell he was torn between worrying over her tears and enjoying every other sensation that was zinging through their bodies.

She opened herself up to him even more, raising her body up to his to take him even deeper, loving the way he felt on top of her, the weight of him, the width of his shoulders, the muscles in his thighs and his arms, his body very much a man’s, hard and lean and strong. She’d never really been with a man and gloried in it. He rocked back and forth against her, feeling so good inside of her, crazy good. She didn’t understand how she’d waited this long to be with him, how she’d resisted him at all.

“Are you okay?” he whispered to her.

She nodded, holding him tighter.

"I just wanted you to know," he said, his voice gravelly and deep, the words seeming to require a great deal of effort to get out, "before we did this. I wanted to promise you those things."

She blinked back more tears, holding his face down to hers. "I'm fine."

He looked as if he wasn't sure he believed her, but she didn't want that right now. She just wanted to be with him, to make him feel everything that she was feeling. He made her greedy, made her crazy, made her feel like no matter how much she had, she'd never get enough of him and being with him this way.

Deep inside her, this crazy, overwhelming energy was growing, building, spreading out in waves throughout her whole body. She just needed him so much, wanted so much more. She had to have it. It was like her whole body throbbed in time with his.

He started moving with more strength, more abandon. Reached down and got his hands under her hips, palming them and using his own strength to hold her body hard against his. His palms were hot on her skin, insistent, and then he got one hand between their bodies, finding the most sensitive spot of all, and that was it. She was gone, all those lovely sensations exploding inside of her. She cried out, clung to him, her body shaking, throbbing, weak as could be.

She looked up into his eyes in that moment, saw that huge, starry sky behind him and a hard stamp of satisfaction on his face. He knew exactly how he'd made her feel.

And then he lost every bit of control he'd exercised to that point, crying out her name, burying his face in her neck, thrusting one more time, then again and then collapsing on top of her, his body hard and spent.

* * *

They stayed that way for a long time, his hand tangled in her hair, her tears falling silently as she lay there with him on top of her, not letting him move, even though it was a little difficult to breathe. She stroked a hand lazily up and down his bare back, watched the stars and thought about dreams coming true, a man she could trust, a man who would stay.

Eventually he rolled onto his back, pulling her along with him and settling her against his side and his chest, then grabbed one end of the blanket and pulled it over both of them.

He wiped the remaining tears from her cheek, then backed up enough so that he could look her in the eye, and said, "I want you to know that I meant what I said. I meant all of it, I swear. Tell me you believe me, Amy."

"I do," she promised him as fresh tears came.

He brushed those away, too. "The last thing I wanted was to make you cry. What did I—"

She touched her finger to his lips to quiet him. "It was perfect," she told him. "What you said, it was absolutely perfect, and I just…you just make me feel so much, so much I don't think I can stand it at times. Do you—"

"Yes," he said, that look of heartfelt satisfaction back again. "I do. Every time I'm with you. More than I thought I was capable of feeling, of wanting, of needing."

And then he made love to her again, the stars twinkling overhead, more dreams coming true.

They crept back into the house just before dawn, having fallen asleep in each other's arms outside. Tate opened the back door for her and then lingered there, watching her, wrapped up in that blanket, her clothes and shoes in a bundle in her hands.

She felt heat creeping into her cheeks, couldn't help it, and her whole body was tingling with the loveliest, warm, soft, so-relaxed-she-could-hardly-stand-it sensation. She was surprised she'd been able to move, even with the threat of the sun coming up soon.

"Go. Go to your bed," she told him.

"Come with me," he said, tempting her mightily.

"I can't. I don't even know where Max is."

"He's not in the bedroom down here. Eleanor wouldn't leave him down here alone. He's probably in the room next door to hers again."

"Which means she knows I never made it home last night."

"Which will make her extremely happy," he pointed out.

"I know, I just…I'm not ready to share that much information with everyone yet. If we could just—"

"Keep sneaking around a little longer?"

"Yes," she said, although she was sure that was not what he intended for her to say. "I want to sneak around a little bit longer. And I know that's kind of silly, with you right over there in your bed and me in mine, at least when morning comes. But…that's what I want. Okay?"

"Amy?" he asked, smiling beautifully. "Haven't I been giving you exactly what you want in this relationship?"

"Well, yes," she admitted. "Is that a problem for you?"

"No, I have no problem with waiting you out." And looked pleased about doing it, too.

"Waiting me out?"

He nodded. "Because I know, one day, you're going to give me exactly what I want, too."

"I thought I just did," she told him.

"Oh, you did. But there's more. I want more. And you're

going to give it to me." He looked as if he had no doubt at all about that. "And you know exactly what I'm talking about. But I bet you're not ready to have this conversation yet, right?"

"Right," she agreed.

"So I'll go to bed now." He kissed her one more time and turned and left.

Amy slipped inside, down the hallway and into the kitchen, intending to get a glass of water, and found Eleanor there instead, looking very pleased indeed. Here was Amy, creeping in near dawn, wrapped up naked in a blanket with her clothes in her hands, her hair no doubt all over the place, blushing for all she was worth. Of course Eleanor wouldn't miss this.

"Good morning, dear," Eleanor said, as if they greeted each other this way every morning. "I thought you might be looking for Max and I wanted to tell you he's sleeping in the room next to mine."

Amy nodded. "Thank you."

"Anything you'd like to tell me, dear?"

"No. Not really."

"All right, dear." Eleanor gave Amy a little hug, blanket and all. "And don't worry. That boy of mine knows how to be patient. He'll wait."

Amy looked down at herself in the blanket. They certainly didn't look as if they were waiting anymore. She gave Eleanor a questioning look.

"To marry you, dear," Eleanor said.

It seemed Eleanor did indeed know everything that went on in this house.

Amy was afraid—and thrilled and happy but afraid—marriage was exactly what Tate wanted.

Epilogue

Eleanor decided she truly couldn't give up her home. It held too many memories, and the only reason she'd left in the first place was because she was lonely. The obvious solution was to fill the place up.

"Weddings?" Amy said, groaning inside six weeks later when Eleanor walked into the kitchen, where Amy was baking, and told Amy her plan.

"Destination weddings are big these days," Eleanor explained.

"You mean...like everyone coming for a long weekend, which includes a wedding, here?"

Eleanor nodded, beaming at Amy.

"But the last one was... Eleanor, it was just crazy. You know that!" Amy tried.

"I thought it was just lovely," Eleanor insisted. "And everything worked out just fine in the end. That's all that matters."

Amy made a face.

Eleanor laughed.

"You can make money on a business like that? Just weddings?" Amy tried instead.

"Not just weddings. High-end corporate retreats, seminars, luncheons, fundraisers. The house should be enjoyed. We'll fill it with people again, and I don't really need to make money. I just need to make enough to offset the expenses of keeping the house. So this is perfect."

"Well, if that's what you really want, then of course I want you to have it."

"And since all of these people coming to the house will need to be fed, I'm going to have to have someone take charge of the kitchen. And I know how much you've become attached to the kitchen here."

"Okay, there it is. Still matchmaking," Amy said.

"I am simply trying to set up a business," Eleanor claimed. "Of course, if you don't want the job, that's perfectly fine, too. If you'd rather continue with your specialty dessert business, that's fine with me. I'll simply buy desserts from you."

Amy had been baking like mad over the past six weeks, still here in Eleanor's huge, beautifully equipped kitchen, trying to figure out if she could make a go of a specialty-dessert business, supplying freshly made baked goods to various restaurants around town.

She'd kept trying to take Max and leave Eleanor's house, but Eleanor, Tate and Max had all conspired together to get her to stay, the final enticement being a chance for her to try starting her own business, living here at Eleanor's house for a couple of months and using Eleanor's kitchen.

It had always been Amy's dream—her own specialty-dessert business—and of course, Tate had found that out and then Eleanor had jumped at the chance to help make it happen with an offer of free room and board for two months during the start-up phase, when she had no idea what kind of income she might have to work with.

They hadn't done anything but present the opportunity, making it all sound quite simple and logical, and it had simply been too enticing for Amy to refuse. She loved feeding people, loved making people happy, and they were almost always happy eating her cooking. It was as simple as that for her.

"Amy, you can't tell me you haven't been happy here," Eleanor said finally.

"No, I can't."

"And Max is certainly happy."

"Yes, he is," she agreed.

"Well, I'm happy, and I know Tate is happy. Can't we all just be happy together? It seems so easy."

"It's... Eleanor, it's just that life has never been easy for me," Amy said finally.

"Oh, my dear. I know. Truly, I do." Eleanor gave her a big hug. "And I promised I wouldn't meddle anymore."

Amy laughed at that.

"And I think I've been doing an admirable job of sticking to that promise," Eleanor claimed.

"Yes, actually, you have been, and I know how hard it was for you to resist. So thank you for that. Thank you for everything. Truly. I don't know how Max and I lived through all these years without you."

Eleanor sniffled. Her bottom lip started to tremble, then she started to cry in earnest.

"Oh, no," Amy said, hugging her this time. "Don't do that—"

"It's just my dear late husband and I weren't able to have children, and then Tate's mother died, and I felt terrible for all of us, losing her, but Tate has always been such a delight.

If I'd ever had a son, I would have wanted him to be just like Tate. And if I ever had a daughter and a grandson, I'd want them to be just like you and Max. My life just feels so full and happy right now that I can hardly stand it."

"Well…I'm happy, too, of course. My grandmother died when I was five. It was terrible. Everyone needs a grandmother."

Eleanor nodded, tears still falling from her face and Amy's as they held on to each other.

The back door opened. Tate and Max walked in. Although both women tried their best to mop up their tears, Tate knew something was up when he came in.

"Hey, what's this?" he asked. "What's wrong?"

"Nothing," they both claimed in unison, still sniffling and wiping away tears.

He stared back at them, then turned to Max. "Max, my man, I think we're going to have to step up our plan. I think it's time. Right now."

Max nodded, then whispered, "You said they might cry after."

"I know," Tate said. "I got it backward. Men do that sometimes. Especially with women."

"Okay, but—" Max looked down at his school clothes, jeans and a T-shirt, not quite clean now at the end of the day "—we don't have our stuff on."

"I know." Tate turned to Eleanor and Amy. "Ladies, we're going to get our stuff. Don't go anywhere."

"But—" Amy said.

"No questions," he insisted. "We'll be right back."

Amy was sure Eleanor would know all about what was going on, but she swore she didn't. And Amy got more and more nervous every moment Tate and Max were gone. Eleanor just grinned, like a woman about to get exactly what she wanted.

"Just remember to breathe," Eleanor told her as they watched the two well-dressed males walk back from the guesthouse toward the house.

They were wearing matching outfits. Suits. Maybe even tuxes. Black slacks and matching long coats, Amy saw as they got closer, starched white shirts, black ties. Someone had even smoothed back Max's unruly head of hair for him.

"Look at them. They're absolutely perfect together," Eleanor said. "Both handsome and adorable."

They were indeed, a matched set, dressed for a very fancy party.

Or a wedding.

Amy's heart thudded inside her chest. She'd known this day was coming, had wondered how long Tate would hold out and even exactly how he'd pop the question. She hadn't guessed he'd include Max in it, although now that she thought of it, it shouldn't have surprised her, as close as they'd become.

Her two men walked in the back door together, looking so polished and pleased with themselves, Max grinning from ear to ear.

"I have smell-good stuff on, too," Max whispered to her. "Man smell-good stuff."

Amy leaned down close to him and sniffed. "Oh, Max. You smell divine."

"And quite manly," Eleanor added.

"He smells good, too," Max said nodding toward Tate.

Tate's grin was every bit as big. "What? No one's going to check out how I smell?"

Eleanor took him by the arms, kissed his cheek and said, "I think I'm going to leave this to the three of you."

"You're kidding?" Tate said, then laughed, watching her go.

Amy was trembling as she watched Eleanor leave and noticed again how happy Max looked. He'd never had a father. She wasn't sure he ever would have one. And she'd wanted that for him even more than she'd wanted a man for herself. She'd doubted ever finding someone who was both wonderful to her son and as wonderful and enticing to her.

"She's crying again," Max told Tate.

"It's okay," Tate promised. "She's happy. Women cry when they're happy, too."

"Do we do it now?" Max asked.

"Yes, now."

They both got down on one knee in front of her, Tate taking her hand in his and putting his other arm around Max's shoulders.

"Amy," Tate began. "Max and I want you to know that we've already had our talk about this, and Max is all for it."

Max nodded, grinning.

"You asked Max first?"

"Well, Max was ready. And I know that anything that happens between you and me, well, that it's not just you and me. And you and me and Max are all in this together. So it just seemed right that I would need to ask Max, too. I mean, he's as big a part of this as you and I are. And we both want you to know that this is what we both want. Max has agreed to be my best man, in fact."

Again Max nodded eagerly, then asked Tate, "Is it time now?"

"Yes, it's time, Max."

Max dug into his pocket and pulled out a tiny jewelry box and handed it to Tate. "That's gonna be my job," Max told his mother.

Tate pulled the box open, took out the ring and held

it out for her to see. It looked old-fashioned, a delicate, scrolling band with a single, clear, sparkling stone in the middle of it.

"It was my mother's," he said. "I thought it suited you."

Amy nodded through her tears, let him take her hand again and slip the ring barely onto the tip of the third finger of her right hand.

"Amy, Max and I would like very much for you to marry me and for the three of us to become a family."

"You forgot the 'ever part," Max whispered.

"Oh, yes." Tate looked a little misty-eyed himself. "Forever. That last part's important to us. It's forever."

Max nodded, obviously satisfied this had been done correctly, as planned, then said, "She's still cryin'."

"I know." Tate reached out and started wiping her tears away for her. "Amy?"

"Mom?" Max said.

"Yes," she said, laughing through her tears. "Yes. I couldn't say no to the both of you."

Tate slid the ring on her finger.

Max gave her a big hug and a kiss, then said, "I'm gonna go tell Eleanor!"

He disappeared, leaving Amy alone in the kitchen with Tate, where it had all started. He looked very pleased with himself, taking her into his arms and giving her a slow, sweet, steamy kiss.

"Sometimes things just work perfectly," he said.

"Yes, they do," Amy agreed.

* * * * *

"How far along are you?" Ethan asked, his tone deceptively mild.

"Ten weeks." Sloane watched him closely while he flashed through the math, waiting to see anger light his eyes, denial tighten his jaw. She didn't see either of those emotions, though. Instead, there was something else, something she had no idea how to read.

He set his shoulders. "Is it mine?"

She nodded, suddenly unable to find words. Hormones, she thought as tears sprang to her eyes. Stupid pregnancy hormones.

Wonderful, Ethan thought. That made two women he'd driven to tears that week.

He hadn't expected this. Not once, in all the times that he'd thought of Sloane, had he imagined that their one night together had led to a baby. A baby that was half Hartwell genes.

Half a potential for such a disaster that his breath came short.

THE MOGUL'S MAYBE MARRIAGE

BY

MINDY KLASKY

First published in Great Britain 2013
by Mills & Boon, an imprint of Harlequin (UK) Limited,
Eton House, 18-24 Paradise Road, Richmond, Surrey TW9 1SR

ISBN: 978 0 263 90638 7
ebook ISBN: 978 1 472 01207 4

23-0613

Harlequin (UK) policy is to use papers that are natural, renewable and recyclable products and made from wood grown in sustainable forests. The logging and manufacturing processes conform to the legal environmental regulations of the country of origin.

Printed and bound in Spain
by Blackprint CPI, Barcelona

Mindy Klasky learned to read when her parents shoved a book in her hands and told her that she could travel anywhere in the world through stories. She never forgot that advice. These days, Mindy works and plays in a suburb of Washington, DC, where she lives with her family. In her spare time, Mindy knits, cooks and tries to tame the endless to-be-read shelf in her home library. You can visit Mindy at her website, www.mindyklasky.com.

To my fellow Arent Fox summer associates—
who laughed with me as Sloane was born

Chapter One

Ethan Hartwell was not accustomed to waiting.

He glanced over in annoyance, not bothering to hide the action from the sour-faced assistant who guarded the inner office. His BlackBerry buzzed and he accepted another appointment for that afternoon. He forwarded a scheduling notice about his Seattle trip the following week.

Hartwell Genetics couldn't afford to get left behind, not with domestic and international demand exploding for the company's gene-based medicines.

If he was going to be kept waiting like a recalcitrant schoolboy outside the principal's office, then he might as well get his homework done.

Another buzz. More email. Ethan cleared his throat to get the attention of the gray-haired Gorgon. "I'm going back to my office," he said.

Before he could carry through on the threat, the door

guard raised a talon to her ear. She nodded at whatever secret message she received, then leveled cold eyes toward Ethan before intoning, "You may go in now."

Games. If he'd announced his decision to leave fifteen minutes earlier, then he would have been granted admittance that much sooner. He shoved his BlackBerry onto his hip and twitched the legs of his trousers into perfect place. For full effect, he shot the cuffs of his shirt, making sure that his wristwatch glinted in the overhead lights. He told himself that his deep breath was to complete the image, to cement the vision of Ethan Hartwell, M.D., MBA, third-generation president of Hartwell Genetics and the most eligible bachelor of Washington, D.C., for three years running.

In reality, he merely needed a moment to clear his head before he entered the inner sanctum.

The handle turned smoothly under his lean fingers, and the door glided open in silence. Ethan's black wingtips left deep impressions in the cream carpet as he crossed the room. He ignored the framed pictures on the wall, photographs taken with the President, with political and business leaders from throughout the civilized world. The United States Capitol was centered in the picture window behind the massive mahogany desk, as perfect as a movie backdrop. With the force of long habit, Ethan crossed behind that desk, approaching the imposing throne that housed the office's lone occupant.

He bent at the waist and settled a faint kiss on a cheek that smelled of baby powder and lilacs. "Good morning, Grandmother," Ethan said.

Margaret Hartwell's eyes gleamed like agate chips as she waved him to one of her uncomfortable Louis XIV chairs. "Will you join me for a cup of tea?"

Ethan swallowed a sigh. It was faster to accept his

grandmother's hospitality than to argue with her. He poured with the ease of familiarity, placing a gleaming strainer across her china cup, dropping in two cubes of sugar, adding a generous dollop of milk. He took his own black, strong and bitter. Determined to conclude their conversation and get back to work, he said, "Grandmother—"

"I finished reading the newspaper this morning, before I came into the office," she interrupted.

He, too, had skimmed the *Wall Street Journal* and the *Financial Times* while his chauffeured car had been stuck in morning traffic. "The new treatment is performing well," he said. "We should move on to stage-two trials next month."

As if he needed to tell his grandmother about pharmaceutical development. As Hartwell Genetics's former president and current chairman of the board, Margaret Hartwell chased down medical news like a ravenous greyhound. Maybe that was why she had the capacity to annoy him so much—they were too much alike: driven, determined and downright dogged about pursuing every last business lead.

"I'm not speaking about stage-two trials," she said acerbically. "I was referring to the gossip page."

Ethan raised one eyebrow. He and his grandmother might be united on the business front, but they were miles apart where his personal life was concerned. "Grandmother, we've had this discussion before. You know that I can't control what the papers print."

She settled her teacup in her saucer with a firm clink. "You *can* control the fodder you give those imbeciles. I've told you until I'm blue in the face—your actions have a direct effect on this company."

He shoved his teacup away. "I hardly think that my

drinking champagne on a hotel rooftop is going to influence our second quarter earnings."

"She's a *showgirl,* Ethan."

He laughed and rose to his feet. "There haven't been showgirls since you were a debutante, Grandmother. Natasha is an *actress.* And don't worry. She flew back to California this morning."

"You will *not* walk out of my office while I am talking to you!"

He shouldn't have been surprised by the iron in his grandmother's voice. He knew that he brought out the worst in her, and vice versa, for that matter. All of a sudden, he was an abandoned little boy again, being chastised by the only relative who had stuck around to raise him. He was the sixteen-year-old who had been expelled from Washington's finest private school—again—for playing tricks with the headmaster's public address system. He was the twenty-year-old who had been thrown off the college tennis team for sneaking his girlfriend into the tournament locker room. He was the twenty-seven-year-old who had celebrated receiving his medical degree and his business degree on the same day, only to crash his Porsche into the Tidal Basin.

He was the thirty-three-year-old corporate executive, standing before his chairman of the board.

"Ethan, enough is enough. Your parties and your women are bringing down this company. They're distracting you. And they're not even making you happy." His grandmother gave him the flinty stare that had sealed a thousand legendary business deals. "Ethan, I want you married by no later than my birthday."

He laughed.

"This isn't a joke." She leaned forward across her desk. All of a sudden, Ethan became aware of the deep lines beside her mouth, the bags beneath her eyes. Her fingers were knotted as she laid them flat against her gold-scrolled leather blotter. Did they tremble because she was angry with him? Or was something more going on? He barely resisted the urge to reach across her desk, to fold his fingers around the pulse point in her wrist, to measure her heart rate. Was she keeping track of her medication? Was she managing the high blood pressure?

"Grandmother," he said, purposely striving for a soothing tone. "I'm a grown man. I'll decide when it's time to marry."

"I wish I believed that." Her voice quaked, spiking his own blood with a touch of true concern. "I've tried to be patient, Ethan, but I'm terrified that I'll die without knowing our family will continue." She raised one trembling hand to silence his automatic protest. "I know that you're afraid. But we can *test* now. We can be absolutely certain that any child you father is spared the genetic mutation."

He had never seen his grandmother cry before. Not when two grandchildren had died—Ethan's siblings. Not when Ethan's mourning parents had incinerated their marriage. Not when Grandmother had been left with the responsibility of managing the company that the family had originally founded to research an end to their long-kept medical secret. Not when she had buried her beloved husband of fifty-one years.

But she was crying now.

"You have a responsibility, Ethan. To the Hartwell family and to this company. To yourself. It's time for you to settle down." She must have read the automatic rebellion in his expression. She sat up straighter, staring at him with the hazel eyes that were the more benign manifestation of his Hartwell heritage. "And if you're not willing to do that, then I'll have no choice but to step down from the board and transfer my shares in Hartwell Genetics."

Her shares. Enough stock to influence every major corporate decision. If someone else owned Grandmother's interest, Ethan would be forced to fight, to keep the secret of his own genetic heritage. He'd be bound to waste countless hours cajoling along new business colleagues, educating them about the corporation's diverse pharmaceutical initiatives, all the while keeping secret its one dear mission. Ethan could kiss every one of his short-term goals goodbye while he adjusted to the change. And under a new regime, his long-term plans might never coalesce.

"You don't mean that," he said.

"I do. I need to know that I've built *something* that will last, Ethan, something that will outlive me." He heard every one of her seventy-nine years in her voice. "Ethan, I need to know that you can step up to your obligations. That you will guide Hartwell Genetics through its next fifty years. If you can't prove that to me—if you're not married by January fifth—then I'm celebrating eight decades by transferring my entire estate to the American Foundation for the Advancement of the Arts."

AFAA. His grandmother's longtime pet charity.

This was even worse than he'd thought a moment ago. AFAA had no interest in medicine. They would view a massive infusion of corporate stock as a conservative investment. They would do their best to challenge every decision Ethan made to expand the corporate mission, to bring Hartwell Genetics into new markets. They'd argue for safety and security and preservation of their newfound wealth, at all costs.

Ethan sighed. He'd escorted Grandmother to the foundation's annual charity auction only a couple of months before, at the luxurious Eastern Hotel, the one with the bar that overlooked the Washington Monument.

He swallowed hard, his mouth suddenly dry. He'd bought a drink for the auction coordinator that night. A drink, and then a hastily arranged suite on the penthouse level of the hotel.

Sloane. Sloane Davenport.

He could still see Sloane's delicate, self-conscious smile as she admitted that she'd never done anything like that before, never gone off with a man she'd just met. He had silenced her confession with a kiss, not willing to admit to himself just how much her innocence attracted him, how much her shyness drew him in.

Since the auction, he'd picked up the phone to call her half a dozen times, but he'd never followed through. He hadn't wanted to hear regret when he identified himself. Hadn't wanted to think about the conversation they'd shared in the dark, the talk that had gone on, sleepy and comfortable, long after their bodies were sated. Hadn't wanted to remember waking up alone, with just a memory of her honeysuckle scent on the pillow.

He cleared his throat and shifted his weight, ordering his body to relax, to forget the only night that stood out from the past year's slideshow of one-night stands. "AFAA," he finally forced himself to say.

His grandmother's eyes glittered as she tapped a thick manila folder on her desk. "I have the papers here, Ethan. Zach drew them up."

Zach Crosby. Ethan's best friend. His grandmother's personal attorney.

Ethan turned on his heel and left, ignoring his grandmother's sharp remonstration, ignoring her secretary's petulant frown, ignoring the buzz of his BlackBerry.

Seven months to find a bride. And he had absolutely no doubt that his grandmother would follow through on her threat if he failed. He was certain of that. She loved him, and she would do whatever she thought best to save him. Even if he didn't want to be saved.

Sloane Davenport gasped as her computer screen flickered, giving one heart-stopping moment of blue-screen warning before it died. Damn! That was the third time today. And she had no way of knowing if her email had been sent before the stupid machine crashed. No way of knowing if her résumé was heading out toward a prospective new employer. No way of knowing if she might finally be making her way out of the mess that enveloped her.

She stood slowly, bracing her palms against the kitchen table before she folded her fingers into fists and rubbed the small of her back. The dull, throbbing pain had returned. She grimaced and picked up a saltine from her chipped plate. Nausea swirled through her belly, but she forced herself to chew slowly, to swallow an entire glass of water when she was done.

Two and a half months. She should be past the morning sickness any day now. That's what the book said, the dog-eared volume that she kept on her coffee table like a family Bible.

She shrugged and reached for the stack of papers beside her computer. Bills. Fortunately, she kept her checkbook on paper. No chance for her ancient computer to ruin *them*.

Not that the curling slips of paper offered any great comfort. At least she'd managed to send her rent check on time. She glanced at the air conditioner that chugged along in the kitchen window of her tiny basement apartment. Her landlord covered utilities. No need to worry about electricity or water.

Student loans, though, were another matter. She'd sent off a tiny payment, along with a note explaining that she'd send more, as soon as she was able.

Like *that* was going to happen anytime soon. Expenses related to the baby had barely begun, and Sloane was already overwhelmed. Soon, she was going to have to buy some new clothes. She wasn't showing yet, but it was only a matter of weeks. Her jeans were already snug in the waistband, and she'd left the button unfastened as she worked at her kitchen table.

She'd have to get some decent groceries, too, as soon as she could keep down more than crackers and ramen noodles. For now, she had to hope that her expensive prenatal vitamins were doing their job. She glared at the white bottle on the counter.

And she'd have to scrape together money for a doctor.

She'd fit in her first prenatal visit just before her insurance ran out. Two months had gone by, though, two visits that she owed herself, owed her baby. She tried to believe that she could wait until she had a new job, until she was insured, but as every day passed without her landing a new position, she became more and more afraid.

She rubbed her fingers across the thin fabric of her T-shirt, letting them curl over the tiny life that lurked inside. Would she have handled things differently with AFAA, if she'd known that she was pregnant?

Her cheeks flushed as she remembered taking the subway home from the Eastern that morning after the auction. She had tottered down the steps to her apartment, her feet pinched in unaccustomed high heels.

Despite her exhaustion, despite the awkwardness of slipping out of the hotel suite unseen and unheard, despite the heart-catching memories from the night before that kept drowning her, she'd caught herself with a goofy smile on her face. She had sung out loud in the shower as she got ready for work. Silly songs. Love songs.

Oh, she knew that Ethan Hartwell didn't love her. He *couldn't* love her. He was famous and rich and the toast of the gossiping town.

But there had been *something* in his eyes when he'd come to stand beside her at the bar, where she'd granted herself a well-deserved break after managing the most successful fundraising auction in AFAA history. There'd been something in the set of his jaw as he gestured for the bartender to make her another vodka gimlet. Something in the curve of his lips as they bantered, as she flirted.

As *she* flirted…

Sloane sighed, remembering how easily the words had come to her, as if she were blessed by some daring goddess of romance. For once in her life, it had been simple to talk to a man, to tease him, to taunt. A little amazed, she'd watched Ethan lean close to her. She'd lowered her voice, bit her lip, dipped her head. When he'd settled a finger on her chin, raising her face to his, she'd felt the promise radiating from his hand. She'd registered the heat that had cascaded over her body in a sudden, astonishing wave.

She'd tasted whiskey on his lips, smoky liquor that swirled through the clean citrus tang of her own drink. Without conscious thought, she'd drunk in more of the flavor of his cocktail, of him. The touch of his tongue on hers had sent an electric tingle down her spine, and she'd shuddered, grateful for his firm hand on the small of her back, steadying her, drawing her closer.

One hour, another drink and much banter later, he'd turned away to the bartender, said something that she couldn't quite catch. She'd seen the flash of a silver credit card pass between the men, and minutes later, the exchange of a plastic room key.

Another kiss had sealed his invitation, that one rocketing across the tender velvet of her mouth, curling through her belly, trembling into the vulnerable flesh behind her knees. She'd found some witty words to reply, and then she was grateful for the fiery hand that he cupped against her nape, for the scorching iron of his body next to hers as he led the way across the bar, to the elevator, to the penthouse suite that he had so effortlessly secured.

His ease had given her the confidence to do all the things she wanted to do. She didn't need to wonder if she should say *this,* if she should do *that.* Instead, she'd trusted herself. She'd trusted him. For one perfect night, she was more comfortable than she'd ever been with a man. It was more than just the sex, more than the amazing things he made her body feel. They had actually *talked,* hour after hour, lying next to each other in the dark, sharing stories of their very different pasts. Everything just felt…right.

In the morning, though, she'd snuck out before he was awake. That's what women did—at least according to movies, according to the newspapers, to the tabloids that feasted on men like Bachelor of the Year Ethan Hartwell. She'd snuck out, gone home to shower, made it in to the office no more than thirty minutes late.

Thirty minutes that her boss had spent waiting for

her. Thirty minutes that he'd spent building a furious argument.

Didn't Sloane know that AFAA had an image to uphold? AFAA project coordinators could not fraternize with prominent playboy bachelors in public bars where donors—discerning donors, *conservative* donors—could see them. AFAA project coordinators certainly could not slink off with their conquests, leaving nothing to the imagination about their destination. AFAA project coordinators could never threaten the long-term success of an organization as traditional and staid and sedate as the foundation—not when offended donors threatened to rescind their pledged funds because of the immoral behavior of AFAA staff.

AFAA project coordinators could be replaced without a second's hesitation.

Even now, weeks later, Sloane grimaced at the memory.

Before she could collect her notes and head to the library with its working computer terminal, her doorbell rang, making her jump in surprise. She never had visitors. When she looked through the peephole, she nearly sank to the floor in disbelief.

Ethan Hartwell. As if she had summoned him with her recollection of that one night.

That was absurd, though. She'd thought about that night almost nonstop since March. Mere *thought* had never brought Ethan to her door before.

Heart pounding, she ran her fingers through her hair. Thank goodness she'd taken a shower that morning, brushed her teeth, even remembered to floss. She glanced down at her trim navy T-shirt, took a second to fiddle with the button on her jeans, sucking in her breath to camouflage her incipient baby bump. He couldn't tell, could he? Not yet. No one could, she reasoned with herself.

The doorbell rang again, long and insistent. She set her jaw against the demand. What did Ethan Hartwell want with her? Why had he come now? She thought about not answering, about letting him go away. He could phone her, if he really needed her. Her number was listed.

But then, she remembered his hazel eyes, the ones that had first snagged her attention at the Eastern. She remembered his rich voice, reverberating to the marrow of her bones. She remembered his broad palms, curving around her hips, pulling her closer....

She threw open the double locks, just as he was raising his fist to knock.

"Ethan," she said, proud that her voice was steady, bright, with just the perfect brush of surprise.

"Sloane." He lowered his hand to his side. His eyes flared as he took in her face, as if he were confirming a memory. He licked his lips, and then he produced the same devastating smile that had completely sunk her back at the hotel. "May I come in?"

Silently, she stepped to the side. She caught his scent as he strode past her, something like pine needles under moonlight, something utterly, completely male. She waited for a familiar twist of nausea to leap up at the aroma, but she was pleasantly surprised to find that her belly remained calm.

Not that her body didn't react to him. Her lips tingled as she sucked in a steadying breath. Her heart raced enough that she half expected him to turn around, to glare at her chest, disturbed by the noise. The thought of his eyes on her chest only stirred her more. She bit her lip as her nipples tightened into pearls, and she crossed her arms over the navy jersey of her shirt.

Faking a tiny cough, she asked, "Can I get you something to drink?" She couldn't make him coffee. She didn't trust her rebellious stomach around the smell as it brewed. "Some tea?" she asked.

He shook his head. "No," he said. "I'm fine." He strode to her couch as if he owned the place.

She'd lived in the apartment for nearly three years. In all that time, she'd never realized how small the space really was, how little air there was in the room. She watched his gaze dart toward the diminutive kitchen, to the tiny table with its mismatched pair of chairs, to the narrow counter. He glanced toward her bedroom, and she had a sudden vision of him literally sweeping her off her feet, carrying her through the doorway, easing her onto the double bed's crumpled sheets.

She flexed her fingers and reminded herself to breathe. Gesturing at the living room, she said, "Not quite the Eastern, is it?"

He ignored her question. "You left the foundation."

She bridled at his tone. "I didn't think I needed your permission to change jobs."

He ignored her sarcasm. "I tried to reach you there, yesterday morning. All they'd say was that you left a couple of months ago. I guess the auction was your last fling?"

She flushed. He had no way of knowing that the night they'd spent together was special to her. Precious, in a way that words could never make him understand. Her vulnerability rasped an undertone of challenge across her voice. "Why do you care? Why were you calling me, anyway?"

In the dim light, his hazel eyes looked black. "Your

name came up in conversation. I wondered how you were doing."

"My name came up," she said, fighting a tangle of disbelief and excitement. "After two and half months? Just like that?" She hated the fact that her voice shook on the last word.

He closed the distance between them, settling a hand on her arm. She knew that she should pull away, keep a safe distance. But she didn't entirely trust her suddenly trembling legs.

"Let's try this again," he said. "Sit down." He must have heard the note of command beneath his words, because he inclined his head and gestured toward the sofa as if it were something elegant, something worthy of royalty. "Please."

She took a seat, pretending that the action was her own idea, even as she was grateful for the support against her back. She longed to cradle one of the throw pillows in her lap, to hide behind the cushion. Instead, she folded her hands across her belly, trying to summon a calm that she could not feel past her pounding heart. As he sat beside her, she tried to think of something to say, anything, some everyday conversational gambit that would pass for normal between two consenting adults.

He spoke before she did, though, his tone deceptively mild. "How far along are you?"

She clutched at her T-shirt. "How did you know?"

"The vitamins." He nodded toward her kitchen counter, toward the white plastic bottle that announced its contents in bright orange letters. "The book." She blushed as his gaze fell on the coffee table. He insisted, "How many weeks?"

"Ten." She watched him closely while he flashed through the math, waiting to see anger light his eyes, denial tighten his jaw. She didn't see either of those emotions, though. Instead, there was something else, something she had no idea how to read.

He set his shoulders. "Is it mine?"

She nodded, suddenly unable to find words. Hormones, she thought as tears sprang to her eyes. Stupid pregnancy hormones.

Wonderful, Ethan thought. That made two women he'd driven to tears that week.

He hadn't expected this. Not once, in all the times that he'd thought of Sloane, had he imagined that their one night together had led to a baby. A baby that was half Hartwell genes. Half a potential for such a disaster that his breath came short.

They'd used protection, of course. He wasn't an idiot. But he *was* a doctor, and he knew the statistics. Condoms failed, three percent of the time. Three percent, and after a lifetime of luck, of practice, of protection, he'd just lost the lottery.

He had come to Sloane that morning with mixed emotions, determined to maintain his independence, even as he gave lip service to his grandmother's edict. He had thought that he and Sloane could get to know each other better. After all, in the past year, she'd been the only woman he'd thought about once he'd left her bed. The only woman he'd ever wanted to confide something in, confide *everything* in. Which, of course, had made him vow never to contact her again.

Except now he needed a woman. He needed a *wife.* And Sloane had been the first person to cross his mind when Grandmother issued her ultimatum.

He had fooled himself, thinking that everything would be simple. They could go out on a few proper dates. Stay out of bed, difficult as that might prove to be. Even as Ethan had built his plan, he'd been wryly amused by the thought that Sloane worked at AFAA. If, after a month or two of testing the waters, he found that he and Sloane truly *were* compatible, then she would be the perfect ironic tool to rein in his grandmother's plan. He would put a ring on Sloane's finger, and AFAA would lose the potential for a controlling interest in Hartwell Genetics.

Except the stakes had just been raised. Astronomically. And Sloane didn't have the least idea what was going on. She had no concept of what heartbreak her future might bear. Ethan set his jaw. There were tests, as his grandmother had reminded him. Tests that could be run as soon as Sloane reached her fourteenth week.

He'd let the silence stretch out too long between them. He had to know. "You're alone here?"

Again, she nodded. He tried to identify the emotions that swirled into his relief at that saving grace: pleasure, coupled with a surprisingly fierce possessiveness. She was alone. *Unattached,* he knew they both meant.

"Good," he growled.

The single word sparked a fire beneath Sloane's heart. Sure, she'd dreamed about sharing her news with him. She'd written silly scenes inside her head, of Ethan finding her a few years from now, after she had built a career, had proved to herself and the rest of the world that she was strong and independent. She had let herself fill in the impossible details— she would be playing in the park with their baby, their happy and carefree and perfect child, when Ethan just happened to walk by, taking a stroll on a brilliant spring morning.

But in her heart of hearts, she had known that could never happen. Ethan would never be there for her, would never share this baby with her. They'd only spent one night together, and they'd taken every precaution to make sure that she would never end up in this precise condition.

Besides, she'd done her research after the night they'd spent together, following up on all the gossip that she had vaguely recalled when she saw him at the Eastern bar. She had forced herself to read the articles about his playboy lifestyle, the stream of women in his life, the flirtations that splashed across the society page.

Sloane's daydreams had to be impossible. Right?

"Sloane," he said, breaking into her swirling thoughts. "I should have been in touch before. I know this sounds sudden, but I've been thinking about you since that night. A lot. When I woke and you had left, I figured that I would accept what you obviously wanted."

He reached out and settled his broad hand across her belly. The tips of his fingers ignited tiny fires beneath her shirt, and she caught her breath in pleasure and surprise. He flexed his wrist, using the motion to glide near, to close the distance between them. "But everything is different now."

His mouth on hers was unexpected. She felt the power within him, a coil of energy. Her body reacted before her mind could parcel out a well-reasoned response. She leaned toward him, drawn to his touch like a starving woman to a feast. His tongue traced the line between her lips, and she yielded without any conscious decision. Her fingers fluttered from the shelter of her lap, tangled in his hair, pulled him closer to her.

The motion of her hands seemed to free his own; his fingers were suddenly hot as they slipped beneath her T-shirt, searing as they danced across her still-flat belly. He cupped one sensitive breast with his hand, rasping the lace of her bra against her flesh. Her body had never been so responsive, and she gasped in surprise. She folded her fingers over his. "Just a moment."

Ethan dropped his head to her shoulder, cradling his cheek against the pulse that pounded by her ear.

This was madness. He'd come here, planning on being the perfect gentleman. He'd intended to wind back the clock, to give them both time to get to know each other, space to explore their true potential together. He'd meant to build on the amazing foundation they'd established back at the Eastern, that endless night of talking and loving and talking some more.

He couldn't help himself, though. Even knowing that she was carrying his baby. *Especially* knowing that.

He tensed his arms and pushed himself away just enough that he could look into her eyes, into a blue so deep that he felt like he was drowning. He spoke before he even knew that he was going to say the words. "Sloane. Marry me."

"What?" Sloane couldn't believe that she had heard him right. He reached out to trace a finger along her lips, but she turned her head aside. How could he have read her daydreams? How could he have known the secret stories that she told herself, just as she was drifting off to sleep?

"Marry me," he said again, as if those two words made all the sense in the world.

He couldn't mean it.

Sure, she'd imagined him proposing, once he found out the truth about their single night together. She'd pictured red roses and dry champagne, a sparkling diamond ring fresh out of some teenager's fantasy.

But in her dreams, they had known each other for longer before he proposed. They had indulged in a thousand conversations, countless discoveries of every last thing they had in common. They had filled days—and nights—with laughter, with secrets. They had built a flawless base for their future. He had left behind his reputation for womanizing, finally content to stay with one true…love?

That was all a wonderful dream. But dreams never did come true. Certainly not *her* dreams, not the dreams of a foster kid who'd spent a lifetime being shifted from unloving home to unloving home. Her old defensiveness kicked in just in time to save her, to remind her that she had to protect herself and her baby, that no one else would ever do that as well as she could. She tugged her shirt back into place, willing her flesh to stop tingling. Roughening her voice, she demanded, "Are you insane?"

His eyes flashed as he drew himself to his feet, and she tried to read the expression on his face. Guilt. Or embarrassment. "I'm trying to do the right thing," he said, his voice strained.

She wanted to believe him. She wanted to think that this could really be happening to her. But seriously. Ethan Hartwell? Hartwell Genetics billionaire? Bachelor of the Year?

Her silence seemed to feed something within him, something angry and hard. His jaw tightened. He reached into his back pocket and pulled out a sleek wallet. Two fingers scissored out a business card, a perfect white rectangle. He crossed to her kitchen table, and she tried to read what he was thinking from the tense lines of his back.

His eyes were hooded when he turned around to face her. "Think about it, Sloane. I want to do what's right. A paternity test, and then a proper wedding. You won't get a better offer." He didn't wait for her to reply. Instead, he let himself out the door, closing it with a crisp finality.

He truly *must* be nuts. One minute, he was the astonishing, charming man she'd met at the Eastern, the man who had convinced her to spend the night with him, all because of his easy smile, because of the instant kinship that had sparked between them.

The next minute, though, he was a cold professional. A doctor and a businessman, driving a hard corporate bargain. Demanding a paternity test! He didn't believe her. He thought that someone else could be the father, that she made a habit of picking up random men in hotel bars.

She'd show him. She'd take that business card and tear it into a hundred pieces. She'd flush it down the toilet. She'd grind it up in the garbage disposal. She stormed into the tiny kitchen.

Her tirade was cut short, though, drowned by the sight that met her astonished eyes.

Ethan's business card was centered on her dead laptop. Beneath it were five crisp hundred-dollar bills.

Five hundred dollars. More money than she'd seen since AFAA had kicked her out the door. Money that Ethan had no obligation to leave. Money that he could have made conditional, could have held out to demand her submission.

In one heartbeat, Sloane's anger turned to shame. Really, what reason did Ethan *have* to believe her, about paternity or anything else?

Sure, they'd shared the most intimate night two people could share. She was carrying a baby as proof. But had she found the courage to contact him in the intervening ten weeks? Had she summoned the internal strength to reach out to her baby's father, to tell him the truth? What if Ethan hadn't come to her that morning? How much longer would he have gone on, not knowing? Weeks? Months? Years?

All things considered, Ethan had actually reacted quite well.

What had he just said? He wanted to do what was *right.* Even after she had shut him out. Even after she had kept him from learning the truth. His first instinct had been to take care of her. To take care of their baby. He'd acted nothing like the playboy she'd read about, nothing like the man-about-town who was splashed across the gossip sheets.

Tenderness blossomed inside Sloane's chest, unfolding like a snow-white rosebud. There *was* something between them, some emotion stronger than all the half-truths, deeper than all the avoidance and uncertainty.

The corners of her lips turned up as she heard his earnest tone. *Marry me.*

Could he really mean it? Did she dare say yes?

She didn't have any model in her past for *marriage.* She hadn't grown up with a happy mother and father, with the sort of easy family life that she dreamed about after watching movies, after reading books. She couldn't imagine what it would be like to trust someone enough to want to spend the rest of her life with him.

To love someone that much.

Oh, it was far too soon to say that she loved Ethan. She knew that. But she could say that she was powerfully drawn to him. That he made her feel safe. Protected. And, more than that, he made her feel desirable. Desired. He made her feel more alive than she ever had before.

Biting her lip, Sloane picked up the five crisp bills and folded them lengthwise, creasing them between her thumb and index finger. The sleek business card continued to glint its challenge from the table's surface.

Did she have the courage to make the phone call? Did she have the strength to reach out to Ethan, to tell him what she was thinking? After a lifetime of tamping down any strong emotion, of shutting down her feelings to protect herself, could she possibly take the next step?

Chapter Two

He'd made a complete mess of that.

From the instant that Ethan settled into the back of his chauffeured Town Car, he knew that he'd made a horrible mistake.

But something about Sloane made him lose his famous business composure, softened his infinitely sharp entrepreneurial edge. *"Marry me."* Where the hell had that come from? The words had been out of his mouth before he could think how abrupt they would sound to Sloane. He'd been filled with the thought of Sloane carrying his child. He'd been captivated by the notion that all of this was *meant* to be—the one incredible night they'd spent together, the pregnancy that had resulted. His grandmother's ultimatum.

Fresh from his grandmother's office the day before, Ethan had phoned AFAA, only to find that Sloane had left the organization. His next call had been to his private investigator. In less than twenty-four hours, Ethan knew that Sloane had been fired. At least he had her home address. And a credit report that told him she was in dire need of assistance. Only one piece of data had been missing—the pregnancy…

Ethan's plan had made so much sense. Tweak his grandmother and her ridiculous notions of marital propriety, at the same time that he figured out if there really *was* something there with Sloane.

But all those calculations had flown out the window when he'd actually seen Sloane standing in the doorway. When he'd looked into those ocean eyes, acknowledged the flash of surprise as she greeted him. The hint of uncertainty. The sudden flicker of arousal that beckoned to his own scarcely banked flames. He'd watched the blush paint her cheeks when he stepped inside the apartment, when she crossed her arms over her chest, trying to hide her body's blatant response to him.

And that was before he'd realized that she was pregnant.

Marry me. He'd said it, just like that. Out of the blue, without any prelude, any explanation whatsoever. He hadn't even taken the time to tell her that she wasn't just one of his flings, that she was *different.* He hadn't told her that they had connected on some level that he'd always thought was imaginary. Their midnight conversation had been the sort of thing that women read about in their pink-and-lace books, watched in their silly damp-handkerchief movies. It couldn't be real.

But it was.

Even now, he could remember every word they'd shared. He'd told her about Hartwell Genetics, about how he wanted the company to continue growing, to change the world. How he longed to help millions with the cures his empire was developing. How he loved the challenge, the struggle, the fierce competition in the often-ruthless business world.

And she'd told him her own dreams. What did she call it? The Hope Project, the website she wanted to build. Art therapy. Foster kids. He'd been truly touched by her unwavering determination, by her certainty that she could make a difference.

He couldn't go back now and reduce all that to nothing. He couldn't admit that his grandmother had ordered him to take a wife. And he definitely couldn't tell her the real reason for his demand, for the so-called paternity test. He'd never told anyone about the family curse, about the brother and sister who had each died before their third birthday.

No. He'd proposed, and then he'd left his ugly cash lying on the table. As if he could buy her. As if he could make Sloane do whatever he wanted her to do.

He swore, wondering how a man who was a proven genius in the business world could make such a spectacular mess out of his personal life. There had to be a way to make Sloane understand. A way to take everything back. To start over again.

He closed his eyes and forced himself to take a steadying breath. If this were a business deal going sour, he'd figure out a way to reset the discussions, to return to square one. He would offer up an olive branch. He pushed a single button on his BlackBerry, summoning his assistant.

He already had the beginnings of a plan....

The package was leaning against the door when Sloane got back from the library. She had forced herself to get out of the apartment, to take a break from the jumble of hope and confusion that she felt every time she glanced at Ethan's business card. The last time she had acted rashly where he was concerned; now, she was determined to *think,* to make decisions with her brain, instead of with her heart.

That was the plan she'd made as she had stared at the library's public access terminal, resisting the urge to call up articles about Ethan, his company, his philanthropic efforts. His hard-partying ways.

As much as she wanted to tell Ethan everything she was thinking, everything she was feeling, she needed to slow things down. Think things through. She needed to remember that she wasn't making decisions just for herself anymore. There was the baby to think about. There was a reason—the *best* reason—not to be impulsive.

She had to be certain that Ethan was truly more than the socializing playboy she had read about in the paper. She had to know that he had shared more with her than he had with the other women whose names were tied to his in the newspaper. She had to force herself to look past her—admit it!—infatuation, her utter physical attraction to him.

Returning home, she spotted the envelope immediately. She recognized the Hartwell Genetics logo on the address label. Her heart started pounding, but she forced herself to unlock her front door, to pour herself a drink of water from the pitcher in the refrigerator and sit down at the kitchen table. She thought about returning the envelope unopened. She could just write "return to sender" and drop it in the mailbox, couldn't she?

Except that he hadn't sent it through the mail. There wasn't a postmark. He'd had it hand-delivered.

Taking a fortifying breath, she slid her fingers beneath the flap.

"Sloane," the note said. Even though she'd never seen his writing before, she could picture his fingers curled around a pen, slashing out the letters on the heavy white paper. "Give me another chance? E." A ticket was nestled inside the folds of paper.

Swan Lake, the Bolshoi Ballet, opening gala for the dance season at the Kennedy Center. Friday night.

She sank back in the hard chair. What was she getting herself into?

But that wasn't really the question, was it? The question was what *had* she gotten herself into? Two and a half months before, when she'd given in to the magnetic power of the man she'd met at the Eastern, when she'd let herself be drawn into the thrumming, driving force that had risen between them like a river overflowing its banks.

She laid her hand across her belly, across the child that grew inside her.

Sure, she could tell him that she had other plans for Friday night. She could send back the ticket. After all, she was healthy and happy, and she already loved her baby with a sharp fierceness.

But what, exactly, was she going to do, long-term? How was she going to raise this child?

Marry me.

Independence was important to her. It was the one thing that she had always carried with her, the one certainty she had clung to, no matter what had happened in her turbulent childhood, in her confused adolescence. She had built a life for herself, built a dream. Self-reliance had made her the woman that she was today.

Marry me.

She'd scoured job sites every day since leaving the foundation, but there weren't a lot of paying opportunities for psychologists focusing on art therapy for foster kids. That was why she'd ended up at AFAA as a project coordinator in the first place. How much longer would it take for her to find something? How much longer would her meager savings hold out?

Even if she spent the five hundred dollars that he'd left, even if she accepted the money as a gift and not an insult.

Marry me.

He couldn't mean it. He had to have spoken out of surprise, the shock at discovering he was going to be a father. Shock. But why *hadn't* Sloane told him? What had she been proving to herself? To him? That she didn't need him? That she didn't need anyone? Once again, she saw the earnest look in his eyes as he proposed to her, his solemn hazel gaze as he turned his own life upside down. He had not hesitated an instant. He had reached out to her with all his strength, all the certainty that had sparked off him at the Eastern during that fateful night. She could learn to depend on that strength. She could learn to bask in it.

Marry me.

She was crazy to even consider it. Crazier than he'd been to offer. But what better option did she have for her baby? How else could she give her child the comfort, stability and security it deserved?

She stared at the gleaming ticket. What could it hurt, going to the ballet? What did she have to lose?

Her stomach growled as she read Ethan's note again. For the first time in days, she was actually hungry. A burger with cheese and bacon sounded wonderful. And for once, she didn't have to worry about whether she could afford an extra large order of fries.

* * *

Ethan forbade himself to check the time once again. Either she would show up or she wouldn't, and staring at his watch wasn't going to change anything.

The musicians were warming up in the orchestra pit. Violins chased each other in discordant flurries. Horns blared repeated trills of notes. Ethan tapped his program against the arm of his chair, wishing that the theater box was large enough for him to pace.

Opting for the best alternative under the circumstances, he stood. He shot his cuffs and glanced at his wrist again, before he remembered that he wasn't going to check the time.

And then the door to the box opened. For one moment, he could only see the dark shadows of the antechamber. Then, a tentative hand reached out, creamy flesh with perfect crimson nails that sent a reflexive shiver down his spine. Sloane followed the promise of that hand, gliding into the light, a dizzying contrast of sophisticated innocence, of steely vulnerability, all enfolded in a demure, floor-length cobalt gown.

He murmured her name, unable to manage more.

She glanced at the half-dozen chairs arrayed in the box, and the shadow of a frown darted across her lips. "Who else is coming?"

"No one," he said. "I wanted to make sure we had some privacy. The box is ours for tonight."

She blushed and looked away from him, obviously nervous. That surprised him. She'd chosen to come here, to accept his peace offering. And she certainly knew what he was capable of, what they were capable of together. He could recall perfectly how she had responded to his touch, how she had trembled when he traced the line of her collarbone with the tip of his tongue. He could remember the instant that she shifted her hips beneath him, that she matched her thighs to his. He could see the arch of her throat as her breathing quickened, as he guided them closer to the edge of their first delicious peak.

And yet there was more to discover with this woman. More to learn about her. About him *with* her. That notion was strangely arousing. Hoping to put her at ease, he said, "I'm glad you're here."

And he was.

Her hair was piled on top of her head in a simple twist, held in place by some invisible woman's magic. The sleek lines made the column of her neck impossibly long. Impossibly vulnerable. His fingers itched to follow the path of the chaste fabric V across her chest. Instead, he settled for gesturing toward her chair, offering her the best seat in the box.

As she stepped forward, he saw that the modest front of her dress lied. The back was cut low, swooping to bare the twin wings of her shoulder blades, the polished marble of her spine. Awareness of that body, of that perfect flesh, shot through him like an electric wire. She took her seat gracefully, apparently unaware of the havoc she was wreaking inside him, the sudden blow she had dealt his composure.

Sloane had known that Ethan would be in a tuxedo. Nevertheless, the formal suit tugged at her memories, catapulted her back to that night at the Eastern. All too easily, she could see his bow tie stripped loose at his throat. She could picture the tiny onyx studs sprung open down his chest, his cuff links freed to reveal the tight muscles of his forearms.

With perfect recall, she could see those satin-striped trousers pooled on the floor, as if he'd just shed them.

But that wasn't what this night was about. That wasn't why she'd agreed to meet Ethan Hartwell here, at the Kennedy Center. She needed to remember her focus. She needed to remember her goal. She needed to remember that her baby deserved medical care and protection, safety and security, things that she could not afford to provide.

Sloane was grateful she'd taken the time to pin up her hair and paint her nails. And she was thrilled that she could still fit into the improbably perfect dress that she'd found years before, at Goodwill, in Chicago.

She'd never been to the Kennedy Center before, had only seen it on television. The rich crimson of the carpet made her feel like a princess. The gold accents on the light fixtures picked out the blond in Ethan's hair, highlighting the unruly strands that made him look like a slightly naughty boy. She blinked, and in the darkness behind her eyelids, she pictured him balanced over her, nothing at all like a boy, supporting himself on his wiry fingers as he whispered her name.

Sudden longing clutched at her belly. Fortunately, the lights dimmed at that very moment, and she was spared the need to say something, to explain. Instead, she filled her lungs with cool, calming air. She leaned back in her chair as the music began to play. She ordered herself to forget about the man who sat beside her, the monumental force that radiated awareness at her side.

The curtain rose.

The music and the dance carried her away, transformed her. She ached with longing as Prince Siegfried rebelled against his forced marriage, as he fell in love with his forbidden princess. She laughed as the swans frolicked, boastfully completing their duets and trios.

She shivered as the evil Odile appeared, as the lovers' eternal happiness was threatened.

And when it was over, when the curtain fell, Sloane leaped to her feet. The audience joined her, roaring its approval, calling for the dancers again and again. A giant spotlight flooded the center of the stage, and the main dancers stepped out from behind the curtain, sinking into graceful bows, collapsing into flawless curtsies.

"Ethan," she said, when the house lights finally came up. "That was incredible!"

She was incredible.

Ethan had stood with the rest of the audience, and he'd added his applause for the dancers. The entire time, though, he was watching Sloane. His gaze had settled on her waist. There was no sign yet of the child that she carried. *His* child.

He wanted that baby to be healthy. He *needed* it to be healthy.

He brushed his fingers against his breast pocket, reassuring himself that the velvet box was still safely hidden away. He could follow through on this. He *had* to follow through. The stakes had gone up exponentially back in Sloane's grimy little apartment. This was no longer a sparring match with his grandmother. This was something more. So much more.

Sloane was biting her lip as she turned her back on the now-curtained stage. He was startled to see tear tracks on her cheeks, silver trails that glistened in the theater's golden light.

He closed the distance between them, settling a hand just beneath her elbow. "What's wrong?"

Sloane raised her hand to her cheek and was somehow surprised when her fingers came away wet. "I—"

she started to say, but her emotions were still perilously close to the surface.

Ethan produced a flawless handkerchief from his pocket, scarcely taking a moment to shake it out before he handed it to her. She smiled her thanks, not ready to trust words yet, and she dabbed the cloth beneath her eyes, careful not to touch her mascara. Thank heavens she'd splurged on the waterproof stuff.

Her emotions had been jangled ever since that night at the Eastern. She slammed her mind closed to the memories that cascaded over her, to the image of sheets as white as the handkerchief she now clutched.

"I thought that we could head up to the roof terrace," Ethan said, smoothly filling the silence, as if she'd been conversing like a normal human being. "The breeze is always nice in June."

He waited until she nodded, and then he gestured to the door, settling one hand against the small of her back. She could feel the heat of his touch through her dress. Somehow, his presence calmed her, gave her strength.

The audience had dispersed, eager to find their way to the garage, to their cars, to their homes. Ethan, though, led her to a deserted bank of elevators. He punched the call button with authority, as if he owned the place. The doors opened immediately, and Sloane imagined that the car had been waiting just for them.

Upstairs, in the rooftop lounge, a kaleidoscope of people spun through a huge white gallery. Waiters hovered with trays of champagne and miniature desserts, ready with a constant supply of napkins. The gala, Sloane remembered belatedly. These people must be donors to the Kennedy Center, to the Bolshoi dance company. Wealthy donors, like the ones who had been so offended by her going off with Ethan after the AFAA auction.

Clearly unaware of her flash of guilty memory, Ethan guided her through the crowd with silent determination. A handful of men glanced at them, nodding like solemn butlers. A half-dozen women were more aggressive, flocking toward Ethan like exotic butterflies, turning from chattering conversation to raise glasses of sparkling wine, to smile open invitations.

One dared to separate herself from the crowd, slinking forward in a crimson dress that looked like woven sin. "Ethan," she cooed, stepping directly in front of him and spreading her talons across his chest. "You promised that you'd call after Chase's party last week. You still owe me dessert." She licked her pouty lips, making it clear exactly what she intended to eat.

Sloane's fingers tightened around the handkerchief she still held. Here it was. The moment when everything changed. The moment when Ethan went back to his playboy ways, to the behavior that made him the darling of every gossip columnist this side of the Rockies.

Ethan, though, merely slid his hand around Sloane's waist, pulling her close in a way that left no doubt about his intent. "I'm sorry, Elaine," he said. "I've been busy."

The woman's face twisted from seduction to cold anger. "Ellen," she spat. "My name is Ellen."

Ethan shrugged, using the motion to pull Sloane even closer. "Ellen," he repeated, as if he were accepting some minor point of clarification in a business meeting. The woman spluttered, obviously lost for words, and then Ethan nodded. "Good evening," he said, concluding the conversation with perfect courtesy.

Three steps farther on, a photographer materialized

from nowhere. "Mr. Hartwell," he said. "Something for the *Washington Banner?*"

"No comment," Ethan snarled, striding forward with a long enough gait that Sloane had to skip three short steps to catch up.

The photographer looked surprised, then angry. He scurried in front of them and took a half-dozen photos, letting his flash spawn a dizzying array of bright white spots. Ethan stepped forward, his shoulders squaring, but the photographer hopped off before the situation could escalate.

Sloane grabbed for Ethan's arm, as much for support while her vision cleared as to calm him down. No one else approached them before they reached the twin glass doors that led to the outdoor terrace. "Something to drink?" he asked, before they could escape.

Sloane nodded.

"Go ahead, then. I'll be out in a moment." He stalked toward the bar before she could change her mind, before she could beg him to stay beside her.

She stepped onto the terrace alone. The June night was balmy, and she stared at the moonlit landscape. This was the beautiful Washington, the vibrant one. Her basement apartment, with its dim light and clunky TV, was a lifetime away from this grace and elegance. She relaxed a bit, watching the golden lights of a boat moving silently up the Potomac River, toward the wealthy enclave of Georgetown. Everything was golden here—lights and laughter and endless, glowing potential.

The doors opened behind her, releasing a clamor from the party within. Sloane tensed at the noise, or at the presence of the man who glided up to her side. Ethan didn't speak as he passed her a glass, a champagne flute. She caught a hint of lime amid the tiny bubbles, and a single sip confirmed that he'd brought her sparkling water. She was grateful that he'd thought of the baby.

He kept a highball glass for himself. His wrist tensed, and he swirled ice cubes in some amber liquor. Scotch, she remembered from the Eastern. The finest single malt the bar could serve. She remembered the smoky echo on his tongue, and her breath caught at the back of her throat.

"Thank you," he said, staring across the water.

"For what?" She was astonished.

"For coming here tonight. For trusting me that much."

She'd trusted him a lot more, back at the Eastern. She'd trusted him the way she'd never trusted another man. But in the past three days, as she'd thought about his offer, about their future, she'd realized that she needed to give him more than just her body. As crazy as it seemed, she needed to give him her future. The future of their child.

She held her glass against the pulse point in her right wrist. She wished that she had the courage to reach for his drink, for the ice cubes that she longed to sacrifice against the fever he lit inside her blood. She wasn't going to acknowledge that heat. She couldn't. This conversation wasn't about that sort of satisfaction.

So far, so good, Ethan thought.

She wasn't running away from him. She hadn't been frightened off by that bird-brained idiot, Elaine.

And Ethan hadn't wasted too much time back inside. Stepping away from the bar, he'd been cornered by Zach Crosby, who had raised an eyebrow at Ethan's two glasses. "You work fast, my man. Who's tonight's lucky lady?"

"Who's asking? My best friend? Or my grandmother's attorney?"

A frown had clouded Zach's face. "You know I can't talk to you about that. I *can* tell you that I advised her against drawing up the papers, though. No hard feelings?"

Ethan had sighed. Zach had been placed in an impossible position. Margaret Hartwell was his biggest client, by far. Besides, the men's friendship had survived a lot worse, from elementary school escapades to college pranks. "No hard feelings," he'd said grudgingly.

"So you'll introduce me to the woman of the hour? Give me a chance to warn her about you?"

"Absolutely not." Ethan had smiled, but he'd continued walking toward the door, toward the balcony where Sloane waited.

"Hey!" Zach had called after him. "What about the silent auction?"

Damn. Zach was in charge of the ballet fundraiser. Ethan had already promised to place a bid, to make a sizable donation. "Put me down for something. You know my limit."

Zach had laughed, and Ethan had escaped to the terrace.

Now, he watched Sloane sip from her champagne flute. Her throat barely rippled as she swallowed. He wanted to trace the liquid with his tongue, to edge aside the dark V that shielded her breasts.

She felt his attention on her. She'd never had any man so aware of her, so focused on her every move. It made her feel…treasured. Protected. Bold enough to say, "What's this all about, Ethan?"

"What do you mean?" A caged wariness flashed into his hazel eyes.

She set her champagne flute on the ground at her feet, as if she could distance herself from the perfect night, from the old dreams that had spun awake as the dancers twirled upon the stage. "I mean, the view is beautiful, and the ballet was gorgeous, and I really appreciate your bringing me here." She let the brightness fade from her voice. "But why do you want to marry me? You're not exactly the type to settle down. We spent *one night* together."

"It was a damned good night," he growled.

The heat behind his words kindled a slow fire inside her, and she had to concentrate to say, "I've read about you, Ethan, over and over again, in all the papers. You've had nights like that before. You've been with lots of other women, but I've never heard of you proposing to one of them."

The simple truth was that not one of those other women had been anything like Sloane. Ethan had thought long and hard since leaving her apartment three days before. *Something* had broken through his usual reserve to make him say those terrifying two words. *Something* had driven him to speak out. *Marry me.*

He'd tried to shrug it off, to tell himself that he was merely overreacting to his grandmother's absurd demand. His grandmother was being manipulative. She was pushing his buttons. She was overstepping her bounds.

But he had a lifetime of practice ignoring his grandmother.

Besides, only a fool would completely ignore a trusted confidante. And as infuriating as Grandmother could be, she *had* raised him. She knew him better than any person in the entire world, better even than Zach. Ethan had seen the honest concern on his grandmother's face; he had recognized the heartsick worry that had softened her to tears when she spoke her mind about his womanizing. If she truly believed that his spending mindless time with a shifting parade of women made him a weaker businessman—a lesser man—then he had to give some credence to what she said. He had to accept the business argument.

And who better to settle down with than the woman who stood beside him? Sloane was *real.* She had true dreams, actual goals. If he closed his eyes, he could still feel her nestled beside him in bed at the Eastern, her body as spent as his but her mind still restless, still intent on sharing, on telling him what she wanted to build, how she wanted to make the world a better place.

Not one of them has been like you. He longed to emphasize his words with a touch. He could see the vulnerable curve of Sloane's jaw. Just trace it with a finger… turn her toward him, tilt her head, slant her lips beneath his own.

But he couldn't touch her now. This had to be about more than simply the lust of his body for hers.

He forced himself to swallow a raw mouthful of Scotch, to substitute one heat with another.

Sloane filled the silence that had stretched out for far too long, making herself say the painful words, the difficult admission that she'd thought about for three straight days. "We had a single night, Ethan. I'm no different than those other women are. I'm not going to hold you to some promise that you made on the spur of the moment. I'm not going to use our baby to force you to do anything you don't really want to do." There. She'd said it. She'd voiced her greatest fear. Whatever Ethan said now, she would know that she had been true to herself. True to her child.

As if in answer, he set his glass next to hers before reaching inside the pocket of his jacket. In the darkness of the terrace, it took a moment to decipher what he took out. The black velvet nearly disappeared into the night. He offered it to her on his open palm, his fingers extended as if he were trying to gentle a wild animal.

She plucked the box from his hand before she was fully aware of what it was. The hinge was stiff; one curious touch threw the box open to the moonlight and the stars. She caught her breath as she saw the most stunning diamond ring she'd ever imagined. An emerald cut, perfect in its simplicity. A platinum band. Two carats, at least.

"Ethan," she breathed, half-afraid that the ring would disappear as she broke its magic spell.

When he'd blurted out his proposal on Tuesday, she hadn't really believed him. She couldn't. Things like that didn't happen to her, had *never* happened to her.

But a diamond ring was different. A diamond ring, offered to her here under the stars, meant that he'd thought this whole thing through. He meant it.

If she passed the paternity test, a nasty voice whispered at the back of her mind. But of course she would pass it. And he'd be a fool to take her word that the baby was his, without medical proof. She'd already seen the swarm of women waiting for his attention back there in the gallery. He had to protect himself.

The negative thought, though, fed her other insecurities. How could she be certain that he would stay with her? Sure, he said that she was different, that the night they'd shared was special. And, in a way, it was. It had resulted in a child. But the baby was one truth, placed in a balance against all the other truths she had learned, all the articles she'd forced herself to read. Ethan Hartwell was not the kind of man who settled down. He wasn't the kind of man who married.

But he was the kind of man who could pay for visits to an obstetrician. And for a pediatrician, after that. And for all the other things that Sloane desired for her baby. For Ethan's baby. For their child together.

She looked down at the stunning engagement ring. Her hands started to shake, hard enough that she was afraid she would drop the velvet box. With a comforting smile, Ethan rescued the ring from its midnight bed. He snapped the box closed, then made it disappear in the pocket of his trousers. His burning fingers grasped hers, steadying her, pouring some iron behind her trembling knees. Carefully, like a surgeon performing a delicate operation, he slid the band onto the ring finger of her left hand.

It fit perfectly. The metal melted into her flesh, as if it had always been a piece of her. The diamond collected all the light in the heavens above, casting it back at her dazed eyes in a thousand tiny flashes.

Ethan thought that the ring looked even better on her hand than he had imagined when he'd selected it at the jewelers. Watching the wonder spread across her face, the wash of joy that echoed the pure physical bliss they'd shared at the Eastern, Ethan folded his hands around hers. She blinked as he covered the brilliance of the ring, almost as if he were breaking some spell. He stepped closer to her, tucking her captured hand against the pleated front of his shirt. He felt the flutter of her pleasure through his palm, measured the solid drumbeat of his own heart through her flesh.

"Sloane Davenport," he said, his voice a husky whisper. "Will you be my wife?"

This time her tears remained unshed, glistening in the night. "Yes," she whispered. "Yes, I will."

He folded his arms around her. Her bare back seared

through his sleeves. He had to hold her, had to feel her, had to crush her against the entire length of his body, so that he could truly believe that this was happening, that she was real. His lips found hers, and he drank deeply, swallowing her incredulous laughter as his tongue demanded more. He closed his teeth against her lower lip with a surge of passion, barely heeding the internal rein that reminded him to be careful, to protect her, to spare the woman who bore his child.

"Ethan," she gasped, finally tearing away from the pressure of his kiss. Her lips felt bruised, swollen, pulsing with the hot blood that he had sucked into them. For a dozen heartbeats, he fought to reclaim her mouth, pressed himself into her, seeking to slake his apparently never-ending thirst.

She couldn't let him, though. She couldn't let herself forget her decision, the why and the wherefore of it. She had to be strong, and true to her baby. "Ethan," she said again, finally managing to lay her palm along his jaw. Her left palm. With the diamond ring winking beside his midnight stubble. "I'll marry you, but there's one condition."

"Yes," he said immediately, the single word a promise and a plea.

She bit back a smile. "No." She shook her head. "You need to listen to me. You need to decide."

His fingers clenched on her hips, but she held his gaze steadily. She had to say this. Had to make sure that her heart knew precisely what she was doing and why she was doing it. She had to make everything absolutely clear.

If she had learned nothing else working on the Hope Project, she had learned this: Children deserved to be with families that loved them. Families that functioned healthily, without parental angst, without adult trials and tribulations constantly undermining stability. All of the art projects in the world could never create what every baby should have from birth: a stable, loving home.

And Sloane couldn't think of anything more likely to turn a relationship upside down than sex. Sex with Ethan had been wonderful, more fulfilling than she'd ever dreamed. But it had made her lose sight of her goals. Sleeping with Ethan had cost her a job. She wasn't going to let a physical relationship take away more—not when her child was at risk.

"If I marry you, Ethan, it can't be because of what happened at the Eastern. It can't be because of…this." She looked down, managing to convey both their bodies, the crumpled clothes between them. "It can't be about… about sex. I won't go to bed with you until after we're married. We both need that break. That separation. We both need to be certain that we're getting married for the right reason—for our baby."

He understood what she was doing. Despite her finding the courage to meet him tonight, she was unnerved by their passion, by the animal need that had drawn them together, that hummed between them, even now, like the echo of a gong.

But that was why he'd been drawn to her in the first place, wasn't it? The freshness of her innocence. The honesty that she'd brought to bed with her. That was what had intrigued him, made him realize that she was different from every other woman he'd ever had. It had been a pure bonus to discover that there was more to Sloane than a beautiful face, a gorgeous body. Her passion for her work had been like a decadent dessert after a sating meal—stunning because it was unnecessary. Unexpected.

If only Sloane still wanted *him,* after she learned the truth about his Hartwell genes. If only she kept her promise to marry him after the fourteenth week, after the testing that would disclose whether Ethan was as cursed as his own parents had been, twice. He couldn't let himself think about that, though. Couldn't think about losing Sloane.

Better to play the role she was expecting. Better to pretend that he knew there would always be a happy ending. Better to give in to the passion that he could barely restrain when she was anywhere near.

He raised her wrist to his mouth. His lips hovered above her trembling pulse, barely touching her throbbing flesh. He heard the moan that she caught at the back of her throat, and then he darted out his tongue to taste her. He clamped his fingers around her arm when she jumped away in surprise, and he used the motion to pull her close to his chest.

"You'll change your mind," he said. "After a few weeks? Months? How long do you think it will take to plan a wedding?" He leaned down and whispered against her lips, "I promise. You *will* change your mind."

She shook her head, her eyes gone round. "I won't," she whispered. "I can't."

"You will," he said. "You already have. And when you admit that, you'll have to tell me. You'll have to ask for what you truly want."

She shook her head, her throat working, but no words rose to the surface.

He pulled back, settling for planting one last kiss in the palm of her hand. "Remember this," he said. "Remember now. You will."

Chapter Three

When Sloane awoke, her bedroom was dark, even though the clock said 9:27 a.m. She sighed and rolled onto her back. It must be raining outside. She usually got *some* glimmer of light from the front room.

She flicked on the bedside lamp, and her gaze was snagged by the ring on her finger. Collapsing against her pillow, she turned her wrist in the wan yellow light. It was real, then. Not some fevered dream.

Ethan had proposed to her. And she had accepted.

It had seemed like magic the night before, edged in fog, lost in impossibility. Following Ethan's smooth certainty that she would keep their relationship physical, that she would yield to the powerful temptation he provided every time he was within a hundred yards, Sloane had insisted on returning home alone. She'd needed to make that point. Needed to prove something to him. To herself.

With a tolerant smile, Ethan had acquiesced, instructing his driver to ferry her through the city streets. She supposed that he'd taken a cab to his own home. Sloane had walked from the dark Town Car to her front door, certain that she was going to wake up at any moment, positive that she was going to discover this was all some strange dream. But the ring was still on her finger, even in the gloomy light of a rainy summer morning. She was engaged to be married.

Sloane Hartwell.

Mrs. Ethan Hartwell.

She tested the names against the brittle edge of her emotions. Getting engaged was supposed to be one of the highlights of her life. She was supposed to call her mother, her girlfriends. Well, no mother to call, that was for sure. And no real girlfriends, either. Unless she wanted to count the librarian who helped out with the public access computers. As a child, she had never brought friends home to her foster families; life had been too chaotic. As an adult, she had been focused on juggling college and work, on fighting for the Hope Project to become a reality. While Sloane had plenty of acquaintances, she was poorer than she liked to admit when it came to true friends.

She sighed and settled her ringed hand on her belly. "Well, little one. We'll just have to be happy for each other, won't we?"

As if in answer, her stomach rumbled, reminding Sloane that she'd been too nervous to eat dinner the night before. She threw her feet over the side of her bed and tugged on her ratty terry-cloth bathrobe. The fabric had rubbed completely bare across the elbows, but there was never anyone around to notice, so she hadn't bothered to replace it.

Stumbling into the kitchen, Sloane filled the teakettle and put it on the stove. It took three tries before the burner lit; she'd have to call her landlord to have him fix the silly thing. Again. She glanced at the minute patch of window left visible beside the hulking air conditioner. She'd been right—it *was* raining, the steady tropical downpour that often hit D.C. in the summer.

As she waited for the water to boil, she heard a rustle outside her front door. Her landlord's cat had probably gotten trapped in the alcove, driven to seek a dry corner in the midst of the torrential rain. The sweet calico had sought refuge from summer storms before. Sloane could let her nap on the couch until the storm passed. Sloane braced herself to get her feet wet as she completed Operation Cat Rescue.

"Sloane!"

"Ms. Davenport!"

"Sloane Davenport!"

The alcove was filled with people, with the flash of cameras, with a half-dozen microphones. Sloane stared at them, slack jawed. Where had they come from? And what could they possibly want with her?

One voice soared above the others, as harsh as pumice. "Sloane, show us your ring! Tell us how you caught the most eligible guy in town!"

Reflexively, she clutched at her robe, pulling it across her belly. Even as she glanced down, frantic to make sure that she was covered, that no one could see her faded pink nightgown, she realized that she might be sending some sort of signal to the press, telegraphing the presence of the baby. She dropped the terry, as if it had burned her fingers.

All the while, cameras continued to flash, and the crowd jostled for position on the three narrow steps.

Sloane's throat started to close; she couldn't draw a full breath. She didn't want these people here, didn't want them anywhere near her.

A terrific flash of lightning, brighter even than the cameras in her face, made her squeeze her eyes closed. Instinct made her hunch her shoulders close to her ears, waiting for the inevitable boom of thunder. When it came, it drowned out the reporters' chatter. All of a sudden, she remembered the way Ethan had handled the photographer the night before. She took a deep breath, determined to make her voice as steely as possible. "No comment," she said.

She closed the door before anyone could protest, before someone could tell her that *she* didn't have the right to refuse to talk. The teakettle chose that moment to reach its boiling point, the shriek of its whistle sounding like a train racing toward her. She rescued the kettle before it could deafen her permanently, setting it onto a cold burner before she crept back to the front door.

Leaning against the wooden panels, she could hear the horde shifting outside. They called her name a half-dozen times, as if she might change her mind and come back out to play. There was only one thing to do. It took her a couple of minutes to find Ethan's business card. She had stashed it in the folder with her working papers for the Hope Project. Her fingers were trembling by the time she punched in the ten digits.

"Ethan Hartwell's office," a woman answered on the first ring.

Sloane gritted her teeth. Given the fact that it was a Saturday morning, she had hoped Ethan might answer his own phone. Feeling absurd, she said, "This is Sloane Davenport, calling for Mr. Hartwell." What sort of woman called her fiancé Mr. Anything?

"I'll see if Mr. Hartwell is in his office." The secretary didn't give the faintest hint of recognizing her name. Classical music filled the silence, and Sloane fought the urge to hang up.

"Sloane." Ethan's voice was warm as honey. "Good morning." He managed to make the standard greeting sound seductive.

That unspoken promise in his tone shattered her taut emotions. "Ethan!" His name turned into a sob.

"What's wrong?" His demand was immediate. "Sloane, are you all right? Is it the baby?"

"No," she gasped, shocked into realizing what a fright she was giving him. "No, I'm sorry. I…it's just the people. Paparazzi. They're outside. I heard them out there, thought it was my landlord's cat. I shouldn't have opened the door. They won't leave me alone!"

Ethan swore, the words low and fluid and unerringly precise.

"I don't know how they found out about us," Sloane cried. "I don't know what I did!"

Even as anger flashed crimson behind Ethan's eyes, he consciously gentled his voice. "You didn't do anything, Sloane. This isn't your fault."

"But how…" She trailed off, and he could hear her gasping for a full breath, struggling to regain control.

"This isn't your fault," he repeated. But he knew whose fault it was. He knew that his driver last night was new, had only been hired two weeks before. The man had been cleared by Hartwell Genetics's security team, and he'd possessed all the required credentials, up to and including U.S. Marines evasive driving training. But that didn't mean the guy was above selling information—especially valuable gossip, like a Hartwell date going home with a diamond ring on her left hand.

Ethan wondered how much the driver had gotten from the rabid press corps. Not enough. The man would never work in D.C. again.

But none of that mattered. Not now. Not with Sloane sobbing on the other end of the line.

"I'm sorry," he said. "I thought you'd have more time."

"More time?" There. That was more like it. She was already getting herself under control. Just as well—she wasn't going to like the rest of this conversation.

"You saw the photographer at the gala last night. Now that your name is out there, it'll be like blood in the water. The sharks won't back off until they've fed."

"Ethan, why do they care about *me?* I'm no one!"

"You're someone to me," he said. He thought about adding a smooth line, something to make her blush. He was certain that he'd be able to tell that she was flustered, even over the phone. But this wasn't the time. He might as well rip off this Band-Aid. It was going to be the first of many. "I'm sending over a man, Daniel Alton. He's the head of corporate security here."

"Ethan, I don't think that's necessary."

"I do." He wasn't in any mood to listen to arguments. Not when he knew he'd win them all in the long run. "Daniel will canvass your apartment. His assessment will help the movers."

"Movers?" He heard the shock in her voice, but he steeled himself against her protest.

"Pack a suitcase now, whatever you need for the next twenty-four hours. Daniel will bring you to my home this morning. The rest of your belongings will be transferred tomorrow."

Sloane glanced at the telephone handset. He had to

be kidding. Pack an overnight bag and leave her entire life behind? "Ethan, I can't do that."

"Yes," he said. "You can."

She could picture him now, standing behind whatever massive table passed for a desk in his office. He would have taken off his suit jacket when he arrived at work. His stark white sleeves were rolled up, revealing the dusting of golden hair on his forearms.

Forget about his forearms!

Sloane swallowed a strangled noise. She tested her voice inside her head before she spoke, and when she delivered her words they were measured. Even. "I agreed to marry you, Ethan. I didn't agree to let you run my life. And I certainly didn't agree to enter a prison."

She expected him to argue with her. She expected him to thread steel into his voice. She expected him to respond with the utter control, the absolute mastery she'd already seen him exercise in other aspects of his life.

She was unprepared for the catch in his throat as he said, "I know you didn't, Sloane." Quickly, though, his words grew urgent, intense. "I need to keep you safe, though. I want to keep you away from those reporters, from people who will take away your freedom. Our freedom. Trust me on this. Move into my house. Let me protect you. You and the baby."

The baby.

That was the key, wasn't it? If Sloane were alone, she could do whatever she wanted.

But she wasn't making decisions just for herself anymore. She couldn't act blindly. She'd lost that ability when she'd chosen to follow Ethan to his hotel suite, when she'd given in to the fiery compulsion, to the impossible certainty that he was the man she wanted to be with, *needed* to be with.

When she'd said that she would marry him.

"Okay," she said.

Ethan exhaled slowly, all of a sudden aware that he'd been holding his breath. "Thank you, Sloane." He shuddered and shifted back to professional mode. "Daniel will be there in an hour. He'll call from his cell when he's outside your door."

By the time Ethan hung up the phone, he was already reviewing everything that needed to be done. One call to Daniel, dispatching him to Sloane's apartment. Another call to the house, telling James to prepare the guest suite. He paused, then, his fingers poised over the speed-dial button, as he weighed making a third call.

By now, Grandmother had to know that Sloane existed. There was certainly some notice on the newspaper gossip page, probably a picture from that obnoxious photographer at the gala. But Grandmother was used to reading about his liaisons, used to discounting them. She wouldn't believe that Ethan had actually chosen a wife until he told her, himself. And she would never imagine that her long-awaited great-grandchild was truly on the way.

Sloane had enough on her plate for now, without meeting the Hartwell matriarch. Ethan *could* give his fiancée a reprieve, and so he would. Just like with the genetic testing.

Grandmother might be unhappy when she learned the truth. But Sloane's happiness was far more important to Ethan now. Grandmother would just have to wait.

Sloane knew she should be grateful. Precisely as Ethan had described, Daniel retrieved her from her apartment, lifting her suitcase with one hand, firmly grasping her elbow with the other. He led her past the soaking-wet reporters, growling the "no comment" that she'd already come to understand was now her standard way of life. He settled her in the back of yet another Town Car, taking the driver's seat himself.

James greeted her at the house. Sloane had to smile. The older man looked like somebody's uncle. He wore neat khakis and a polo shirt that barely managed to cover his potbelly. He took Sloane's bag from Daniel, nodding an amiable dismissal, and then he ushered her into the kitchen. A cup of chamomile tea and a fresh-baked cinnamon roll later, Sloane was almost ready to believe that being transplanted to Ethan's home was a good thing.

She had the better part of the day to think about it, and the evening besides. Ethan sent a message through James. Some production matter had come up at the Swiss plant, and he was going to be late coming home.

A production matter. On a Saturday.

Sloane shivered in the aggressive air conditioning.

What was she getting into? Who was this man she had agreed to marry? A workaholic who spent his entire life at the office? She needed better for their baby. She would fight for more.

James showed Sloane into the library. He helped her log on to a laptop computer kept for the convenience of guests. She sighed at the springy touch of the keyboard, so unlike the brick that she'd rescued from her own apartment. She was eager to get back to work on the Hope Project. But tomorrow would be soon enough. She had even more important work to do. She needed to organize her thoughts.

Taking a deep breath, she clicked on the button that

launched a word processor. Half an hour later, she was still staring at an empty document. What, exactly, did she want from Ethan? What did she expect to get out of their marriage? And why was she so afraid to commit anything to a silly computer file?

Ethan Hartwell, she finally typed across the top of the screen. To delay a little more, she retyped his name, in all capitals. She made the font bold, and she underscored the two words, hitting the enter key twice to place the cursor at the beginning of a new line.

Unable to delay further, she typed a new word. *Trust.* She needed to trust Ethan. Needed to believe that he would always be there for her and the baby, that his days of playboy escapades were over forever.

Respect, she added. She needed Ethan to respect her. To appreciate what was important to her—the Hope Project, for example—even if he never fully embraced it himself.

Friendship, she typed. She stared at the cursor blinking after the word. What did she mean by friendship? She didn't have enough practice to understand the concept herself. Shaking her head, she backspaced carefully.

Partnership, she wrote instead. She and Ethan needed to be equals. They needed to talk, to share, to accept each other on level ground.

Trust. Respect. Partnership.

That sounded more like a formula for a business arrangement than for a marriage. But what else could she type? "True love"? How could she demand that? How could Ethan promise it? True love was something that either happened or it didn't; it couldn't be subject to negotiation.

Sloane sighed, and then she typed something else, at

the bottom of her list. A date—a deadline for their wedding. The baby was due at the end of December. Add three months to get back in shape. Another three months to actually plan the wedding. June 1 of next year. That was the earliest that they could get married, the first possible date that made any sense at all.

Sloane leaned back against her rich leather chair. Here it was: a foundation for her entire relationship with Ethan. She glanced at the broad desk situated beneath the mullioned windows. A wireless printer waited to do her bidding. A flurry of keystrokes, and she had a crisp sheet of paper in hand. She read over her words one last time before she folded the document into thirds and tucked it into her purse.

Just as she was beginning to get hungry, James appeared with a chicken sandwich on a tray. He seemed to understand that Sloane needed time alone though, time to process the changes in her life. He left her in the mahogany-and-leather library until nearly sunset, when he carried in another tray, this one sporting a lightly dressed shrimp salad. "Sloane," he said, interrupting her as she checked her email. "I'll be heading home for the evening."

"Home?"

He gestured out the window, across the spacious yard. "I live in the carriage house, out back."

"I thought—" She'd just assumed that James lived in the house. He clearly was responsible for every aspect of the mansion's smooth operation. Sloane had already come to count on his presence. She'd even considered that James would be a sort of chaperone as she got used to living with the man she was going to marry.

"This works out better for everyone," he said, with a twinkle in his eye. "A little privacy can go a long way.

Every phone in the main building has a direct line to the carriage house. Just press zero if you need me, and it will ring out there."

Sloane nodded, but she couldn't imagine having a property large enough to sport a carriage house. And she certainly couldn't imagine having a—what? A butler? A housekeeper? A *friend?*—at her beck and call. "Thank you," she said a little belatedly. "I appreciate everything you've done for me."

"It's not often that we have such a lovely visitor in the guest suite." James winked and left her to her own devices.

Lovely visitor. Ha. Ethan Hartwell had plenty of lovely visitors. Sloane wasn't about to forget that.

But James had no doubt chosen his words carefully. *In the guest suite* he'd said. Ethan's usual "lovely visitors" must not stay in the suite. Ethan probably sent them home in the dark of night, before they could get any ideas about settling in for a long stay.

Sloane closed her eyes, letting her memories catapult her back to the terrace at the Kennedy Center. She remembered the shock of electricity that had jolted through her as Ethan kissed her palm, the liquid heat that had tempted her to change her mind then and there, to dismiss the promise that he had just made, the promise to curb the need that shimmered between them like a physical thing.

No. She was right to insist on that restraint. She had to prove to Ethan that there was something more between them, something deeper than the pure physical attraction that sparked whenever they were in the same room. She needed to be certain—for herself, and for the baby.

Sloane closed the laptop, making sure that it was

firmly latched. She'd grab a book and head upstairs to her room. There was no telling when Ethan was coming home, and she certainly wasn't going to wait up for him like an overeager puppy. Or a mistress. Heading over to the shelves that she'd studied so many times that day, she picked up *Cannery Row.* She'd never read the Steinbeck classic, and it looked light. Enjoyable.

James had left a trail of lights on, guiding her from the library to her suite of rooms. Stepping over the threshold, she took a deep breath, filling her lungs with the scent of roses. A riot of three-dozen long-stemmed beauties overflowed a cut-crystal vase on the dresser. White, pink, yellow and peach. Someone had studiously avoided sending any message with red.

Had Ethan ordered the flowers? Or had James taken care of the detail, just another one of his homey services? Were not-red roses the standing order of the day where "lovely visitors" were concerned?

She could see that James had turned down the sheets on the king-size bed. She half expected to find a mint left on her pillow. Shaking her head, she turned to unpack her suitcase. She'd been lazy all afternoon; she should have hung up her clothes before now. Well, better late than never.

Except that her suitcase was nowhere to be found.

She looked on either side of the bed. Under the massive wooden frame. Behind the bedroom door.

At last, realization dawned on her. She crossed to the large closet that James had indicated when he'd first shown her around the house. Opening the door, she discovered a room that was nearly as large as the entire apartment she'd left behind.

And there, huddling like refugees in a border camp, were her clothes. A quick check of the bathroom confirmed that her drugstore toiletries were displayed on the counter like crown jewels, looking sad amid luxurious towels and gleaming fixtures. Sloane shook her head. This was too much. It was all too much.

After finishing in the bathroom, she sighed deeply as she climbed into the bed. The mattress was twice the size of the beaten-up old bed in her apartment. The peach-and-honey-colored sheets were crisp and cool, even on this muggy June night. A featherweight comforter settled over her body with a whisper.

She lay back on the pillow and forced herself to take a dozen deep breaths. She imagined the picture she would draw if she could fire up her computer, if she could use the Hope Project's specialized software. There'd be a mommy and a daddy and a baby, all standing on Ethan's front lawn, all happy and healthy and together.

The wind picked up outside, and a tree's wooden fingers scraped against her window, shattering the bright image she was painting inside her mind. It was going to be a long, long night.

Ethan paused outside the door of the guest suite. He glanced at his watch. A few minutes past two. Well, no reason that he *should* expect to see a glint of light under the door, was there?

He sighed in frustration. This wasn't the way he'd planned on having Sloane arrive at his home. Oh, it certainly seemed that things had gone smoothly once Daniel had gotten her out of that godforsaken apartment. He hoped that she wasn't going to insist on bringing along any of her furniture; none of it deserved even a brief afterlife in some college dorm room.

James had reported that Sloane had settled in well.

With the nonstop rain, she shouldn't have minded being cooped up in the house. Too much.

But Ethan regretted having spent the entire day at the office. The Swiss production problem should never have taken so long to resolve. At least everything would be back online by Monday morning.

In fact, he'd managed to turn the Zurich fiasco into a good thing. Grandmother had insisted on heading over there to monitor the new quality assurance process for a few days. The quick trip would be a win-win. His grandmother could exercise her iron will over the Swiss plant, and the foreign engineers would learn just how serious Hartwell Genetics was about its demands. At first, Ethan had worried about the strain of travel, but that concern faded after he managed to convince Grandmother to spend a few weeks in her Paris apartment before she came home.

Those would be a few weeks that Ethan could spend getting his own life in order, getting past the all-important genetic testing with Sloane. He carefully hid his true concerns, convincing his grandmother that he only wanted Pierre and Jeanette to pamper her in her luxurious Seventh Arrondissement home. Looking out at the Eiffel Tower, she could get all the rest that she deserved.

Rest. He could use some himself. He should go to bed, get some sleep, wait to see Sloane in the morning. But he couldn't resist opening her door.

The sight inside made him catch his breath.

Sloane had kicked the summer comforter onto the floor where it huddled at the foot of her bed like a lumpy ghost. Her sheets were tangled, nearly tied into knots. Even in the silvery moonlight, he could see that her feet were caught in the twisted mess. Her hair was splayed across her pillow, like seaweed trailing on a beach. Somewhere in her sleep, she must have heard his soft grunt of amazement. She rolled from her side to her back, her arms lashing out in the darkness. "No," she moaned, rubbing at her face. "Please. No."

He stepped into the room before he was consciously aware of moving. As if she could sense his presence, Sloane grew more agitated. Her breath caught in a sob, and she pushed away the confining chains of her sheets. Her fingers snagged in the colorless cotton of her nightgown, and she struggled like a desperate child.

The scent of roses filled the room. He saw the flowers that he'd ordered, faded to gray in the moonlight. He thought he'd been so clever, choosing chaste flowers. He had thought it would be their joke, their secret, a floral memory of the silly, brave promise she'd extracted from him the night before. Now, though, the roses looked like rotten rags and their perfume reminded him of a funeral parlor.

The dead oak tree outside the window swayed in a sudden breeze, scraping its branches against the window. The sound grated like fingers on a chalkboard, and it raised the hairs on the back of his neck. The screech must have penetrated Sloane's nightmare, because she started sobbing in earnest, her words drowned in hopeless, helpless sorrow.

He was beside the bed before he could think.

"Hush," he whispered, settling his palm against her cheek.

She fought like a wild thing, thrashing against the sheets, flinging herself away from him. "Sloane," he murmured, trying to wake her gently, to ease her out of her nightmare. He gathered up the sheets that bound her, shoving them toward the foot of the bed. Her feet were still tangled, and he edged his hands past her thighs, along her calves, fighting to free her ankles. "Sloane," he said again, sitting on the edge of the bed, folding his arms around her, gathering her close to his chest. "I'm here. It's all right. You were having a bad dream."

She shook her head, still dazed, obviously confused. He tightened his grip, pulling her onto his lap. Her head rested on his shoulder; her fingers clutched at the crisp broadcloth of his shirt. "Hush," he said again. "I'm here. You're fine."

The oak fingers scraped against the window again, and she tensed in his arms. He fought the urge to swear out loud. The damned tree had been struck by lightning the summer before. James had hoped that it would recover, but Ethan would have it cut down in the morning.

"It's just a tree," he said. "Just a dream." He started rocking her, gently easing his hand down the trembling plane of her back. He was relieved when her sobs quieted, when her breathing started to slow.

Sloane forced her fingers to loosen their death grip on Ethan's shirt. What had she been thinking? How had she gotten so lost inside her dream? Even now, the nightmare was fading; she could scarcely remember the horror that she'd been fighting. She was awake enough to feel foolish, absolutely idiotic as she sat on Ethan's lap, clutching him as if she were a child, listening to him whisper meaningless phrases.

She didn't feel like a child, though. Ethan's fingers were firm. His right hand gripped her steadily, keeping her anchored, secure. His left palm stroked her back with a soothing pressure.

No. Not soothing. There was more than that.

His flesh spoke to hers. He had dragged her back from the brink of a nightmare, his steady hands returning her to her body. He had brought her to wakefulness, and then to something more.

Another stroke. Her spine quivered, eager to meet his touch. Heat leached through her body and she sighed, releasing the last tendrils of her dream. She melted beneath his ministrations, soaking into him. She shifted, trying to put her arms around his neck.

He froze. His fingers gripped her tight, tattooing the flesh above her hips. She heard him catch his breath, felt every muscle of his body harden into iron.

Ethan grimaced in the dark. One minute, he'd been offering chaste comfort, trying to ease a frightened soul. The next, that frightened soul had sprung to full, sensual life beneath his fingertips, arching to meet his hand, reflexively seeking the pleasure they'd shared in the past.

The last thing Sloane needed now, though, was to realize just how much pleasure he longed to give her. The last thing she needed was to discover how completely she'd aroused him, how hard he was, just beneath her warm, supple flesh, with only a few layers of fabric between them. "Sloane," he breathed, as she pulled back enough to look into his eyes.

"Please," she said, her voice still faintly blurred from sleep. "Kiss me."

The trust in her moonlit gaze nearly made him lose control. It would be so easy to shift her. So easy to fall back on the mattress beside her. So easy to rip away that cotton thing she was wearing, to see her body, ready and ripe, waiting for him, *eager* for him.

The unbearably rough fabric of his silk boxers taunted him. The feel of her across his lap was almost enough to spring him, to release him from the delicious tension that threatened all his logic, all his higher senses.

Sure, he had told her that she was the one in control.

He had said that she must ask him before he'd give in to his temptation. And he'd heard her words, just a heartbeat before, heard her beg him to touch his lips to hers.

But this wasn't right. This wasn't how he'd envisioned her coming to him. Inviting him, giving up her silly, stubborn rules. She was still dazed, confused by her dream. She wasn't capable of making a true decision.

Summoning the last vestige of his control, he lifted her from his lap. The motion brought him dangerously close to her throat, to the devastatingly smooth stretch of flesh that begged to be tasted, nibbled, nipped. Clenching his teeth, he settled her on the bed. Before she could register the change in their positions, before she could protest, he got to his feet, sucking in his breath against his body's own complaint. He was actually in pain as he made himself move to the far side of the bed, as he gathered up her sheets, as he aired out the linen between them, using it as a shield.

By the time the fabric had drifted on top of her, by the time it had billowed and collapsed and revealed her lithe form, he had enough control over himself that he could speak without groaning. "There's a night-light in the bathroom. I'll turn it on." He matched action to narration, relieved to find that he could walk without betraying his arousal. With half the room between them, he dared to look back at her. She was propped up on her pillows, enthroned like some sort of devastating princess. He could just make out the blue of her eyes in the glow of the night-light from the marble room.

"I'll have James call someone about the tree tomorrow."

"Thank you," she said, and he could hear the confusion in her voice, the question that she was afraid to ask, the invitation that she wanted to issue again. The invitation that he could not accept honorably. Not that night. Not under those circumstances.

"Good night, Sloane," he said as he crossed to her bedroom door.

"Good night," she whispered.

He closed the door behind him as softly as he could. A part of him longed to stand there, to listen until he heard her even breaths, to peek in once she was safely dreaming.

Another part of him, though, knew that he would never be able to walk out of that room again. Not without claiming everything she had to offer. Not without taking away the promise he had given her the night that she had agreed to become his wife.

He curled his hands into fists and made his way down the hall to his own lonely room.

Chapter Four

Sloane poured herself a cup of peppermint tea from the pot that James had set on the countertop. The man had greeted her cheerfully when she padded into the kitchen, her clothes cautiously chosen, hair carefully brushed. A cardamom coffee cake rested on the center island, fragrant as it cooled to eating temperature.

"I hope that you slept well," James said, gesturing for her to pull up one of the nearby bar stools.

Sloane settled onto the comfortable chair and forced herself to take a soothing sip of tea. She wished she could have a healthy dose of caffeine, something to help her wake up after her long night of tossing and turning. She made some noncommittal noise, though. There was no reason to tell James about her strange dreams. No reason to mention Ethan's late-night visit. Before she could weave a polite lie, though, Ethan's unexpected voice sliced across the kitchen. "I want that oak tree down by nightfall, James."

Sloane's gaze shot up from her stoneware mug. Her stomach flipped at the sight of Ethan, framed in the doorway to the kitchen. She'd seen him in a tuxedo, of course. Twice. And in a business suit. But this was the first time she'd seen him in casual clothes. His jeans were snug around his waist, just tight enough to suggest the muscles she knew stretched beneath them. His arms were akimbo, as if he expected to be challenged about the tree. She swallowed hard, trying not to think about the hard abs beneath his hunter-green shirt, the pecs that she had felt under her cheek the night before.

"Of course," James said, his voice calm and respectful. "I'll make the call now."

"It's Sunday," Sloane said. She couldn't imagine what an emergency tree crew would charge on a weekend. "Surely it can wait until tomorrow."

"No," Ethan contradicted. "It can't." He nodded to James, and the caretaker hurried away to solve the problem. Sloane drowned her discomfort in another sip of peppermint tea.

Ethan took advantage of the uneasy silence to pick up the palm-size box on the corner of the center island, the one he had deposited there when he'd returned home from the office the night before. "Here," he said, passing it across to Sloane. She looked up in surprise, peering at him over the rim of her mug. The pose made her look impish. Attractive, in a coltish way.

Damn! What *didn't* make her look attractive? For the hundredth time, he wondered where he'd found the willpower to walk away from her the night before, to honor his promise to stay chaste.

"What's this?" she asked.

"A cell phone. One where the paparazzi can't track you down. My private number is already programmed in."

She picked up the phone with an air of caution. "It's Sunday morning. I just called you yesterday, and you worked until midnight. When did you have time to pick up a new phone?"

He snorted. "That one came under the category of 'security.' Daniel took care of it when he got back to the office, after bringing you here." He reached into his back pocket, taking out his sleek leather wallet. An extra credit card was nestled beside his own. "Now *this* took a little more doing."

He passed the silver card to her. Recognition dawned as she read her name in the raised letters across the bottom. "You can't—" she started to protest.

"I have." He shook his head firmly. "It's a lot easier than my leaving hundred-dollar bills lying around, isn't it?"

There. She was blushing again. He *knew* that he'd made a mistake when he'd left her the money. Then again, if his misstep could bring that defiant sparkle to her eyes…

"Ethan," she said, trying to give him back the card. "Really. This is too much."

He closed his fingers over hers, trying to ignore the hum that her skin ignited in his. "Don't say that. You're going to need it. You have a lot of work ahead of you."

"Work?"

"Daniel took care of the press yesterday. And they definitely know better than to try to get in here." He paused, giving her a moment to think about what he was going to say. He felt guilty for having created the public spectacle that had already changed her life. His past was catching up with him—all those nights of flirting with the press, of tweaking his grandmother's sensibilities, just because he could. If he hadn't invested so much energy and effort into squiring meaningless women around town…

But he hadn't known that he'd meet anyone worth leaving the games behind. He hadn't known Sloane Davenport.

"You're going to need a whole new wardrobe," he said. "Invitations will come in once we announce the engagement, once we make it more official than this morning's gossip columns. Cocktail parties, dinner parties… Your dance card will be full. Buy what you want. Just make sure that one outfit is…sedate."

"Sedate?" She almost laughed, almost thought that he was teasing. But she could hear the tension in his voice. "Why sedate?"

He swallowed hard. "You'll wear it to meet my grandmother. She can be…a challenge."

Sloane almost laughed at the uneasy expression on Ethan's face. She wasn't afraid of Margaret Hartwell. She'd learned all about the woman, before the AFAA charity auction. As project coordinator, Sloane had discovered Margaret's favorite drink was gin and tonic, with extra ice and three limes. She knew that Margaret preferred ballpoint pens to roller balls, that she chose black ink over blue. Margaret's favorite color was green, and her birthday was January 5.

"I'm sure I'll find something she'll approve of," Sloane said. Even if she had to look in the maternity section of the store.

Ethan nodded, as if he were checking off another item on his efficient to-do list. She watched as he crossed the kitchen, then opened a drawer to select a knife. He carved up James's coffee cake with flawless efficiency, placing a generous slice on a plate and passing it to her.

"Oh, that's too much," she said. "I don't usually eat breakfast."

"Well, that will change now."

She bristled at his peremptory tone. "I can decide what I want to eat and what I don't want to eat."

"You could, when you were making decisions for yourself. You've got the baby to think about now."

She made a face. "And the *baby* wants me to eat cardamom coffee cake?"

"Good point. I'll tell James to forget about baking for the next six months. Protein will be good for all of us."

She thought about arguing—she *liked* cardamom coffee cake—but she knew that Ethan was right. In fact, she was secretly pleased that he was concerned about her and the baby's health. And she loved the way that he said "all of us." Loved it so much that she almost missed his question. "Did you get any sleep at all?"

The question was innocent enough—almost the same as James had asked—but it made her remember the feeling of Ethan's arms around her, the heat of his hands burning through her cotton nightgown. She couldn't control the blush that painted her cheeks as she fumbled for an answer. "Yes," she managed. "After a while." After he'd left. After the blood pounding in her veins had finally calmed to a dull roar. She forced herself to meet his gaze. "Thank you," she said.

Thank you for waking me from my nightmare, she meant. Thank you for holding me when I felt like a lost child. Thank you for leaving, when I forgot my promise to myself, when I forgot that I can't have you. Not until we're actually married. Until I'm certain that this is real.

She wanted to say all that. All that and more. But the words jumbled together inside her head, tumbling over one another, until she wasn't sure that she could ever make him understand.

"You're welcome," he said gravely.

She sighed in contentment. He *did* understand. Just as he had when they'd spent hour after hour sharing their thoughts, their secrets, their dreams.

He kept his eyes on hers as he said, "New beds can take some getting used to."

There. That was another conversational gift. He was giving her an option. She could take the easy way out and say something simple and sly and sexy about new beds. They'd laugh together. She'd probably blush.

But he was inviting her to tell him something more. He was opening the door to a deeper conversation, to an admission about the roots of her nightmare. She swallowed hard, then raised her chin, meeting his eyes with a new-forged determination that felt almost like defiance. "You'd think I would have learned to adjust when I was a kid. I was in and out of a lot of foster homes."

She saw the way he was listening to her. She was certain that he'd been about to pour himself a cup of coffee. Instead, he took a casual seat on one of the high stools, hooking his toes under the footrest. His voice was mild as he said, "That must have been difficult."

Trust, Sloane had written. She wanted to trust the man who was going to be her husband. Respect. Partnership.

She needed to make those words happen before she could even tell him that she'd put them on the list, that she'd created a list in the first place. Trust. She raised her chin and said, "There was a woman I used to call Angry Mother."

Ethan merely met her gaze. Sloane hurried on, before she could think about the fact that she had never told anyone about Angry Mother. "That was my third foster home. The house was a wreck, and the windows were all crooked inside their frames. It was freezing at night, all of January, of February. And every morning, Angry Mother told me I was bad, because I tried to sleep in my blue jeans. She put me back in the system because of that. She said I wasn't good enough to keep."

"I'm sorry," Ethan whispered. "No child should have to experience that sort of thing."

It hurt him to see the way that she swallowed, the way that she fought to meet his gaze. Then and there, he promised himself that he would never do anything to make her look that bleak again. Gently, he said, "Your parents..." He trailed off, giving her the option of picking up the words, of sharing more of her story, her past.

"I never knew my father. I think he was a lot older than my mother. He was long gone by the time I was born." He watched Sloane's fingers curl over her belly, as if she were protecting their baby from an ugly truth. Her voice was a lot harder when she said, "My mother was only seventeen when she had me. She was an addict and she'd already been in and out of treatment for three years when I came along. She stayed clean, though, the entire time she was carrying me."

"She must have loved you very much." He said the words because he knew they had to be true. It twisted his heart when Sloane shook her head.

"She put me into foster care before I was a year old."

She tried to be matter-of-fact, but he heard the carefully trained acceptance in her tone. Old doubt was transparent in her eyes; it weighted down her shoulders. He tried to keep his own tone light as he contradicted. "But she put you first, for nine months. Keeping away from drugs for her pregnancy couldn't have been easy, especially when she was only a child herself. She wanted you to be healthy. Safe."

Sloane had never thought about it that way. All these years, she'd thought about her mother as a weak person, a sick woman, unable to face the new life that she'd created through her own mistakes. Sloane had never once seen her mother as strong or brave. Doing what she thought best, even when everyone had turned against her, had left her on her own.

As Sloane met Ethan's steady gaze, another piece of the puzzle dropped into place. "She wanted to get me back. She put me in foster care because she thought that she'd get better, that she'd get well enough for us to live together. She could have put me up for adoption, but she hoped..."

Hope. The word was a strange one when applied to Sloane's childhood. *Hope* wasn't a word that Sloane associated with the dark-haired woman she barely remembered. *Hope* wasn't part of her foster family patchwork.

But it was, of course. It had been all along. That was why Sloane had named her internet work the Hope Project. That was why she had designed her system, to help children like she had been.

"Thank you," she said to Ethan. "I hadn't really thought about things that way before."

She was warmed by his easy smile. "Glad that I could be of assistance." He lifted the teapot that James had left on the counter, gesturing toward her mug. "Can I heat that up for you?"

She edged the stoneware closer to him. "You're spoiling me."

"That's my intention."

She flushed at the purr beneath his words. She would have gulped down her tea, but she knew that it would burn her tongue. She settled for using her fork to tamp down stray crumbs from her coffee cake. When the silence ticked a dozen points closer to unbearable, she blurted out, "What about you? You said that your grandmother raised you?"

Damn. Ethan would rather spend the morning teasing her, bringing out that blush on her cheeks. He'd even prefer talking about *her* past, navigating the thicket of her tangled family ties. Turnabout was fair play, though. "My parents got divorced when I was seven. Neither of them was prepared to raise a…challenging child alone, so Grandmother stepped in."

"Challenging?"

"Let's just say that I didn't like to follow the rules very much."

"Didn't?" She raised her eyebrows and extended her hand toward him, so that her engagement ring sparkled in the morning sunlight. "I don't think that's changed very much, Mr. Hartwell. You and rules still seem to be pretty much strangers to each other."

"Why change when something's working for you?" he retorted with a shrug. She should smile more often. It brought out the sparkle in her eyes.

"Seriously," she said, taking back her hand before he could think of something distracting to do with those long fingers. "What sort of trouble did you get into?"

"Let's just say that my grandmother ended up on a first-name basis with the principal." Sloane's lips quirked in amusement. "At all five schools I attended." She grinned. "And the Coast Guard commander who tracked down my sailboat when I tried to run away from home." She laughed. "For the third time."

He'd gone too far there. Told too much. Sloane wasn't a fool; she obviously heard the darker story beneath his joking. She immediately seemed to grasp that no boy caused *that* much trouble unless there was something very wrong in his life. A frown ironed a crease between her eyebrows. "Why so desperate to get away?"

He still could laugh it off. It wasn't too late to make up something ridiculous about being a bad boy, about playing a rogue-in-training. He had planned to keep things light, to make everything easy, for another three weeks at least, until the prenatal testing could be done.

But Sloane would remember this conversation when he finally told her the truth. She would recall all the things he'd told her, and the huge, important things he'd left unsaid. She would conclude that he had lied to her, by omission, at the very least. He took a deep breath, wishing that it was late enough in the day to break out a bottle of Scotch, to fortify himself for this conversation that he absolutely did not want to have, that he'd never wanted to share with anyone.

Sloane felt Ethan's mood shift, as if a cloud had scudded across the sun. Even though he didn't move, she felt him withdraw from her. For just a heartbeat, she thought that he was going to slip beneath the mask of Bachelor of the Year, to shift back to the good-times-guy she had read about in the paper, the one who belonged at AFAA charity auctions every night of the year.

Instead, he reached for her hand, folding his fingers around hers with an urgency that sent her heart leaping into her throat. "Sloane," he said. "We have to talk."

She forced her lips to turn up at the corners even though the fake grin made her throat ache. "No good conversation ever started that way."

She tried to pull her hand away, but he wouldn't let

her go. Instead, he took a deep breath, then exhaled on a count of five. "I wasn't an only child, Sloane. I had a brother and a sister, but they both died, before I was five. That was what pulled my parents apart. That was why I spent so much time acting out."

She heard the sorrow behind his words, still raw after all those years. She blinked, taking in the grand kitchen, the fine mansion that surrounded her. Of course, money truly couldn't buy happiness. It hadn't been able to spare the Hartwells from tragedy. "What happened?" she asked, her mind skirting over a dozen terrible accidents.

"My brother and sister were born with a genetic mutation, trisomy. She lived for almost three years, but he survived only a few days."

Genetic mutation.

The words were ugly, frightening—all the more so for the irony that Ethan's company was Hartwell Genetics, a forerunner in creating cures for terrible diseases. No, Sloane realized. It wasn't ironic at all. Those poor siblings were the reason that Hartwell Genetics flourished. Ethan had devoted his life to saving other families the agony that his own had suffered. Ethan, and his grandmother, too. How long had the company been in existence? How long had they fought to find a cure?

Sloane suddenly realized what Ethan was going to say next. Her fingers clutched at her blouse, closing over the delicate life that grew inside her.

No. She had to be wrong. *Ethan* was fine. He didn't have…what was it? Trisomy? It couldn't kill every child in the family. It couldn't put an end to the entire Hartwell line. It absolutely, positively couldn't affect the baby she had already come to love so much.

She forced herself to ask, "It runs in your family, then?"

He nodded, his hazel eyes nearly black. When he spoke, he sounded as if he were making a solemn vow. "Sloane, I never meant for this to happen. I never intended to have children at all. You know I took precautions—" His throat closed around that last word, and all she could do was clutch his fingers where they still grasped hers. He steadied himself with another deep breath, and then he squared his shoulders. "There are tests now. They can do amnio at fourteen weeks."

"Fourteen," she said, trying to absorb everything he had told her. That left three weeks hanging in the balance. Three weeks of not knowing.

He nodded, raising his free hand to her cheek. "That was why I told you I wanted the paternity test. That is what I really need to know."

Sloane felt light-headed. She had been so worried that Ethan didn't trust her. She had tried to convince herself that his insistence on a paternity test was to protect himself, to protect the Hartwell family fortune. Now, her heart leaped at the notion that *trust* wasn't the issue at all. Ethan *did* believe her.

But any relief was crushed by darker thoughts. Their child could be in the worst kind of danger. She pulled away from his caress, extracting her hand from his grasp. "Why didn't you tell me before?"

"I didn't want to worry you. I didn't want you to be afraid."

"Ethan, I think this is something worth worrying about! This disease has destroyed your family! I had a right to know!"

"How was that supposed to work?" he snapped. "What was I supposed to say? 'Marry me? And by the way, our babies might all die'?"

She heard the self-hatred behind his words, recognized the emotion for what it was. Nevertheless, she said, "You could have held off on the 'marry me' part! At the very least, you could have told me the truth!"

"You don't understand! I watched this thing ruin my parents' marriage! I watched it tear them apart! I wanted to prove that I could do this. That I could be better than they were."

"All the more reason that you should have told me, Ethan." He started to interrupt, but she pressed on. "You're right, you know. Our story can be different from theirs. I'm not your mother. You're not your father. Our baby isn't your sister or your brother."

She saw that his immediate reaction was to fight. As she watched, though, he swallowed one retort, then another. He spread his fingers across the granite countertop, as if he were seeking strength from the cool stone. He nodded slowly, and then he said, "You're right. I should have told you. And in the interest of full disclosure now, you should know that I've made an appointment with Dr. Morton for three weeks from tomorrow. I'll need a copy of your obstetrician's reports from your other visits. I want to get those to Phil tomorrow morning."

"Phil?" She could think of about a dozen things wrong with Ethan's request, but the first word to splutter from her lips was the unfamiliar name.

"Phillip Morton. He's the leading obstetrician in D.C. He knows my family history. He'll take over your case now."

She wanted to say that she was perfectly content with her own doctor. She wanted to say that she had everything under control.

But she didn't.

She'd only been to the doctor once since finding out

she was pregnant. That was all she'd been able to afford. She swallowed hard and met Ethan's eyes, fully aware of the fact that she was about to make her own uncomfortable disclosure. "Fine. I'll switch to Dr. Morton. But there aren't a lot of records. I've only been to the obstetrician once."

He couldn't have been more surprised if she'd slapped him. "What?" he asked, half expecting to find that he'd misheard. A woman as fiercely devoted to her unborn baby as Sloane… Only going to the doctor once in her entire first trimester? "Standard medical protocol—" he started to recite.

She cut him off. "Standard medical protocol has insurance. At the very least, it has a job. I've been doing everything that I'm supposed to do," she said. "I've read all the books, and there are all sorts of communities online. I was very active in one of them before…"

He barely smothered his sigh of frustration when she trailed off. "Before what?"

"Before my computer died." She looked away, as if she were confessing infidelity. "I've been going down to the public library, though. Everything I've experienced with this pregnancy has been textbook perfect. They could write a book about me."

He heard a suspicious brightness behind her tone, and he wondered if she was trying to convince him, or just herself.

He had a choice. He could push her about the doctor visits, about the limited care that she'd provided for their child. He could lambaste her for managing her life so poorly that she had nothing in reserve, no savings to fall back on. He could vent some of the fierce possessiveness that clenched his fists, the driving need to keep her safe, to protect her, to ease her way. He could take out on her all of his fear about the Hartwell genetic curse, all of his anxiety about the unknown state of their baby.

Or he could let it go.

There wasn't any way to change the past. No way to pick up the missing appointments. Besides, who was he to say that *she* had been irresponsible? She'd managed to keep a roof over her head for nearly three months, without a job. She'd done the best she could under challenging circumstances. He exhaled slowly and forced himself to release the tension that torqued his shoulders. "Okay," he said. And then, because she was sitting there, obviously nervous and clearly still processing the bombshell he had dropped in the middle of their Sunday brunch, he asked, "Did you bring your computer from your apartment?"

She nodded. "It's upstairs."

"I'll take it into the office tomorrow. Someone in the computer department should be able to fix it. At the very least, they can transfer everything from your hard drive to a new machine."

He made the offer so casually. Just as he'd presented her with the cell phone, with the credit card. Sloane had spent weeks worrying about her failing computer; she'd wasted hours wondering what she was going to do when the thing finally refused to turn on at all. She was so close to launching the Hope Project….

And just like that, he could give her back all the tools she needed. He could make things right.

If only their visit to Dr. Morton resolved problems as easily… "Ethan," she said, but then she realized that she didn't know what she wanted to ask. She smoothed her blouse over her belly, wishing that the pregnancy was already further along, wishing that she could feel the reassuring flutter of a new life inside her.

He settled his hand over hers. Strength flowed through his fingers. Strength and an iron-firm resolve. “Ask me any questions, Sloane. I’ll tell you the truth, as best I can.”

She wanted numbers. She wanted absolutes. She wanted guarantees. But she knew that he could never give her those. “We’ll know the test results in three weeks?”

He shook his head. “Phil will do the amnio then. It takes time for the cells to be cultured, for results to come in. Probably another ten days.”

She had to ask the next question, even though she dreaded the answer. “And if we get bad news?”

A nerve twitched beneath his right eye. She saw him withdraw, disappear into his memories, into the past of a family torn apart by *bad news*. When he answered, his voice was barely a whisper. “I can’t do it, Sloane. I’m not strong enough to be a father for that kind of child. A child that we know we’re going to lose, probably much sooner rather than later.”

She knew she should be grateful that he was answering her honestly. She should welcome the unvarnished truth, even though it hurt him to say the words, even though her heart pounded in her chest when she realized what he meant. She had to answer him, though. She had to tell him how *she* felt. “Ethan, I am never giving up this baby.”

“Sloane, you don’t understand. You can’t imagine what it’s like—”

She wasn’t angry with him. She wasn’t afraid. She wasn’t even overwhelmed by sorrow. She just knew that she was determined, that she was absolutely, one hundred percent certain. “No, Ethan. That isn’t a possibility.”

He ran his hand through his hair, making the golden strands stand on end. "Let's wait and see. Let's wait until we have all the facts."

She didn't need anymore facts.

Before she could drive home the point, though, the doorbell rang. Sloane heard James greet someone in the foyer. There was easy laughter, comfortable familiarity. She glanced at Ethan, saw his face brighten. He shot Sloane a quick glance, and she shrugged. They could finish their conversation another time. Not that there was anything left to say. Not before they had test results in hand.

"Zach!" Ethan exclaimed, as a man walked into the kitchen. The newcomer was Ethan's opposite in every way. His hair was dark where Ethan's was light; his eyes were ordinary brown instead of Ethan's complicated hazel. Zach was short, and he could easily stand to lose twenty pounds. His T-shirt was wrinkled, as if he'd pulled it out of a laundry hamper, and his jeans slouched around his hips.

"Zachary Crosby, this is Sloane Davenport. Sloane, Zach." Zach's hand was soft in hers, but he smiled as he said hello. As Zach reached for a coffee cup, Ethan said wryly, "Make yourself at home." The newcomer was clearly familiar with the Hartwell kitchen; he wasted no time collecting a plate and a fork, cutting himself a generous slice of the cardamom coffee cake.

He downed a huge bite, chasing it with a hefty swallow of coffee. He might act like a starved teenager, but Sloane quickly realized that there was more to the man than met the casual eye. His glance darted to the cell phone that still sat on the center island, to the silver credit card beside it. He scarcely missed a beat before zeroing in on her left hand, on the diamond ring that glinted in the morning light.

"Then the rumors are true. I take it congratulations are in order," he said, shifting his gaze from Sloane to Ethan.

Ethan stared at him for a long moment. Some silent communication passed between the men, an entire conversation, made easy by their obvious familiarity. Ethan finally said, "Sloane and I got engaged on Friday night."

"Have you set a date yet?"

Sloane thought the question was a little odd, especially since it was directed at Ethan. Dates were something women asked about, girlfriends, excited about a wedding in the offing. She thought about her list. June 1—the earliest date that made any sense at all.

Before she could decide whether or not to say anything, Ethan replied, "Nothing certain." His tone was terse.

Another glance passed between the two men, another flash of communication. Sloane wasn't certain what Ethan was saying, what the meaning was behind his words. That was silly, though. There wasn't any secret meaning. They *hadn't* decided on a date.

Zach just nodded, as if he'd expected the answer. "Don't worry," he said. "I'll have my best man's toast ready, whatever date you choose." His sudden smile brightened the entire room. "Just think of the stories I can finally make public...."

Ethan rolled his eyes as he said to Sloane, "Don't believe a word this guy tells you. He's the worst liar I've ever known."

Zach only laughed. "Twenty-five years of being your best friend, and this is the way I'm treated?" He passed his mug to Ethan, waiting for a refill. "Besides, you should be especially nice to me today. I brought you a present."

"I can't wait," Ethan said dryly.

Zach glanced toward the foyer. "James! You can bring her in!"

Her?

Afterward, Sloane couldn't have said what she had thought she would see. There was always the specter of Ethan's old girlfriends. Or his grandmother. Or even some business associate, waiting to steal him away for whatever was left of the weekend.

But Sloane had never expected a *puppy.* A fuzzy, black-and-white bundle of fur, with paws the size of dinner plates.

"What the—" Ethan exclaimed, even as Sloane knelt beside the excited dog.

"May I present Heritage Sacre Bleu Chevalier? Or, you can just call her Daisy."

"What type of dog is she?" Sloane asked, as the puppy licked her fingers with unbridled enthusiasm.

"A purebred Old English sheepdog. Eight weeks old." Zach laughed as Ethan swore under his breath. "You won the silent auction bid, and now she's all yours. I've got her official papers out in the car, along with a leash and some Puppy Chow. Congratulations."

"You can take your official papers, and—"

"The Ballet Fund is truly grateful for your very generous gift, Mr. Hartwell."

Zach sounded as pious as an altar boy. James chuckled from the doorway. Sloane caught her breath, waiting to see what Ethan would do, how he would react to the surprise.

For a moment, his face was dark, frustration twisting his features. But then, he looked at Sloane. She felt him measure her smile. She saw him register her fingers already twined in the puppy's soft fur. She watched him turn to Zach, shaking his head. "You're going to owe me for this one, buddy. Owe me, big time."

Daisy chose that moment to deliver one short bark, as if she understood every word of the mock threat. Sloane watched in amusement as Ethan Hartwell, M.D., MBA, president of Hartwell Genetics knelt down beside her, accepting a slobbery canine kiss from the newest member of his family.

Chapter Five

Three nights later, Sloane plucked at her blouse, removing a glistening white strand of Daisy's fur from the aquamarine silk. Ethan grinned openly at the gesture; he had already fought his own good-natured battle against the puppy's long fur before they'd left the house. "I thought that Old English sheepdogs don't shed," Sloane said.

"They don't lose their winter coats all at once in the spring, like some dogs. Instead, they drop hair all year round."

Sloane raised her eyebrows. "It sounds like you've been doing some research."

"What else would a responsible dog owner do?" Ethan shrugged as he helped himself to a generous bite of his duck à l'orange.

Sloane smiled at his offhand acceptance of the responsibility that Zach had thrust upon them. Ethan might have grumbled about the puppy initially, but he'd certainly been in a great mood for the past three days.

His impromptu invitation to a Wednesday night dinner had come as a complete surprise. At first, Sloane had protested when he named the restaurant—the French country inn was known to be one of the most expensive places in the Washington area. Ethan had insisted, though, saying that he wanted her to try the white asparagus in one of the inn's famous appetizers.

He'd been right, of course. The food was incredible. Her scallops were divine, in their complicated sauce of shrimp, oranges and olives. "How is your duck?" she asked.

Before Ethan could answer, though, Sloane's cell phone rang. She wrinkled her nose in embarrassment, realizing she should have put the thing on vibrate before they even set foot inside the exclusive restaurant. The ringtone grew louder as she rifled through her handbag, taking some things out to speed her getting to the phone. A hand mirror jostled the spoon beside her plate, quickly followed by lipstick, a pen and a carefully folded piece of paper.

At last, she got to the phone, only to see the cheerful icon that told her she had missed a call. She glanced at the phone number and realized it started with 1-800—no one she actually knew at all.

"Sorry," she said ruefully, thumbing the switch to set the phone to vibrate.

"No problem." Ethan's smile was easy. She started to squirrel away her possessions, but he reached out to grab the sheet of paper. "What's this?"

Her stomach plummeted. "It's nothing," she said, trying to keep her voice light.

"It has my name on it."

Of course it had his name on it. She'd typed his name when she'd made up the list, the catalog of what she wanted out of their relationship. She had kept the page in her purse, afraid to leave it anywhere that James or Ethan or anyone else could stumble upon it.

Just as Ethan had done now.

"Please," she said. "It's nothing. It's just a stupid note I wrote to myself."

His voice was gently teasing. "Should I be offended that my name is on a 'stupid' note?"

She felt color flood her cheeks. *Respect.* That was on the list, wasn't it? She needed Ethan to respect her. Even when she did silly things like write up a list of traits she needed for their marriage to work. Well, this would be a great test.

She swallowed hard, and then she nodded toward the paper. "Go ahead, then. Read it." She gulped at her sparkling water as he took his time absorbing the five words. Five words and a date.

His hazel eyes were serious as they met hers. "What does it mean?"

"It's what I want, Ethan. What I need. If we're ever going to make this work, really work, long term."

"Trust?" he asked, and his voice was surprisingly, impossibly gentle.

If he'd taken any other tone, she would have challenged him. As it was, his tenderness made her feel shy. She stared down at her plate, as if she could make out some magic reply amid the seafood. "You frighten me," she finally said.

Out of the corner of her eye, she saw him draw back, pull away as if she'd burned him. She glanced up just in time to catch the look of shock on his face, of something stronger—something she might even call horror.

"No!" she hastened to clarify. "Not frighten me, like I'm afraid you'll hurt me." But then she had to explain some more. "Not hurt me physically. I know you would never do that. But Ethan, I know your reputation—the women, the parties, the constant social life. I knew it when I met you and I'm so afraid that nothing has changed. That nothing will ever change."

His eyes softened as she fumbled for the words. "Sloane," he said, reaching across the table to twine his fingers between hers. "There isn't anyone else. There hasn't been since you agreed to wear my ring. There won't be. Not ever. I promise."

When she still hesitated, he reached into the breast pocket of his jacket, fished out his personal cell phone, the one that he used for private calls, separate and apart from Hartwell Genetics business. Still holding her gaze, he dropped it into the ice bucket beside their table, using her bright green bottle of sparkling water to push the electronic device to the bottom of its icy grave.

"Ethan!"

"If I kept an actual little black book, I would give it to you to burn."

"Ethan, you didn't have to do that!" But she was laughing.

"That brings us to…" He looked back at her creased page. "Respect."

Amusement died on her lips. "I'm never going to be famous like all those other women you've known. I need to know that you can respect what I am—a simple woman who wants to help people, help children. A woman who is never going to be an actress, or a model or anybody special."

Anybody special. Did Sloane have any idea what she was saying? Ethan saw the earnestness in her face, felt her urgency like a palpable thing as she waited for him to respond.

His first instinct was to laugh. Of *course* he respected her. How could he not respect a woman who knew what she wanted in life and took the difficult steps to get there? She had paid her own way through college, through graduate school, all so that she had the credentials she needed to make her dream come true. She had taken a meaningless gofer job and turned it into a dynamic position at the foundation, a coordinator's post that had netted hundreds of thousands of dollars for the organization in a single night.

But laughter would destroy Sloane now. Laughter was the last thing that she needed from him. The last thing that he would ever give her. He leaned over the table, lowering his voice so that she needed to move closer as well, so that she met him partway.

"Sloane Davenport, I respect you. I respect you, and everything that you are trying to do. I respect your work on the Hope Project."

He couldn't leave it at that, though. Because he did respect her mind, he did respect her drive, but she pulled an equally strong response from him in other ways. He roughened his tone until his words were almost a growl. "And I respect the fact that you got me to make a promise up there, on the Kennedy Center terrace. You got me to vow not to take you into my bed until after we marry. Any woman who can drive a bargain that…" He cleared his throat, making his meaning absolutely, perfectly, one hundred percent clear. "That…persuasively, gains my absolute, undying respect."

She blinked hard at the innuendo behind his words. His tone, though, freed something inside her. Like a zipper easing down, metal foot by metal foot, she felt tension flow from her shoulders. She had not realized how much she wanted to talk to him about her list, how much she had needed to share her needs. Her desires.

That sense of release gave her the courage to say, "That leaves us with the last thing. Partnership. I need to know we're equals in this."

"Does that mean you're offering to walk Daisy when she gets up in the middle of the night?"

Her smile was fleeting. "I mean it, Ethan. We need to work together, to know each other well enough that we can stand side by side, through anything."

He leaned back in his chair, shrugging and spreading his hands to either side. "Fine. Ask me anything. What do you want to know?"

There were a thousand things, of course. She started with the first thing that came to mind. "What was your favorite toy when you were growing up?"

"My chemistry set. After Grandmother got over the first three explosions."

"What's your favorite book?"

"John Steinbeck's *East of Eden.*"

"Your favorite color?"

"Blue."

"Why didn't you have a vasectomy, years ago? Why did you ever take a chance at getting some woman pregnant, if you were so worried about passing along the genes?"

The question surprised her as much as it surprised him. She had been thinking it for days, though, ever since he had told her about the danger. Ever since he had sparked the constant gnawing uncertainty about the health of their baby, the niggling fear that would not be put to rest for several more weeks.

"I'm sorry," she said, when she saw the stricken look on his face. "You don't have to answer that."

"No." He drew a deep breath, and then he took a healthy swallow of his burgundy. "I do." He rubbed his hand across his mouth, as if the gesture would help him to collect his thoughts. "I never had the surgery because it would be permanent. It felt like giving up. Like admitting that we'll never find a cure."

"After what? Fifty years?"

He heard what she was doing with her voice, the way she tried to be gentle with him. The way she tried to say that there might not ever be a cure. He appreciated the effort, even as he pushed away her specific question.

"In fifty years, Hartwell Genetics has brought hundreds of new pharmaceuticals to the market. We've found cures for a dozen different diseases. We've helped millions of people. We just haven't helped my family. Yet."

"Yet," she said, purposely hardening her voice to match his certainty.

He nodded, and then he rubbed his hands together, obviously closing the door on that part of their conversation. *For now,* he amended mentally. Until Sloane decided that she needed to talk about it again. He would answer any questions that she had, whenever she had them. He would do that for her.

"Your turn," he said with a devilish smile. "What's your favorite dessert?"

"Chocolate mousse," she said. "No, wait! Crème caramel!"

"Let's see what we can do about that then, shall we?" He raised his chin, claiming the attention of the waiter on the far side of the room.

Hours later, well after crème caramel and coffee

and several long, lingering kisses, Sloane was falling asleep in the privacy of the guest suite when she remembered the last thing on her list—the June wedding date. Oh, well, she thought, already slipping into the fuzzy warmth of a dream. There was plenty of time to set a date…months and months and months.

Sloane caught her tongue between her teeth, holding her breath as she pressed the enter key on her computer. A progress bar appeared on the screen, racing from left to right, and then a model of the Hope Project home page blinked into existence. Every photograph was in place. The fonts were correct. Three columns marched neatly across the screen.

"Yes!" she cried, pumping her fist in the air. She was startled to hear laughter from the doorway. "Ethan!" she exclaimed, looking up. "How long have you been standing there?"

He ignored her question. "I take it the Hope Project is going well?"

He looked perfectly relaxed in his broadcloth shirt and tailored trousers, as if he'd left the office hours before. She wondered what he was doing home in the middle of the day, on a Friday no less. Glancing back at her computer screen, she grinned. "I finally got the front page to look the way I want it to. It's taken about a hundred tries, but everything is finally falling into place." Ethan started to walk across the library, but she shielded the screen with her palms. "No! You can't look at it yet. It's not ready for prime time."

He held up his hands as if to prove that he was innocent. "The computer's working all right, then?"

"It's wonderful." She couldn't help but caress the sleek silver edge of the casing. The new machine was ten times faster than the wreck she'd brought from her apartment. Ethan had assured her that the computer was just something he'd had lying around the office, that it hadn't cost him a penny. Reluctantly, she'd accepted it, telling herself that she needed *something* to help her fill the long hours that he spent at the office. Speaking of which… "What are you doing home?"

"Don't we have Daisy's appointment this afternoon?"

The puppy's first visit to the veterinarian, a simple checkup to make sure she was in general good health. "I thought I was going to take her," Sloane said. James had already told her that she could take the SUV from the garage. Sloane had looked up directions to the vet's office, telling herself that she would have no trouble navigating the unfamiliar streets. No trouble, that was, if Daisy behaved herself.

Ethan shrugged easily. "It didn't seem fair for me to stick you with the hard stuff. Partnership, right? We're in this together."

If Ethan had harbored any doubts about coming home early, they were banished by Sloane's brilliant smile. He really *should* be back at the office, but there would always be time to schedule another meeting with the in-house trademark lawyers.

He watched Sloane's fingers fly over her keyboard, saving whatever she had just completed on her internet project. He was glad that the new machine was working out well. The technology guru back at the office had laughed when Ethan suggested repairing Sloane's old computer. "It'll cost more and take longer for me to order replacement parts for this ancient thing than for you to just buy something new, something top-of-the-line." The guy had shaken his head as if he were studying some museum exhibit on the history of home computing.

Top-of-the-line it had been, then. Getting the new computer was simple enough. And it made Sloane happy.

Ethan produced a ring of keys from the pocket of his trousers. "Do you want to drive? Or should I?"

Sloane told herself that she was silly to feel so relieved. Of course she *could* have made it to the veterinarian's office on her own. Nevertheless, she laughed as she said, "You drive. Our fearless watchdog is in the kitchen, sleeping on her new bed."

She switched off her computer and led the way out of the library. She was pretty sure Ethan was watching her as she walked in front of him. Normally, the thought would have made her self-conscious, but that afternoon, she felt empowered. She had just taken a major step toward completing the Hope Project. She was managing her life, accomplishing her goals. *And* Ethan had remembered the words that she had typed on that slip of paper. He had been the one to say *partnership.*

She let her hips sway a little more than usual as she walked down the hall. She couldn't help but run her fingers through her hair. She slowed her pace, just a fraction.

She widened her eyes with mock innocence, as she tried to convince herself that it wouldn't be *her* fault if Ethan came up close behind her. *She* wouldn't be responsible if he nuzzled that sensitive place at the side of her throat, if he started to play with the buttons on her floral blouse. If he tempted her to forget every single promise that she'd made to herself and to the baby inside her. At least, it wouldn't be *entirely* her fault. Would it?

Before she could decide just how far she was willing to tempt her fiancé, she was distracted by the sharp yap of an excited puppy, newly energized by a nap.

"Yes," Ethan said, brushing against Sloane before he knelt on the floor to wrestle with the barking hellion. His hand lingered against Sloane's hip for just long enough that she was certain he had been reading her mind. He didn't follow through on that tingling promise, though. Instead, he crooned to Daisy, "I'm home. And you're glad to see me. You know how to welcome a man back to his house."

As Sloane watched, Ethan continued talking to the fluff ball of a dog. He growled at Daisy in mock ferocity as he eased the animal into her harness, double-checking the fastening to make sure the puppy couldn't escape, couldn't come to harm on his watch. The click of Ethan's tongue was automatic as he summoned the dog to walk beside him to the garage. He was a natural at controlling Daisy, at giving her the length of leash she needed, at pulling back to keep her manageable and secure before he put her into a travel crate.

Ethan handled the car with the same smooth efficiency, winding his way through the shady summertime streets. As he braked to a stop at a traffic light, he asked Sloane, "So, how close are you to finishing the Hope Project?"

"Getting that template to work this afternoon was a major step forward. I still need to test the algorithms, though, to make sure that everything works as well online as it does on paper. I'd like to think that it will function perfectly, but there's a huge difference between design and reality."

"Tell me about it." He sighed, heading back into traffic.

"What does that mean?" she asked. "Are you having computer problems at work?"

"Not a computer." He shrugged and glanced in the

rearview mirror before changing lanes. "There's a new drug that showed a lot of promise in the lab. Turns out it's not nearly as effective in our first round of human test subjects. It's safe, not going to hurt anyone. But if it worked as well as it did in the last round of testing, we could wipe out an entire class of diseases."

She heard the disappointment in his voice. There was something else there, though, something that ran even deeper. It took her a moment to process his words, to figure out what she was responding to. Ah, that was it. *Determination.*

Ethan was determined to make his drug therapy work, no matter how many times he had to go back to the drawing board. No matter what it cost him financially, emotionally. He was invested in Hartwell Genetics, and he wouldn't give up until the new drug functioned flawlessly.

Maybe that was what had drawn her to him in the first place. Okay, she reasoned with herself. In the *second* place. She'd been drawn to him in the first place by his incredibly sexy smile, by his ruffled hair, by the smoky way his eyes had tracked her when she'd walked into the Eastern Hotel bar.

His determination was what had convinced her to take the chance of a lifetime, to jump into the deep end by agreeing to marry him when her entire life had turned upside down. Ethan was a man who could make things happen. He could get things done.

Her fingers inched across her blouse, gathering up the fabric in tiny hills and valleys. There were some things, she knew, that even Ethan couldn't accomplish. Their baby was growing, with or without the Hartwell genetic flaw. Ethan couldn't change that. Not now. Not ever. And she dreaded the fight that she knew was coming if all her hopes came to nothing, if all her dreams crumbled to ash with the amnio results that Ethan dreaded. Sloane could barely imagine what life would be like if she were pitted against the very determination that had drawn her in so deeply at the start.

"I lost you there," Ethan said, and she was flustered to realize that he had pulled into a parking space. She had completely lost track of their drive, of the careful twists and turns that had brought them to the vet's office.

"Sorry," she said, flashing him an automatic smile. She wasn't about to tell him all of her worries. No reason to borrow trouble. Not now. As if to emphasize Sloane's resolve, Daisy yipped from her crate in the back of the vehicle. "I didn't mean to zone out like that."

She undid her seat belt with her own gesture of determination. Ethan shot her an appraising look, as if he knew that she was ducking out of an unpleasant conversation. He didn't press the point, though. Instead, he easily maneuvered the latch on Daisy's crate, bundling up the wriggling puppy, laughing as the dog tried to smother him with sloppy kisses.

Soon enough, an only slightly subdued Daisy was standing on the veterinarian's examination table, shaking her head at the scope Dr. Johnson used to inspect her ears. With the vet's right hand firm on her neck, the puppy submitted to having her teeth inspected. "Her gums look good," the vet said. "She should start to lose her milk teeth in a couple of months. She'll chew on things constantly as her adult teeth come in. Make sure she has toys, or you'll find yourself out a pair of shoes or two."

Sloane laughed. "No problem there. She has all the toys a puppy could ever need." Ethan had seen to that, bringing home a wide selection of playthings earlier in the week. Zach might have strong-armed him into accepting the puppy, but Ethan was taking his responsibilities as a pet owner seriously.

Dr. Johnson moved her hands down Daisy's back, apparently pleased with the alignment of the puppy's spine. She reached around to the belly, palpating and nodding to herself. "No masses in the abdomen," the doctor said, before she slipped her stethoscope buds into her ears.

Ethan approved of the doctor's smooth actions. The woman was clearly comfortable with puppies. It was obvious that she liked them; the vet had exclaimed over Daisy as if she were the only dog on the schedule for the entire afternoon.

Comfort, though, and enthusiasm, weren't enough when it came to medical care. A good doctor was thorough. Able to diagnose problems from the subtlest of hints.

Dr. Johnson moved her stethoscope around, finding a better placement on Daisy's chest. A tiny frown tightened around the woman's lips, and she planted the medical instrument again. Another shift, another angle for the stethoscope's round plate.

"Is there something wrong, Doctor?" Ethan made himself keep his voice even, but he felt his brain shift into businessman mode. As an officer of Hartwell Genetics, he was accustomed to dealing with medical professionals who bore bad news. As an expert in human genetics, he was prepared to discuss anatomical anomalies, contraindications, complex diagnoses.

Sloane must have recognized the change in his focus. He heard her breath catch at the back of her throat. Wishing that he could spare her whatever the doctor was about to say, he stepped closer, weaving Sloane's fingers between his own. Her hand was cold, slack, as if she already knew that the veterinarian had bad news.

Dr. Johnson only shook her head, taking several long minutes to listen further to Daisy's chest. When she finally removed the stethoscope from her ears, her face was grave. "I'm sorry," she said. "At first, I wasn't certain what I was hearing—I didn't expect to find it in a puppy this young."

"Find what?" Sloane asked the question before Ethan could, her voice impossibly fragile.

"Daisy has a heart murmur. The valves of her heart aren't functioning the way that they should, so her heart isn't pumping blood as efficiently as normal."

"What grade?" Ethan snapped. He'd read enough laboratory studies over the years to know that there were five grades of heart murmur. Grade one or two, and Daisy was fine; she'd likely grow out of the problem. Three or four, though, and the poor dog would have problems, meaning she'd likely require medication. And five…

"Five," the vet said grimly.

"But what—" Sloane started to ask, her voice breaking before she could complete the question.

"You'll do an EKG to be sure?" Ethan asked. The electrocardiogram might give them valuable information. Let him control the situation. Manage everything that was going wrong.

"Of course," Dr. Johnson said. "And an echocardiogram might get us more information as well. Maybe some X-rays, if it seems like they can give us more facts."

"You have the equipment here?"

"Yes," the veterinarian assured him. "Of course, the tests can become rather expensive—"

"Just do them," Ethan cut her off.

Dr. Johnson flashed him a pleased smile. "Some people aren't willing to invest in a new pet, a puppy they've hardly gotten to know."

"Do whatever tests you need to do," Ethan said.

The vet gathered up the squirming puppy. "Come on, you. These tests aren't going to hurt. And you just might get a treat when we're done." She turned back to Ethan and Sloane. "We'll probably need an hour or two. There's a coffee shop next door, if you want to wait there."

If Ethan had been on his own, he would have insisted on waiting right there in the examining room. Keeping himself front and center, he would have made the vet's staff work harder, complete the tests sooner, interpret the results just a little faster.

One glance at Sloane, though, told Ethan that it would be a mistake to stay there. Her face was rigid with worry. She was already looking at the instruments in the examining room as if they were tools in some medieval torture chamber. It was better for Sloane to get away, to wait somewhere else.

"Thank you," Ethan said stiffly.

The veterinarian smiled, as if she knew the battle he had fought. "Just leave your cell phone number with the receptionist, and we'll call you as soon as we have any results."

This was a nightmare, Sloane thought as she watched the doctor carry off Daisy.

Any minute now, Sloane was going to wake up. She would hear the oak tree scraping against her window, smell the roses on the writing desk. She would realize this was all a bad dream, and she would laugh at herself.

But the oak tree had been cut down almost a week

ago, the very same Sunday that Zach had brought Daisy into their lives. The roses had been replaced with a new floral display, a riot of color that no one could ever confuse with a funeral arrangement.

She felt Ethan's fingers tighten around hers, and she realized that they were still holding hands, had been ever since the veterinarian had begun to examine poor Daisy. Sloane let Ethan guide her out of the bright room. She stood beside him while he recited his cell number to the receptionist. She waited with him while a bored barista served up two cups of coffee—a dark roast for Ethan, decaf for her. She watched as he doctored her cup, adding a healthy dose of cream, stirring in a single packet of sugar.

She roused herself enough to carry her own cup to the table, and she was vaguely conscious of Ethan holding her chair for her, waiting to make sure that she was settled before he folded himself into his own seat. Reflexively, she started to drink, but the beverage was still too hot. Nevertheless, Ethan managed to swallow his.

She waited until he'd returned the paper cup to the table before she finally asked, "What are we going to do?"

"Let's wait until we hear what the doctor has to say."

"Grade five," she said, finally getting to the question she'd been unable to choke out back in the examining room. "That's serious, isn't it?"

She saw the discomfort on his face and realized that he wanted to duck the truth, to lie to her. She also recognized the moment that he decided to face the problem head-on, the moment that he embraced the first word on her list. Truth. "Yes," he said. "It's serious."

"What will happen?" She could see that he longed to avoid responding, that he was going to tell her to wait for Dr. Johnson's report. She pushed urgency into her voice. "Assuming the worst. Assuming that all the tests come out wrong."

"We might be able to treat her with drugs. She'll probably have a shortened life, depending on what the underlying cause is."

He ticked off the possibilities, falling back on his medical training. He wasn't a veterinarian, of course, but he'd seen enough lab results based on animal studies. Treatment options spread in front of them like some sort of strange tree. Dr. Johnson would report back with specific information, which would open up new courses of action. They'd make a decision, shutting off some possibilities, opening up others.

Cold. Mechanical. Manageable.

He saw the way his tone was affecting Sloane. She curled into herself. She probably wasn't even aware that she spread her fingers across her belly again, as if she were protecting their child, shielding their baby from bad news about the puppy.

He should reach out to her. He should take her hand, offer whatever comfort he could. He should tell her that they'd make it through this, no matter what happened, no matter what the doctor said.

But he'd fought too hard to build a wall around himself, to protect himself from ever having to say words like that, to anyone, under any circumstances. Not after what he'd seen his parents go through. Not after losing first his sister, then his brother. He'd only been a child himself, but he still remembered the pain.

Damn Zach and his idiotic silent auction! Who gave away puppies in a ballet fundraiser, anyway? And what sort of breeder ended up with puppies this sick? He'd sue the breeder. File an action before sunset tonight. Make

Zach draw up the papers—otherwise, what good was it to have a lawyer for a best friend?

He reached for his phone, but he was distracted by Sloane taking a sip of her coffee. She set the cup down with absolute precision, as if moving carefully would earn her precious "good girl" points, something she could cash in for a miracle.

He sighed. He'd have time to sic Zach on the breeder later. For now, he owed it to Sloane to be present for her. To help her through whatever was going to happen. He forced his tone to be light as he asked, "Did you have any pets when you were growing up?"

Sloane heard the question, felt it pull her back from the whirlpool of despairing thoughts that threatened to carry her away. *Don't borrow trouble,* she reminded herself. *Just wait until you know what's actually going on.* She tried to picture some of the bright drawings in the Hope Project, the smiling suns and giant tempera flowers that children painted when they were happy. When they were safe.

"A few," she answered Ethan, forcing herself to take a deep, steadying breath. "When I was in fourth grade, my foster family had a goose."

"A goose!"

She'd surprised him with that. The thought made her smile, despite her worry about Daisy. "It lived in a screened-in porch, on the side of the house. It was huge—its beak came up to my chest, when it straightened its neck. It was better than any watchdog. It would make a racket if anyone even drove up the driveway."

"What do you feed a goose? Goose chow?"

She laughed at his incredulous expression. "Cracked corn. Weeds from the garden. Some canned cat food, for protein. The family had owned Gertrude since she was a gosling."

"Gertrude? You're pulling my leg!"

"I'm not! Scout's honor!" She raised three fingers, as if she were taking some solemn vow. "I was terrified of her when I first got there. She would hiss whenever she got excited, and she'd flap her wings around. After a while, though, we sort of became friends. I'd talk to her every night. Tell her about my day at school, about all the cute boys I liked."

"Cute boys, hmm?" He gave her a mock-ferocious glare. "Anyone I need to worry about?"

"I don't think Billy Burton is going to ask me to the school dance any time soon."

"He might," Ethan pushed.

"Last I heard, Billy was married to his high school sweetheart, and they had four children—two sets of twins."

"Sounds like the man might want to get away from all that," Ethan growled. "Maybe I should get a goose or two, to make sure he stays off my property."

Sloane laughed despite herself. It felt good to hear Ethan teasing her. Good to hear his possessiveness. No one had ever fought for her before, not even in jest. "What about you?" she asked. "What pets did you have?"

His lips twisted into a wry smile. "Grandmother isn't exactly a 'pet' type of woman."

"What does that mean?"

"She wasn't about to let an animal track dirt into her home. It was bad enough having an unruly boy around. Besides—" he ratcheted his voice into a falsetto that was obviously supposed to represent his grandmother's speech "—no housekeeper could possibly be expected to keep up with the fur a dog or cat would shed."

"You poor thing," Sloane said, reacting more to the child he had been than the man who sat across from her now.

His hazel eyes glinted as he took another sip of coffee. "You understand, then. I had no choice but to bring home a snake."

"A snake!"

"It was harmless, an albino corn snake," he said, and she could hear the remnants of the enthusiasm he must have felt as a boy. "I set it up in a terrarium, with a heat lamp and a rock. I fed it a live mouse once a week."

"That's terrible!"

"Only for the mouse," he said, pinching his fingers together as if he held a tiny rodent. He shook the make-believe creature in front of her, and she couldn't help but cringe, laughing all the while. He dropped the imaginary mouse, twisting his fingers to grab her wrist, to pull her closer to him. His lips were surprisingly soft against hers, and she found herself leaning closer, wanting more, needing some solid reassurance as she was capsized by another wave of worry about Daisy. He cupped her cheek with his palm, and she leaned against his smooth skin, closing her eyes to take a steadying breath.

"Ethan," she said, back to asking herself the questions she knew he wouldn't answer.

He said, "We're great caretakers for a puppy, aren't we? With only a goose and a snake between us, for past experience?"

"We can learn," she said. Suddenly, her response seemed unbearably important, much more relevant than any single thought about any single little dog. "We can always learn."

His eyes darkened, but he didn't have a chance to respond because his phone rang. She leaped back in her chair, as if she'd been bitten by his harmless albino corn snake.

Ethan answered before the ring was complete. "Hartwell," he snapped. "Yes. Fine. We'll be right there." He terminated the call and started to collect their cups, not meeting her eyes.

"Ethan?" she asked.

"Let's go."

He held the doors for her, the one leading out of the coffee shop, the one going into the vet's office. But she felt him pull away emotionally. She knew that if she reached for his hand, it wouldn't be there. Her fingers would twine around empty air.

Dr. Johnson was waiting for them in the examining room. She'd clipped X-rays onto a light box, and she'd spread out an array of papers on the table—medical charts, spiky test results that clearly detailed heart function.

Daisy was overjoyed to see Sloane and Ethan. The puppy yipped a greeting, then danced onto her hind paws, begging to be cuddled. Sloane gathered up the animal automatically, burying her face in the dog's black-and-white curls. She heard Ethan demand a full report, and Dr. Johnson responded like a battlefield medic.

Stage 5 heart murmur. Cardiomyopathy. Breed prone to the disease. Medication. Shortened life expectancy.

The words flowed over Sloane, sweeping her aside like eddies on a dangerous river. She caught a sob at the back of her throat, managing a strangled hiccup that made Daisy tilt her head to one side in adorable confusion. Sloane scratched the sweet dog's neck and cut off some technical question that Ethan was posing, some request for obscure medical details. "Is she in any pain?"

The vet turned to her with a sympathetic smile. "No. She'll get fatigued earlier than a healthy dog would. She may develop a cough. Of course, you won't be able to breed her."

"But it isn't cruel to keep her with us? To keep her alive?" Sloane's voice broke on the last word, but she forced herself to look directly in the doctor's eyes.

"Not at all. You should have a few good years with her, given proper medication, and adapting to her needs for a relatively quiet life."

That was all Sloane needed to hear. She let Ethan ask his questions, then, technical things about the chambers of the heart, blood tests, biochemical profiles. She heard the answers, understood them, but they didn't matter. Not for now. Not when she knew that she could have some real time to enjoy Daisy's companionship.

Ethan nodded as the doctor finished her explanation. He requested a complete copy of the medical file, including the X-rays. He'd have everything reviewed by one of his own veterinarians, by one of his trusted Hartwell Genetics staff, but he had no reason to doubt what Dr. Johnson was saying.

He shook the vet's hand, thanking her for giving them so much of her time. He watched Sloane gather up the puppy, cuddling the thing against her chest as they headed out. He produced his credit card without thinking, signed the receipt automatically. It was second nature to hold the door for Sloane, to open the back of the SUV, to work the latch on the dog's crate.

The animal turned three instinctive circles before she collapsed on the soft bedding, sighing as if she'd had a thoroughly satisfying outing. Sloane laughed and chucked the dog under her chin, and then Ethan secured the latch, tugging twice to make sure the animal was safe. He opened Sloane's door, waited for her to settle, closed the door and headed for the driver's seat.

He was already composing an email to Zach. If Ethan were able to act alone, he would insist on the breeder taking back the damaged animal. Let someone else be responsible for the rest of this miserable story. But one look at Sloane made him certain that she would never accept that action.

He was stuck with a creature that was doomed to die well before its rightful time. And there was nothing he could do about it. Nothing at all. Except refuse to be taken in. Refuse to get attached. Refuse to get anymore involved than he already was.

Ethan turned the key in the ignition, closing his ears to Sloane's crooning as she comforted her puppy on the short drive home.

Chapter Six

Two and a half weeks later, Sloane sat in another medical office, glancing uneasily at the clock. Dr. Phillip Morton was running late—half an hour so far. Of course, he was an obstetrician, and he couldn't control emergencies that came up among his pregnant patients.

Sloane glanced down at the forms she had completed, the endless pages that asked for shockingly personal information. It always bothered her to fill out medical documents. She had so little information about her parents, no real family history to include. Most doctors looked at her with suspicion when they saw how many questions she left blank. She never got used to that pause before she could explain, before she could say, "I didn't know my father, and I only have limited information about my mother."

At least Ethan had taken over for some of the forms. He had filled in all the blanks that related to insurance, to money, to the cost of the medical care she was about to receive. He completed his own profile as well, dashing off information about his personal health, diseases that ran in his family. He filled in the box labeled "other," recording details about the genetic anomaly that underlay this entire office visit.

She'd half expected him to leave as soon as the paperwork was complete. He had delivered his insurance card to the front desk, though, and then he'd sat beside her. His keys jangled in his pocket as he settled into his chair. He'd insisted on driving them to the doctor's office, powering his own luxury car through the crowded city streets and giving his driver the morning off.

Sloane was just grateful that they hadn't taken the SUV. She would always associate that vehicle with Dr. Johnson, with Daisy, with the sad news about the puppy's cardiomyopathy. Not that the little dog seemed to understand anything about her illness. The Old English sheepdog had taken to jumping up on Sloane's lap whenever she could, curling up as if she were a lapdog. Daisy was putting on weight every day. Between the puppy's size and Sloane's own expanding waistline, the practice couldn't continue, but it was certainly fun while it lasted.

Not that Ethan had even noticed. He now ignored Daisy whenever he could, acting as if the sweet little animal was invisible. He no longer scratched behind her ears, and he'd stopped taking her for walks. Come to think of it, Sloane couldn't even remember the last time he'd referred to the dog by name.

Sloane wasn't a fool. She knew what he was doing. He was protecting himself, keeping his heart safe from future pain. But he was also missing out on all the fun and joy that Daisy could give them—potential years of canine love and affection.

Sloane glanced at Ethan, wondering if she dared raise the issue while they waited. He was stunning in his navy suit, the fabric offset with the faintest pinstripe. His shirt was bright white, almost blinding across his chest, at his wrists. He wore a conservative burgundy tie, perfectly knotted, as if he were expecting to be photographed at any minute.

Which, if the press ever found out what they were doing that morning, would certainly be the case.

Her belly churned with anxiety. She wanted to stand up, to pace across the room, to work off some of the nervous energy that sparked through her body. Instead, she recrossed her legs. There was nothing to do but wait.

She clenched her hands in her lap, rubbing her right thumb against her left palm. She'd never imagined that she'd be sitting here in the office of one of the world's foremost obstetricians, waiting for a test that could dictate the entire future of her life.

Not that anything would change. She was going to keep this baby no matter what the test results showed, even if they confirmed the worst possible news, the strongest form of the Hartwell genetic curse.

She almost wished that she was innocent again, that she still believed that the amnio was only necessary to prove that Ethan was the father of her child. Then she could have believed that everything would work out perfectly. One quick medical confirmation of a fact she knew could never be in doubt, and all would be settled.

But in reality, everything was tangled. Everything was confused. Three weeks ago, at Ethan's insistence, Sloane had phoned her landlord and told him that she was breaking her lease. She'd agreed to have her furniture donated; she didn't even know where it had been sent. James had taken care of that. James had taken care of everything, dispatching movers to collect one more suitcase of clothes, her favorite coffee mug, a handful of trinkets.

Two medium-size boxes. That was all she owned. If today's test came back with devastating news, and she took the stand she knew she had to take, Ethan might very well throw her out of his house. She could put all of her belongings into the trunk of a taxi. But where would she tell the driver to take her?

She closed her eyes and leaned her head back against the wall. She was just nervous about the procedure. Everything was going to be fine. Even if the amnio revealed Ethan's worst fears, he wasn't going to kick her out. She had to believe that.

"Are you all right?" His voice was low, vibrating with an edge of concern she'd never heard before.

Her eyes fluttered open. "I'm fine. Just nervous."

"The procedure isn't supposed to hurt."

She managed a wry smile. "That's what all the fathers say."

His face shuttered closed, and he shifted in his seat, increasing the gulf between them. Before she could think of something to tell him, something to smooth over the awkward silence, a nurse appeared across the waiting room. "Ms. Davenport?"

Sloane grabbed a deep breath and got to her feet. She took two steps before she turned back to Ethan, ready to tell him that he should feel free to take a walk, to get out of the waiting room, that he should just go into his office, and she would call a cab to take her home.

He was right behind her, so close, in fact, that he reached out a hand to steady her, to keep her from falling backward. His fingers on her arm were cold, like granite.

"I—" she said, flustered.

"I'm coming with you."

There was no way to argue with the grim determination on his face. She swallowed and turned back to the waiting nurse, trying to pretend that Ethan was always by her side, that he was always her companion. That she had no doubt they would stay that way for years and years to come. *Partnership,* she thought grimly. She was the one who had put the word on that damned piece of paper.

Ethan barely noticed the hall they walked down. The procedure room was the same as thousands he'd seen before, the same as all the other offices where Hartwell Genetics worked its magic. An examining table covered with fresh white paper. A chair. A hanger on the back of the door. An ultrasound machine, lights already blinking to show that it was ready to serve. The nurse delivered her standard patter, handing Sloane a paper gown, telling her to leave it open at the front, departing with an efficient swirl of papers.

All too soon, the two of them were alone, and Sloane had donned the flimsy paper garment.

He could see that she was terrified. She was putting on a brave face, pretending that nothing would go wrong, but he could read her tension in the set of her jaw, in the line of her lips as she swallowed noisily.

His palms itched. He wanted to close the distance between them. He wanted to kiss those pale lips, whisper against her cheek that everything was going to be fine, that he would be there for her, no matter what the tests revealed.

He couldn't do that, though. He couldn't make a promise that he wasn't certain he could keep.

He was spared the need to drum up small talk by a sharp knock on the door. Sloane jumped as much as he did before the door opened and Phillip Morton glided into the room.

"Phil," Ethan said, smoothly stepping forward and extending his hand.

"Ethan."

Phil was an old business colleague. They had sat on advisory boards together, played more than a few rounds of golf. Ethan had chosen Phil because he knew the man had impeccable credentials and hands-on experience to match the sterling diplomas on his wall. More than that, though, Phil knew the Hartwell family history. He understood the science behind Ethan's greatest fear.

The obstetrician reached out to shake Sloane's hand, offering her a professional smile, automatic reassurances. The nurse returned to assist with the procedure, and Ethan moved to the far side of the examining table, trying to stay out of the way.

Sloane had grown stoic. Her nerves were more apparent now. She fiddled with that ridiculous paper gown, tracing her fingers back and forth along one edge. She answered Phil's questions with as few words as possible, her voice pitched half an octave higher than usual. Several times, she took deep, isolated breaths, as if she were reminding herself to fill her lungs, to exhale her fear, to relax as best she could.

Soon enough, she was reclining on the table. Her eyes widened in alarm as the nurse applied gel to her belly, preparing her for the ultrasound that would guide the doctor's needle. Sloane swallowed, the sound clearly audible in the sterile room. For the first time, Ethan could see the gentle swell of her changed body, the soft curve that told him that there really was a baby, that there really was a new life that they'd created.

He couldn't do this for her, couldn't place his own body on the table instead of hers. But he could help her. He could do his best to ease her fear.

Snagging a chair with his wingtip-clad foot, he sat down close to her head. With one hand, he reached out to smooth a stray lock of hair from her cheek. With the other, he captured her own hand, twining his fingers between hers.

She turned to look at him, tears filming the saturated blue of her eyes. "It's okay," he whispered, leaning down to place his lips against the shell of her ear. A rush of tenderness threatened to close his throat, and his voice grew rough as he said, "Everything is going to be fine."

The words were a prayer for him, an invocation for everything that was good and bright and kind within the universe to preserve him, to keep him from being a liar, now, when the words were the most important he'd ever uttered in his life. He passed his free palm over Sloane's forehead, trying to soothe away the worried lines he found there. "Relax," he said. "It's almost over."

Phil nodded in approval as Ethan spoke. The doctor's hands moved smoothly, with the ease of familiarity. He narrated his actions, letting Sloane prepare for the slight pinch as he inserted his needle, telling her that everything was going as expected, that everything was routine.

Soon enough, they were done. Sloane heard Dr. Morton's patter. She felt the nurse wipe away the ultrasound gel. She understood that she was supposed to wait for fifteen minutes, then sit up, get dressed, meet Dr. Morton in his office down the hall. The door to the examining room closed.

"Ethan," she whispered, turning her head to see him.

"Thank you," he responded in the same subdued tone. "I'm sorry." He lifted her hand, the one that was still wrapped inside his stony fingers. His lips across its back were dry, nearly weightless, like a memory of autumn leaves.

He lowered his head to her shoulder.

Sloane wanted to stroke the golden strands of his hair, wanted to tell him that everything was going to be fine, that he had no reason to apologize, that he hadn't done anything bad or evil or cruel. She knew he wouldn't listen, though, knew he wouldn't believe her. She stared up at the ceiling instead, reminding herself to take deep breaths, waiting until it was safe for her to stand, to get dressed, to carry on as if nothing whatsoever had happened.

Dr. Morton was waiting for them in his office, a veritable forest of mahogany and brass, with deep leather chairs that looked like they belonged in an antique boardroom. "We'll have results in ten days," he said.

Ethan cleared his throat. "Surely you can expedite this."

Dr. Morton shook his head. "Some tests take time to run, Ethan. We can't rush nature." There was a mild sharpness to the doctor's tone, a hint of rebuke. That sting, though, was gone when Dr. Morton returned his gaze to Sloane. "Take it easy for the rest of the day. Stay off your feet as much as possible. Drink plenty of fluids. No sex for twenty-four hours."

Sloane studiously avoided looking at Ethan. No sex for a lot longer than that. Not until after they were truly married.

Dr. Morton shook their hands as they stood to leave. He spared a grave smile for Sloane. "Ms. Davenport, please don't hesitate to phone me if you have any questions. Any questions at all."

"Thank you," she said, liking his solemn sincerity. Ethan had been right. Transferring her care to Dr. Morton was a good thing. It was a tremendous comfort to know that she could schedule her monthly appointments, that she could follow through on everything that was good for the baby.

Ethan held the door for her as they left the office. He wished that he could do more, that he could make the next ten days disappear, that he could write a check, empty a bank account, open a vein to guarantee the results he craved.

Instead, he was reduced to idiotic, everyday tasks. He insisted on pulling the car around to the elevator lobby so that Sloane wouldn't have to walk even the short distance through the parking lot. He opened the door for her and hovered a protective hand above her head as she gracefully eased herself onto the seat. He barely resisted the urge to lean across, to tug at her seat belt to make sure that she had secured it properly.

Once he was back in the driver's seat, he double-checked his mirrors. He made his way through the streets like a model citizen, observing every speed limit, gliding to a perfect stop at every red light. He felt as if he were making a bargain with heaven, that he was offering up his good behavior in exchange for his dreams.

As he helped her out of the car, he caught a whiff of her scent, the honeysuckle freshness that always surrounded her. Unconsciously, he braced himself for the tug in his groin, for the hot lance of lust that she awakened in him without any effort at all. Instead, he felt a throbbing ache in his chest, a terrifying surge that nearly stopped his heart.

She was so brave. So determined. So willing to sacrifice for him, for their child.

He only hoped that he had not betrayed her, that his genes had not paved the path for the destruction of everything good that was growing between them.

Inside the house, he trailed after her, up the stairs to the guest suite. Feeling like a stranger in his own home, he glided over to her bed. The comforter felt foreign beneath his fingers; he might never have seen it before. The sheets were crisp, clean, but they held no familiarity, no saucy temptation of heat, of memory, of passion. He folded them back as if he were completing a ritual, a prayer.

Ethan's navy suit was incongruous as he worked; he stood out like a preacher at a motel. A strangely luxurious motel, but a motel all the same. Only when he'd run out of things to do, when he'd finished all the business of seeing to her comfort did he actually meet her eyes.

"Ten days," she said, betraying the thought that had nagged at her all the way home.

"And then we'll know." He raised his hand, settled his chilly palm against her cheek. A shudder crinkled down her spine, even as she turned her head to lean against his fingers. "Get some rest," he whispered. "I'll have James bring you some lunch."

"Ethan? Will you bring Daisy up here? I'd like to have her beside me while I sleep."

His shoulders stiffened, and she knew that he wanted to refuse. He didn't want anything to do with the puppy, with a living, breathing reminder that genetic mishaps did occur. She knew that she needed to talk to him, needed to tell him that he was wrong to ignore the dog.

But she couldn't. Not right then. Not when she was so tired that she could barely keep her eyes open.

Ethan's voice was gravely courteous as he said, "I'll have James take care of that."

That. A living, breathing puppy was reduced to "that." Sloane swallowed hard, and Ethan ducked out the door before she could make any verbal response.

As soon as he was gone, Sloane slipped out of her summer sundress. She'd gone on the shopping spree that Ethan had recommended. New clothes hung in her closet, spanning the range from casual to formal. Her dresser drawers were filled with satin and lace; she had splurged on intriguing lingerie that had made her blush even as she imagined what Ethan would say when he finally saw it.

For now, though, she dug to the back of the drawer, shoving aside garments that still bore their price tags. Her fingers closed on her old cotton nightgown, and the softness of the fabric nearly brought tears to her eyes. She shrugged it over her bare shoulders, relishing the familiar feel. She yawned as she climbed into bed. The morning had been so emotionally fraught, so charged, that she felt as if she'd run a marathon. She was asleep before James arrived with his tray. His tray, and Daisy.

Once Ethan was certain that Sloane was sleeping soundly, he headed for his office. He knew that James would call him if anything went wrong, if there was anything at all that he could do back at the house.

Watching Sloane's grim determination that morning had made him realize that he was long overdue in attending to his own difficult matters. It was time to confront his grandmother, time to declare that he was marrying Sloane Davenport.

Of course, there was the usual rigmarole in the waiting area outside his grandmother's office suite. The grim-faced secretary waved him to a seat, treating him like he was some unwelcome petitioner. Well, Ethan wasn't going to put up with that. Not today. Not when he had such an important message to deliver.

Ignoring the squawk of professional outrage from the secretary, Ethan marched straight into the lion's den.

Grandmother was on the phone, nodding her head at something that was being said on the other end of the line. She took one look at Ethan's face, though, and she interrupted whoever was talking. "I'm sorry, Richard. Something has come up here. I'll call you back later." She hung up the phone without waiting for a response, as if she were an actress in a movie. "Ethan," she said levelly.

"Grandmother."

The trip to Paris had not been as beneficial as he had hoped. Dark circles still stood out beneath the hazel eyes that matched his own. Grandmother's cheeks were still pale, and he couldn't help but dart a glance to her hands, taking quick measure of the tremor there. As if she knew exactly what he was doing, she folded her fingers into her palms, drawing herself up to her fullest height. "I tried to reach you in your office this morning," she said. "I wanted to discuss the supply figures from Singapore."

"I was out," he said. "At Philip Morton's office." He saw the flash of recognition in his grandmother's eyes, the instant that she registered the name of the prominent obstetrician.

"I assume from your tone that you had a personal reason for being there? Not some study you're asking him to conduct for the company?"

His tone. Ethan had been accused of using the wrong

tone ever since he was a child. Well, he was long past the age where he would roll his eyes and click his tongue in teenage exasperation. Instead, he harnessed all of his skills as a successful business executive, every lesson he'd ever learned about meaningful communication, about driving home his personal agenda in a dog-eat-dog world.

Because there was nothing more personal than his relationship with Sloane Davenport.

"Grandmother, you told me that you wanted me married by January. I'll meet your deadline, with a couple of months to spare."

There. He'd caught her by surprise.

But it only took a moment for her to follow his words to their logical conclusion, from Philip Morton to her damnable birthday ultimatum. "So, you got a girl in the family way, and now you're going to marry her. Is she one of your actresses? Or is she a model?"

He shook his head, resisting the urge to protest the way she always thought the worst of him. Then again, he hadn't given her a lot of reason to think otherwise, not where his personal life was concerned. "Her name is Sloane Davenport. We met at the AFAA auction. She used to work for the foundation."

"Used to? Where does she work now?"

He hedged his answer, knowing precisely how his grandmother would interpret the unvarnished truth of Sloane's unemployment. "She's a freelancer, working in the area of child psychology."

"Ethan." She turned his name into an essay of warning. "What do you really know about this woman?"

He bristled at the implied accusation. "I know that she's no gold digger, Grandmother. She's not staying with me because she expects a share of the Hartwell fortune, if that's what you're worried about."

"And the baby?" Grandmother sounded like a particularly troublesome shareholder in the midst of an annual meeting. "Does she know about the risk?"

What kind of man did his grandmother think he was? "Of course she knows. That's why we were at Phil's office this morning. We'll have the test results in ten days."

"And will she stick around if the results are bad?"

"Grandmother—"

"I'm just asking, Ethan. You're talking about spending the rest of your life with this woman, and I want to know if she has what it takes to handle bad news. The worst."

His own parents hadn't. They'd abandoned him when the going got tough. Sloane was different, though. She was more determined than Ethan was himself. He knew that, even though it frightened him to admit it. "She'll stay with me, Grandmother. No matter what the test shows."

"Very well," Grandmother said after a long pause. She nodded as if they'd just decided to change the color of their corporate logo. "You'll bring her to the *No Comment,* on Independence Day?"

Grandmother's yacht. Site of her annual Fourth of July party, where scores of friends and business associates would gather for the finest catered foods and the best view of fireworks over the Potomac River.

"Of course," he said. "There's nothing we'd like more."

She didn't bother to call him on the lie. Instead, she let him turn on his heel, let him cross all the way to the office door. As he settled his hand on the knob, though, she called out his name. "Ethan, I have to warn you. If

I find this girl wanting, if I think that she's only trying to use you for your name or your money, I'll follow through on my original plan. I can still step down from the board and donate all my shares to AFAA."

He turned back to meet her gaze, hazel eyes to hazel. "Of course you can, Grandmother. You'll do whatever you have to do. Sloane and I will see you on the Fourth."

He left before she could get in the last word.

Chapter Seven

Ethan told himself that he didn't need to worry. He'd attended Independence Day celebrations on the *No Comment* for years. He was used to his grandmother's sly power plays, to the barbed comments she made, all in the name of family love. This year wouldn't be any different.

Except it was. This year, Sloane was with him.

She looked stunning as she stood at the boat's railing, the picture of health in a bright blue sundress. He had no idea what sort of fabric that thing was, or how a designer would describe the cut. All he could say was that the color set off the glow of her eyes, made her hair seem even darker in the brilliant late-afternoon sun. He came up beside her, handing over a glass of sparkling water before he leaned against the railing. "Compliments of the *No Comment,*" he said.

She flashed a smile at him. "I've never been on a boat large enough to have a 'below.'"

"I'm sure Grandmother would love to show you around. Just brace yourself to answer a thousand questions in payment for the privilege."

She gave him a concerned look. "Maybe we shouldn't have come, if you feel so strongly about her."

He just shook his head. There was a lot that Sloane had to learn about the Hartwell family. A lot that he should tell her. But not yet. Not now. Not while they were still waiting for news about the amnio, about the baby's health. There'd be time enough to give her the full background on Grandmother and the old woman's ridiculous, controlling demands.

He smiled to ease the frown that was starting to settle onto Sloane's lips. "You need to meet each other, and there's no time like the present. I just wish that we didn't have to stay on this boat until the fireworks display ends. There are better ways to spend a summer evening."

She quickly took a swallow of her drink in a fruitless attempt to tame the blush that leaped to her cheeks. Over the past month, Ethan had scrupulously honored their agreement; he'd never come close to pushing her beyond her comfort zone, sexually. He certainly wasted no time, though, teasing her, alluding to the things that he would do once her ban on bedroom play was lifted. Even now, he stared at her with an amused hazel gaze, taking careful note of the way she settled her ice-filled glass against the hot pulse point in her wrist. "Let's go downstairs," he said. When she raised her chin in surprise at his proposal, he laughed. "Grandmother is down there. She'll hold court in the air-conditioning, until the sun sets."

"Well," she said, trying to muster the composure that she knew he could destroy with a single wicked glance. "I wouldn't want her to think I was afraid of her."

"Oh, she'll never think that," Ethan said.

He slipped his fingers between hers easily, holding her hand as if they'd known each other for years. Sloane looked around, surprised to realize that so many people had joined them on the yacht's deck. There must be thirty altogether, gathered in clusters of three and four. Sloane tilted her head back to look at the raised deck, where the captain was just beginning to maneuver the *No Comment* out of the marina.

"Ethan!" a voice called out. Sloane turned around to find Zach Crosby approaching. The two men shook hands, and Zach leaned in to settle a quick kiss on Sloane's cheek. "I'm glad that both of you could make it," Zach said, directing a concerned glance at Sloane. "Ethan said you weren't feeling well earlier this week?"

She resisted the urge to settle a protective hand over her belly. Instead, she smiled at the honest worry on the man's face. No reason to fill him in on the amnio test, on the nerve-jangling wait for results. "I'm fine, now."

"Ethan told me about Daisy. I was so sorry to hear about her condition. I certainly never intended to cause any problems for you."

Sloane made herself smile again, hoping to ease the earnest frown on Zach's face. "*You* didn't cause the problems. Sometimes these things just happen. No one's to blame." She glanced at Ethan, hoping that he'd say something to smooth things over. He didn't oblige, and she fought the urge to chide him.

At least Zach seemed to miss the momentary tension between them. "Thanks for your understanding," he said. "Hey, did Ethan tell you about the Fourth of July when we brought firecrackers on board the *No Comment?* We were thirteen, and we thought we were in charge of the universe."

She laughed at the energy in Zach's voice, at the image of two mischievous boys, wreaking havoc on the boat's deck. "I think he forgot to mention that one."

"Zach—" Ethan warned, but there was no deterring his best friend.

"Ethan bought them in the first place, but it was my idea to bring them on board."

"I don't think Sloane wants to hear—" Ethan started to complain, but there was resigned laughter behind his words.

"Oh, no," Sloane protested. "I'm very interested in this. Go on, Zach. Tell me more."

"Ethan figured out how to rig them under the starboard railing. He wanted to see what would happen if all the guests ran to one side of the boat at the same time."

"It was a study in physics," Ethan said piously. "Newton's third law. Every action causes an equal and opposite reaction."

"That's not what your grandmother said when she caught us."

"My grandmother didn't appreciate the finer points of the scientific method."

Zach's eyes sparkled. "She appreciated free labor, in any case. It took us three whole days of summer vacation to scrub down the deck after the party. The worst part, though, was that she insisted on checking our pockets for the next three years, whenever we got anywhere near the boat."

Sloane was pleased to hear Ethan laugh at the memory. To hear him talk about his childhood, there had been so much that was dark, so much pain. It was a revelation to discover that Ethan actually had some good memories.

"What do you think of Margaret?" Zach asked Sloane.

"Actually, I haven't really met her yet. Just shaken her hand at the AFAA gala and thanked her for coming. I'm sure she doesn't remember me at all."

Ethan said, "We were just heading below."

Zach nodded, directing a warning to Sloane. "Don't believe everything he tells you. Margaret Hartwell isn't really a tyrant. It's been years since she had anyone flogged on board the *No Comment*."

"Enough!" Ethan exclaimed in mock exasperation, and then he said to Sloane, "Shall we?" He settled a hand on her hip and pulled her away with a tantalizing hint of possession.

He glanced quickly at Sloane before he led the way down the stairs. She'd had the good sense to wear flat sandals—no chance that she'd lose her footing on the narrow steps. Nevertheless, he felt anxious each time she settled her feet. He wished that he could gather her into his arms, that he could carry her through the passage ahead. Of course, if his hands were anywhere near her bare flesh, he and Sloane might not make it as far as Grandmother's sitting room. He just might wander into one of the bedrooms, by "mistake."

The stairs negotiated, Sloane came to stand beside him. They entered the dragon's lair together.

As he had expected, Margaret Hartwell was sitting on her favorite throne, the massive armchair that faced the doorway of the elegantly appointed room. She must have come fresh from the hairdresser that morning; he could still smell the hairspray that held her white aura in place. She wore a classic summer suit, all in navy. Her fingernails were painted the same orange-red that she'd worn forever, perfectly applied and a single shade too bright.

"Ethan, dear," she said, tilting her face for him to kiss. He was pleased to see some color in her face, and she looked a little less fatigued than she had earlier in the week.

"Grandmother." He brushed his lips against her cheek. "May I present Sloane Davenport? Sloane, this is my grandmother, Margaret Hartwell."

He brought Sloane forward, fighting the urge to roll his eyes at his grandmother's formality, at her turning a simple meeting into an audience with a queen.

For one insane moment, Sloane wondered if she was supposed to curtsy. There was something about the awkward way Ethan was holding himself, the stiffness that jammed his spine, that turned him into a man she'd never seen before.

Margaret, though, offered her hand and a smile, the very image of a perfect hostess. "Sloane, dear. How very nice to meet you. I must say, you look very familiar to me…"

Sloane hoped that her own fingers weren't trembling too much as she shook hands. "We've met before, very briefly. At the AFAA Spring Gala."

"Of course!" Mrs. Hartwell exclaimed. "Ethan told me that you are no longer with the foundation. He said that you're doing something related to…child psychology?"

Sloane flashed an uncertain glance at Ethan. How much had he told Mrs. Hartwell about Sloane's ignominious dismissal from the woman's pet charity? She tried to sound confident as she said, "I'm developing a computerized art therapy system, to help children adjust to foster care."

Margaret nodded with something that looked like approval. "That sounds quite complicated."

"It is," Sloane said, "but there's a real need out there."

"I would love to hear more about your work. Have you looked into market distribution, anything like that?"

Ethan finally stepped forward, shattering his own awkward stance with an exasperated sigh. "Grandmother, we didn't come here expecting to be grilled by a venture capitalist."

"I don't mind—" Sloane started to say, but Mrs. Hartwell cut her off.

"You're quite right, Ethan. We shouldn't mix business with pleasure. Could you be a dear and get me a drink? A gin and tonic with—"

"Extra ice and three limes." Sloane heard the bored familiarity in Ethan's tone, and she expected him to smile indulgently. His face was grim, though, and he hesitated before heading over to the stairs. Sloane nodded at him, trying to convey that she would be fine, that she could handle further chat with the woman who was going to be her…grandmother-in-law?

As soon as Ethan was out of sight, Margaret patted the chair beside her. "Please, dear. Sit down. I imagine you're still getting tired easily? I assumed that you were well past morning sickness, or I'd never have suggested that Ethan bring you onto the *No Comment*."

Sloane tried not to look surprised. She parsed the tone of the old woman's words, fearful that she'd hear disdain or disapproval. Neither was present, though. Just good old-fashioned solicitude for a guest. "I—thank you," she said, sitting down. "I've felt much better the past few weeks."

"I trust that my grandson is taking good care of you?"

"Of course, Mrs. Hartwell."

The old woman tsked. "Now doesn't *that* sound stuffy. And 'Grandmother' sounds like something out of a British drama, even coming from Ethan. Why don't we try 'Margaret.'"

"Margaret," Sloane said, smiling. "Yes, Margaret, Ethan has been quite kind to me."

"Kind." Margaret tilted her head to one side, like a magpie evaluating a particularly sparkly treasure. "I see that he bought you a lovely ring."

Self-conscious, Sloane extended her hand. Margaret grasped her fingers lightly, turning her wrist to get a better view. "It was such a surprise," Sloane confided. "I never expected anything so beautiful." She stopped, realizing that Margaret might interpret her words as a criticism of Ethan. "I mean, Ethan has wonderful taste. Of course, he'd choose a beautiful ring. I just meant…"

She trailed off. What was she going to say? Her engagement to Ethan had been a business arrangement? A way for both of them to provide for the well-being of their child, the baby that neither of them had anticipated on that breath-stealing night at the Eastern?

No. Margaret definitely did *not* need to know anything about the Eastern.

The old woman released her hand. "My grandson seems quite taken with you, dear. I hope that you won't take this the wrong way, but I've seen him with any number of women over the years, squiring them around town. He's never been quite as…attentive as he is to you. And, of course, he never actually proposed to any of the others."

Sloane heard the unspoken questions behind Margaret's statements. The older woman was honestly perplexed to find her grandson engaged. She was fishing for details. Sloane obliged by saying, "He proposed to me on the balcony of the Kennedy Center."

That wasn't quite the truth. Ethan had first proposed in the living room of her ratty basement apartment. But the proposal that mattered, the proposal that she'd *accepted,* had been at the famous landmark.

"I trust my grandson had the good sense to treat you to some romantic show first."

Sloane blushed, as if she were speaking with a girlfriend. "It was the ballet gala," she said shyly.

Margaret nodded, as if she were seeing the pieces of a jigsaw puzzle coalesce into a single coherent design. "That was Zach's event?" Sloane nodded, and Margaret said, "Poor Zach told me about the silent auction. He feels absolutely terrible about your puppy."

"He shouldn't," Sloane insisted. "Daisy is adorable, and she's doing fine, for now. We'll have some hard times ahead, but doesn't every pet owner?"

Margaret raised her eyebrows, as if Sloane had just imparted brilliant words of wisdom. "I suspect that Ethan doesn't feel quite the same way."

Before Sloane could reply, Ethan's voice came from the foot of the stairs. "Feel the same way about what?"

Ethan forced himself to keep his voice light, but he was annoyed. There'd been three people in front of him at the bar upstairs, and there hadn't been any polite way to force himself to the front of the line. He'd hated leaving Sloane alone here, hated subjecting her to one of his grandmother's famous inquisition sessions.

"Nothing, darling," Grandmother said. "We were just talking about your new puppy."

Every muscle in his body tightened. That creature was the last thing he wanted to talk about in front of Grandmother. Well, he amended, suddenly flashing on the memory of Sloane submitting to the amnio test in Philip Morton's office, the *second to last* thing. "What about it?" he asked flatly.

"Her," Sloane said.

"Excuse me?" He glanced between the two women, wondering what he was missing.

"What about *her,*" Sloane said. "Daisy isn't an *it,* she's a *her.*"

The intensity in Sloane's voice astonished him. He'd heard that tone before—when she spoke about the Hope Project—but he couldn't fathom what made her feel so strongly about the damned animal.

He glanced at Grandmother to see if she understood where Sloane's argument was coming from, and he immediately recognized the expression on her face. It was a small, wry grin, a raised-eyebrow expression that had always made him feel like he was being called on the carpet. She'd used it when he was a boy, when he was forced to face the consequences of some misbehavior, demerits or detention or some more drastic punishment. She still brought it out in business meetings, when she thought that a competitor was getting the better of him. She had leveled it against him in personal discussions, when one of his past indiscretions came home to roost.

He hated that look. And, even more, he hated the fact that Sloane was seeing it now.

He harnessed all the dispassion of his medical degree, all the cool logic that he'd learned in business school, and he said, "Her. If that's what you prefer."

Sloane bristled at the concession. Still, she might have let everything drop, if she hadn't caught the glance that Margaret shot at her. Ethan's grandmother was actually *inviting* Sloane to challenge him. Practically demanding it. And Sloane had to admit, it felt good to say, "You haven't touched that puppy since we got the diagnosis."

Ethan glared at Margaret, as if he were aware that she was some sort of instigator in this conversation. Sloane didn't care, though. This confrontation had been weeks in coming. "You think I'm an idiot for getting attached to her."

"I don't think you're an idiot!" His voice shook with some emotion. "And I don't think that we should be having this conversation here. Now." He sparked a meaningful glance toward Grandmother.

"Don't mind me," the meddlesome old woman said. Had the two of them worked this out, in the little time that he'd been upstairs? Had they banded together to force him into this?

Ethan scowled at Margaret, barely wiping the expression from his face before he turned back to Sloane. "I don't think you're an idiot," he repeated. "I just don't want you to be hurt."

"You don't get to decide that! Besides, I can't be hurt by loving something that loves me back, the way that Daisy does!"

Ethan raised his hands in a placating gesture. "You don't understand what I'm saying."

Sloane's fingers clutched at the crisp cotton that covered her belly. She raised her chin and chilled her voice until it met the temperature of Margaret's gin and tonic. "Ethan Hartwell, I understand every single word that you're saying."

It was all there. She knew that Daisy frightened him because they were ultimately going to lose her. She knew that the baby terrified him even more. The baby, and the decision that they might have to make. The decision that she would never, ever accept.

Ethan's throat worked. He started to reply to Sloane's indignant protest, seemed to decide that it was actually impossible to continue talking in front of Margaret. He stopped. Tried another approach. Stopped again. It was the first time she'd ever seen him without an easy answer, without some glib reply. At last, he gave up speaking to her at all. Instead, he glared at Margaret and said, "I hope you're happy now, Grandmother."

The old woman sighed. "No, darling. I'm not happy at all." Sloane heard the endless sorrow beneath her words—disappointment at the current situation certainly, but more than that. Sloane could only imagine how many fights there had been between the two of them, how many disagreements when a headstrong boy, now an iron-willed man, had vented his frustrations with life's unfairness.

Ethan snorted in disgust. "I don't believe that for a moment."

Sloane cut him off. "Don't you dare take this out on her!"

"She—"

"She asked a simple question," Sloane said, feeling the fragile hold she had on her own emotions start to fray. "She asked about the night you proposed to me. About the gala, and Daisy. Good things, Ethan. Nothing that *hurt*."

Ethan stared at her, hearing the frustration that she dumped on the last word. And suddenly, he realized that he should have trusted her more. He should have believed that Sloane could devote herself to Daisy, that she would be able to cope with the puppy's ultimate demise. Sloane was stronger than he'd ever given her credit for, infinitely more resilient.

"—so pleased to have made your acquaintance," she

was saying, extending her hand to his grandmother. "I'm afraid I need some fresh air."

"Dear," Grandmother started to say, but Sloane was already halfway across the room. Ethan started after her, only coming to a stop at the sword-sharp note in his grandmother's voice, calling his name.

He took his time turning around, using the pause to freeze his voice. "Yes, Grandmother."

"What were you thinking?" she said. "All these years, chasing after anything in a skirt, and you haven't learned the first thing about how a woman's mind works?"

"Sloane has nothing to do with my past, Grandmother!"

"And if you're not careful, she'll have nothing to do with your future. It's the Fourth of July, Ethan. You have six months to be married. Don't make anymore mistakes."

He started to tell her that he knew the date. He started to tell her that he hadn't made a mistake, that he'd acted in Sloane's best interest. He started to tell her that he was through with manipulation, with games.

But he couldn't waste the time. He had to find Sloane.

She had found a space on the railing, toward the back of the boat. The other guests had swarmed the luxurious buffet tables, taking advantage of the festive red, white and blue plates that encouraged everyone to indulge in gourmet picnic food. Apparently, everyone was accustomed to the notion that Margaret didn't attend her own party. Or at least that she arrived late.

Sloane didn't really care. The only thing she wanted was to get off the boat. She glanced up at the sky. The color was deepening to indigo in the east. Another fifteen minutes, maybe, before the sun actually set. An hour after that, before the fireworks were over. And yet another hour to get back to the dock.

As if she knew what she was going to do then. She certainly couldn't face going home with Ethan. Not when she had finally dared to call him on his greatest fear. Not when she had challenged him in front of his grandmother.

Maybe she could rent a hotel room downtown. As if anything would be available over the holiday weekend. She sighed and ran her fingers through her hair, suddenly feeling wilted by the July heat.

"Why don't you come sit down?" She hadn't heard Ethan come up behind her. His voice was solicitous.

"I don't want to sit down," she said. She realized that she was still angry with him. He had backed them into that impossible corner in Margaret's room, forced them into a conversation that should never have been started on board the *No Comment.*

"Come below," he whispered. "We can have some privacy there, in one of the bedrooms."

"I will *not* go into a bedroom with you!" Her voice was louder than she'd planned. She darted a look around but, mercifully, no one seemed to have heard.

Ethan sighed and shifted his weight, resting his forearms on the railing. He couldn't say anything right. He would just have to wait for Sloane to change her mind. Wait for her to get over the peak of her anger.

The guests swirled in little pockets behind them, exclaiming as they found each other in the growing twilight. Waiters passed trays of bite-size desserts, along with after-dinner drinks. Grandmother finally made her appearance, raising a round of applause and carefully orchestrated fawning by the partygoers.

Throughout it all, Ethan stood beside Sloane, locked

into her silence, riveted by her fury. The worst part of it was that she looked so beautiful. Her profile was stark against the night sky. She held her chin high. A breeze caught a few stray tendrils of her hair.

Each breath carried her unique scent to him, the combination of her delicate skin and whatever soap or perfume or fragrance she wore. In the past month, he thought he'd grown accustomed to the gentle aroma, but now he found that it awoke his own senses, heated the pads of his fingers, scratched across the back of his throat. He longed to pull her close to him, to crush the crisp fabric of her dress beneath his needy hands, to absorb her essence through his palms.

The first fireworks startled her. A quick explosion, and a spatter of crimson and white, high in the sky above them. Sloane caught a yelp at the back of her throat, even as she realized what was happening. Even as she felt Ethan tense beside her.

A dozen more blasts followed in quick succession. The concussions were nearly deafening over the river, the sound echoing back toward the shower of light. Scarlet and silver, cobalt and emerald. The guests oohed and aahed over each display, catching their collective breath in astonishment at the beauty.

Sloane tilted her head back for a better view. Her eyes filled as she watched. It was so beautiful. The entire evening could have been so beautiful, everything about it. Instead, it had all been ruined by a stupid fight. Stupid, but necessary. Because Sloane knew that she was right.

A tear snaked from the corner of her eye, trailing into her hair. She wiped at it with her palm, hurried, embarrassed. Another followed, though, and another—she couldn't stop herself from crying.

"Sloane," Ethan breathed, but she shook her head furiously.

Finally, with a grand finale that left her half-deaf, the fireworks display was over. The other guests cheered and clapped. Someone launched a chorus of "She's a Jolly Good Fellow," and Margaret made a little speech, thanking them all for joining her, exclaiming that she could never ask for more than an enjoyable night with friends and loved ones. The boat's engine finally thrummed to life, and they made their slow way back to the marina, to the dock. To freedom.

Of course, Margaret was waiting at the head of the gangplank, bidding farewell to each guest. Sloane longed to slip past her, to huddle off the boat anonymously, lost in a group of strangers. Margaret, though, made a special point of reaching for her hand, of closing her aged, knotted fingers over the sparkling diamond that had given Sloane so much pleasure only a few hours before.

"I'm sorry that we didn't have a chance to chat more, dear," Margaret said. Her voice was kind, and she waited for Sloane to meet her gaze. "I'm so glad that you came this evening."

"It was lovely," Sloane said mechanically. She was positive that Margaret was studying the remnant tracks of her tears.

Margaret reached out for her grandson's shoulders, pulling Ethan close in an awkward embrace. Sloane couldn't hear what the woman murmured, but she caught the urgency behind the words.

Ethan was astonished when his grandmother hissed, "Make this right."

"I—" he started to protest, barely remembering to keep his voice down. How could he ever have worried about Grandmother's health? She was as sturdy as an ox, pinning him with her agate eyes.

"Now," she ordered. "Make this right."

He shrugged and pulled away. Certainly Grandmother could issue her edicts. She'd been doing it her entire life. But Sloane wasn't some merger or acquisition. Sloane wasn't a government review board to be convinced about the safety and efficacy of a new treatment. Sloane wasn't an investor to be charmed into parting with millions of dollars.

Sloane was the woman he loved.

As soon as he thought the words, he knew that they were true. He should have realized it weeks before, when they had spoken together, laughed together, shared stories of their torn and tangled pasts.

It had taken arguing with her in front of Grandmother, though, hurting her in a way that he'd never intended. It had taken watching her standing at the boat's railing, pretending that she was fine, that their fight hadn't driven her to real tears....

Ethan had felt his own heart shred at her pain. They weren't playing some game, acting out some parts for Grandmother's benefit, for the investors and business partners invited to the party. This was reality. This mattered. This was life.

Sloane Davenport was the mother of his child, the woman that he loved. The woman he had hurt. And he didn't have the first clue about how to fix things.

The car was waiting for them at the end of the dock. Ordinarily, he would have been grateful for his driver, for the luxury of someone else to deal with the crowded streets, with the throng of other fireworks-viewers, everyone returning home after a long, hot summer evening. Tonight, though, Ethan regretted that he couldn't get behind the wheel of the car himself. At least driving would have given him an excuse for the unending silence between them, the jagged stillness that sucked up oxygen like a dying fire.

Why was this so difficult? Why couldn't he just talk to Sloane? After all the words they'd shared, all the conversations they'd had, why was he struck mute now?

But he knew the reason. It kept repeating inside his skull. He loved Sloane. And he had no idea how to prove that to her.

Finally, he let them into the house, working the alarm code with the ease of long familiarity. By the time he turned away from the keypad, Sloane was halfway up the stairs. He longed to follow her, but he knew that he could not. Until he found the right words, he had to let her go.

Sloane slumped against the bedroom door as soon as she had closed it.

She didn't want to be this woman. She didn't want to be so angry. So scared. So alone.

That was it. Loneliness. The loneliness of the child who had feared Angry Mother. The girl who had befriended a goose rather than figure out how to interact with human companions. The woman who had made herself so busy with school, with work, that she had never bonded to close friends. Loneliness—that was the emotion beneath all the turmoil, beneath everything else that was swirling through her head.

She shook her head and stepped out of her sensible sandals. She stripped off her dress, left it draped over the chair in front of the vanity. She added her panties, her bra. Suddenly, she was exhausted. Too tired to dig in her dresser drawers for a nightgown. Too tired to do anything but snap off the overhead light, cross the room, worm her way beneath the sheets.

As she lay naked in the darkness, she cupped her hand over her baby bump. The swell was real. She was going to have this child.

Alone.

She twisted at her engagement ring. She couldn't keep that lie on her finger. An engagement ring was a sign of trust, of promise. Ethan didn't trust her. He didn't think of her as an equal. He certainly didn't love her—he'd never come close to saying anything about love.

She couldn't wear his ring.

The stupid thing was caught on her finger. Her hands must be swollen, from the pregnancy, from standing in the heat all night. Nevertheless, she tugged harder, suddenly consumed with the notion that she had to get the platinum band off her hand. Her heart started pounding in her ears. She closed her eyes, trying to force herself to calm down.

She remembered the last time she had felt this helpless, when the reporters had confronted her on the doorstep of her sweet little apartment, the apartment that was long gone. After she left Ethan tomorrow, she would have nowhere to retreat, no place to escape to. Her lungs constricted, and her breath started to come in short, sharp pants.

It wasn't just her personal life that was ruined, either. Her professional life was going to be a wreck. She'd already lost one job because of Ethan, the AFAA. How could she move ahead with the Hope Project now? With the gossip from the past month smeared all over the internet, any potential investors would think that she was just another in a long trail of women who had ridden on Ethan's coattails, who had thrown herself into a short-lived relationship for a good time and the thrill of reading her name in the tabloids. She'd never launch Hope, never grow the website from a dream to reality.

Her heart squeezed tight, sending a spear through her chest.

Her hands curled into fists. She was having a heart attack. Here. Now. With the baby inside her, innocent and helpless. Sloane scrambled for the telephone on her nightstand. Zero. That was the only number that she needed to press. James would answer. He would help her. Save her. Her and the baby.

Her hand swung wide, knocking the bedside lamp to the floor with a crash of shattered glass. Sobbing, she fumbled for the phone again, found it, dropped it, tried to pick it up one more time.

Ethan heard the clatter from the hallway. Unable to bear the thought of exiling himself to his bedroom, he had slumped against the guest suite door. In the darkness, he'd replayed the entire disastrous night. "Make this right," Grandmother had said. Just how did she expect him to do that? How could he admit to Sloane a truth that he was nearly afraid to admit to himself?

Ethan was launching Round 731 of how his grandmother had made his life miserable when he heard the crash. Adrenaline spiked through his veins as he recognized the sound of glass breaking, the jangle of a phone smashing against the floor.

He sprang to his feet and slammed his hand against the doorknob, hurtling into the room.

His eyes were dazzled by the moonlight streaming through the window, so much more light than he'd had in the hallway. As if Sloane were illuminated from within, he could see her reaching for the nightstand, clutching her fingers over empty air. She was choking, gasping for breath, kicking against her sheets. Even as he flew across the carpet, she worked one foot free, then the other. Flailing, she cast her legs over the side of the bed, toward the sprawling phone. Toward the shattered glass.

"Sloane!" he cried, leaping onto the bed. She flowed through his arms like water, drifting away. He adjusted his grip, closed his fingers around her waist.

She fought him, her voice rising in a terrible, wordless moan. He could hear her breath stutter from her lungs, feel the heat rising off her as she writhed in panic. Flattening his palms against her hips, he pulled her back onto the bed, onto him. He folded his arms around her, pinning her hands to her sides, wrapping his legs around her, enveloping her in the fortress of his body.

"You're all right," he said. "Sloane, you're all right. Listen to me. Breathe. You're all right."

His words came to her as if she were awakening from a nightmare. She felt the iron bands of his arms holding her close against his chest. She was entwined in his legs, captured, stilled. She felt his strength against her back, his deep breaths that reminded her to take her own, to fill her lungs.

The arrow that had pierced her heart finally crumbled.

"Breathe," he said again, and she followed his instruction. "Breathe." Her chest remembered how to expand. "Breathe." She forced herself to swallow, to hold one of those deep breaths, to stop. His hands moved from her waist. He stroked the hair off her face, smoothed it back, twisted it away from her neck. "Breathe," he reminded her one last time.

"I—" she whispered, her voice broken. "I thought I was having a heart attack."

He pitched his voice to match her own, so low that she had to calm herself more to hear it. "A panic attack, more likely."

"My chest," she said.

"Do you feel any pain now?" She barely shook her head. "Numbness?" Another shake. "Tingling in your arms?" Another one. "You're going to be fine," he said.

She closed her eyes, feeling foolish. What was she doing, working herself up like that? It couldn't be good for the baby. Or for herself. And she certainly wasn't doing any favors for the bedroom. She winced. Had she really broken the lamp? And probably the phone? James was going to have a mess to deal with in the morning.

Ethan slid his arms closer around her, cradling her against his chest. Lying in the dark, listening to Sloane growing calm, Ethan knew that he had to do something, had to *say* something. *Make this right,* Grandmother had commanded.

He knew how to make business right. At Hartwell Genetics, in the office, at the helm of a Fortune 500 behemoth, Ethan knew that he had to keep information to himself. He needed to parcel out the truth, keep his employees on a need-to-know basis. He needed to outsmart his competitors, keep them in the dark about markets, about the future.

But Sloane wasn't his employee. She wasn't his competitor. She was the woman who was going to be his wife. He needed to share with Sloane. He needed to treat her as an equal. *Trust. Respect. Partnership.* She'd taught him the words weeks before, when she'd first shared her list with him.

"Sloane—" he started, but he had to stop, had to clear his throat. As much as he longed to confess everything to her, to admit his love, to tell her all the truth that he now knew, he had to apologize first. He had to make it right. "Sloane, I am so sorry. I was wrong to pull away from Daisy, to ignore her. I acted out of fear, but that is no excuse. I blocked her out of my life, and you, too. I had no right to decide how you should handle the bad news, to even try to control you that way. I am so, so sorry."

She grew absolutely still as he spoke. He felt her listening, absorbing every word. He waited for her to say something, anything.

But while he waited, his body betrayed him. His noble thoughts were cheapened by his body's realization that the most desirable woman in the world was lying, naked, in his arms. The sudden heat in his groin made him shift to relieve the pressure against the confining cloth of his trousers.

As long as he was shifting, he might as well leave the room altogether. He'd said everything that he could say. Done everything that he could do. Offered his best bid to *make it right.* She would never believe anymore words that he said, not when he'd been betrayed by a body that would never tire of Sloane's beauty.

Before he could leave the bed, though, her fingers clutched at his. Her hand folded around his, pulling him closer, keeping him near.

Sloane had felt his body stiffen; she recognized the heat of his desire, sudden and firm against her back. She knew that he was leaving in defeat, in shame.

But she also knew just how much his words had cost him, how deeply he'd been moved as he whispered to her in the darkness.

His confession hadn't come from the Ethan Hartwell of the boardroom. No. He'd spoken as the Ethan Hartwell that she'd first met in the Eastern Hotel, that she'd recognized as some sort of kindred spirit within minutes of their first words at that fateful hotel bar. This was the Ethan Hartwell who had opened his life to her.

She'd heard the remorse in his voice, heard the devastating emotion behind his confession. He was doing the best that he could. He was admitting his own fear. He was sharing, reaching out to her.

She twisted, turning to her side, letting him roll with her so that they lay on the bed, face-to-face. "I'm strong enough to do this," she said. "I'm strong enough to love Daisy. To love our baby. No matter what happens. You have to believe me. To trust me."

He brushed the hair back from her face, his fingers impossibly gentle. "I do. I understand that now." And then he knew that he could say the rest, that he *had* to say the rest, no matter how his flesh had tried to lead him astray before. "I trust you, Sloane, and I love you."

He made the words sound new, fresh, as if they'd never been spoken by any human being in the entire history of the world. Sloane might have thought that she was dazed, that she was dreaming, if she hadn't seen his lips form the syllables. Those last three words filled her, capsized her, steadied her again. She held herself perfectly still as she whispered, "I love you, too."

Only then could she lean forward to kiss him. At first, she merely brushed her lips against his. The instant that their mouths met, though, passion leaped high inside her. She parted her lips, yielded to the velvet of his tongue.

She arched her back as he ran his hand down her arm; she shivered at the heat he spread all the way to her fingertips. He raised her wrist to his lips, drank deeply of the pulse point that pounded there. "Sloane," he breathed after teasing her with the tip of his tongue. She heard her name catch in his throat. "I love you," he said, as if he were discovering the words all over again.

She laughed, a little breathlessly. "And I love you."

His teeth teased the pad of her thumb. "Say it," he growled. "Admit that you've changed your mind."

Suddenly, she was standing back on the balcony of the Kennedy Center. She was enchanted by moonlight, by the magnetic power of the man beside her. She was determined to stand fast, to be absolutely, positively, one hundred percent certain that she was doing what was best for her child. Not necessarily for her. Not for her body that sparked and sighed, that longed for pure, physical release.

Not yet. He loved her, and she loved him. But she had made a promise outside of their relationship, beyond the magic that bound them together. She had made a vow for their child. She would not, could not, give in to her driving need until she was well and truly married.

She sagged back against the mattress, fighting to catch her breath.

Of course, Ethan understood her decision. She heard his own ragged sigh as he released her wrist. She recognized his muffled groan as he pulled away from her, as he eased up the sheets from the foot of the bed, as he covered her with all the chaste care of a nursemaid.

But then he lay down beside her. With crisp cotton between them, he gathered her hair to her nape, smoothing it down her back. He folded an arm around her, spreading his fingers across her shielded belly. He whispered for her to relax. To trust him. To sleep.

And she did.

Chapter Eight

Five days later, Sloane sat on the flagstone patio at the back of Ethan's home, trying to convince herself that she was enjoying the book she was reading. The day was unseasonably mild, absent of D.C.'s legendary humidity. Sloane had staked out one of Ethan's chaise longues, settling in with a tall glass of decaffeinated iced tea, a poor substitute for the double espresso she craved.

Her attention wandered from her book, and she gazed out at the brilliant emerald lawn, at the black-and-white patch that was Daisy, sleeping in the shade beneath a crape myrtle tree. The puppy had insisted on a long game of fetch, repeatedly chasing after a tennis ball that Sloane had obediently thrown, over and over and over, thrilled that the animal's heart murmur wasn't inhibiting her play. For now. Finally exhausted, Daisy was snoozing, something that Sloane wished she was able to do.

She hadn't slept at all the night before, and not much for the entire week before that.

She had set her cell phone on the table beside her chair, its ringer turned to maximum volume. She had no idea whether Dr. Morton was going to phone her or Ethan, but she didn't want to risk missing the call.

The days of waiting for amnio results had crept by, stretching and contorting, drumming on her nerves until she'd thought that she would go mad. Every morning, she had stared at her new computer, telling herself that it was time to dig into the Hope Project, to finish the website. Every afternoon, she had glanced at her electronic files, tried to concentrate. Every evening, she had given up, telling herself that there was plenty of time, that she could work on Hope later.

Matters weren't helped by Ethan's near-total absence from the house. After their reconciliation on the Fourth of July, he had practically disappeared from her life. She knew that he didn't regret telling her that he loved her. He wasn't punishing her for her decision to stand by her vow. He sent messages through James, and he'd found time for a few bantering emails. It was just that he had to work late one night, and then he got called out of town to Mexico on an emergency production matter. That trip merged into a long-scheduled conference in San Francisco, another two nights of absence.

Sloane knew that Ethan had returned to Washington the night before. She'd heard him walk down the hallway after midnight, pause outside her door. She'd waited for him to turn the knob, to look in on her, to say something, anything. But he'd walked away without disturbing her. He'd been gone by the time she rose for breakfast, and she'd eaten yet another egg-white omelet, with only James for company.

Five days. Five days of loneliness, of uncertainty, of desperate, aching worry about the child inside her. Was this what her entire married life would be like?

Sighing as her tension ratcheted even tighter, she climbed to her feet and walked to the edge of the patio. To her left, she could see a patch of bright green grass, the sod that the gardeners had laid down once they'd rooted out the dead oak tree. The edges of the new grass were already starting to blur, to melt into the flawless expanse of the rest of the lawn.

She heard the door to the house open behind her, but she didn't bother to turn around. It was certain to be James, coming to ask her what she wanted for lunch. She appreciated his kindness, but she wasn't sure that she could stand another hour facing his patient smile, another meal sharing meaningless stories. Maybe she would just take Daisy for a walk, a long, meandering exploration of the neighborhood.

"Sloane."

Ethan's voice. Her name on his lips jolted through her like an electric wire. She whirled to face him as he closed the distance between them, holding out a single sheet of paper like an invitation to the prom.

She could see the energy lighting up his face, read the excitement that sparked his hazel eyes. The sunshine caught the gold in his hair, spinning back to her like confetti. Her fingers trembled, even though she knew what was written on that paper, even though she understood that it had to carry good news, given Ethan's reaction.

He watched as Sloane took the medical report from him. He saw her glance at the heading, acknowledge her name on the appropriate line, his name beneath. She barely paused when she got to the baby's gender, to the unequivocal statement that they were having a daughter.

It took her longer to parse the dense medical jargon of the next paragraph, the complicated confirmation that their little girl was healthy. No Hartwell genetic curse. No problems at all.

Sloane looked at him, her blue eyes wide, her chin tilted to a defiant angle. "Just as I said," she declared.

Even as she teased him, Sloane's exhaustion crumbled away. She felt as if she were awakening from a long, dream-torn sleep, like she was blooming in the fresh light of dawn. She laughed as Ethan closed the distance between them. His lips slanted over hers with a new urgency. It seemed as if he was kissing her for the first time, building new bonds, tying her closer than she'd ever been to any man.

A lifetime later, he finally broke away. Her knees trembled at the sensations he'd raised within her, and he gathered her close, folding her into his rock-solid arms. One confident hand spread across the back of her head, soothing, supporting. She buried her face against the white broadcloth of his shirt and breathed in the woodsy smell that was uniquely his.

She was comforted by his gesture, reassured. Ethan truly understood her need for there to be a complete emotional bond between them, something greater, something deeper than the constant thrum of physical excitement that beat inside her anytime he was near.

He laughed as he gathered her close. Certainly it had not been his first instinct to break off that kiss. He longed to let his hands roam, to ease beneath her green blouse, to tweak the pebbled nipples that he knew stood out against her bra. But fair was fair. He had promised.

And that promise had led to a miracle. A healthy baby girl. *His* healthy baby girl.

For the first time since he had learned that Sloane was

pregnant, Ethan actually let himself enjoy the thought. He allowed himself to picture a future, a life shared for decades. He finally let himself think beyond the mock marriage he'd stumbled into, the pretend commitment that he'd told himself he could walk away from if his worst fears had been confirmed. This was Sloane he was thinking about, the woman that he loved. The woman who, impossibly, had said that she loved him back. He couldn't leave her. Not now. Not ever.

He only had one more hurdle: meeting Grandmother's January deadline. Now that he and Sloane were united in their happiness, there should be no problem defeating that absurd ultimatum. He wasn't a fool, though. He wasn't going to tell Sloane about Grandmother's ridiculous requirement. There was no reason to disturb her with facts that had absolutely no shred of meaning.

Instead, he murmured against her hair, "That just leaves one small thing."

"Hmm?" Sloane murmured, unwilling to break the perfect moment, to topple the steady, comforting balance that had settled over them.

"We need to set a date for the wedding. I've been thinking about September sixth."

She started to laugh, thinking that he must be joking. When she pulled away enough to see his face, though, she knew that he was completely serious. "September sixth? Why?"

"It's the Sunday of Labor Day weekend. Our guests will have time to travel here, time to return home on Monday."

"But it's less than two months away!" She caught his hand and guided him back to the chaise longue. They sat at the same time, as if they were beginning a formal business negotiation.

He shrugged at her protest. "We can get everything done between now and then. I was thinking that we'd get married here at the house. That limits access for the press, and we don't have to worry about securing a facility on relatively short notice. It won't be a problem to line up caterers, of course. That's just a financial transaction."

Just a financial transaction. Sloane settled a hand over her waist. Over her *daughter.* "I'll be as big as a house by September!" She'd never considered herself a vain woman, never thought that she would care about appearances like that. But she was only getting married once in her life. Only building a family once in her life. A part of her wanted everything about that experience to be absolutely perfect. "I assumed that we'd wait until after the baby is here. Get through the first few months of chaos with a newborn, and then get married in June."

His eyes darkened, as if she'd suggested something impossible. For just a moment, she saw him consider some argument, contemplate words that he discarded with a tense shrug, with a quick bite of his lip. Instead, he settled his fingers over hers, rippling a fresh wave of energy through her. "I don't care if you're the size of the Taj Mahal. Sloane, I made a promise to you, back at the Kennedy Center, and you know that I'll keep it. But I'm not going to lie to you. I want you. Now, here, on this patio, on the grass, in my bed." He cupped her face with his free hand, snagging her gaze with an intensity that rocked her to her core. "Don't make me wait until next summer. Don't do that to me, love. To us."

Her skin was on fire where he touched her; every nerve ending sparked with energy. She was catapulted back to their night at the Eastern, the night that had created their daughter. Everything had been simple then.

She had listened to her body, trusted its desires. Trusted Ethan.

He shifted the hand that spread across her belly, raising his fingers to her neck. Seemingly without effort, he found pressure points above her nape, tiny anchors of tension. He kneaded away stress that she hadn't realized she was carrying, caressing her with all the care he had shown her as a lover. She closed her eyes and let her head fall back, let her body luxuriate in the attention.

Floating on a sea of warmth, she knew that she wanted more. She wanted to feel his skin against every inch of her, wanted to press herself against his broad chest, twine her legs between his. She was melting beside him, longing transforming her into a mindless puddle.

September. She pulled her thoughts together enough to focus on September. She could wait until then. Just.

She settled her ready mouth on his, shuddering at the unexpected sensation as his teeth closed on her lower lip for a single, fleeting moment. She barely managed to pull away from the reeling kiss. Somehow, though, she found the wherewithal to say, "You drive a hard bargain, Mr. Hartwell."

His rough laugh against her throat nearly made her demand an overnight elopement. "You'll do it, then? We can marry in September?"

"September," she said, the three syllables getting lost in a sigh of pleasure. Ethan folded his arms around her, leaning her back against the chaise longue, cushioning her body as his embrace became even more enthusiastic.

Sloane nearly lost herself in the waves of sensation washing over her body. Before she could summon the will to pull away, though, before she could restore them both to the promise they had made, she was startled by a chorus of hysterical yapping.

Daisy.

The puppy had awakened from her nap. Seeing Ethan, she had galloped toward the patio. Now, she was bouncing up and down as if her legs were spring-loaded. She acted as if she hadn't seen her beloved master for years.

Ethan collapsed his head against Sloane's shoulder. "Quite a little chaperone you have there, Ms. Davenport."

Sloane laughed a bit unsteadily. "She has our best interest at heart."

Heart. The word should have made them both cringe, should have reminded them of the illness that would eventually steal Daisy away from them. That future, though, was far away on this sunny July afternoon, on the day when they had discovered that their daughter was going to be healthy, was going to be born with a complete life ahead of her. No cloud could spoil the joy of the letter that Ethan had delivered from the doctor's office.

"Sit," Sloane said to Daisy, adding a hand signal to emphasize the command. The puppy was too excited, though, to mind. "Sit!" Sloane repeated.

Ethan smiled indulgently as the silly little dog kept up her barking. He pushed himself off Sloane carefully, taking care not to harm her in any way. When he turned to the bouncing Daisy, he pushed authority into his voice, "Sit, Daisy," he commanded. The dog dropped to her haunches as if she'd been trained in the circus.

Sloane laughed. "Well, I guess we know who she thinks is the pushover, don't we? There's no reason for her to listen to me."

Ethan ruffled the puppy's ears, telling her that she was a good dog. The words came to him automatically, easily, but his mind was already drifting elsewhere. Sloane had agreed to the September date. He would meet Grandmother's deadline, with months to spare. He couldn't imagine being a happier man.

The following Monday, Hartwell Genetics released a formal engagement announcement, officially confirming all the gossip of the past several weeks, declaring to the entire world that Sloane and Ethan were getting married on September sixth. Sloane still felt they were rushing things, but she understood, and even appreciated, Ethan's reasons for moving forward. He certainly reinforced their decision often enough—cornering her in the kitchen with a few well-placed kisses, passing her in the hallway with a knowing caress that turned her knees to jelly, and often, oh, so often, repeating the words that made her heart soar: I love you.

By noon on Monday, Hartwell Genetics's marketing department had already secured the finest caterer in town, booked a band and arranged for a photographer. Ethan's wealth made so many things easy.

It also, though, made things complicated. By midafternoon, the phone calls started at the house. These were contacts from the legitimate press—the business papers and magazines that would never have stooped to report the earlier gossip. James handled them all, answering with a reserved "No comment," politely but firmly refusing to provide any additional information about where Mr. Hartwell had met Ms. Davenport, about where Ms. Davenport was currently residing, about rumors that a baby might be on the way, rushing the date of the nuptials.

Retreating from the jangle of phones, Sloane closed the door to the library. It was comforting there in the dark, wood-paneled room, surrounded by books and the heft of heavy leather furniture. She curled up on the dark green couch with her laptop, grateful for the chance finally to dig back into the Hope Project.

She made the mistake of checking her favorite news site before she began her work. Her engagement was splashed all over the page. It turned out that a lot of people had an interest in Ethan Hartwell and his matrimonial plans. The financial pages all discussed the likely impact on Hartwell Genetics. The health care reporters speculated on whether any new products would be brought to market in the fourth quarter. The gossip pages continued to report their usual mash of confused half-truths, focusing on Sloane's mysterious background. She didn't know whether to be pleased or annoyed that she was painted as a conniving fortune hunter by one publication, an innocent victim of Ethan's playboy ways by another and a business partner in disguise by yet a third.

As she shook her head in disbelief, her cell phone rang. She glanced at the Caller ID. Ethan.

"Surviving the storm?" he asked. She could hear the smile in his voice, picture the curve of his lips as he formed the question. Immediately, she pictured those lips put to better use, and she had to shake her head, to return her concentration to the matter at hand.

"I had no idea that so many people would care about what we do with our personal lives!"

"Just imagine what would happen if they knew the *truly* personal details I could share with them." His growl ignited a blush that tingled from the roots of her hair to her toes. "Where are you now?" he asked.

"In the library." She made her voice as prim and proper as she could. If she gave in to the invitation barely hidden behind his words she would never get any work done that afternoon.

"What are you wearing?" he whispered.

"A white blouse buttoned up to my neck, a black skirt with a bustle that hangs to my ankles and tiny boots that pinch my feet," she said, smoothing her hand over her T-shirt and shorts.

"Are the boots made out of leather?"

She couldn't help but laugh at the hopeful note in his voice. "How's work?" she asked. "Are you able to get anything done, with everyone digging for more information? James has been fielding calls here nonstop."

"I've issued my 'no comments.' I've also accepted a half-dozen invitations."

"Invitations?"

"Drinks here. Dinners there. I'm only saying yes to the ones I absolutely can't afford for us to skip. Do you hate me?"

She laughed at the worried note in his voice. "How could I hate you? Just make sure I end up with all the dates in my calendar."

"The most important one is in a month. Grandmother is throwing a cocktail party in our honor. At her apartment, downtown."

"Her apartment? Fine. I assume there will only be a handful of guests?"

"You haven't seen Grandmother's apartment. She has the entire top floor of the Waverly."

Sloane's enthusiasm flagged, but she knew that they'd both be happier if she kept a positive attitude. "A cocktail party for a hundred of our closest friends. Sounds grand. It'll cost you, though. I'll need something appropriate to wear."

His chortle thrilled her over the phone line. "Whatever you desire. Speaking of which, let's get back to those leather boots…."

Ethan drank deeply from his beer, grateful that he and Zach were viewing the Nationals baseball game from the air-conditioned comfort of the luxury box owned by Zach's law firm. "You owe me, buddy," he said. "Owe me big time."

"Wait a minute," Zach said, gesturing around the well-appointed room. "I thought *you* were supposed to be grateful to *me,* for bringing you to the game."

"I consider this a small down payment on the real debt, my friend." Ethan paused to watch the visiting pitcher step up to the plate. Three pitches, and the Nationals had nailed the third out of the inning. Music started to play as the team ran in from the field.

Zach sighed in mock apology. "And what have I done this time?"

"Made a small fortune for the Good to the Bone dog obedience school." Ethan pretended to glare as Zach laughed. "I've had one of their instructors on call for a week. Whenever Sloane heads out on an errand, James squeezes in a quick session with Daisy. So far, she's mastered sit, stay and down. I just hope that she gets the hang of 'heel' pretty soon. That one's harder to practice, without Sloane figuring out what we're working on."

"I never thought I'd see the day when Ethan Hartwell was worried about training a puppy."

"Yeah, well, there are a lot of things I never thought I'd be doing." Ethan stared out at the baseball diamond, losing track of the pitch sequence as he thought about the night before. He had taken to walking Sloane to her bedroom each night. He stood on the threshold of the guest suite like a high school kid hanging out on a front porch, worried that his girlfriend's father was standing just inside the front door.

Like that overeager teen, he had leaned in to kiss Sloane good-night. Before he was fully aware of what he was doing, he had eased his hands beneath the loose T-shirt that she wore. The garment was casual, but her hidden bra was not. He had caught his breath as his palms passed over a line of lace that left little to his overheated imagination. Immediately, he could picture her breasts straining to be free. Trying to ignore the arrow that tugged at his groin, he had eased his fingers beneath the fabric edge, gliding around to Sloane's back, to the delicate clasp that kept her covered, kept her safe. She had sighed as he flicked the fastener open, her delicate breath immediately reminding him of the way she had lain beneath him at the Eastern.

Another minute, and it would have been too late. Another minute, and they both would have cast away their silly vow of chastity. He'd recognized the powerful need on her face, the desire that had welled up in her eyes like an entire conversation.

And then Daisy had come bounding up the stairs, eager for her last walk of the night and her usual dog biscuit treat. Ethan had managed not to swear as he bent down to ruffle the excited puppy's ears. Sloane had actually laughed, closing her door before either of them could walk down a tantalizing—and thoroughly physically satisfying—road of regrets.

Now, Zach whistled, long and low. "You are a total goner, aren't you? And here I thought you were never going to give up your title to Bachelor of the Year."

Ethan shook his head, forcing his thoughts back to the stadium, back to the good-natured ribbing of his best friend. "Believe me, I never thought I'd do it, either."

"Then it's not just because of Margaret? Not because of the stock transfer?" The two men rarely talked about Margaret Hartwell. Zach took attorney-client confidentiality seriously. In this case, though, they were both fully aware of the transfer provisions that would benefit AFAA if Ethan failed to conform.

Ethan's lips curled into a sardonic grin. "It started that way. I figured I could kill two birds with one stone—keep Grandmother's stock in the family, and push every single one of her controlling, manipulative, marriage-minded buttons—all by choosing a woman she never expected me to marry."

"But now?"

"Now, I just want Sloane. If Grandmother disapproved and said that she was still going to donate her stock, I wouldn't care. I'd still marry Sloane. Tomorrow, if we could."

"Man," Zach said, shaking his head and popping open two more beers. "You really have it bad." Ethan heard a faint touch of jealousy in the other man's voice. He laughed, and they turned back to the ball game, just as the Nationals' cleanup hitter knocked a home run out of the park.

Sloane picked up her purse and hurried back into the library. "Jeanine," she said. "Thank you for being so patient!"

The skinny redhead glanced up from Daisy, who was sitting quietly in the middle of the thick Turkish rug, eyes focused intently on the trainer's right hand. "No problem!"

"Should I make out that check to you, or to Doggie-B-Good?"

"The company name is fine," Jeanine said. Then she turned back to Daisy and snapped her fingers. "Good Daisy," she said, releasing the pet from the "sit" command. Daisy started to wag her entire hind quarters in excitement at the praise.

Sloane laughed. "I cannot believe how she's caught on to all of the commands!"

"Some dogs just learn really quickly," Jeanine said. "They all *want* to be good. That makes everything work out in their pack. Isn't that right, Daisy? Don't you want to be a good puppy?"

For answer, Daisy yapped once. Sloane handed over the check. "I really appreciate your coming over here at such crazy times. It's just that I want this training to be a surprise, for Ethan. It would be easy enough if I just had to wait for him to be out of town, but I don't want James to know, either. He'd spill the beans, for sure."

"I completely understand. You'll call me when you're ready to schedule our next lesson?"

"Absolutely," Sloane promised. She walked the dog trainer to the front door, then settled back on the couch.

As she adjusted her laptop computer across her legs, Daisy whined from the floor. "Down!" Sloane commanded. The little dog dropped to the floor like a pro. "Good dog," Sloane said. She would have loved to have the puppy on the couch beside her, but she knew that would only create problems when the Old English sheepdog reached her full growth. A little discipline was good for a dog.

Discipline was good for computer programmers, too. Sloane had spent the past week trying to work out yet another problem with the Hope Project website. She knew the drawing module that she wanted to link to the front page. The software worked exactly as she intended when she used it in isolation. But every single time that she plugged it into one of the diagnostic packages, it locked up the entire website.

"Okay, Daisy," Sloane muttered under her breath. "I am *going* to figure this out. I'm not going to bed until this section works."

Two hours later, Sloane regretted her rash promise. Her eyes felt sandy. She was thirsty. Her back twinged from sitting too long in the same position. She was about to give up on the entire evening, declare the night a loss, when she heard Ethan's key in the front door.

Daisy leaped up and skittered into the hallway, yipping a greeting. "I'm in here!" Sloane called out, when she could make herself heard over the din. She set her computer on the floor and swung herself into a sitting position.

Ethan came into the room, Daisy at his heels. "Sit!" he said to the excited dog, and Sloane was secretly proud to see how quickly Daisy responded. Sloane couldn't wait to show Ethan all of Daisy's tricks, to put the little dog through her paces. Soon enough… All they needed to master was the command to heel.

Ethan sank onto the couch beside Sloane. "You're not still working, are you?"

She smiled ruefully. "I have gone over every single line of this program a hundred times. I *cannot* figure out why it won't launch properly."

He made a comforting noise and shifted beside her. When his strong hands fell on her shoulders, she melted against him. He started to knead her taut muscles, backing up his gentle touch with just enough strength to force out the knots she'd acquired in a long evening of frustration. "Why don't you tell me what you're trying to do? Sometimes talking about something makes it all come clear."

She shifted a little, giving him access to her shoulder blades, to the middle of her back. His questing fingers obliged, and she let the rhythm that he established guide her thoughts. "Everyone who wants to use the drawing module has to register when they come onto the website. It's a security step, to keep individual children anonymous within the system, and to let users save their work between sessions."

He made a wordless sound of understanding, walking his fingers down another few vertebrae. She hadn't realized how tight her spine had become. She let her head fall forward, stretching out the muscles in her neck, and then she continued. "The registration sets correctly whenever users immediately go into the drawing package. But if they stop first at one of the information pages, then they're locked out of the entire system."

She started to tighten her hands into fists, falling back into her frustration, but Ethan's gentle touch reminded her to exhale, to let her body relax. It was as if his hands had the power to wash all of her thoughts out of her mind. He could clear her memory with nothing more than the tips of his fingers and the smooth, steady sound of his breath.

Clear her memory.

The art program cleared its memory every time it was called up, giving each user a clean slate for creating pictures. That was a feature, an easy way to let children start each session fresh, without being dragged down into whatever drawings they had made before, whatever problems they had been working on in the past.

"That's it!" she said. "I just have to tell it explicitly

to remember the password! It should forget everything else but remember that information!"

Energized by her breakthrough, she pulled away from Ethan, snatching up her computer from the floor and typing away on the program.

Ethan watched her single-minded enthusiasm as she worked. He loved the way that she focused on the monitor, the way her eyes narrowed just a fraction as she worked through each line of text. Most people would have walked away from the Hope Project by now. Most people would have given up, written off the idea as a good one, but too complex, too difficult to make real.

But not Sloane. She was willing to fight for what she believed in. She was willing to do whatever had to be done.

And Ethan had to admit that he found that drive, that devotion, more compelling than anything else about the woman he was going to marry. Sure, he enjoyed showing her fine things, introducing her to the ballet, to the best restaurants in Washington. Absolutely, he reveled in her body, as much as she was willing to share. But her mind was what truly captivated him—her absolute dedication to her beliefs of right and wrong, and her certainty that she could change the world for the better.

With a flourish, she pressed a key, hunching forward as she waited to see if the program would finally work. Ethan caught his breath as she did, waiting, hoping. When a bright rainbow spilled across the screen, Sloane shouted her laughter. "That's it!" she cried. "You solved it!"

He caught her close as she flung her arms around him, embracing him with the enthusiasm of a high school cheerleader. "I didn't have anything to do with it," he protested until she stopped him with a kiss. "But if that's the way you want to thank me," he continued when he'd surfaced from her energetic attention, "I'm happy to pretend."

"Pretend!" She pulled him close in another overwhelming hug. "That's what I love about being with you. Neither one of us has to pretend a thing!"

She pulled away so that she could show him how the art package functioned, how a child could use it to work through worries and fears. Ethan listened to every word. He had to. He was trying to drown out the little voice that clamored at the back of his head, nagging him to tell Sloane about his grandmother's ultimatum. He should stop pretending, once and for all.

And he would. Very, very soon, he promised himself. For now, he concentrated on the Hope Project, and everything that Sloane was going to accomplish.

Chapter Nine

The next two weeks flew by. Ethan had three business trips—to San Francisco, to Paris, to Montreal.

Sloane missed him while he was gone, but every reunion was sweeter than the last. Each time, he entered the house like a returning hero, finding her on the patio, in the bedroom, staking claim to her with kisses that threatened to steal her breath away forever.

Coming back from Canada, he found her working in the library, her legs stretched out on the green leather couch, her laptop balanced across her thighs. Daisy greeted him with enthusiasm, wriggling with excitement, as if he'd been gone for years rather than forty-eight hours. Nevertheless, the puppy complied with his command to sit; she behaved like a true show dog.

Sloane started to stand up when he came in, but he quickly settled beside her. He took her bare feet onto his lap, finding the tender point at each arch, smoothing away tension with the unerring weight of his thumb.

"Mmm," she said, scrunching lower on the couch so that her head rested against the padded arm. "Do I know you?"

"How quickly they forget," he growled in mock disdain. His fingers tickled up her bare legs, tracing the hem of her shorts against her thighs. "Or maybe you have an endless line of men, waiting to rub your feet?"

For answer, she shut the computer, making sure that the lid snicked closed before she set it on the luxurious Turkish carpet. She would hate to lose hours of hard work. The Hope Project was nearly done; she'd be ready to have beta testers work through the website in another week or two.

Her hands free, she knelt on the couch, enjoying the flare of pleased surprise in Ethan's eyes as he realized that the top two buttons of her blouse were open. His hands settled on her waist, steadying her, pulling her closer.

The action triggered a flutter deep inside of her. "Oh!"

"What?" he asked, only the tightening of his fingers over her hipbones betraying anxiety.

"The baby! I felt her move!"

The look of joy that spread across Ethan's face filled her heart even more than the sudden realization that her baby—their daughter—was growing, was ever closer to joining them. Another flutter rippled through her insides.

"Is this the first time you've felt her?" Ethan asked. He kept his voice low, even though he knew the baby couldn't hear them, even though he knew that he could not possibly disturb their daughter.

"I thought I felt her move, maybe a week ago. And again, the morning that you left for Montreal." Sloane's smile was wide, her blue eyes bright with laughter. "This is the first time I've been certain, though."

Reaching underneath Sloane's blouse, he settled his palm across her belly. He felt a sudden tremble ripple across her skin, but he knew *that* motion was caused by him, summoned by his touch. He waited, holding his breath.

"There!" Sloane said.

He shook his head, trying not to feel cheated, not to feel left out. "Nothing," he said. "Not yet." Still, seeing the excitement that flushed Sloane's cheeks, he found himself laughing. "Soon enough, though. Give our little ballerina another couple of months, and you'll be begging her to sit still for a while."

"Never!" Sloane's laughter filled his chest with a fierce protectiveness, and he gathered her close to his side, kissing the top of her head, all the while maintaining contact with their baby.

"I hope she doesn't bother you too much at dinner tonight."

Sloane shook her head. Of course the baby wouldn't be a bother. Then, she remembered. "That's right! We're meeting those board members, for dinner downtown!" She looked at her watch. "Another engagement party. That's why you're home early."

The smile that he turned on her was as lazy as a summer afternoon. "That, and I wanted to see you."

He was rewarded with a deep kiss. A deep kiss, and her hands roaming over his back, and then the confession, "I missed you."

"All of this travel has been ridiculous. It'll slow down for the rest of the month. Washington practically goes to sleep in August. We used to travel, Grandmother and I, to a different country every year."

"I can't imagine what that would be like!" She sighed, thinking that their daughter would get to enjoy that sort of life, would thrive on exciting experiences.

She shivered as Ethan's inquisitive fingers did something thoroughly unapproved with the waistband of her shorts. She caught his hand in hers, needing to protect herself from his distraction. "Which was your favorite trip?" she asked, as if his childhood travels were the most fascinating thing in the universe.

He laughed, but he played along, knowing full well what she was doing. "Paris, probably. Grandmother and I spent an entire day in the Musée d'Orsay, looking at the Impressionist paintings."

"I had no idea you were such an art lover."

"I wasn't," he admitted. "But the tour guide Grandmother hired was a totally stunning French girl, with the sexiest accent..."

Sloane hurled a throw pillow at him.

"What?" he protested. "I was fourteen years old, and very impressionable."

"I can only imagine," she said dryly.

"What about you? What was your favorite summer?"

She paused before she answered, really thought about the question. Summers were always a challenge when she was young; the long days seemed to add a special strain to life in a foster family. But when she was a teenager, she had volunteered at the Art Institute of Chicago. "The year I turned sixteen," she said. "I spent every day down at the art museum. I developed a series of tours for little kids, five-minute lectures that taught them the basics of art history. I just loved seeing the connections those kids made, the way they figured things out."

"And the Hope Project grew from there," he said.

"With a few thousand steps in between."

"I guess it really is the things that spark for us when we're young," he said. "My grandfather and I used to play Monopoly. He was absolutely cutthroat at the game, wouldn't give an inch, even when I was just starting to learn the rules. But I ended up loving everything about it—the deals we'd make to swap properties, the strategy of building hotels on some squares and not on others."

"You don't talk about your family very much. I've never even heard you mention your grandfather."

"He died ten years ago. I was only twenty-three. Sometimes I wonder what he'd think about me. About the person I've become."

Sloane heard the yearning in Ethan's voice, the desire to be accepted. To be loved. "I think he'd be very proud," she said.

Ethan cleared his throat and pushed himself to his feet. The movement caused Daisy to dance backward and forward. "We should get ready, if we're going to get to the restaurant on time. I'll walk this fierce beast before we go."

They made it to the restaurant with ten minutes to spare, and they had a charming evening with the board members. As they did three nights later, when they got together with Ethan's med school roommates and their wives. And Ethan's business school friends a few nights after that.

Sloane was consistently astonished that Ethan knew so many people. He shrugged it off, as easily as he shrugged off his enormous fortune, the tremendous success of Hartwell Genetics. He'd lived lots of lives, he said, first as Margaret's grandson, then as a doctor, then as a successful entrepreneur. There were a lot of social circles to intersect.

A lot of dinner parties to attend.

Sloane needed to put Ethan's credit card back in circulation. At five months and counting, she was truly beginning to show. She felt marvelous, full of energy, as if she were only now coming fully awake after those first few months of nausea and discomfort. She suspected that, down the road, she'd be awkward and uncomfortable, but for now, she was thrilled by the ease of her pregnancy, by the simple presence of her ever-growing daughter.

Her increased energy let her finally finish the Hope Project. In fact, she was just saving the final computer file, when her cell phone rang. She glanced at the unfamiliar number, surprised that anyone was tracking her down that way. Suspecting that Ethan might be trying to reach her from an unknown line, she answered. "Hello?"

"Ms. Davenport?"

"Yes. Who is this please?"

"My name is Lionel Hampton. I'm afraid we haven't met before, but Margaret Hartwell suggested that I give you a call."

Sloane's heart leaped into her throat. Lionel Hampton. The executive director of the American Foundation for the Advancement of the Arts. Her ex-boss's boss's boss. "Mr. Hampton," she said, hoping that she hadn't let too many seconds tick away as she battled her surprise.

"Is this a good time for us to talk?"

Sloane glanced at her computer screen, at the culmination of five years of work, all wrapped up in the Hope Project. "Yes," she said, and then she realized that she'd made her statement sound like a question. She cleared her throat. "How can I help you, Mr. Hampton?"

"I had lunch with my dear friend Margaret this afternoon. She informed me that you and Ethan Hartwell are to be married next month. Please accept my very best wishes."

"Of course," Sloane said, feeling her forehead crease as she frowned. What had Margaret done?

"I don't have to tell you that Margaret is one of your biggest fans." Sloane wasn't about to say otherwise, even if the news was something of a surprise. Mr. Hampton went on, as if Sloane had agreed wholeheartedly. "I was just telling Margaret that we are trying to expand our mission here at AFAA, that we want to have more of an impact on the world beyond the traditional four corners of cultural stewardship. As soon as Margaret mentioned your art therapy project for at-risk foster children, I knew that we had a perfect match."

"A perfect match?" Sloane wondered if her mind was playing tricks on her, if she was hearing things.

Mr. Hampton cleared his throat. "With Margaret's generous assistance, AFAA is about to create a new center, a division that will specialize in advancing the arts curriculum for children. Margaret speaks very, very highly of you, Ms. Davenport. I would love to offer you a position as the director of our new program."

Just like that. Margaret wrote a check, pulled some strings and Sloane landed the job of her dreams. Months of résumés, frantic nights wondering whether she would ever find another job, all erased by her wealthy future grandmother-in-law's largesse.

Even if Sloane could accept such a gift, there was one substantial problem. "Mr. Hampton, are you aware of the fact that I worked for AFAA? That I was dismissed from my position back in March?"

"Oh, yes. That." A prim sound rattled over the line, a cross between a cleared throat and a cough. "I understand that there was some confusion about our Spring Auction, and that one of our managers may have acted a little precipitously…."

Sloane shook her head. She couldn't believe what she was hearing. "I was fired out of hand, for something that had nothing to do with my performance."

"And I wish that I'd been made aware of the circumstances at the time. Ms. Davenport, I do hope that you can set aside any negative feelings that you might have about our organization. To that end, I'd love to meet you for lunch, say next Monday? We could discuss this matter further, along with the possibilities of our exciting new center. I do hope that you'll say yes."

Sloane considered her options. She could refuse to meet with the man. She could send him back to Margaret in defeat, mostly likely returning a large check.

Or she could meet with him. She could talk to him about his new center. She could explain, in her own words, just what her project was about and what she knew she could accomplish.

Sure, they might not be able to get past her prior experience at AFAA. But she'd be a fool not to try. Wouldn't she?

"Thank you, Mr. Hampton. I'd love to discuss this matter further."

She heard the gratitude in his voice as he specified a restaurant, as he thanked her for agreeing to consider the possibility, as he offered her his very best wishes for a wonderful weekend. Sloane stared at the phone for a long time after she hung up from the call.

So. This must be what it was like, to have the power and prestige of the Hartwell name behind her. This was what she could anticipate for the rest of her life, as Ethan's wife. This was the way that doors would open for their daughter.

As if in response, the baby chose that moment to kick against her insides. Sloane smiled. She couldn't imagine what her meeting with Mr. Hampton would be like. She could hardly give him the details about why she'd been dismissed from AFAA. Of course, if the man had done his homework, then it wouldn't be necessary to give him any information at all. And if Margaret's check had already cleared the bank, the entire matter would be moot. The only thing that Sloane needed to do was thank her future grandmother-in-law.

Three days later, she had the opportunity, at the engagement party Margaret was hosting for Ethan and Sloane.

Sloane took greater care than usual dressing for the party, feeling like a debutante, poised on the edge of her formal introduction to polite society. Sitting beside Ethan in the back of the Town Car, she stared out the window as the streets of D.C. rushed by. She ran over names and faces in her mind, hoping that she didn't stumble over any important introductions.

Ethan laughed when she asked him to fill her in, one more time, on the names of the Hartwell Genetics board members. "Relax. It's a cocktail party. We'll have a couple of drinks, and then we'll leave."

"Easy for you to say." She sighed. "You actually get to drink something with alcohol. Just one glass of wine… that would make this so much easier."

"What if you had something to look forward to?"

His arch tone was enough to bring a blush to her cheeks. Good. The color brought out the sparkle in her eyes. "Like what?" she asked, faking a tone of perfect innocence. She knew exactly what she was doing to him. She laughed as he shifted beside her, adjusting his suddenly uncomfortable summer-weight trousers.

God, she was beautiful tonight. The forest-green of her dress set off her eyes, complemented the jet-black hair that she wore down, perfectly straight, a challenge to all those women who thought that primping and preening would make them more attractive. Her body was responding to the baby's needs; every curve that had initially sparked his attention was more voluptuous than ever.

He considered ordering the driver to take a detour. After all, what would his grandmother do if they were late? She couldn't very well interrogate him in public, could she?

Ethan shook his head. Grandmother could do exactly that. And she would, too.

No. Better to go to the party. Hear a few short speeches in honor of himself and the woman who was the mother of his child. Eat some incredibly overpriced appetizers. Drink some of the world's finest alcohol. And then come home, to see what he could do about raising another smile on Sloane's lips.

Ethan's obvious appreciation of her appearance made Sloane a little less apprehensive as the car pulled into the sweeping circular driveway of the Waverly condominium. A doorman helped her out of the backseat as Ethan gave brisk instructions to the driver.

As they stood in the elevator, Ethan took her hand, twining his fingers with hers. He squeezed once, meeting her eyes in the mirrored door, and she smiled back at him, cursing herself for feeling nervous about a simple party.

Every building in Washington was subject to a height restriction. There were only twelve stories to travel in the privacy of the elevator car. All too soon, the door opened. All too soon, they were ushered into a stunning apartment. All too soon, Sloane was swept up in the chaos of a party in full swing.

It seemed as if a dozen men waited to shake Ethan's hand, to offer him their hearty congratulations. She pasted a smile on her lips as he was pulled away from her. Before she could begin the hard work of finding someone to chat with, Margaret glided across the room.

The older woman wore a dramatic pink suit with wide lapels and a cinched waist. Sloane couldn't imagine anyone else wearing the outfit. She also couldn't imagine anyone questioning Margaret's choice—not with the triple strand of pearls that hung halfway down her chest, an authoritative reminder of Margaret's wealth.

Sloane was surprised that Margaret folded her into an embrace. She could smell baby powder on the older woman, along with just a hint of lilac. Margaret spoke first. "You look lovely this evening, dear."

"Thank you," Sloane said, a little surprised by the warmth of the greeting. "It's so kind of you to throw a party in our honor."

"You're feeling well?" Margaret glanced at Sloane's waist, her smile indulgent.

"Very well, thank you."

Margaret switched her attention to Sloane's face. The older woman's gaze was intense, as if she were suddenly communicating in some secret language. "I want you to know how much I appreciate what you've done for Ethan. He's a changed man since he met you."

"Oh, I don't think—"

"I do," Margaret said firmly. "I can see it in his face. In the way he walks down the hallway at work. He's more relaxed, more *confident* than I've ever seen him before."

Sloane could hardly imagine Ethan being anything other than confident. Nevertheless, grandmothers viewed their grandsons through different lenses than did the rest of the world. And Sloane certainly wasn't going to argue with her hostess.

"Oh, bother," Margaret said. "The senator is waving me over. I really should be a proper hostess."

"Please," Sloane said. "Don't let me keep you." She watched, a little awestruck, as Margaret floated across the room to shake hands with one of the most influential men in Washington.

Only then did Sloane remember that she hadn't mentioned Lionel Hampton, hadn't thanked Margaret for her donation to AFAA. She gritted her teeth in exasperation. Well, there'd be another opportunity at some point in the evening.

Sloane looked around the room. This was a different world, far removed from the foster homes and uncertainty she'd known as a child. How could anyone growing up in this *not* be confident? Sloane saw Ethan standing near the grand piano, surrounded by a circle of dark-suited men. She recognized the junior senator from New York, and a Supreme Court justice, both offering their hearty congratulations.

"So much power, all in one living room."

Sloane started at the voice. She turned around to see Zach, a friendly smile brightening the lawyer's face. He held a highball glass, filled with some amber liquid and ice. His suit looked a little rumpled, and there was a spot on his tie. Sloane caught herself liking the easy-going man more than ever. She said, "Do you ever feel like you're caught up in a masquerade, and any minute now someone is going to rip off your mask?"

"Every day," Zach said, taking a sip from the glass in his hand. "Every single day."

"But you've been coming to this sort of thing for years! Don't you get used to it?"

Zach shrugged. "In a way. Ethan used to invite me when we were kids. Margaret always let him have one friend along, so that he wouldn't get *too* lonely among all the grown-ups."

"From what I hear, Margaret was probably hoping that your good behavior would rub off on him."

"It didn't work out that way. I just learned bigger and better ways to get into trouble."

Sloane answered dryly, "I can see how that would happen."

Zach laughed at her tone. "You can see why Margaret worked so hard to get Ethan to settle down. She just wanted to host one single cocktail party where he didn't cause a scandal. After all those years, I could hardly believe it, when she finally found the magic key."

"Magic key?"

Zach drank again. "You know, the whole ultimatum thing." He curled his fingers into quotation marks, as if he were reciting something Margaret had said. "A wedding by her birthday, or she was stepping down from the Board and giving everything to AFAA. I never thought it would work, but she proved me wrong. It made all those weeks of writing the stock transfer agreement worth it."

Margaret's birthday.

Everything to AFAA.

No wonder Ethan had pushed for a wedding before the baby was born.

Sloane felt the blood rush from her face. She made some halfhearted excuse to Zach, something that might actually have sounded like a joke, and then she stumbled off to the edge of the room. She needed to sit down. Needed to catch her breath. Needed to make sense out of the nightmare words Zach had just cast off so blithely.

Before Sloane could escape, though, Margaret was at the front of the room, summoning her guests to silence. Ethan broke away from his coterie of friends, crossing to Sloane with an easy smile. His fingers were light on her elbow as he said, "Time to sing for our supper."

Ethan was astonished at how pale Sloane had become. Maybe he'd been wrong to bring her here, wrong to let Grandmother plan this ridiculous party. It was so tiring to be on display, to meet and greet business acquaintances and friends. He should have put his foot down. He should have insisted that they forget about the party, about letting Margaret show them off to everyone.

Too late now.

He settled one hand across the small of Sloane's back. She shied away from him, though, as if she were burned by his touch. As if she resented his dragging her here. He scowled toward his grandmother, annoyed to see that she had finally succeeded in breaking through the cocktail party chatter. All eyes were on Margaret Hartwell.

And her eyes were on him. On him and Sloane. He leaned close and whispered, "Are you all right?"

For answer, Sloane merely pulled her arm away from him. She followed him to the front of the room, though, and he had to be content with standing next to her, fighting the urge to give her his arm to lean on, to make their excuses and get them out of the damned room altogether.

Apparently unaware of Sloane's distress, his grandmother said, "Friends! I thank you all for joining me this evening, to celebrate an event I never thought I'd live to see."

Ethan heard the good-natured laughter of the guests, heightened by the drinks they'd already enjoyed. His grandmother went on, spinning out a story about how Ethan had been a wild little boy, how he had always refused to mind her, how he had run away and hidden from her in the National Museum of Natural History. She made people laugh, recounting Ethan's first experience in the Hartwell Genetics boardroom, when he had refused to give in to a strident board member, matching age and money with his own unique brand of stubbornness.

Grandmother's voice grew suspiciously thick, though, as she lifted her glass in the air. "I see that my grandson was only conditioning me to accept his headstrong ways, preparing me to rejoice in the finest decision of his adult life. My darling Ethan has chosen to bring Sloane Davenport into our family. Ethan, Sloane, may you have many joyful years together!"

"Hear, hear!" cried the guests, and Ethan inclined his head as dozens of glasses were raised in his—in *their*—honor.

Knowing what was expected of him, he leaned down to kiss his grandmother's cheek, murmuring, "Thank you."

Her eyes sparkled as she settled a dry hand along his jaw. Her lips trembled with a surprising show of emotion. He had to admit, though, that she looked happier than she had in years. Happier, and healthier—as if she could live another eighty years.

Ethan smiled at the crowd as he slipped his arm around Sloane's waist. She felt stiff as a board next to him. Poor thing. She hadn't been in this spotlight before, hadn't been the center of attention for dozens of well-wishers. He wished that he could say something private to her, that he could whisk her away. Just a few more moments, though, a few more polite words. Then they would be done with the formal part of the evening. He'd be able to get them out of the room in half an hour, tops.

He cleared this throat before addressing the waiting guests. "I suspect that my grandmother has been saving up a lifetime of stories, waiting to bring them out when my daughter is born, to teach her all the ways that she can make my life miserable. Or I should say, *our* lives miserable. Sloane, I suppose I'm lucky that you didn't hear any of these tales before you foolishly agreed to marry me. It's too late now! No changing your mind."

Sloane heard the crowd's appreciative chuckles. She felt Ethan's right hand fold over hers. She saw him raise his glass. She heard him say, "I ask each of you to drink to my continued good fortune. May I always be as lucky as I was the day that Sloane Davenport agreed to be my wife."

Sloane looked down at their joined hands. She knew that the guests would think that she was being shy, demure. She suspected that even Ethan would think that she was simply overcome with nerves at being the center of this spectacle. As their daughter delivered a strong kick, though, Sloane realized that she was counting the seconds until she could escape.

Margaret's birthday. Stock transfer agreement.

Zach's words kept pounding through her brain. Her engagement, her pending marriage, Ethan saying that he loved her—it was all one grand charade. It was all a business deal. Her hand in marriage. Margaret's stock for Hartwell Genetics. AFAA left out in the cold.

Not entirely in the cold. The foundation would get the consolation prize of Margaret's grand gift. The check that the old woman had written to cover Sloane's Hope Project.

This must be the way that big money did things. I'll scratch your back; you scratch mine. You marry my grandson; I'll give you back your job.

Sloane's head was reeling. With the speeches done, guests surged around them, offering congratulations to Ethan, best wishes to her. Sloane responded with a lifetime of learned politeness, smiling absently, making all the expected replies. The crowd eased between her and Ethan, and Sloane was relieved to have some space, to get away from the complete *awareness* that she felt whenever he stood next to her.

Ethan grimaced as he finished shaking hands with a congressman from South Carolina. He'd somehow agreed to meet the man for breakfast the following week, to discuss the possibility of opening a manufacturing plant just outside of Charleston.

By the time Ethan managed to shrug off the politician, he realized that Sloane was halfway across the room. She was steadier on her feet now, but his heart twisted in his chest as he saw just how vulnerable she looked. Her graceful shoulders seemed so inadequate to the task of navigating the crowd....

He took two steps to follow her, ready to spirit her away to the Town Car and home and a restorative dinner of scrambled eggs and toast, alone in the privacy of their kitchen. Before he could follow through, though, he heard his grandmother's voice, piercing the tangle of party conversation. "Ethan, darling. There's someone I want you to meet."

He shot one more look toward Sloane's disappearing back. She must be heading down the hallway, toward Grandmother's living quarters. Sloane could put her feet up there, take a break from the chaos of the party. He'd rescue her soon enough.

He remembered to curve his lips into a smile before he turned back to the newest business connection his grandmother was presenting.

Sloane reached the elevator, relieved that her escape had gone undetected. She'd been prepared with an excuse for anyone who stopped her—she just needed to lie down for a few minutes, put her feet up in one of Margaret's grand guest rooms. No one had noticed when Sloane left the living room, though. No one cared. The wheels of big business just kept on turning.

She clutched her handbag close to her side as the elevator descended all twelve stories. She was grateful that she'd brought the purse; all too often in the past couple of weeks, she had let herself depend on Ethan entirely, let herself trust him to be ready with tips, with credit cards, with whatever financial arrangements were required.

That night, though, for Margaret's party, she'd wanted to be perfect. She'd needed a lipstick for mid-party touch-ups, and a couple of acetaminophen in case the crowd brought on a headache. It had been second nature for her to slip her wallet into her sleek clutch purse as well.

Second nature. And good fortune.

Sloane crossed the empty lobby, pleased that she

didn't encounter any late-arriving guests. Not that any of them would even recognize her. Sloane was just a prop for the bigger drama that was unfolding upstairs. Just a conveniently needy woman for Ethan, someone he could use to meet Margaret's birthday ultimatum.

She had to say, Ethan was an excellent actor. He knew exactly what to say to keep Sloane by his side. He hadn't planned on their fighting on Independence Day. He hadn't meant to endanger his deal. That was when he'd finally confessed his so-called love—when she had most threatened his boardroom arrangement. And she had fallen for it, hook, line and sinker.

Sloane had been a business proposition, all along. A cold, hard bargain, driven to preserve some insane family obligation.

The thought flashed through her mind that she was wrong. She knew Ethan better than that. They understood each other more completely. But then she remembered how he had reacted to Daisy's illness. He had been perfectly capable, perfectly *comfortable,* cutting the little dog out of his life entirely. He could turn his emotions on and off like a spigot.

He had lied to Sloane every single day for the past two months, every instant that he let her believe that he was giving up his Bachelor-of-the-Year ways for her, for their daughter. *Truth. Respect. Partnership.* Those were just words for him. Meaningless syllables.

For the first time since Sloane had stood on the Kennedy Center terrace, she was one hundred percent grateful that she had insisted on maintaining *some* distance from Ethan—physical, if not emotional. How much worse would it have been to hear Zach's words, if she and Ethan had spent the past two months in the intimacy of a physical relationship? How much worse would it be to realize that he had lied with his body as well as his words?

Approaching the heavy glass door to the outside, Sloane realized that Ethan's driver would pull into the circular driveway the instant that he saw her pause on the threshold. She never gave the guy a chance, though. Instead, she exited as if she had a distinct destination, turning to her right and rushing toward the sidewalk without any hint of hesitation. With any luck at all, the driver wouldn't recognize her in the few seconds before she slipped into twilight shadows. He wouldn't be able to report to Ethan. Couldn't turn her in.

She walked two blocks before she got to busy Connecticut Avenue. Three taxis passed by her raised hand, already ferrying passengers to their own destinations. The fourth one, though, pulled to a stop. She opened the back door reflexively, settled into the seat, fastened the belt.

"Where to?" the driver asked, glancing at her in the rearview mirror.

Sloane moved her purse onto her lap. Her wallet held the five hundred-dollar bills that Ethan had left for her that first morning, the day that he had tracked her down in her dingy basement apartment. She had intended to use them on a wedding present for him, buying him something sweet and sentimental, something that marked some inside joke that only they could share.

Well, there was nothing sweet or sentimental about their wedding.

Unable to think of a destination, increasingly aware of the driver's exasperation, Sloane said the first thing that popped into her mind. "Take me to the Eastern Hotel, please."

Chapter Ten

Sloane huddled against the headboard, the snowy-white hotel duvet pulled up to her chin. It had been easy enough to get a room. Not the penthouse suite that she and Ethan had shared; her cash wouldn't stretch that far, by any means. But a regular room, with a king-size bed and a view of Pennsylvania Avenue, America's Main Street. A retreat.

She'd slipped off her uncomfortable shoes and hung her party dress in the closet. The rich terry-cloth robe, so thoughtfully provided by the Eastern, felt like a memory of the childhood she'd never had, a whisper of comfort as she wrapped herself inside its modest warmth. Despite the robe, though, her teeth had started to chatter.

She'd adjusted the thermostat in the room, turning off the whispering air conditioner. She'd run her hands under the hot water faucet in the bathroom, holding them in the stream until they turned red. She'd looked lon ingly at the Jacuzzi tub, but she knew that she couldn't indulge in a steaming hot bath. She had to protect her daughter. Had to do what was right for both of them.

It had been so easy to slip into the dream represented by Ethan Hartwell. So easy to believe that she could live in a nice house, surrounded by nice things. She could talk to kind people like James. She could eat gourmet breakfasts, work in a complete library, surrounded by wonder-filled books.

But she wasn't supposed to be that woman. She wasn't supposed to have that sort of good fortune.

Sloane Davenport was a misfit kid, a foster child. She was the girl without a real family, without real friends.

That's what had happened with Ethan, she now realized. She'd been so eager to make things perfect. So eager to live the life she desired. She'd told herself stories, told herself *lies.* Made herself believe lies told to her. He loved her. Ha. Any idiot could see that Ethan Hartwell would never be interested in *her,* not in the long run. Not when he had every model and actress in the world to choose from. Not when he could buy whatever companionship he desired.

She closed her eyes and shook her head. It had all seemed so *real.* In the darkness behind her eyelids, she could see Ethan leaning over her. She could feel his lips on hers, teasing, taunting, seeking admission to the heat of her mouth. She could feel his fingers, raising heart-trembling reactions from her flesh. She could smell the pine scent of him, the fragrance unique to the man she had loved.

when he'd given her the engagement ring. It had all been a game, a play, a performance put on for Margaret's benefit. He had always known, in the back of his mind, that he was working to meet his grandmother's ultimatum. He had always been lying to Sloane.

Forget about *truth.* Forget about *respect.* And don't even mention *partnership.*

Sloane forced herself to take a calming breath. Another. Another.

Maybe she was being ridiculous. Maybe she was making the proverbial mountain out of a molehill.

But she couldn't get past one simple fact: Ethan could have told her about Margaret's demands at any time. He could have shared the truth. They could have laughed about it together. If their relationship were real, wouldn't Ethan have done that? Wouldn't he have trusted her?

Zach had saved Sloane from a lifetime of misery. Her lips twisted into a grim smile. Perhaps she should pay Zach for his time. Whatever astronomical hourly wage the lawyer commanded, it couldn't be too much, given the value of the lesson he had taught.

As if Sloane had two cents to pay a high-priced lawyer.

She curled her hands into fists. Everything had *seemed* so much better. Sloane had enjoyed a roof over her head, food on the table, medical care for herself and her unborn daughter. She had looked forward to her new job at AFAA, to the fruition of all the hours she'd spent on the Hope Project.

She could never take that job now. She'd been a fool even to consider meeting Lionel Hampton for lunch. The job was as tainted as all the rest of it—a treat dangled by Margaret, to lure Sloane into the bizarre web of Hartwell family deceit.

Miserable, Sloane reached for her purse on the nightstand. She dug out her cell phone, thumbed through the last few entries until she reached Mr. Hampton's phone number. She pressed the button to reply to his call. One ring. Two. Three. His voice mail picked up halfway through the fourth ring.

She didn't pay attention to his authoritarian message, didn't bother to hear how sorry he was to have missed her call, how she could reach his assistant. Instead, she waited for the mechanical beep, and then she said, "Mr. Hampton, this is Sloane Davenport. I'm afraid I won't be able to meet with you next week after all. Thank you for your interest in my project. I hope that the foundation does well in the future."

She hung up before she could change her mind.

After that, she didn't have anything more to do. There was no one else to call. No one to talk to. No one to share the mess she'd made of her life.

She pulled the robe closer around her body, slashing the belt tight with a series of tight motions. Her teeth started to chatter again as she pulled the duvet up to her ears.

No one could find her here. She'd paid with cash. She was anonymous. She could sleep until morning, until she needed to check out, until she needed to leave the Eastern and figure out a new place to live, a new way to find food, clothes. Tomorrow would be soon enough for all of that. She started sobbing, well before she managed to fall asleep.

e woke to the sound of pounding on the door.

couldn't remember where she was. The room

rk, so dark. This wasn't the bright guest suite of

home.

She rubbed her hand across her face, rasping her skin with loops of terry cloth. Memory flooded back to her; she was in the Eastern, hiding from everyone, from everything. She blinked hard and glanced toward the window. She could see that it was bright outside; a chink in the blackout curtains revealed summer sunshine.

The pounding began again, and she swung her feet over the edge of the bed. She fumbled for the reading lamp on the nightstand, took three tries to find the switch. Dull yellow light washed across the room.

Her mouth was dry; she tried to figure out what she would say to whoever had awakened her. She must have slept past checkout time. She hoped that the hotel wouldn't charge her for a second day. She had no way of paying. Not without using Ethan's credit card. And she was never going to use Ethan's credit card again.

Abruptly, the noise at the door stopped. Sloane drew a deep breath, grateful for the reprieve. She could take a shower. She could get dressed. She could have a few more minutes before the sanctuary of the Eastern was taken away from her.

In her rush of relief, she almost missed the sound of the key card whispering through the door's lock. A solid *snick,* though, indicated that the mechanism had released. Two men were silhouetted in the cold light that flooded in from the hallway.

Ethan's relief was so sharp that he needed to steady himself against the door frame with one hand. The sight of Sloane stole his breath away, left him literally unable to speak. She stood beside her rumpled bed, clutching her robe closed at the neck. The folds of fabric hid the gentle swell of her belly, protecting her modesty perfectly.

Her hair was mussed, as if she'd had a bad night's

sleep. He could see a faint crease on one cheek. Her eyes were blurry, their sapphire brilliance hidden for once, as if she were still dozing, still dreaming whatever crazy nightmare had brought her to this place.

He turned to the manager, intensely aware of the privacy of this moment, of his need to be alone with the woman who was going to be his wife. "Thank you," he said. "That will be all."

The manager bristled. "Sir, you said that this woman's health is in danger. It is certainly not the policy of the Eastern to burst into guests' rooms unannounced—"

Ethan turned to Sloane. He could see the confusion on her face, the frown that pulled down the corners of her mouth. Taking a single step closer, he could see the faint puffiness beneath her eyes, silent, accusing proof that she'd been crying. "Sloane," he said, and he was astonished to hear his voice break across her name. "Please…"

She blinked, obviously still confused. The manager's thin lips twisted in disdain. "Sir," the man said. "You will leave this room immediately, or I'll be forced to call security." He backed up his threat by setting one firm hand on Ethan's biceps.

Ethan resisted the urge to shrug free. He had to prove that he was here to help Sloane. That she would be safe with him. "Sloane," he said, and this time his throat worked properly. "I spoke with Zach. He told me what he said. That you misunderstood. *Please.*"

Sloane shook her head, more in disbelief than in denial. Now that she was awake, she could see how limited her options were. By the light of day—a new day, when she would owe new fees for the hotel room—she realized just how little she could do to get her life back on track.

She also knew, though, that Ethan wasn't any physical threat to her. From the look on the manager's face, the police might be getting involved at any minute. She found the presence of mind to nod once, to send a grateful smile at the hotel official. "Thank you," she said. "I'll let him stay."

"Madam," the manager said, puffing out his chest. "I assure you that the Eastern takes every guest's safety as a matter of utmost concern. I would never have let this man in here if he had not convinced me that it was a matter of life or death, that your physical safety was endangered at this very moment."

She barely glanced at Ethan. She couldn't bear to look at him. "I understand. He can be very convincing."

"Madam?"

She had to cut him off. Had to stand up for herself. Had to take the first steps down the long road of the rest of her life. "Thank you. I'm not afraid of him. He can stay."

The manager stared at her for a long minute, obviously weighing whether she was making her decision freely and without duress. He must have approved of what he saw, though, because he finally stepped out into the hall. "You can reach me at any time, simply by pressing zero on any hotel phone."

Zero. Just like in Ethan's home.

Sloane nodded her appreciation, then waited for the door to swing closed behind him. She gathered her robe closer about her, stepping back toward the bed, trying to put as much space as possible between Ethan and herself. The silence stretched between them, long and dangerous. She tested a dozen thoughts, tried twenty conversational openings, but nothing was right. Nothing fit.

He read the indecision on her face as clearly as if she were shouting at him. He had to say something, do something to let her know that she *could* trust him, that he hadn't just been making an excuse for the manager. "Thank you," he said, putting solid emotion behind the words.

He glanced at the reading lamp beside the bed, at the feeble pool of light that it spread across the floor. He needed to change that, needed to bring her out of whatever dark place she'd retreated to. "May I?" he asked, nodding toward the window.

She hesitated a moment, but she nodded. He took longer than he needed to, crossing to the curtains. He pulled the shades slowly, giving her time to adjust. Time to grow comfortable with the change.

He turned back to face her, and he caught the tail end of a nervous gesture, of her running her fingers through her hair. The black cascade over her shoulders tightened his throat. He spread his fingers wide, forcing himself to take a steadying breath, to relax, to keep from frightening her further.

"How did you find me?" she asked. What had she done to betray herself? She thought she'd been so careful, purposely avoiding using his credit card, being tracked by his driver.

He nodded toward her cell phone on the nightstand. "Hartwell Genetics security," he said. "You made a call last night, to AFAA. We could trace it from the office."

She swallowed hard. The foundation, catching her once again. She forced herself to meet his eyes. "Ethan, I placed that call to cut my ties. I told the foundation that I wouldn't work for them. Wouldn't take Margaret's money."

He nodded, as if he had expected as much. Nevertheless, he asked, "Why?"

She stared at him, incredulous. "Do you have to ask? I can't work for them. Not when the job is only another round of charity. Not when it's just another manipulation, another way of Margaret reining you in."

"Me?" He sounded astonished, but she refused to be drawn in to another round of his game playing.

"You said that you spoke to Zach. Then you know that he told me all about Margaret's ultimatum. You need to be married by Margaret's birthday or you lose everything. I understand that."

She rubbed her arms, fighting off the deadly chill that nearly made her teeth chatter. She wasn't losing anywhere near as much as Ethan was. Not control over a corporation. Not a family fortune. She was only walking away from luxury that she'd enjoyed for a couple of months.

Of course Ethan had made his choice. Of course he'd agreed to his grandmother's demands, kept them secret in case Sloane even thought of protesting. She couldn't blame him. Wouldn't blame him.

He eyed her steadily. "Sloane, I made my choice. I chose you." He closed the distance between them, standing so close that she could feel the heat from his body, could feel a human warmth that she thought would never be hers again. "I chose you and our daughter."

He made it sound so simple. So easy. She bit her lip, trying desperately to maintain her concentration. "No. If you had truly made up your mind, you would have told me about Margaret's demands. You wouldn't have waited for some lawyer to betray your secret. You would have shared the truth."

As soon as she said the words, he saw the piece of

paper she had created, her carefully folded marriage manifesto. *Truth. Respect. Partnership.* For the first time, he completely understood how deeply he had betrayed her. He had failed on every one of her counts.

Truth. He had lied by omission, every single time that he chose not to tell her about Grandmother's demands.

Respect. He had treated her as if she were an incompetent, a child, a fool, someone who could never understand the real pressures in his life.

Partnership. He had never let her be his equal, never relied on her to stand beside him, to work with him, together, to solve the problem of Grandmother's demands.

He could try to explain the twisted way his mind had worked. He could try to tell her that he had been working to protect her, to keep her safe from emotional harm. He could repeat the words that he had taken so long to say, reiterate the simple, unassailable fact that he loved her. That she was the one woman he had ever loved.

His excuse wasn't good enough. His reasoning was completely flawed. She had given him a rulebook, a simple formula, and he had utterly, completely failed. He wanted to reach out for her, to touch her, to convey the perfect truth of his understanding with the language of their bodies, the only language that he'd ever made work between them. But for now, the only thing that he could do was struggle with unwieldy words.

"Sloane, I should have trusted you. I was wrong in a hundred different ways. You told me, you wrote it down in black and white, and I still didn't understand. I was an idiot, Sloane, but you have to believe me when I tell you that I love you. I love the way you fight for what you believe in. I love the way you build your own life, making it what *you* want it to be. I love the way you make your lists, the way you set all the world's wild, confusing emotions into simple, straightforward words. Trust. Respect. Partnership." His voice broke on the last word, and then he whispered, "I'm a better man when I'm with you, Sloane. Let me be with you. Let me stay with you. Let me love you."

She had to shut her eyes against the sight of him. This was not an Ethan Hartwell she had ever seen before. This was a man who was stripped to his bones, who was bare to the world. "Ethan," she whispered, not trusting herself to say more.

"Sloane." His voice was so husky that she felt the words more than heard them. "Grandmother's birthday doesn't matter. It's just a date. If you want, I'll wait until next year, until June, or whenever you agree to marry me. I don't care about stock transfers, about corporate obligations. If there isn't room for me at Hartwell Genetics, I'll build my own company. *We* will. Please. Just tell me that you will marry me eventually. Not today, not tomorrow, but some day, when you can trust me again. I love you, and I'm begging you. Will you be my wife, sometime, in the future, with no more games between us?"

Her heart stopped beating. Her breath froze in her lungs. She was suspended in a cocoon of silence, of space. All of her fears shimmered on the edge of her vision, all of her dark thoughts whispered at the very limit of her hearing. Ethan stared at her, perfectly still, hope indelibly written across his features.

The baby stirred inside her, reminding her to speak. Ethan had said everything, had confessed everything, had made every argument he could ever make. And in the end, she had to embrace the essential truth: she loved him. She loved him as much as he loved her.

"Yes," she whispered.

He crushed her to him. Apparently freed by her acceptance, his body moved to enfold her, to gather her close, to show her that she was his and his alone. His kiss was devastating, igniting her lips, sparking across her tongue. She clutched at his back, wrapped her fingers in his hair, pulling him closer, deeper.

The ice that had bound her shattered into a million shards, bursting with all the force of frantic, pent-up love. Fire thrust into her belly, making her heart kick hard in her chest. She moaned against his lips, barely managing to form his name in her gasping desire.

She slipped her fingers into the waistband of his trousers, pulling him toward her, toward the rumpled bed. As she fumbled at his already loosened tie, she realized that he was still wearing the suit he'd worn to their engagement party. He'd spent the entire night seeking her, tracking her, desperate for her; he hadn't gone home, hadn't taken any creature comfort.

She smothered her remorse as she pulled off his shirt, laughing as his eager fingers helped her. The laughter turned to a gasp of shock as he stripped away the belt from her robe.

He buried his face in the hollow of her neck, nuzzling the tender flesh with such perfect attention that she was forced to squirm away, to pull back, gasping for air. Her hands found his, though, and she pulled him to the bed, tugging him down beside her.

Her robe slipped open as she tumbled into the sheets, and he lost no time measuring the perfect flesh of her body. He was overwhelmed by the need to know her, to feel her, to understand every inch of her. His lips followed his fingertips in exploration as he traced the dark circles that accented her breasts, as he discovered the perfect beads waiting for his attention.

She writhed beneath him, tightening his groin. He shifted, trying to maintain contact with her sweet flesh, trying to fill his lungs with the honeysuckle scent of her, with the warmth that radiated from every exposed inch of her.

The power of his need was simply too great, too painful. He tore at his trousers, kicked them off, banishing them to the floor with a grateful gasp.

That relief, though, was short-lived. Sloane reached out to help him, edging her slim fingers beneath the elastic waist of his boxers. The touch of her hands on the full length of him nearly made Ethan shout her name; he had to bury his face in the soft valley between her breasts, had to smother his instinctive cries. He forced himself to breathe deeply, to calm his raging need, to ease the throbbing pressure that threatened to convulse him.

Sloane laughed in pure delight. She had never imagined that she could have this much power over a man, that she could bring such a powerful creature completely under her sway. Feeling wicked, she traced one fingernail from the forest of tight curls to his velvet tip, rejoicing as Ethan's entire body shuddered.

He tried to pull away, but she only let him get far enough that she could strip off the last garment between them, that she could send his boxers to the floor with the rest of his clothes. He succumbed to her decision, and she thought she was in control, until he wrapped his arms around her, rolling her so that his back was cushioned by the mattress, so that she was sprawled across his chest, her robe finally lost in the chaos of the sheets.

He took advantage of their new position, raising his head to suckle at her right breast. The touch of his lips on her tight nipple sent waves of heat rolling over her body, ripples of pure sensation that drew her in, focusing her on a single circle of pure, flawless pleasure. She thought that she'd never felt anything as wondrous, anything as perfect, and then he shifted his attention to her other breast. Whimpering, she threw her head back, nearly overwhelmed by the intensity of the feeling he raised within her.

With velvet tongue and satin lips, he fed the fire within her. Red-orange-gold flames flowed through her body, eddied in her veins, pooled deep inside her core. Backfires were kindled by his fingertips digging into her waist, by the firm grip of his hands as he held her steady, held her close, locked her in to the pure pleasure he delivered.

Overcome by the intensity, she tried to arch away from him, tried to give her body the cool break that she thought she needed. He merely doubled his attention, though, adding tiny nips from his perfect teeth to accent the sensations that flooded through her breasts. She shuddered at the new sensation, crying out in surprise. The solid touch of his palms against her flanks reminded her of the child inside her, of the daughter they had created, of the unexpected, perfect beauty they had shared months before. His hands were anchors, pulling her closer to him, securing her body to his.

One more tug of his teeth, one more tickle with his tongue, and she crashed over the precipice she'd known was terrifyingly close. She cried out his name, drowning in the sudden whirlpool that roared through her core. The entire world around her disappeared; she was reduced to the brilliant fire that he sparked inside her, billowing wave after billowing wave of endless, mindless heat.

In that moment outside of time, Ethan thought that his

heart might break from the beauty he saw before him. Sloane's hair surrounded her face like a midnight halo. Her eyes were closed, hiding away the brilliant intelligence that had drawn him to her in the first place. Her lips had tightened into a perfect circle in the instant before he gave her the release that she craved; now, her mouth was relaxed, swollen, begging him to drink as deeply as he dared.

He felt the aftershocks ripple through her body, the shuddering descent as she returned to awareness, to reality. The iron muscles of her fingers, her hands, her wrists unlocked, and she telegraphed the final waves of her sweet tension to the broad muscles of his chest.

That secret message, those unspoken words, reminded his proud flesh that he had sacrificed for her pleasure, that he had denied himself even the faintest hope of release. His body shifted of its own accord, and her eyes opened wide, suddenly filled with understanding.

"Ethan," she breathed.

He couldn't keep from touching her. He couldn't restrain himself from brushing the hair off her face, from tracing the delicate line of her lips as she hesitated. He'd hurt her. Hurt her in ways that he hadn't understood, that he'd never intended. He would spend the rest of his life making that up to her, giving her whatever she wanted, whatever she needed, now that she'd agreed to stay with him forever. "Yes, love," he said, lifting one of her hands from his chest, brushing his lips across the sweet silk of her palm.

"I want to feel you," she said, holding his gaze. She set each word between them with perfect precision, just as he had once predicted she would, on the night he had proposed. She wasn't asking for a kiss. She wasn't asking for simple physical release. "All of you," she said. "Like we did before, before all of our misunderstandings, all of the confusion. Please, Ethan. I need you inside me, now."

He had no intention of making her ask again.

His arms were firm around her as he pulled her to his side, as he shifted so that she felt his body against hers, his legs stretched beside her own. The rasp of the hair on his thighs awoke new sensations in her, stirring her to an awareness she would have thought impossible only a few heartbeats before. She thought that he had shown her all the pleasure of her physical self, that he had taught her everything she could enjoy, but now she knew his lessons were only beginning.

As if he sensed her uncertainty, he kissed her. This was not a kiss of passion, not a kiss of endless, reeling sensation. Instead, it was a pure bonding, a seal of all the promises they'd ever made to each other, of all the vows they'd ever taken, ever were going to take. There was a sweetness on his lips, an infinite tenderness, and she knew that he had never meant to hurt her, would never hurt her again. That kiss made tears rise in her eyes, happy tears, joyful tears, and he wiped the moisture from her cheeks with a gentle touch.

Still holding her gaze, he lowered his hand to her waist. He found her damp folds without hesitation, stroking once, twice, coaxing her to open. She shifted her hips, responding to his call, biting her lip at the sensations he stirred within her.

Slowly, with perfect deliberation, he ran a finger over the most tender pearl between her thighs. Pure sensation jolted through her, arching her spine against him, driving her to seek immediate release.

He shook his head, though, smiling with the intensity of an explorer about to discover a whole new world. His fingers touched her again, ignited her again, and she closed her eyes against the sheer physicality of the sensation.

"No," he whispered, and the command was as gentle as the last kiss they'd shared. "Watch me. I want to see your eyes."

She swallowed hard, wondering if she dared. Another pass of his fingers. Another blast of pure, grasping pleasure. A new energy, a new force, as she managed to maintain eye contact, as she read his promise of eternal, perfect devotion.

Knowing that she was ready, knowing that he had primed her to take the length of him without harm to herself, to her body, to the precious child that she bore, he raised himself above her. Her gaze was steady. Trusting. She was ready for this new life between them, the new shape of love between their bodies, between their souls.

For just an instant, he hovered, feeling the sweet softness of her entrance, sensing the magical need that chimed through her veins and sang to his flesh. And then, he eased himself inside.

He moved as slowly as he could, giving her time to adjust, to accept, to envelop the full length of him. The tightness of her feminine muscles nearly undid him; he would have lost control, if not for her pure, unshuttered gaze. His hips met hers, and they were joined completely, in perfect balance, in perfect trust.

Careful, watching her for any sign of pain, he started to withdraw. Her fingers scrabbled on his back, coaxing him forward with a new urgency. He yielded to her silent request, dipping back into the honeyed sweetness of her core.

She felt the rhythm grow between them, the ways their bodies adjusted to each other. Heat poured from him into her, spiraling deeper inside, winding past all of her inhibitions, any lingering thoughts of right and wrong. Overwhelmed by the sensation, by her emotions, she closed her eyes, the better to concentrate on the power expanding between them.

"Sloane," he whispered, summoning her back. His fingers traced the line of her jaw, and she forced her eyes open, locked on to the steady agate of his gaze.

She'd thought that she could not find release again, not so soon after the utter dissolution of her body. He worked his magic, though, as if he'd known her flesh forever; he tightened the muscles of her belly, of her thighs. He filled her inner channel, drawing her closer, deeper, further inside an aching tunnel of need. One long stroke, deeper than any before. Another. One last thrust, and she was shuddering, toppling over a cliff of pure, rolling sensation, clenching every muscle in her body before opening up in blinding release.

He saw the wonder in her eyes as she reached her cliff, saw the moment just before he let her go, saw the instant that her body was flooded with exquisite freedom. He rode out the storm beneath him, giving her every last instant of pleasure, willing himself to hold back, to deliver more, to share every heartbeat that he could.

When the storm was finally fading, though, she shifted her hips, jolting him to a new level of awareness. He had restrained himself for so long that only the slightest movement was necessary to hurtle him toward his own edge. Catching a single ragged breath, he pulled back, nearly deserting the heaven of her ready core. Then, he plunged deep inside her, one last thrust unlocking all of his reserve, freeing him to fill her.

He nearly broke his own rule then, nearly closed his eyes, but the sparkling joy on Sloane's face kept him fully aware. He clutched her shoulders as his power pulsed out of him, drawing her closer, closer, never losing the lifeline of her gaze.

She held him until the end, overcome by the pure physicality of the life force that they shared. At last, he collapsed beside her, his breath as rapid as if he'd run a marathon. She kissed him, letting her lips tremble against his. She pulled his arm around her, relishing the weight, the power, the unbroken security.

She knew that they would be together now. They would follow through with the mechanics of marriage, with a license, with vows. But they had more than that. They had the power of true love, of shared destiny. They had kindled a new life, a new person, to symbolize their joined and perfect love.

Sighing, she burrowed close to his side. And then, they slept.

Epilogue

Ethan watched with pride as Sloane adjusted Emma's blanket. The baby didn't stir, even though she was the centerpiece of attention.

"Ready, Gran?" he asked, turning to Margaret Hartwell.

"Ready," she affirmed. The photographer swooped into action, moving in with his camera, directing the matriarch as no other man dared to do. He ordered the proud great-grandmother to turn her head, to tilt her chin, to gaze down at the infant in her arms.

Ethan stepped back, awed at how readily the old tyrant complied. Sloane was watching, a smile on her lips. He settled his arm around her waist, drawing her in close to his side. Sloane sighed and said, "I can't believe how good she's being."

"Gran always did rise to the occasion," he said, with purposeful misunderstanding.

"Ethan!" Sloane whirled toward him in disapproval, but settled for a quick kiss as reprimand.

Other photos had already been taken, one formal composition, with Ethan and Sloane together, looking down at their perfect child. Another, with Gran holding the baby, while Ethan and Sloane gazed down from behind her thronelike chair. A series of Sloane holding a wakeful Emma, maternal joy radiating with a purity so brilliant it had captured Ethan's breath and he'd needed to look away. A portrait of the entire family, including Daisy, who had sat at perfect canine attention, through a half-dozen camera flashes.

Sloane watched as the photographer turned Margaret to another angle, focused his soft floodlights to drive away shadows. She whispered to Ethan, "I can't believe how many he's taking! It's been hours!"

He smiled indulgently. "Not as long as he would have taken to capture our wedding, if you'd let me give you a real ceremony."

She caught her lip between her teeth at his teasing tone. They'd never had this conversation; it hadn't seemed necessary at any point in the past four and a half months, since they'd emerged from the Eastern Hotel and gone directly to a justice of the peace in Virginia. "Do you really care? Did you really want a full wedding?"

He laughed, loudly enough that Daisy scurried to his side. The photographer cast a quick scowl in their direction, and Sloane meekly pulled them toward the back of the room, away from the busy work of capturing the perfect portrait. One quick hand command guaranteed that Daisy followed suit, staying out of the thick of things.

When they were safe in the privacy of the corner, Ethan slipped his hands around Sloane's waist, drew her close with a firmness that promised more, that reminded her precisely how well they fit together, how perfect they were for each other. "The only thing that matters to me, Mrs. Hartwell, is that you agreed to marry me. That you signed the paper, in front of the justice of the peace and two legal witnesses. That you wear my ring. And that you rock our daughter to sleep at night, with me standing right beside you."

She sighed and settled her cheek against his chest. She could hear his heart beating through the fabric of his shirt, a steady reminder of the power of his love. As if to horn in on the sweet domestic scene, though, Daisy raised a paw to scratch at Ethan's leg. At the same time, Sloane and Ethan both commanded, "Down!" The dog dropped to the floor immediately.

Sloane laughed before she looked up at Ethan. "You know," she said. "I have a confession to make."

His smile was easy. "I can't wait to hear this."

"It's about Daisy. When we first got her, when she was just a puppy, I hired a trainer to come out to the house. I wanted Daisy to be perfect, so that you'd fall in love with her as much as I had." She was startled by the volume of Ethan's laugh. "Wait!" she exclaimed. "It wasn't *that* funny. I mean, I did a decent job, didn't I?"

"A decent job," he finally said, but he shook his head as if he didn't believe her.

"What? She sits when we tell her to. And she knows *come* and *stay* and *down*."

Ethan looked fondly at the dog. Daisy, for her part, was cocking her head at an angle, glancing between her two humans as if they were creatures of great mystery. Ethan said, "But she's not much good at *heel*."

Sloane frowned. "We tried. The trainer and I just couldn't get her motivated to stay by my side."

"I didn't have any better luck myself."

"What?" Sloane took a step away, even as Ethan started to laugh again.

"I hired my own trainer. I worked on the same commands. I wanted to show you that I believed in Daisy. That I understood she had a future with us."

The dog chose that moment to spring to her feet, overcome by the obvious good cheer of her master and mistress. Sloane said in disbelief, "Then she managed to wrangle double treats from us, to master the exact same tricks."

"She's smarter than we ever thought, isn't she?"

Before Sloane could respond, her cell phone rang. She jumped at the intrusion but quickly plucked it out of her bag. One glance at the number, and she shook her head.

"Take it," Ethan said.

"This is family time! It's Margaret's birthday."

"Take it," he said again, and she complied, her smile letting him know just how eager she was to answer the call.

"Sloane Hartwell," she said, after pushing the button that completed the connection.

Ethan watched as Sloane nodded. She found her handbag, fished out a pad of paper, a pen. Bright spots of color accented her cheeks, and her eyes sparkled as she mustered her arguments. "No," she said, stepping out to the hallway. "If the foundation is serious about implementing the Hope Project, it's going to have to…" Her voice trailed away as she closed the door behind her.

At last, the photographer finished with his grandmother. Ethan stepped forward to take the baby, marveling at the way a month-old child could sleep through any disturbance. "There, Gran," he said. "You've had your way, once again. You've got your pictures of Emma."

The old woman spared a fond smile for the baby before she leveled her hazel eyes on him. The determination there was utterly familiar; he'd seen it in his own mirror, every day of his life. "I think that family photos were a perfectly reasonable request for a birthday present. It's not every day that someone turns eighty, after all. Besides, you know I only do what I think is best for those I love."

Ethan heard the familiar acerbic note beneath her words. "Of course, Gran. Everything you do is good for someone else."

"You can't complain about the rules I set for you." Her gaze was a direct challenge.

He wanted to argue. He wanted to tell her that she'd been headstrong, unreasonable. He wanted to say that she'd had no business interfering with his personal life, setting deadlines, tying him to an arbitrary timetable.

But when he looked down at his daughter, he knew that such a complaint was meaningless. He couldn't be happier with the way things had turned out. He wouldn't change a thing.

Nevertheless, he couldn't let Gran think that he was growing soft. "You had no right—"

"No right to make you sit up and pay attention?" She cut him off, and he could see now that she had planned this confrontation. She knew precisely what she wanted to say.

"You treated me like a business venture," he protested.

"One that needed a tight rein," she said sourly. "One that had to be brought into line." Emma chose that moment to squirm in her blanket, to stretch out her arms before settling back to sleep. Ethan was surprised at the stark love that he found on his grandmother's face. He was even more startled by her words. "I knew that you needed this, darling. I knew that you were too afraid to step forward on your own. You needed me to push you."

"Over a cliff," he said wryly.

"Into the arms of a good woman," she retorted.

"Who is going into whose arms?" Sloane asked, gliding in from the hallway.

Margaret looked at her, those hazel Hartwell eyes bright with mischief. "I was just telling my boneheaded grandson that his grandmother is a wise and wonderful woman."

Sloane looked at Ethan. She could see echoes of disagreement on his face, hints of some argument that he'd planned on voicing. Now, though, he merely shook his head, his lips curling up in a resigned smile. When he gazed down at his daughter, that expression transformed, became a look of wonder, of sheer fascination. "Listen to her, Emma," he said. "One day all that Hartwell wisdom will be yours."

Still cradling the baby, he held out one hand to Sloane. As she laced her fingers between his and drew close to look at their daughter, she knew that her life could never be more perfect. "Listen to your father, little Emma," she said, brushing a fingertip against the infant's cheek. "Listen to the entire family who loves you so much." Daisy gave one sharp bark of agreement, as if she understood every single human word.

* * * * *

Have Your Say

You've just finished your book.

So what did you think?

We'd love to hear your thoughts on our 'Have your say' online panel
www.millsandboon.co.uk/haveyoursay

- Easy to use
- Short questionnaire
- Chance to win Mills & Boon® goodies

Visit us Online

Tell us what you thought of this book now at
www.millsandboon.co.uk/haveyoursay

YOUR_SAY